Praise for Anne O'Brien

'O'Brien cleverly intertwines the personal and political in this
enjoyable, gripping tale'
The Times

'[A] fast-paced historical novel'
Good Housekeeping

'Anne O'Brien has unearthed a gem of a subject'
Daily Telegraph

'A gripping story of love, heartache and political intrigue'
Woman & Home

'There are historical novels and then there are the works of Anne
O'Brien – and this is another hit'
The Sun

'The characters are larger than life…and the author a compulsive
storyteller'
Sunday Express

'This book has everything – royalty, scandal, fascinating historical
politics'
Cosmopolitan

'A gripping historical drama'
Bella

'Historical fiction at its best'
Candis

The Shadow Queen

ANNE O'BRIEN

HQ

ONE PLACE. MANY STORIES

HQ
An imprint of HarperCollinsPublishers Ltd.
1 London Bridge Street
London SE1 9GF

This hardback edition 2017

1

First published in Great Britain by
HQ, an imprint of HarperCollinsPublishers Ltd. 2017

ISBN:
HB: 9781848455078
TPB: 9781848455221

Printed and bound by
CPI Group (UK) Ltd, Croydon, CR0 4YY

For George, as ever, my love and my thanks for his cheerful tolerance of all things medieval. His appreciation of Joan of Kent's wayward lifestyle was often more balanced than mine. The Fair Maid owes him a debt of gratitude too.

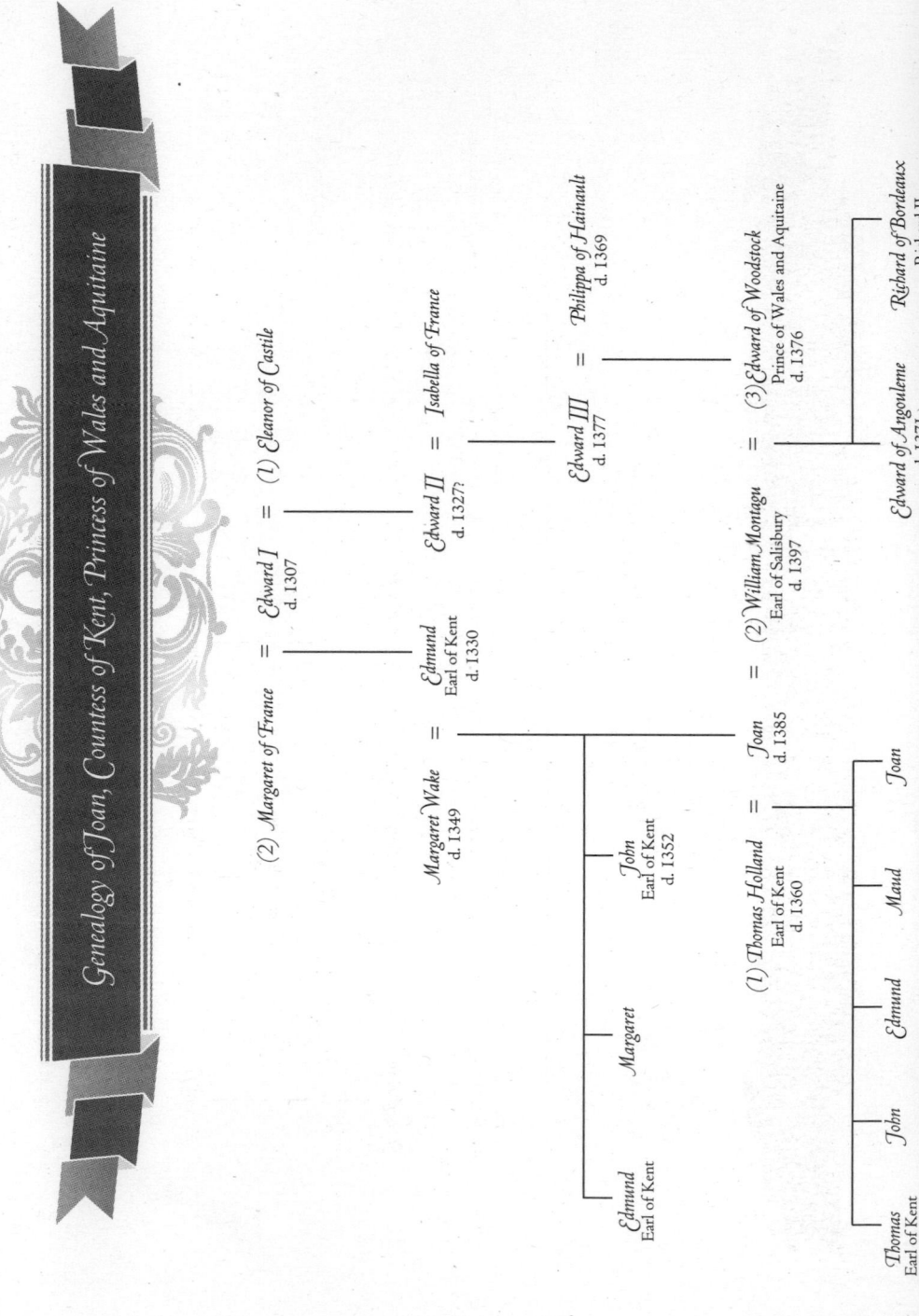

Genealogy of Joan, Countess of Kent, Princess of Wales and Aquitaine

(2) Margaret of France = Edward I = (1) Eleanor of Castile
d. 1307

Edmund
Earl of Kent
d. 1330

Edward II = Isabella of France
d. 1327?

Edward III = Philippa of Hainault
d. 1377   d. 1369

Margaret Wake
d. 1349

Edmund
Earl of Kent

Margaret

John
Earl of Kent
d. 1352

Joan = (2) William Montagu
d. 1385   Earl of Salisbury
d. 1397

(3) Edward of Woodstock
Prince of Wales and Aquitaine
d. 1376

(1) Thomas Holland
Earl of Kent
d. 1360

Edward of Angouleme   Richard of Bordeaux
d. 1371   Richard II

Thomas   John   Edmund   Maud   Joan
Earl of Kent

Descendants of Edward III and the Claims to the English Throne

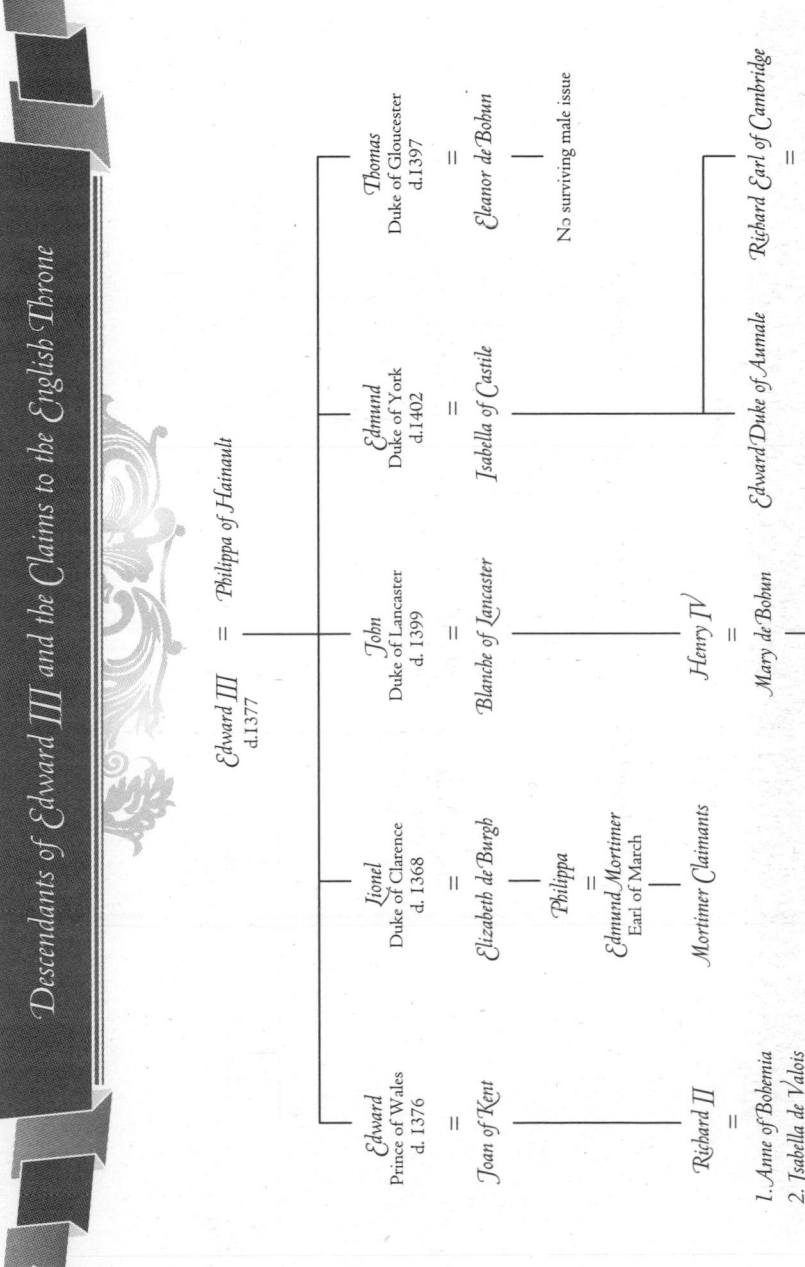

Edward III d.1377 = Philippa of Hainault

Edward Prince of Wales d.1376 = Joan of Kent

Lionel Duke of Clarence d.1368 = Elizabeth de Burgh

Philippa = Edmund Mortimer Earl of March

Mortimer Claimants

John Duke of Lancaster d.1399 = Blanche of Lancaster

Henry IV = Mary de Bohun

Henry V House of Lancaster

Edmund Duke of York d.1402 = Isabella of Castile

Edward Duke of Aumale

Thomas Duke of Gloucester d.1397 = Eleanor de Bohun

No surviving male issue

Richard Earl of Cambridge = Anne Mortimer

House of York

Richard II = 1. Anne of Bohemia 2. Isabella de Valois

No issue

'…the most beautiful lady in the whole realm of England, and by far the most amorous.'

Jean Froissart

'…concerning whose birth (Richard II) many unsavoury things were commonly said (of her), namely that he was not born to a father of the royal line, but of a mother given to slippery ways – to say nothing of many other things I have heard.'

The Chronicle of Adam Usk 1377-1421

'The gentle prince married… a lady of great renown, who kindled love in him, in that she was beauteous, charming and discreet.'

Chandos Herald

'Prudence teaches the princess or great lady how above all things in this base world she ought to love honour and good reputation.'

Christine de Pisan

Prologue

I stared at the reflection, with appreciation. The eyes – bold, self-assured – stared back at me.

To mark the celebration of the day of my birth – I do not recall which year it might have been except that I was still little more than a child – I was given this mirror by Philippa. Queen Philippa, my cousin by marriage, wife of my royal cousin King Edward the Third. I think that I had no gift from my mother on that occasion. My mother had mislaid the celebration amidst all the other burdens on her memory. As for my father, he was dead by an axe reserved for those condemned for treason. But Queen Philippa remembered and marked the day. I valued that mirror highly.

'Don't look in it too often, Joan,' Philippa advised in her kindly manner, when she saw me glance in its silvered surface for the third time within the reading of our daily prayers. 'It will set your pretty feet on the path to vanity and self-will, neither of which are admirable qualities in a young woman.'

It was a beautiful thing, the glass embellished by an ivory mount, the back smooth-carved with two figures of a knight and his lady. She was crowning him with a garland to symbolise their love. The mirror was made to hang from a cunning little hasp at my belt.

Lifting it, now that I was alone and at leisure to do so, I angled it towards the light and studied the face that looked back.

Fair hair, as fair as that of the Blessed Virgin in my Book of Hours, was pleated and pinned and tucked beneath a coif in seemly fashion, so that there was little to see of it, but I knew it was much admired by the women who cared for me. Pale skin without blemish or unsightly freckle. A straight nose. Brows darker than my hair, arching impressively with a touch of female artifice. Eyes that were agate-dark, with lashes that were the envy of my female cousins. A graceful neck. Which was as much as I could see in the small aperture, but it was enough. I enjoyed the experience.

I was Joan of Kent. Joan the Fair. Even now my praises were being sung where men admired female loveliness.

'And in the taverns too, I don't doubt.' My cousin Princess Isabella had a caustic tongue. 'I would not be proud of that.'

'But then, dearest cousin, you can lay no claim to my degree of beauty. Although,' I adopted a nice tone of condescension, 'the ground lily root with egg yolk has been miraculous in ridding your skin of blemishes.'

Isabella, pretty enough, glowered.

Beware conceit, Queen Philippa would admonish. Her beauty was neither in her face nor her figure, rather in her loving heart, but I was too young to acknowledge that allure of the flesh could be of less value than winsomeness of the spirit. How could I not be vain when I had been so gracefully blessed in face and form?

What would the future hold for me?

Whatever I wished it to hold, of course. Was I not of royal blood? I tilted my chin, liking the result as the light glimmered along the fine line of my brow, softening my perfect cheekbones. I must practise looking imperious. I was sure that it would be a most useful attribute.

Chapter One

Late Autumn, 1340: Windsor Castle

A servant, opening the door with well-worn deference, bowed briefly and generally to the crowded chamber. For the most part, inured to such interruptions and intent on our own pursuits, we, the youthful but high-bred occupants, ignored him. There was music, there were books and counter games. There were small animals to be teased and cosseted. The boys were clustered round a longbow in need of repair. We, my sister and female cousins, were draping a length of luridly-vermillion embroidered cloth, discovered in one of the King's Twelfth Night dressing-up coffers, around the short figure of Princess Isabella.

The servant cleared his throat, to no avail.

Who were we, to ignore what would be a summons from some higher authority for at least one of us? We, as we were all supremely well aware, were of the highest blood in the land.

Here in my company, or I in theirs if rank was of supreme importance rather than age, were the royal daughters of King Edward the Third and Queen Philippa, the princesses Isabella and Joan. There, his head bent over a harness, working with ferocious attention at a detached buckle, was William Montagu, heir to the Earl of Salisbury who was at this moment prisoner in France, captured during the French wars. The vivid, dark-haired lad with the bow in his hand, re-attaching the bowstring with some skill, was Edward of Woodstock, the heir to the throne, who should have been engaged with the Master at Arms in polishing his military skills but had escaped to talk battles and horses with William Montagu and my brother John, Earl of Kent, for all his youth. And then there was Lionel, another prince of the King and Queen's growing family, still barely two years and under the close eye of his nurse as he staggered on unsteady legs after his magnificent brother.

The servant, undeterred by our lack of response – for which Queen Philippa would have taken us to task, for nothing excused ill manners in her book of how royal children should be raised – allowed his eye to discover and rest on me. I was sitting on the floor, passing pins to my elder sister Margaret with instructions on how to fit the damask bodice as becomingly as possible to Isabella's flat chest.

The servant loomed over me. I looked up.

'A message for you, Mistress Joan. Your lady mother, the Countess of Kent, has arrived. She wishes to see you. If you will present yourself at her chamber.' When I did not stir, other than to hand another pin to sister Margaret, he added. 'Now, mistress, not some time at your convenience. It might be best.'

So my mother was at Windsor, and it was implied, by being graced by her full title rather than the simpler Lady Margaret, in a hasty mood. My mother travelled often, so much so that I rarely saw her. So why had I been summoned, selected out of her three offspring? No, it would not be politic to waste time. My mother had a temper born out of disappointment and past humiliations brought on by an absent and horribly dead husband.

So I stood, pushing the pot of pins into Margaret's hands. Spurred by curiosity, Isabella detached herself and, trailing velvet damask, accompanied me to the door, pulling at my sleeve when I did not moderate my step.

'What do you suppose she wants?' Isabella, four years younger than I, was considered precocious for her age. 'Have you committed some sin? If you have, I don't know about it.' Her eyes gleamed with the prospect of some conspiracy. 'Tell me!'

I had no intention of telling Isabella, an inveterate gossip, anything at all.

'I will soon know,' I said.

I looked down at my side-less surcoat, pulling it and the sleeves of my undergown into order. I had not dressed with any care that morning, nor had sitting on the floor improved my skirts that were now creased. My mother had an eye for appearances and she was not tolerant. If it was a matter of sin, better not to earn her displeasure before she took issue with me.

'Let me.' Accepting my brusqueness as normal in the circumstances, Isabella stretched up and straightened my coif, tucked my hair almost out of sight before picking the evidence of fur from the small grey cat from my bodice. 'That's better, although red does not become you.'

'Better than vermillion becomes you, cousin.' I became aware that she was looking at me, lips pursed in thought. 'What?'

'Did you go to Mass this morning?'

'No.' She knew very well that I had not.

'Then this might be useful.'

Shrugging aside the damask so that it fell in a heap to the floor, from her bodice Isabella unpinned a jewelled reliquary, far too fine for so young a girl to be wearing but Isabella had insisted. It was hers to wear, given at her birth by an indulgent father who saw no wrong in his wayward daughter. It contained, as we all knew since repeated frequently to impress, the tears of the Blessed Virgin herself.

Isabella's bright face was lit with intrigue.

'I think you should wear this.'

'I am honoured.'

And I was. Isabella did not give possessions willingly. She trans-ferred it from her bodice to mine, where the gold glittered impressively as I moved.

'But why would I need a symbol of such power?' I asked.

'It will keep you safe from sin.'

'I have committed no sin.'

'No, but your lady mother might think that you have.'

She might indeed. I kissed Isabella's cheek.

'But take good care of it,' she admonished. 'I want it back when this interview is over.'

'Quickly if you will, mistress.' The servant, breathing heavily, was still waiting in the doorway.

Following the servant to my mother's distant chamber, I still found the opportunity to linger on the way. I disliked being beckoned in such a manner when she had not seen me for more months than I could recall. She would not have demanded my brother's presence so forcefully, but then, to her mind, sons were of far greater value than daughters.

I stopped by a window, to press my cheek against the cold glass, a luxury on which the King had just spent a fortune in an attempt to ward off the draughts. Since my veils fluttered a little, it had not been a great success.

'Mistress!'

'I am coming!'

I entered her chamber to curtsey with practised precision and innate grace, but if I had intended to make a good impression, I failed.

'Joan. At last.'

My mother. Margaret, Lady Wake, Lady of Badenoch, Dowager Countess of Kent.

Tall and spare, my mother gave off the air of a determinedly held widowhood. Her close-fitting gown was rich but sombre in layers of grey and black and the deep purple of autumn blackberries. Her veil was richly embroidered but not one curl of hair was allowed to show beneath the wimple that she still embraced despite the dictates of fashion. Her face was long, the skin finely grained, but there was no evidence of any humour or pleasure in her existence. Indeed, her stark solemnity with its close folding of her lips was intimidating, as was the heavy musk of her perfume as the satin of her skirts rustled into stillness. She looked older than her years. She had barely more than forty to her lifespan.

'I expected you a half hour ago.'

An exaggeration, of course. My mother did not touch me. The Queen, who had absorbed me into the royal nursery when I was no more than two years old and had supervised my upbringing ever since, would have folded me into her arms after such a lengthy absence. Queen Philippa would have smiled at me.

'I came as quickly as I could, madam. I was reading with the princesses.' The lie came easily, slipping off my tongue. I had lied before. 'Our tutor wished us to have knowledge of the life of St. Ursula who is the patron saint of young virgins, such as we are. We will be celebrating her Feast Day on the twenty-first day of October with a masque before the court. We were commended on our reading.'

My mother had not led the easiest of lives. Some would say a life full of degradation. Perhaps she deserved my pity; when a woman's husband was executed for treason, and that in disgraceful circum-stances, and she within weeks of producing a child and under arrest for her husband's sins, she will not feel blessed. And then there was the resulting loss of lands and titles and pre-eminence as a consequence of that husband being declared traitor. My mother had lived under suspicion because she had set her own hand to some of the treasonous letters.

But that was all in the past. Since a royal pardon had drained away a portion of her guilt but not all of her bitterness, my mother had dedicated her life to the reinstatement of her family. A laudable objective, but sometimes I found it difficult to experience any emotion but resentment.

As now.

'That is good. I approve of St. Ursula,' she said, still seated in the high-backed chair beside the window where the light fell on her unflattering hair-confinement. 'I hope that you are a credit to the Queen and to your governors. Do you take heed of all your lessons?'

'Yes, madam.'

'Do you observe your daily prayers? Do you attend Mass?'

'Yes, madam.'

Standing now, she approached, to walk in a circle around me, before stopping to lift my chin with her fingers. I was not sure that she believed me, but her reply was complimentary.

'Then you are everything I had hoped for in a daughter.'

Released, abruptly, I lowered my eyes.

'I hope so, madam.'

'A beautiful girl, well nurtured, without sin.'

'I make confession, madam.'

I prayed, aware of the weight of Isabella's powerful reliquary against my breast, that my mother could see no colour of culpability in my cheeks. It seemed, from the faintest of smiles that was bestowed on me, that she could not. But then the smile vanished.

'I trust that your behaviour is decorous and seemly when at court, when you are in the company of the King's young knights. I do not wish it to come to my attention that you are of a flirtatious disposition, Joan.'

'My deportment is exemplary, madam. Queen Philippa commends me on it as an example to her own daughters.' My reply was supremely colourless.

'So I have heard.' The Countess returned to her chair, seating herself in a billow of silk, before pinning me with a direct stare. She breathed in, her nose narrowing as it did when she was displeased. 'I can rest assured that you have been well chaperoned.' She considered me, the soft pads of the fingers of her right hand tapping against the Book of Hours that she had picked up and now rested on her lap. 'It is, I think, time.'

When I remained silent under her regard, my mother stopped tapping but instead curled her hands around the fierce animals, carved with open mouths and sharp teeth along the arms of her chair.

'A marriage has been arranged for you,' she announced. 'Your hand has been sought by the most pre-eminent of families.'

There it was, declaimed without warning or fanfare, the announcement I had feared, even though I had always known that in the making of alliances, daughters were of inestimable value. Margaret and I would be expected to marry well, but this was the moment I had been dreading. I swallowed soundlessly, gaze still lowered to the hem of her gown, while the Countess took my silence for demure acceptance.

'I see it is no surprise to you.'

Obviously my dissembling was sufficient, but it was a surprise. Given my young age I had not expected it to be quite yet, accepting that such plans would be postponed for at least another year, perhaps two. And that it would be a lengthy betrothal rather than a marriage. My sister Margaret, older than I by one year, was betrothed to an important Gascon nobleman, Amanieu d'Albret, a man she had yet to meet. There was no talk yet of their actual marriage on the near horizon.

Oblivious to the thud of my heart beneath the Virgin's Tears, my mother was continuing. 'You must have known well what was planned. The King wishes to reward his closest friend, the Earl of Salisbury, sadly still under French restraint and likely to remain there until a ransom is paid. What better way to show royal gratitude for Salisbury's service to the Crown at home and overseas than for the King to give the hand of his cousin, a Plantagenet princess in her own right, to the Earl's son.'

So I was to wed Will Montagu, the boy with the harness. I could think of nothing to say.

'Does it not please you?' The edge in the Dowager Countess's voice was emerging as the silence played out.

What could I say that would not cause an eruption of temper?

'Yes, madam. It pleases me.'

It was the only possible reply.

'It will be an exceptional alliance. The King and Queen are in full agreement. As for the Salisbury boy, you know him well. You have been raised with him. There will be nothing for you to dislike in the match.'

'No, madam.' I decided that I must say something else to deflect the flare of impatience. 'I like William well enough.'

She nodded. 'You are much of an age. You will wed, but of course you will continue to live as you do now, until you are both deemed old enough to take on the responsibilities of marriage in the flesh.'

I kept my face expressionless, my eyes abandoning the hem to focus on the toes of my mother's shoes, expensively gilded.

'In the absence of the Earl, we will meet with the Countess of Salisbury this afternoon when we will sign the contracts of marriage.' At last she managed a smile that was more than a bleak movement of her lips. 'Your father would have approved, Joan. I have carried out this negotiation exactly as he would have wished.' She looked at me. I could feel those eyes searching my face. Her fingers, relaxed in satisfaction, now clenched. 'Have you still nothing to say?'

No, I had not. Nothing to the point. Nothing that would not shake the ground beneath her feet. And beneath mine. My thoughts tumbled over each other, searching to find something appropriate, and failing.

'Thank you, madam.'

My mother sighed as she deigned to explain further.

'William will be a worthy husband. An alliance with the Earl of Salisbury will be nothing but advantageous for our family. It will be a final mending of our reputation.'

I was not aware that it was broken beyond repair. Did the Queen not love me as much as she loved her own daughters? But treason could cast a long shadow, and my mother had had her own unfortunate role in it. There was much that needed to be healed. Yes, perhaps my mother did deserve my pity and my compliance.

'Yes, madam.'

'And you will make a good wife.'

'Yes, madam.'

'Tell your women to dress you as befitting a royal audience. I will fetch you when it is time.'

'Yes, madam.'

'Now you may go. Perhaps you can summon some expressions of gratitude and delight at the marriage before I see you again.'

'Yes, madam. I will.'

At last I got to the door, and outside it, with nausea churning in the pit of my stomach. My mother hoped that I would be instrumental in stripping aside our family's disgrace to finally heal the wounds of the past.

She was doomed to disappointment.

I knew full well what would be my own doom. Many would say that I had brought it on my own head.

I stood outside the door, leaned back so that the wall was cold against my back, and took a breath as I willed the initial panic to subside. Until, that is, I saw in the shadow of a pillar at the far end of the chamber three figures in descending height: William Montagu of Salisbury, Edward the princely heir and my brother John, all of whom had followed me to discover the need for such a summons. They were clearly waiting for me because as soon as I appeared they began to cover the ground between us. Pushing myself upright, with what I considered to be an innocent expression I walked slowly towards them, arranging my thoughts into what I might and might not say.

'What did she want?' John demanded without ceremony.

'Nothing for your little ears, brother,' I said, but my eyes were on the scion of the House of Salisbury.

Did William know the subject of my interview? Had he already been informed that I would join my hand with his in Holy Matrimony? It might well be. Not a word had passed his lips, but William was perfectly capable of keeping his own counsel. I regarded him through my lashes. Here, at our parent's planning, and that of the King and Queen, was my future husband, and since I had not been sworn to secrecy, perhaps it would be a good time for me to comment on the fact that we were destined, by forces beyond our control, to spend our future life together.

Except that sharp fear gripped my throat so that I could not force the words into being.

But William could. He pushed John aside.

'Have you told your mother the truth?'

My eyes narrowed.

'And you need not lie to me,' he continued. 'I know all about it.

I have friends in low places. What possessed you, Joan? Had you no sense?'

Which censure soon restored my voice.

'Have you been listening at doors, Will?'

'Yes.'

'Which doors?' Edward, ignorant of what was passing between us and immediately interested, his eyes were travelling speculatively between William and me. John, interest lost, had climbed onto a window seat where he sat like a crouching gargoyle, hugging his knees.

William nudged Edward, ignored him.

'You have to say,' he ordered me. 'You have to tell her.'

'I know.'

'If you don't, I will.'

Of course I must tell the truth. But when *I* decided, not at the prompting of my betrothed. For a moment I imagined his standing foursquare between our respective mothers, announcing what I had done. I imagined the combined fury of two irate women raining down upon my head.

I took a rapid step: I seized Will's arm. 'You would not dare!'

But William shook me off, in no manner intimidated. 'Not dare? Of course I dare. If I do not, what sort of a fool will I look, when all is discovered? And discovered it must be.'

William could be formidable when he chose, even though our gaze was on a level.

'Shh!' I hissed. His voice had risen in pitch, to echo through the antechamber.

'Tell them Joan, or I will.'

'Tell them *what*?' Edward would not be deflected a second time.

'Be quiet, Ned! You are too young to know anything about it,' I said.

'Only because you won't tell me,' he replied with superb logic. He stopped fidgeting from one foot to another and for a moment looked like a royal prince and with all the pride of his Plantagenet heritage. 'You must tell me. I insist.'

'If Joan confesses,' William said, 'then all can be put right and there'll be nothing to tell.'

'I will tell my mother,' I said, back on my dignity, except for the evidence of my fingers tightening once again on his forearm, making him wince. 'How do you know?'

'A page. A terrified rat who fell over me in his hurry to pack up his lord's armour when we were in Ghent. I picked him up. He was shockingly talkative. Until his mouth clammed shut like a wolf-trap.'

A flutter of rising panic unnerved me. Of course, William had been with us in Ghent. 'Did the page tell anyone else?'

'How would I know?'

All I could do was pray that he had not. I released Will's arm. 'You must promise me you'll not say a word.'

Unimpressed, William strode off with the final sally: 'I promise nothing!', leaving Edward regarding me with what could only be described as haughty demeanour.

'You should not allow Will to talk to you in that manner.'

'I know.'

'You are of royal blood. You are my cousin.'

My thoughts were elsewhere. 'The King is my cousin, not you.'

Ned's brows climbed, his reply was curt. 'As near as makes no difference. You are my family. You must tell me if Will does not show you the respect due to you.'

'Oh, I will.'

And then the arrogance was gone, leaving only a young man growing into his strength and impeccable rank. 'I'll be kind to you, Jeanette.'

'I know you will.'

I patted his shoulder. He might be the only one who was kind when all was revealed.

I walked with him back to the Painted Chamber, brother John running ahead to catch up with William who might prove to be better company, Edward fast forgetting his irritation and making practice sweeps with the new sword, a gift from his father and from which he was inseparable. When we arrived, to my relief, William was not there, nor was my sister, but Isabella was and must have read some emotion in my face for she gathered me into her arms in a quick embrace, stroking her fingers over the amulet at the same time as she ordered her brother to go away. Which he did with a stern nod of his head and a distinct swagger.

'Did it work? Did the Blessed Virgin fill you with grace?'

I shook my head. 'Not noticeably. I think I would like to keep it,' I suggested. 'Until supper. If you would allow.'

I thought I would need the continued offices of the Blessed Virgin Mary before this day was out. Before I could answer any more questions, I was swept up by my women. They had work to do on my person if my mother was to be satisfied. They would not let me out of their sight until I was groomed and polished like Ned's new warhorse.

Who were we, this royal but troubled family? Who was I, to be raised in a royal nursery, yet to be used by my mother to rebuild our future security, to repair a damaged reputation?

There was no question about my royal blood. My dead father was Edmund, Earl of Kent, son of King Edward the First by his second wife, which made him half-brother to the previous ill-fated King Edward the Second, and uncle to the present King Edward the Third. There was no question about my impeccable lineage. As I had reminded Ned, I was first cousin to the King.

My mother Margaret, Lady Wake, was of a lesser rank. A young widow, her hand in marriage had been sought by my father, a marriage that had been frowned on by his royal brother. My mother came from good stock, but one which was neither wealthy nor influential in the politics of the day; she was not the woman King Edward the Second would have chosen for his brother. Notwithstanding, my parents married for love, were ultimately accepted back into the royal fold and produced four children in as many years, of whom I was one. Why would they not enjoy a life at the royal court, under the patronage of the King?

'Why is our blood besmirched?' I asked when my mother had regretted the descent of royal disfavour on her and her children.

'Your father was unwise,' my mother said. 'And I allowed myself to be drawn into a plot that brought us to our knees.'

For my parents became involved in the events that removed the second Edward from the throne, casting government into the hands of Earl Mortimer and the Queen, Isabella, who between them brought the young Edward the Third to the throne as the Mortimer puppet. My father, discovering that his brother King Edward was incarcerated in Corfe Castle far to the west, under the control of Earl Mortimer, became involved in a plot to rescue and restore him to the throne, writing letters to that effect, letters that fell into the hands of Earl Mortimer who used them to rid himself of my father.

So my father was taken prisoner, condemned to death for treason in being part of a plot to oust the rightful King Edward the Third. The new young King gave his assent for his uncle's death, which seemed a cruelty beyond belief to me in my youth but later I understood. For my father to have rescued the old King would have threatened not only Earl Mortimer and Queen Isabella, but would have snatched the newly won crown from young King Edward. My royal father, even before I knew him, was executed outside the walls of Winchester Castle.

Thus ended my father, and thus my mother's perennial discontent. We were all blighted by treason, for she too had set her hand to some of those subversive letters. Our titles were gone, our lands confiscated, my mother's jewels and possessions removed, leaving us in woeful condition. Even when Earl Mortimer and Queen Isabella were overthrown in an audacious coup by the young King Edward, we and our estates were duly cast into the King's vengeful lap.

My mother and my eldest brother, polished for the occasion, made petition for mercy and restitution. Now escaped from the Mortimer iron hand, my cousin Edward was of a mind to be magnanimous. My mother was forgiven her treason, my family pardoned, the lands and title restored to us, but only in the sense of my mother being awarded wardship over a selected few of our estates during my brother's minority. The rest remained firmly in King Edward's hands. We children were taken into the royal nursery at Woodstock under the benevolent dominion of Queen Philippa with the Earl and Countess of Salisbury as our governors.

Was the young King suffering a fit of remorse for allowing his uncle to be executed? I expect that he was. He would make amends, yet it did not salve my mother's wounds. She remained permanently embittered, regretting royal refusal to restore her complete authority over the Kent lands, spending her life in wearying travel to oversee and protect those she had in her keeping. A constant hard-won vigilance to oversee the work of her stewards. It was a heavy responsibility.

For me there was no bitterness. I was too young, too naive perhaps for bitterness. But not for ambition. I was royal. I would never give King Edward reason to regret his recognition that I was a worthy cousin.

How did I see myself in years to come with true maturity? The image was not clear, shrouded in mists. All I knew was that I would be myself. Joan of Kent. Princess Joan. Admired and of fine repute.

My mind was set on it.

At two hours after noon, we met in a festively painted and tapestried audience chamber to formalise the agreements over my marriage to William Montagu, heir to the Earl of Salisbury. Clothed in a tightly buttoned cotehardie, a side-less surcoat of rich satin damask cast over all with a jewel-set girdle to anchor it to my hips, as for a royal audience at my mother's request, I entered the chamber at her side, assessing the occupants who, in various attitudes, awaited us. My mother paused to make effect of her majestic presence, smiled with condescension and pushed me forward, determined to dominate the proceedings and achieve the connection she desired, the Earl of Salisbury being King Edward's oldest and most loyal of friends, a friendship stretching back to the days before he achieved the Crown. Salisbury was the man who had stood at King Edward's side when they had taken Roger Mortimer prisoner. The King's gratitude for this loyalty could not be measured.

Those who peopled the chamber were no surprise to either of us. My uncle Sir Thomas Wake to give some weight and support to his sister in the absence of my father. There was the Countess of Salisbury, Catherine de Grandison, in the absence of the Earl. Will was here, standing stiffly beside his grandmother, the ancient Lady Elizabeth Montagu, who had remained seated at our entrance out of pride rather than advanced age. And then there was our family priest to deal with any matters of a religious content. I studied his benignly smiling face. He had no idea of the cataclysm that was about to fall on his — on everyone's — head.

I allowed a trickle of relief that King Edward was not one of our number. Nor Queen Philippa, which would have been even worse.

I might own a strong streak of defiance, but royal displeasure at close quarters was not something to be sought.

I curtsied to the Countess, as I did every day of my life, for she had the role of Governess over me and all the younger royal household. I curtsied to Lady Elizabeth and was acknowledged by an infinitesimal nod of her ruffled veiling. Momentarily I stared at Will, then looked away. I was still wearing Isabella's reliquary, wishing that I had more faith in the efficacy of the Virgin's tears. She had not preserved me from this marriage alliance. Will, dressed as finely as I, incongruously formal in a knee-length gypon and an eye-catchingly domed beaver hat, complete with feather, was studying his linked fingers. He was deliberately not looking at me.

'We are met today,' Sir Thomas announced, taking control of the proceedings in true Wake fashion, 'to make formal agreement of a marriage between my niece, Joan of Kent, and William of Salisbury. Such fine young people, here with us.'

I curtsied again, staring once more at Will, silently commanding him to look at me. Will bowed, and refused. We knew what was expected of us, and there was a little ripple of pleased concurrence as two servants poured wine into fine silver cups and awaited the direction to carry them round.

'Our lord the King has given his blessing,' Countess Catherine, now seated before the fireplace, remarked. 'So has my husband *in absentia*. I am only sorry that the Earl could not be here, but the arrangements need not wait on his release. We strongly desire this match for our son.'

And so followed a discussion of the extent of my dower. Of legal requirements. Of the publication of banns. Of when the marriage would best be solemnised. Of where we would live and when it would be considered proper for us to live intimately as man and wife. All the complex and heavy detail necessary for a marriage between scions of two important houses. As for when, since the festivities of Christmas

and New Year were fast approaching, it was considered by our priest
to be most appropriate to celebrate our marriage after the festivities
and before the penitence of Lent, which would necessitate abstention.

Taking no part in any of this, because none was required except
for me to stand and look royally obedient and flattered, my thoughts
hopped and churned. I allowed none of it to show on my face, not
even when I felt the sharpest of glances, finally, from my soon to be
betrothed.

The discussion was drawing to an end.

'The two young people know each other well. It will be most
advantageous for both, and for our families to be drawn into this
felicitous alliance.'

My uncle Wake again persuading us all of what we already knew.
At last, business done, I could feel the general smiling regard turned
in our direction.

'At least they will know each other's faults and failings before they
are committed to living together,' Lady Elizabeth observed. 'They
are to be envied. The same could not be said for my own marriage.'

'I deny any faults and failings in my son.' Countess Catherine was
not quite in accord with her mother-in-law. 'William, of course,
will soon soften Joan's sharpness of tongue and unpredictable spirit.'

Now, to my right, I could feel Will's regard, fierce as an eagle, for
so mild tempered a youth. I returned it.

'We will make it a superb occasion. It may be that the Earl is
released, making it a double celebration. Edward and Philippa will
of course attend.' My mother, her habitual caustic utterance overlaid
with bright anticipation, incongruous in her sombre figure.

I saw Will's lips part, his brow furrow.

I frowned at him, even as I knew I must bow to his command. I
could remain silent no longer.

'There is no impediment to this marriage that will require a dispensation,' our priest, Father Oswald, writing down the salient points of our betrothal, spoke quietly and with satisfaction into the august exchange. Within aristocratic circles there were few betrothed couples who were not related within the forbidden degree through family intermarriage over the years. Papal dispensations were a common commodity.

'Which is fortunate,' my uncle Wake said with a grimace. 'The present Avignon holder of the office is notorious for being long-winded and expensive.'

I took a breath.

William scowled.

I swallowed and spoke out.

'There is an impediment to this marriage.'

How strong and clear my voice sounded as I launched the statement into the confines of the room, like a fire arrow winging its destructive path over a besieged castle wall to bury itself in a thatched roof of the stabling, with instant conflagration. A statement that would change everything. That would bring ire and retribution down on my head.

I saw Will flush to the roots of his tawny hair. Well, he could not complain. I had done what I said I would do.

'An impediment?' For the first time throughout all that discussion, my uncle Wake's regard fell fully on me, and without approbation. His voice acquired a rough edge. 'What ill-judged nonsense is this? Of course there is no impediment. Have we not studied the lines of descent of our two families with care? There is no connection between us. There is no complication of consanguinity.' He glanced across at Countess Catherine, an assured smile replacing the severe lines. 'As the Countess knows, there is no obstacle to this marriage.'

'What are you thinking, Joan? This is no time for misplaced levity.' My mother tried to sound amused, and failed.

'It is a highly desirable,' Sir Thomas continued, riding roughshod over any objections that anyone might raise. He thought that I had raised my voice because I did not like Will. Did not like him well enough to wed him. How little he knew of me, to think that I would be guided by so trivial a matter of who I liked or did not like. He did not know me at all.

Taking a cup of wine and emptying it in one gulp, my uncle was saying: 'What could be more comfortable for you than our disposition of your future?' He repeated the decisions, as if I had not heard them for myself. 'You have known each other since childhood. You will both continue to live in the royal household until you are of an age to set up your own establishment. You will receive money necessary to do so. What is there not to like? I'm sure the King will settle a castle on you for your household. There can be no impediment.'

Countess Catherine looked across at her son. 'Have you argued? Is that the problem? Arguments are soon mended.' And then regarding me as she was want to do in the past when I was an errant child who had defied her. 'I am sure that you have a kind nature, Joan. There will be no rift with my son.'

Yes, indeed, as if I were a child who affections could be commanded.

I was no child.

'No, Sir Thomas, my lady, madam my mother.' I curtsied once more. 'I like William well enough. And I think he likes me. There has been no disagreement.'

I had to do it. If I didn't, Will most assuredly would. He was already moving his feet as if finding secure ground to launch his accusation.

I spoke calmly, with faux assurance.

'I cannot marry William. I am already married. I already have a husband.'

If I had ever dreamed of making an impact on a busy room, this was it. Silence fell. The only sound the priest, who, still writing, promptly dropped his pen with a soft flutter to land on the birds and flowers that adorned the painted tiles. I watched the expressions form and change. My mother astounded, then full of recrimination. My uncle expressing disbelief quickly subsumed into fury. Lady Elizabeth and her daughter-in-law both simply perplexed. The priest also full of anxious puzzlement. The servants with their silver flagons and ears pricked for any tasty morsel had been struck into immobility. And Will – William! – full of unholy joy at the debacle I had just created.

'You should know,' I added, 'that I have been married for more than six months. Since April of this year.'

'You do not know what you say.'

My mother took one long step to seize my wrist in her hand. It was not a gentle grasp.

'But I do know, madam. And I have witnesses to my marriage.'

'And who is this husband, of whom we know nothing?' My uncle Wake, his brow thunderous.

I must of course tell them.

'My husband is Thomas Holland. Sir Thomas Holland. A knight in the royal household. You all know him well.'

And in that moment a species of black anger shook me. For my husband of six months had wilfully abandoned me to face this situation alone.

Chapter Two

A hot barrage of question, denial and opinion was levelled at me from mother and uncle, all of which I attempted to answer as Countess Catherine had the good sense to shut the servants out of the chamber, relieving them first of the wine.

'What possesses you to make so outrageous a claim?'

'It is no mere claim. It is the truth.'

'And you have said nothing? All these months?'

'We thought it would be politic to say nothing, until Sir Thomas returns from the war.'

'This is naught but a mess of lies, Joan. Have you no sense of morality?'

To which I would not respond.

'An exchange of foolhardy kisses and foolishly romantic promises, I expect.'

It was more than that. Far more. I thought it was not wise to say so. Countess Catherine was simply looking from one to the other. Lady Elizabeth hid her mouth with gnarled hands. Will smirked.

'This gets us nowhere.' Finally my mother raised her hands and her voice in exasperation. 'Speak to her, Father Oswald. We need to know the truth.'

The priest thus beckoned, so that we moved a little away to the end of the chamber where our only audience was from the stitched birds and hunting dogs, all keen eyes, teeth and claws which seemed uncommonly prescient. He bent his head, his tone a holy reprimand although his eyes were kind. I had known him since I had known anyone in my mother's household. I might even hope for compassion here, unless he lectured me on the penalty for sin. He held a parchment and the recovered pen as if to note down all my foolishness that made my claim invalid.

'My daughter. You must indeed tell me the truth, as if you were in confession. Come now, no one can hear us. I am sure that you are mistaken. What has this young man said to you, that makes you think that you are wed?'

It was so easy to answer.

'He asked me to be his wife. And I agreed.'

'But there were no banns called, no priest to give his blessing. How can this be so, then, that you think that you are his wife?'

I knew exactly how it could be so.

'We made our vows together. We were married because we expressed a wish to marry. We spoke them aloud and there are witnesses to it. Thomas said it would be legal and I know that it is.'

He looked at me, worry on his brow, and lowered his voice further. 'Were you forced, my dear? You must say if you were. There would be no blame on your head if it was against your will, persuaded by an ambitious young man against your better judgement.' The tips of his fingers touched my cheek in compassion. 'Was that the case?'

I thought about the wedding. There had been no force at all. I had been a willing bride.

'No, Father. There was no compulsion. He did not have to persuade me.'

'What did you say to this young man?'

I thought back over the six months, and repeated as nearly as I could recall, what I had said to Thomas and what he had said to me.

'Ah ...!' Father Oswald nodded.

'It is legal, is it not, Father?' I asked as he fell into an uncomfortable line of thought, his face falling into even graver lines.

Upon which he flushed. 'It could well be. But... ' He hesitated, then said, more brightly: 'But, of course. There is another matter to be considered for true legality. The matter of consummation. Without this, there is no marriage at all, my dear girl, no matter what vows were spoken.'

My gaze was steady on his, admitting no embarrassment. 'Our marriage is consummated.'

'Are you certain? You are barely of an age to be wed.' His cheeks were aflame. 'It may be that you are not quite aware of what...'

'Yes, Father. I am certain. I am well aware of what is required for consummation and it is more than a quick kiss. And I am of an age to be wed.'

Father Oswald fretted, his fingers tearing at the quill so that it was all but destroyed. He had written nothing. 'Even so... Your lady mother will not like this. For all sorts of reasons.' He looked back over his shoulder, to where my mother and uncle were in deep conversation with a distraught Countess of Salisbury, and Will looking merely bored. 'Where is he now, the young man in question?'

'Fighting somewhere in Europe. When I last heard.'

There was a faint easing of the consternation.

'And you have not heard from him for six months?'

'No, Father.'

'So it may well be that...'

I did not want to guess at what he was thinking. Six months of silence from a man engaged in warfare could mean any number of things. Mentally I swept them aside, for it was a path my mind had long followed of late.

'Sir Thomas assured me that the vows were binding,' was all I would say. 'He assured me that I am his wife.'

'I am afraid that I agree with him.' The priest sighed, took me by the hand and led me back to the lowering group who had resorted to finishing the flagon of wine.

'Well?' My mother faced us, demanding and expecting a retraction.

'She speaks the truth, my lady,' Father Oswald pronounced with all the authority of Holy Mother Church invested in him. 'She and the young knight arc married. Not in the manner that the Holy Father would smile on, but it is a lawful union and it is in my mind that it will stand up as such in any court.'

'I don't believe it.'

'It is so, my lady.' The priest was proud to display his erudition dropping into impressive Latin. 'A marriage *per verba de praesenti.*' He was nervous but pursuing, sure of his legal grounds. 'The young people expressed their intentions. In the present tense you understand, and before witnesses. I regret but it is a binding union.' He turned his regard to me. 'Who are the witnesses, Mistress Joan? You did not say.'

'Never mind the witnesses. What about the consummation?' My uncle Wake, beyond any sensitivity.

'It was, by your niece's own words, consummated.'

'But it can be annulled.'

'No, my lord, it cannot.' Father Oswald was adamant, enjoying his moment of authority. 'The marriage has been consummated. It was entered into willingly and with no duress. There is no room for annulment here, despite the lady's young age. Unfortunately, a consummation makes the oath doubly binding. If that had not occurred, there may have been room for an annulment. As it is, my lord, on the word of the lady here present...'

If there was silence before on my first pronouncement, it was doubly so now.

My wrist was instantly transferred from the priest's gentle hand once more to my mother's fierce grip, hot with a barely controlled fury.

'I will remedy this.' She swept the room with a regard designed to intimidate. 'The arrangements for this Salisbury marriage are by no means in abeyance. I suggest that you discuss this with no one until the matter is settled, one way or another.' The glint in her eye settled on Will who looked to be about to burst with a need to tell all. 'It would be wise to keep this from any ears but our own. And now Mistress Joan…'

I was led from the room with far less grace than I was brought into it.

Looking over my shoulder before the door was closed at my back, I saw that the faint air of malice or boredom in equal measure had been wiped from Will's face. Almost I could read sympathy there. It made me feel no better. Now I had to withstand my mother's displeasure, as I had always known I must. In that moment I wished that I had confessed my marriage to my mother when it was first done. I had chosen otherwise because I had envisioned it being when I decided would be the best time, of my own free will, most crucially with my new husband at my side to plead my case and smooth over any unpleasantness. I had expected Thomas to be somewhere at least close, with his feet in the same realm. Now I was alone, Thomas Holland wielding sword and lance against the infidel in Lithuania in the name of the Teutonic Knights, where he would have no idea of the repercussions of our wilful actions for me in England. Thomas was not one for either reading or writing letters.

Now, alone, I must face the drums and trumpets of my mother's wrath.

I had misjudged the situation. I should not have allowed myself to be left in so vulnerable a position; rather I should have insisted that we announce the deed when it was done rather than let time pass by. It was enough to make me vow, silently, as I matched my footsteps with the staccato beats of my mother's flat soles, that I would never again act against my better judgement. I would never allow myself to be persuaded to renounce what I knew to be in my best interests.

Was this the decision of a selfish young woman? It was. I knew it and had no compunction in making my private vow. I had learnt from my mother that a woman had to keep her wits and her desires sharp if she were to follow the path of her own choosing. My mother, led into treachery by the man she loved, had been left to make what she could of her life without him. I would do better. It was always better to rely on oneself rather than on the promises of a man, however attractive he might be.

But now all I felt was fear. I might appear undaunted, indomitable even, but what would be the outcome? It was beyond my ability to foresee. Would my mother be able to force me into compliance with her wishes? I feared that she would.

It was in my mind to resist, to deny, to refuse.

Blessed Virgin! Give me wisdom and strength to follow my own path.

'Where is he? Where is the despicable cur who lured you into this abominable contract? This rogue who inveigled you into rank scandal that will shake the foundations of our family?'

My uncle, who had accompanied us, invited or not, his anger crackling across the room like a summer storm as soon as the door was closed, turned on me as if he and I together could conjure Thomas Holland into being. His face was suffused with a venom that reverberated outward to the walls and back again. I could taste it on my lips.

My uncle's fingers stretched and fisted, his hair hung dull and lax in disarray on his brow.

'Where is he? I swear he will face the wrath of the King who will strip him of his knighthood before he can step out of his boots on English soil. This is no act of chivalry worthy of a knight, to take a young woman to his marriage bed without the consent of parent, of guardian or priest. He will answer for this.' He turned on me, looming over me, all attempts at controlling his speech failing. 'I presume he did discover a marriage bed for you to honour this travesty.' His lips twisted. 'Or was consummation nothing but a quick fumble behind a pillar or a squalid hanging, as if you were a servant and knew no better. Or even an act of rape...'

'Tom...' my mother warned.

But he was past warning. 'Holland will answer for this,' he repeated. 'I will hunt him down...'

I stood between mother and uncle, bearing the weight of their joint disgust. There would be no compassion here. But then, I could expect none. My choice that day, my own choice, for Thomas had not inveigled me into anything I had not wished with my whole heart, had tottered on the edge of propriety. On the edge of scandalous impropriety. I had always known what was the expectation for me, and I had thrown it away. Willingly. With heartfelt joy.

There was no joy between these four walls. I could see no joy at any point in the future, near or far. Well, I had done it. No point in retreating now.

I spoke a flat, easy denial, of the one fact in all this complicated weave of which I was quite certain. 'Thomas Holland did not inveigle me, sir.'

It was not so difficult, I decided, being aware of a surge of courage. My spine was as straight as a Welsh arrow, my chin raised, my hands loose at my sides. I was Plantagenet, the blood of kings in my veins, and I would not be cowed by my uncle. I would not be reduced under his displeasure to a trembling puddle of regret and repentance. Queen Philippa had tried her best to instil in me some of her gentleness but to no avail. It was not in my nature. I called on that spirit of rebellion now, even as I vowed to keep my temper under close rein.

'He must have.' My uncle dismissed my calm assertion with a slice of his hand through the air. 'It must have been against your will, for, before God, such an act was against every moral tenet of your upbringing.'

'It was not against my will. I wished it. We both did.'

'You were not raised to be a whore, Joan.'

His lip curled as, disbelieving, I felt the flush of humiliation high on my cheekbones. I was no whore.

'You married this man of no birth, of no family, without permission. How could you be so maladroit?'

So my good intentions died a rapid death. Anger, stoking the humiliation of being branded a whore, spurred me into unfortunate retaliation. 'I am not the first member of this family to wed without permission, sir.'

My mother froze. My uncle burned with ire. This was obviously a day for sharp silences. I did not wait for their response, continuing with the righteousness I felt in my bones, first to my mother:

'You married my father without his brother, the King's, permission, madam. The King was not pleased, as I have heard. And you sir,' I held my uncle's eye, 'married Blanche of Lancaster without her father's permission. In the light of such impropriety, it is not appropriate for you to take me to task for doing exactly the same.'

Perhaps not the wisest of moves to brave these two furious lions in their den. But it was true. Neither marriage had been well received, both denigrated because of the Wake family's lack of sufficient grandeur.

My uncle pounced on the the weakness in my own argument.

'Not appropriate? Your mother's husband was a King's son. My wife was daughter of an Earl. We chose well. We made good marriages. This man that you have tied yourself to is not worthy of our consideration. Your argument is specious, Joan.'

'But at least I cannot be accused of overweening ambition, sir. I wed Thomas Holland for his own qualities. I have heard it said that you and my mother had nothing but your pre-eminence in mind. I am not guilty of self-aggrandisement.'

For the briefest of moments I thought he would strike me, yet I stood my ground. Then my mother picked up the gauntlet and stepped onto the battleground.

'Leave us, Tom.'

'Not until we've shaken some sense into your daughter.'

'If there is any shaking to be done, it will not be done by you. Now go away and leave her to me.'

Ungraciously he went. No sooner was the door slammed behind him than the onslaught began again, each word carefully enunciated in her wrath.

'Do you not realise what you have done? How outrageously thoughtless you have been? You know the ambitions that drive young men of no particular blood or background. You know what they will venture, to find a niche for themselves, to gain land and power, and you have played so magnificently into this man's hands. I know who he is. A younger son, with no inheritance of any merit, a knight of no importance from some insignificant estate in the north if I recall the matter. One of the household knights with a life to make for himself, a handsome face and a soldier's agility, but no prospects other than those he might win on the battlefield. His father was notable for a despicable default in loyalty on the battlefield, leading to his murder by his erstwhile friends. And you have been wilful enough to ally yourself with such a family, wasting your royal blood on a man without name or fortune.'

She stopped, but only to draw breath. Yet before she could continue, in pure self defence:

'So was my father executed as a traitor,' I said.

It was the wrong thing to say. The wrong time to say it, even though there was no doubting it. Whereas my uncle had restrained himself, my mother lashed out with her hand, catching me with a flat blow against my cheek that made me stagger. She had never stuck me before. Verbally yes, but never with such physicality. I read her anger in the engraved lines of her face, as I refused to raise my hand to register the raw impact of the blow. Instead I simply stood and faced her, eyes wide on hers.

'Your father was pardoned,' she said, as if the violence had never occurred. 'His reputation and his name were wiped clean from the filth of treachery by King Edward himself.'

'You were involved also, madam.' The outline of her hand still smarted, so I gave no quarter, whatever the wisdom of it. 'Were you exonerated too?'

'Your defiance is unacceptable.'

My whole body tensed, until my mother grasped at her dignity, threading her fingers together, moderating her tone.

'You know that I was. And you too, or you would not have been given the honour of royal status in the queen's household.' Her fury might be under control but she had still not finished with me. 'Are you so credulous? I did not think a daughter of mine would fall into the hands of a man of no distinction, like a ripe plum into his palm. All he saw was an indiscreet girl with royal connections who could pave his way to some place in the royal court, opening the doors to patronage and wealth and royal preferment. How could you have been so immeasurably foolish?'

'Thomas did not want me for patronage and preferment.'

'Do you say?' Her mouth twisted in an unmistakable sneer. 'He must be the only man in the realm who would not!'

It had more than crossed my own mind, yet still I believed that Thomas Holland saw more in me than a path to royal approval. Love was a powerful bonding.

'Joan!' My mother, abandoning accusation, fell back on a false softness. 'Tell me that he persuaded you with honeyed words. If that is so, this marriage can be annulled before anyone else is the wiser.'

I could not imagine Thomas using honeyed words. Thomas was a soldier, not a troubadour, his knowledge of songs limited to those a troop of militia might roar round a campfire after victory. Or possibly those employed by harlots in a camp brothel to seduce the coin from a soldier's purse.

'I was not persuaded,' I said, 'if you mean lured into impropriety against my will. I gave my full and free consent. I wished to be married to him. I love him. And he loves me.'

But she would not let the battle lapse, driving on with all force. 'You knew it would be unacceptable. So did he. Did he persuade you to such subterfuge? If he was a man of chivalry, a true knight, he would not have wed you in secret.'

'We knew you would not support it. We had no choice.'

'You knew well! I wanted this Montagu marriage, as did the King. Our future would be safe, secure, our inheritance inviolable from attack. Your children would be Earls of Salisbury. I could not believe our good fortune when the Montagu connection looked in your direction.'

I frowned a little.

'But who would attack our inheritance? The King has restored all our father's lands to us. John's ownership as Earl of Kent is unquestioned.'

Were we not safe enough now that the Mortimer treachery had been so ruthlessly stamped out? The King had openly forgiven my father's involvement in the plot to undermine his power. It was all so long ago in the past. I could not truly understand why my mother should still feel so insecure.

'I was not given authority over all the estates. A permanent punishment, a constant reminder that I must watch my step.' Oh, she was aggrieved, and not only towards me. 'Who's to know what the King might be moved to take from us if displeased? How do we read the future?' She turned away as if the sight of me was anathema. 'What do we do now? Accept it? Father Oswald was plain that it was a legal binding if you exchanged vows and with witnesses. How do we circumvent such an appalling outcome? And you confirmed that it was consummated...'

On a thought she whipped round, her whole expression arrested. 'That's it! Did he force you, before the marriage? Was that how it was? Are you carrying his misbegotten child, so that you must wed him?' Her eyes travelled over the flat expanse below my girdle as if she would delight in seeing evidence of my sin. 'No, of course you could not. When did this travesty take place? May? And as he has not been in England since to my knowledge, it's a specious argument.' I could feel my face flame, whereas my mother's was still full of a bright but false hope. 'Yet if he did force you, it would provide grounds for an annulment.'

I read uncharitable anticipation there. My mother would willingly discuss my rape if it could sever the terrible bond with Thomas Holland.

'He did not force me. I did not wed him to save my reputation. I will not cry rape.'

My mother's accusations lurched into a different track as she strode the length of the chamber and then back again. 'Were you so carelessly chaperoned? I cannot believe that the Queen would allow the young women of her household such license. We will send for Holland. We will make him retract his words, the whole disgraceful debacle. We will know the truth.'

'You cannot send for him,' I said, wishing that she could, wishing that I could.

My mother once more stood before me. 'Why not? Where is he? We are not at war. There is a truce. Where is this bold knight who besmirched your reputation but leaves you alone to face the world with the repercussions of your mistakes.'

I told her what I knew. It was not much. 'He has gone, I think, to Prussia. There was an appeal from the Holy Father and the Teutonic Knights...'

I was interrupted. 'A crusade? A knight who follows the cross? God was far from his thoughts in this recent venture. He is mired in sin.' Then once again my mother's eyes lit with a sudden realisation. 'When did you last have news of him?'

'He left after we were wed, in spring.'

'And now it is October. Have you heard from him since?'

'No.' I could read the direction of her thoughts as if they were bathed in golden sunlight, rather than hidden in the black shadow of loss for me. Had I not thought of this possibility, again and again?

Her fingers tapped against her girdle. 'Six months, with no news. Do you suppose that he is dead? It would solve the problem with no more need for our anxiety.' She scowled at me when I made no reply, for how could I? My heart was sore with the foretaste of death on some distant battlefield. Already his body might be reduced to a carrion-stripped carcase, and I not know of it.

'Yes. That is it,' my mother was saying, her voice becoming smooth in her certainty. 'He is dead. Nor do I admit the legality of a form of words, whatever the priest's opinion. There is a way out of this, for all of us.' She took my hand, more gently now. 'You will forget this man. You will forget this day, and the day that you claim you exchanged facile promises. The details of your marriage to William Montagu will be formalised between myself and the Countess of Salisbury, and it will happen.'

I heard her instructions but I would not obey.

'I will not wed William Montagu,' I said.

'You will be there at the altar and you will give your consent.'

'I will not. I cannot. My holy vow is given elsewhere.'

'You will do as I, your mother, command.'

When she released me I closed my hand hard over Isabella's reliquary.

'In the sight of God I am wife of Sir Thomas Holland. I cannot, I will not, wed William Montagu.'

My holy vow is given elsewhere, I had said. I love Thomas Holland, I had said. Was this true, that my heart resided in the keeping of a poor knight on some distant battlefield in Prussia? In those days, love seemed far distant from me, so distant that it sat on my conscience. Was I so shallow, so superficial that I should doubt that love as soon as its power was challenged?

I did not think that I was shallow. I would swear before the Blessed Virgin that my heart had been given honestly and lastingly.

That was not the end to it. I never thought it would be, rather it would be a matter of whose will proved the stronger, mine or the combined weight of the Wake and Montagu families. Furthermore, more persuasive than all the rest, did not this marriage have the blessing of the King himself? I would have to gird myself like any knight to wage this war of attrition, to withstand the siege of my will and my senses.

Or no. This was no siege at all, rather a relentless campaign. It was not a matter of wearing down my assertions in respect of my wedded state. My mother and uncle and the Countess of Salisbury simply rode roughshod over all legal and personal denials. I would wed William Montagu as soon as we could be brought before the altar with the banns called and a priest, ignorant of the true state of affairs, sufficiently acquiescent to record our vows before God.

But I had witnesses, even though they were crusading with Thomas, and some might say their witnessing worthlessly obscure. Yet did I not have the family priest who had declared my marriage valid even though not officially blessed? Would he stand me in no good stead? My mother snapped her fingers in dismissal when, once again, the relevant families met together and I raised my well-versed, frequently voiced objections.

'You have no witnesses, Joan. It is an invalid act. The priest was mistaken.'

I tried no more. What had my mother done, I wondered, to be so certain of her victory? Bribed the priest? Warned him to hold his tongue on pain of dismissal? With my mother and uncle and the Countess of Salisbury united in a determination to tie the nuptial knot between myself and William, the triumvirate once more embarked on detailed discussion, while, drawing him aside, as a betrothed had the right to do, I tested the water with William.

'Do you want me as your wife, Will?'

If he objected, then there was hope.

'I don't see why not.' He looked at me warily but with good humour. 'I know your temper, and how to avoid it. And you are very pretty.'

'I have no fortune to bring as a dowry.'

I had practised every detrimental argument.

'You have royal blood. My mother hopes that the King will dower you substantially.'

'The King is short of money. His foreign matters against France do not prosper, pinned down as he is with sieges of towns that have no intention of surrendering. I doubt he can dower me to any degree.'

William looked at me with owlish bewilderment, his brows forming astonished arcs. He did not believe me. William did not listen to court gossip as much as I.

'I cannot love you,' I said.

I liked him well enough. With his equable demeanour, he would make some woman an excellent and devoted husband.

William grinned, a sudden lightening of his rather heavy countenance. 'My mother says that you will grow to love me. As I will grow to love you. I can sing you songs of love and devotion.'

'You, Will, cannot sing at all, unless you call that raven-like croak singing. And you do not love me.'

'No, but I will be a chivalrous knight. Not like Holland who wed you, bedded you and fled the country.'

I wondered where he had discovered that particular comment. Probably, from the polite tone, from his mother. Not from Lord Wake who tended to be crude in these matters.

'Thomas will come back.'

'My mother says he is dead.'

I felt a lick of temper heat my blood. 'So does mine. Just wishful thinking on their part. And on yours. If you were not a creature of straw, you would support me and refuse my hand.'

'I'm no creature of straw, and there's no point in your taking out your vexation on me, Joan. I am impervious.'

Irritated beyond measure, I tried the final throw of the matrimonial dice. 'Listen to me, Will, not to your mother.' I shook his fur-cuffed sleeve for emphasis. 'If my marriage to Thomas is valid, as the priest says, then mine to you would be invalid. Any heir I bore you would be illegitimate. Any son born between us could never be Earl of

Salisbury when you are dead, and there would be terrible scandal.
What would you think of that?'

His grin fading, Will flushed as bright as a cider apple, but he
replied readily enough. 'My mother says that we will not live as
man and wife for the next few years. By then any legal problems
will have been smoothed out. Besides, Joan, our marriage will be
valid. There will be no scandal, and you must not say anything
that would rouse a breath of it. If you do, they will punish you,
you know.' And then, his brows meeting above his nose: 'They'll
probably punish me too, for not stopping you from spreading false
rumour. I wouldn't like that.'

He had been well schooled. And there at the end the hint of a threat.
When he patted my arm in a clumsy fashion, as if that would make
all well, an unpleasant helplessness gnawed at my determination to
hold out. Will would simply go along with the family demands and
plans. There was no hope of escape for me here.

I released myself from the patting and went to stand at the window
so that I might look out towards the east. I thought of sending Thomas
a letter, paying a courier to deliver it. But how to find him in the
vast expanses of Prussia with the Teutonic knights. And even if I
did, would he drop his weapons and ride hotfoot back to England? I
would like to think that he would. I prayed that he would. I needed
help and time was running out.

I saw more of my mother in those next weeks than I had in all the
previous years of my life since Queen Philippa had been so touched
by compassion at our situation that she took us under her wing. There
my mother had been content to leave me during her extensive travels;
now, with the need to bring the marriage to its conclusion, her lectures
were long and detailed. And so I listened to my mother's instructions
of what was required of me, standing firm under the pinching fingers

of the sempstresses whose task was the sewing of a gown fitting for a future Countess of Salisbury, the rich cloth a present from the Queen.

Meanwhile I survived the clipped animadversions, on which pertinent facts from my past I should forget and pretend never happened. I absorbed the detailed disclosures of what would be my life after this marriage; a wife but not a wife. We would live separately, I completing my lessons and acquiring court polish while William continued to hone his skills for warfare to follow in the footsteps of his gallant father. We would probably be granted money and an estate by the King, in recognition of our married state, for our new household.

I would hold fast to the undoubted fact that I was a virgin. I would never voice the possibility that this was not so.

There were no difficulties foreseen.

'We will make no fuss about this little matter of Thomas Holland,' my mother completed her lecture as if the sempstresses did not exist. 'The least said the better. There will be no washing of the dirty linen of your making in public. Once the marriage to the Montagu heir is witnessed under the auspices of Holy Mother Church, by the Archbishop of Canterbury himself if we can get him, then we can all breathe a sigh of relief. No hint of scandal must reach Edward and Philippa. What they do not know they will not worry about. It is a blessing that they are both still in Flanders.' Philippa and Edward were still together in Ghent in the aftermath of the French truce. My mother almost smiled. 'The war against France has an unlooked-for benefit.'

To which I replied on every occasion, when I was allowed to break the flow.

'I will not marry William. I am already the wife of Thomas Holland, before the law and before God.'

My mother never struck me again, whatever the provocation, and there was much, even though I stood in silence to hear her pronouncements and agreed that the gown with its carved buttons and embroidered hem was superb. She merely ignored what I said as beneath her notice and covered any reticence with her own cold certainty. I would marry as my family instructed, as any well brought up daughter would accept the duty of obedience.

And what did those who gathered in our chamber at Windsor think of my good fortune? Here with the princesses Isabella and Joan, with my own brother John, with Ned and Will and baby Lionel, my marriage to Will was accepted as a natural development of the King's wish to reward the Earl. Will was sworn to secrecy under what threats I could not imagine since, unnervingly, he kept as silent as a Thames oyster.

'Although *I* would never marry a man of my father's choice if I did not like him,' Isabella announced. 'But of course you like William.'

'You would marry exactly whom your father instructed you to marry,' I said, patience wearing thin. But yes I did like William. That was one of the problems. I was in no mind to hurt him or tip coals of fire over his head. He must not be punished for my sins.

'Of course, I will not marry a man unless I have formed a lasting passion for him.' Isabella was not deterred.

'Then I wish you well. I presume that you will take the veil when you reach your thirtieth year and your schemes have fallen flat.'

'But they will not. I have every intention of capturing a lover who will kneel at my feet in adoration.'

'If I might suggest, then, do not lend your reliquary to anyone. You will have constant need of it.'

Oh, I was ruffled beyond bearing.

'I'll not lend it to you again!' Then Isabella's sharpness softened, but I should have known better than to believe that I was forgiven. 'The problem is, Joan, that you are incapable of forming a lasting passion for anyone but yourself.'

She left precipitately before I could think of a suitable rejoinder.

Notwithstanding such minor clashes, all accepted that we would be wed after the New Year and we would all rejoice. Except for Ned who took a moment from riding at the quintain, his hair plastered with sweat to his skull, still clad in mismatched elements of his armour.

'Does Lady Margaret force you to marry against your will, Jeanette?'

Of them all, it seemed that he had seen the anxiety that I had thought well hidden. It surprised me. Ned noticed very little that did not appertain to his own rank and importance or to his future ambition on the battlefield. Also, of them all, he still sometimes addressed me by my childhood nursery name. I did not mind it, from the Prince, the heir to the throne, and for one moment of weakness I considered telling him the truth, until treading that idea firmly underfoot. It was not as if he could do anything to remedy my situation, and he would have forgotten about it after another five minutes in the tilt yard. I would not burden his kindness with an answer.

'Why?' Still I was interested in why he should think so.

'You are quieter than usual.'

So I must remember to chatter mindlessly, to deflect suspicion. 'No,' I lied. 'I am not under duress.'

He did not believe me. 'I understand that you have to marry. Girls do.'

'Yes.'

'You must have expected it. Why should it worry you? And Will's not some disgusting old knight with greasy fingers.'

I wrinkled my nose. There were many I could name who might fit that description. 'No.'

'You could marry me. If you do not wish to marry Will.' For a long moment he stared down his nose at me, registering my reaction, which had been less than flattering. 'No, you could not, of course. My father looks for a princess from Europe with money and connections and a powerful family. There are any number to choose from.'

Which made me laugh.

'Who is it this week?'

'Well, it was the daughter of King Philip of France. Now I think my father has changed his mind. It is to be Margaret, daughter of Duke John of Lorraine and Brabant.' He studied me with some speculation. 'You, Jeanette, are probably prettier than both – not that I have seen them – but sadly you cannot hold a candle to either of them in the round of marriage negotiations.'

Which might be true, but not gratifying to hear. 'I am a princess,' I remarked.

'True,' Ned agreed. 'A princess with no money, no influence and your father's mistakes behind you. I need a powerful family with an army at its back and a fortune in its coffers.'

'Whereas my brother the Earl is younger than I, so hardly likely to ride to my rescue, or yours, in moments of danger,' I considered. 'And I doubt his treasure coffers match your expectations.'

Ned thought about this, scratching his fingers through his drying hair so that it stood up in spikes. 'I would,' he said, enigmatically.

'Would what?'

'Ride to your rescue, of course.'

'Of course you would.' My heart suddenly warm within my chest, I hugged him and he allowed it. He had an affection for me, as I had for him.

'We could not wed anyway.' I planted a kiss on his moist brow. 'We are well connected within the bounds of consanguinity. Your great-grandfather is my great-grandfather too.'

'I know that. But then, I am related to almost everyone. We would get a papal dispensation. It's not impossible.'

'You are very kind.' He was. My heart jumped a little at his thoughtfulness. 'But your mother and father would not like it. Neither would William.'

'William would not care. I would give him one of my tournament horses. He would like that just as well as a bride.'

Which was probably true. It put an end to the discussion which had become frivolous.

'I will dance at your wedding, Jeanette.'

But I would not. It was not in my heart to dance.

The day appointed for my union with the Salisbury heir was growing closer. The banns were called without a breath of rumour raising its head. No one uttered any impediment as to why it should not take place, blessed by God and witnessed by a puissant congregation, while I suffered from a despicable fear. Could I stand up before the altar and announce before the King and Queen, the Archbishop, and the whole royal court that I was not free to marry?

It seemed that I must. It was a matter of loyalty, of honour, of dedication to the man to whom I had pledged my heart and my life. And if my pride was destined to suffer from a blast of unwavering displeasure, then so be it. My marriage to Sir Thomas Holland must be made plain to all.

My path first crossed that of Thomas Holland, through no devising of mine, in Ghent, where I had accompanied Philippa, who did not wish to be parted from her royal husband longer than was necessary despite the uneasy stalemate between France and England. Edward was planning one of his famous tournaments in Brussels with much gift-giving and negotiating under cover of the clash of weapons in mock fight. Since, as we all knew, he was intent on laying claim to the crown of France through the blood of his mother, he needed all the help he could get and had a mind to sign treaties with Brabant and Flanders. He would need allies when the King of France came to hear his ringing acclamation that the French crown belonged by right of birth to the King of England.

Philippa, being pregnant and indolent, was not enthusiastic about travelling to Brussels, and so declined the promised jollity. I was more than enthusiastic, as was Isabella, nor was Edward averse to having decorative females present to grace his ceremonies. Looking round for a likely escort, he beckoned to the first passing knight of the household.

'Sir Thomas will escort you and see you safely there.' And to Sir Thomas: 'Don't let them out of your sight. They are valuable.' And to us: 'Mind you do what Sir Thomas says.'

Sir Thomas bowed. He looked as if he would rather not.

He had masterful features and a shock of dark hair with more than a touch of autumn where it curled against his neck. He was young too. And stalwartly built. With such an attractive prospect, I chose to ride beside him, in spite of my high status that might have pushed Edward into ordering me to make use of the Queen's travelling chariot if he had had the time to think of it. Unused to escorts who would rather be elsewhere, I was intrigued. A man who was unmoved by my renowned beauty was out of the ordinary.

'You don't have to watch over us like a herding dog,' I said, to promote some response.

'I do. My King commands it. My lady.' He stared straight ahead, allowing me a splendid view of his straight nose and clenched jaw.

'Then you could smile. As if obeying the King gives you some pleasure.'

'I could, my lady.' The jaw remained clenched.

'Where would you rather be?' I asked, now with more than a passing interest.

'Back there,' he gestured, 'with my horses and equipment.'

'Do you not have a squire?'

'I do.'

'Then he will look after them for you. Will you fight in the tournament?'

'Of course.'

'Will you enjoy it?' This was hard work, but I imagined that his voice held a pleasing tone when not so brusque.

'I need the money, my lady.'

Of course. He would earn little as a household knight. 'Are you a good combatant?' I asked.

'Yes.'

His confidence was as impressive as his stark features.

'I will give you my favour to wear if you wish,' I offered. 'To bring you good fortune.'

For the first time his head turned imperceptibly towards me. 'Your cousin the King would not approve.'

'Why would he not?' I certainly knew that Philippa would disapprove of this conversation. Which made me smile. I so rarely had the opportunity to converse with a young knight with what might be considered impropriety.

'I am a knight with little to recommend me. You are of royal blood.'

'That is true,' I admitted. 'But are you not a valiant knight?'

'Yes.'

'Then you will be my valiant knight in the tourney.' I became expansive, abandoning the modesty of my upbringing. 'You will be my Sir Galahad.'

His eyes slid fully to mine.

'It would be my honour to fight for you.' It was the first time, I thought, that he had looked directly at me. 'But will you watch me fight? There will be others more worthy of your notice. Some Brabant lordling in gilded armour, I expect.'

So there was a hint of pique in my Sir Galahad. 'Well, if there is a gilded lordling, I will watch him, but I will promise to watch you too.' How cheerfully I set out to destroy his grave displeasure. 'I wager that you will be beaten by some Flemish knight in the first bout.'

Sir Thomas Holland's brows flattened. 'What will you wager?'

'This.' Stripping off my glove, a waved my fingers so that the deep red of a ruby glowed.

'You cannot wager that against my skill.' How uncompromising he was.

'Why not?'

'It is more valuable than all my Holland inheritance put together.'

'It was a gift to me and so is mine to wager.' I smiled at him. 'You must make sure that you win.'

Sir Thomas slowly returned the smile. 'I always win.'

'Is she annoying you?' Following rapidly in our wake, Edward drew alongside.

Sir Thomas rearranged his features into the stern visage of a royal escort. 'No, my lord.'

'Hurry up then. We haven't all day.'

And since Isabella joined us our conversation was at an end. But it was a conversation that remained with me, embedded in my mind, trivial as it was. I had flirted. I had been artful. I had enjoyed it. And so, I decided, had Sir Thomas Holland.

Sir Thomas Holland won his bouts against any number of Brabant and Flemish lordlings, gilded or otherwise. Against English ones too, impressing me with his fighting skills, whether with sword or lance. His lack of wealth and status stood for nought when he beat his opponent to the floor, then with a strikingly gracious elegance offered his hand to pull him to his feet.

In the end I kept the ring.

Miraculously, I lost my heart.

I knew not how it could happen, or when, for I had no experience of such emotion that compromised my breathing and disturbed the beat of my blood at wrist and throat. Somewhere between his kissing my fingers when I pinned a scarf to his sleeve and his kneeling to accept a purse of coin from King Edward, I was smitten with a yearning that he would look at me again, and often. The clouds were low and grey but he shone in my sight. I was ashamed to acknowledge that I watched him to the exclusion of any other knight on the field. I did not understand it, but it was as if some finest of threads had been spun by an invisible hand to connect us, one to the other. Was it a malicious hand, for we were not equal in status? I did not care.

I was desolate when he did not escort us back to Ghent, the task being given to an ageing knight who had nothing to say for himself.

I discovered a need to put myself in my erstwhile escort's way, not difficult in the lax household at Ghent where knights and damsels mingled more freely than at Windsor, and so did royal cousins. Everyone passed through the Great Hall at some point in the day.

'Did you make your fortune, Sir Thomas?'

'No. I did not.'

He was no more forthcoming than on the road to Brussels but he looked at me, a direct stare that stirred a little warmth into my blood.

'But you caught the King's admiration,' I suggested.

'On this occasion it was not the King's admiration I was thinking of.'

He frowned at me, as if he might wish the words unsaid.

The tilt of my chin was unforgivable. 'Who was it that you wished to attract? Some Flemish lady perhaps?'

'No. An English lady.'

'And who might that be?'

'I imagine you know very well.' His stare became fiercer, his response more particular than I had expected. I was considering how to reply when he continued. 'You are far beyond my reach, my lady.'

Indeed I was.

'I think that I am not,' I said.

'The Queen would tell you differently.'

Indeed she would.

'The stories in my books,' I said, 'tell me that nothing should stand in the way of love. I am an enthusiastic reader of the adventures and amours of King Arthur's knights.'

'Your books will tell you that you do not understand the meaning of love.'

'What do you think, Sir Thomas?'

His hands clenched around his belt. 'I think that you are the most beautiful girl I have ever seen. I think that I would consider it my holy grail to wed such as you.'

By now the warmth in my blood had become a heat.

'But that is not a holy grail that you can achieve, until you ask for my hand. Have you asked me to wed you, Sir Thomas?'

'I would not. I dare not.'

Shocked at my own temerity, I placed my hand on his arm.

'Please do, Sir Thomas.'

His eyes, softer now and very appealing, were full of raw emotion. 'If I did, I hope that you would have the sense, for both of us, to refuse me.'

He bowed and walked away, leaving me solitary but unexpectedly exhilarated.

In whirlwind fashion and the spirit of all courageous knights, since once this attraction had gripped us it refused to grant us release, Sir Thomas Holland did ask me. I did not have the sense to refuse.

'Yes,' I said. And always practical: 'When?'

'Now.'

'Can we not wait?' I might be in thrall to him, but this seemed unconscionably fast.

'If we wait, you'll be lost to me. You'll be married to your Flemish lord before the month's out.' A faint line appeared between his brows. 'I wish you were not so young.'

I smoothed it away with a finger. 'Time will take care of that. Do you love me, Thomas Holland?'

'More than you will ever believe. Is my love returned?'

'Yes.'

Which settled the whole affair.

These were the days, back at Westminster, when my thoughts clung to the person and environs of my lawful husband rather than the stitching of my new garments. Where was Thomas Holland? Were his military adventures likely to demand all his concentration, or would they allow him to return home in time to rescue me from the altar? It was in my mind that he would most likely discover yet another battle in which to make his name and fortune. He did not know that his wedded state, so carefully kept secret, was about to be destroyed.

With some investigation in mind, I absented myself from my morning lessons with lute and songbook on the plea that my mother needed me for matters appertaining to my wedding and went to avail myself of my cousin the King's library. A room full of books, leather bound, gilded, redolent of the mustiness of old ink, I entered the silent and empty chamber. But it was not the books that drew me. I was looking for the loose-leafed manuscripts, many of them gifts to the King; maps and charts, old and new, of distant lands as well as tracts closer to home, unbound and highly precious. Edward would not object if I investigated. He might be surprised that my interests had turned to what might exist across the sea, but he would not forbid it.

Discovering the sheets of vellum in a low coffer, I unfolded the leather cover, lifting them them out one by one, spreading them across the table used for such large items. I had travelled more than many

persons my age. Born at Arundel, of which I had no memory, I had
resided chiefly in London since my father's death. Thus I knew the
reaches of the Thames and the palaces along its length. I had lived at
the Tower and at Westminster and at Havering-atte-Bower, Philippa's
favourite manor. Further afield I knew Kennington and Woodstock
and, of course, Windsor where we were now based. I had also travelled
to Flanders with the royal household when Philippa had chosen to
follow the King on his campaigning. I knew Ghent well. But further
than that was a blank space.

A map of England was of no value to me. A painted copy of
Mappa Mundi with Jerusalem at its centre intrigued me when I found
England tucked along the edge but it did not aid me in discovering
where Prussia might be. And even if I found it, I acknowledged in
sour mood, what value would that be to me? It could be years before
Thomas returned with his weapons and horses and coffers of coin.

I slapped my hand down on the precious document, raising a cloud
of dust.

I understood perfectly why Thomas was driven to use his skills in
theatres of war. My mother's slighting of the Holland family had been
more than accurate. Thomas had no claim to greatness other than
the reputation that he could win with his own endeavours. Besides,
he liked soldiering. After the very briefest celebration of our wedded
bliss, Thomas had pledged his everlasting love, packed his fighting
equipment and, with page and squire had taken himself to join the
King, eventually engaging in the Battle of Sluys, the battle where
King Edward had made his mark in a magnificent victory, as well as
taking a French spear in his thigh that kept him to his bed for two
whole weeks. And then, in a matter of days, both King and Thomas
had been engaged in the siege at Tournai that had achieved little but
an expensive truce between England and France.

Edward was now recently returned home from his campaigning

against the French, seething with anger of his lack of money and his discovery of the abominable lack of defence of the Tower of London in his absence, but Thomas was not. Thomas had found a need to go to Prussia. It would avail me nothing to know where Prussia actually was but my spirits were at a low ebb. Abandoning my search, I began to shuffle the maps back into order. I had been chasing a wild goose, and it had escaped me.

'I thought I would be alone here.'

The voice, quiet yet unexpected, made me jump so that I dropped the route between London and Jerusalem, illuminated with tiny pictures of towns on the way, that I was holding.

The King clicked his tongue and picked it up, smoothing it back onto the table, casting an eye over it.

'I was not aware that your interests were in discovery of the world, Joan. Or of going on a pilgrimage to the Holy Sites.' There was a gleam in his eye. 'My advice is to go to Canterbury first, to see if you have a taste for the pilgrim life.'

My cousin, twenty-eight years old now, hardened and bloodied from campaigning, a ruler of supreme confidence and some renown, was laughing at me. The life of a pilgrim with hard travel and noxious inns with their communal beds and lice would not suit me at all.

'No, my lord.' I felt a need to be formal. He might be my cousin but he was King and this was his library in which I was trespassing. 'They are beautiful to look at. I am sorry if I should not have unwrapped them. I know their value.'

His gaze moved from the map to me. 'There is solace in beautiful work, as I know. If I were not King, yet still I would be a collector of books.' Then he smiled so that the sombre lines of his face were transfigured into prints of pleasure. 'I would not have thought you unhappy, with your marriage imminent.' I tensed. Did he know?

Had he some presentiment of the difficulties? 'The Salisbury boy is well favoured and good natured.'

No, he did not know. I breathed out slowly. 'Yes,' I said. 'William is blessed with both face and character.'

'I wager he'll make a good husband. I know of no vices.'

'No, sir.'

I thought that I might tell him, that I might appeal to his judgement for a resolution of my case. Would he not have compassion and rescue me? But Edward was speaking, accepting of my compliance.

'Marriage can be a vital element, particularly if there is love or strong affection. I miss Philippa.' He smiled, a little sadly. 'She will be returned from Ghent before your marriage. She will be here to wish you well.'

He sifted through the documents as I had done, selecting one that showed the stretch of water separating England from Flanders and France. And here was my chance.

'Will you show me where Prussia is, my lord?'

'We are very formal today, Joan. Here.' He turned the map so that I could see where his finger pointed to the east. 'Why do you need to know?' Then fortunately not waiting for an answer, he added: 'There are a number of my English knights fighting there in the crusade. The Teutonic knights are intent on taking this piece of territory from the Slavs and Christianising it. A worthy cause. I know Thomas Holland has gone there after Tournai – making quite an impression too, so I hear. I need more knights with the courage and commitment of Thomas Holland.' He smiled a little wistfully. 'I recall knighting him some years ago now, at the end of the Scottish campaign. He was very young but impressive even then.'

His name, dropped into the conversation, so suddenly, so unexpectedly, wiped my mind of comment. Then again I saw my chance, running my tongue over dry lips.

'Is he fighting bravely?' I asked with all the insouciance in the world. I found that I needed to talk about him, just to hear his name mentioned without vilification.

'Indeed he is. He has been wounded, but nothing short of a spear through his heart will stop Thomas.' Edward massaged his thigh with his fingers. He still felt the spear wound. 'I have had reports that he continues fighting, even with a bandage around his head.'

I inhaled slowly. 'So he is not dead?'

'Very much alive. Making important friends on the battlefield too.' Edward's glance was suddenly keen. 'I had no idea that you were interested in military campaigns either.'

'I am not. Except when it is an English victory. And to know that our English knights are fighting bravely.'

Fortunately for me, Edward's thoughts were elsewhere, his attention claimed by a chart that showed the northern areas of Flanders and France, and his tone became dark with an unexpected foreboding.

'My task is not finished there.' He jabbed at it with a finger. 'I signed a truce with the King of France because I had not the money to continue the siege at Tournai. It was not a bad truce, you understand. I came out of it before my money ran out.' He grimaced. 'What King enjoys defeat? For me the truce had the degradation of failure. But I will fight again. My claim on the throne of France through my mother's blood is one that must engender respect. We will achieve a great victory there one day with the aid of my brave young knights.' His gaze, still centred on the map, softened. 'My son Edward will be a greater warrior than I could ever be. He will make of England a name that will last for ever where tales of greatness and valour are told.'

And in spite of my own selfish preoccupations, I was drawn into his vision.

'I have a thought, you know. Come and look at this.' He drew me away, a hand on my sleeve to lead me to a book that he took down from a shelf. Opening it, he turned to a picture that I knew well, for these stories had stirred the romance in my youthful soul: a vivid illustration of King Arthur, seated around a vast table with the best of his knights.

'It is my thought to create an order of knights,' Edward was explaining, 'the bravest ever seen since the days of King Arthur. Men who will fight for right and justice and wisdom, for the glory of England and of God. I will choose the finest, the most chivalric, just as Arthur chose. It will be a great honour for a knight to be invited to join such an august gathering.' Forgetting about me at his elbow, he was fired with the dream, his eyes alight as he turned the pages to illustrations of Sir Lancelot, Sir Galahad, Sir Gawain and a host of others of repute. 'I see them bearing an insignia which will be known the length and breadth of Europe. My eldest son will be one of the first. William of Salisbury too, my closest friends who have stood in battle with me. Then there are others, young men such as Thomas Holland. We will test their skills in tournaments where they will show their prowess before the whole world. Perhaps even some of the greatest knights from Europe too will be invited...'

It startled me momentarily, that Edward would include Thomas within his pre-eminent body of man. And yet why not? In my eyes he was brave and bold and everything a knight should be. I could see him in my mind's eye with that shining insignia on his breast, whatever it might be, the magnificent cloak, if Edward decided that is what they would wear. I knew well the King's taste for the dramatic in clothing. I was swept along with the glory of it, although Edward was unaware.

'I will have them take an oath to fight against evil, a stern and binding oath to God and St. George. Now *he* will be the best saint for our emblem, would he not? My knights will promise to fight the good fight, to stand firm. What a magnificent achievement it will be!

King Arthur's knights have lived long in song and story. Mine will live even longer. I will even have my own Round Table...'

I nodded to encourage his enthusiasm, my thoughts with distant Thomas, recipient of such glory.

'I have a thought about the insignia. A garter with the words *Honi soit quit mal y pense*. Evil be to him that evil thinks. What do you think to that?'

Again I nodded.

'They will live up to their oath to uphold God's and my law, on pain of dismissal. We will have no more scandal in this land. My reign will be remembered for all time for the honesty of its King and its knights. The law will be sacrosanct. It is a dream I have.'

Edward's words struck home.

An oath. A solemn, binding oath to live a blameless life, full of honour and sanctity.

'I will not have scandal and treachery and dishonour in this land. I will not have such a travesty of God's laws. Any knight who dishonours God dishonours me and will be stripped of his knighthood and cast out of the kingdom.'

It made me shiver.

'But those who are worthy. What do you think, cousin? What colour shall I clothe them in? You have an eye for colour.'

I sought for a reply, while my mind dismantled Edward's dream.

'Blue,' I said. 'The blue of the Blessed Virgin's gown.'

'I knew you would choose well.'

'I am not sure that I have any bearing on your decision, Edward,' fear making my reply acerbic. 'You have made up your own mind. As you usually do.'

He laughed, before sobering quickly, his face once more losing its light. 'I think that you at least would tell me the truth. I am beset by enemies, Joan, men who sit at my own board, eat my bread, yet would wish me ill. The Archbishop of Canterbury, God rot his treacherous soul, has proved to be no friend of mine.'

I pretended not to understand, when in fact the whole court understood. To Edward's wrath, Archbishop Stratford had accused Queen Philippa, that most moral of women, of being in an adulterous relationship, since the child she was now carrying must have been conceived when Edward was engaged in the siege of Tournai.

'Rumour and gossip! How would the scandalmongers know when and where Philippa and I came together to get this child? And were they counting the weeks and months of its gestation?' Edward railed, his low voice rendering his displeasure even more implacable. 'They, with their crude and vicious lies, are the true demons in a well-ordered state. My wife is the most loyal, most honourable woman I know. I'll not allow vicious tales of impropriety to destroy her reputation. You'll do well to mirror your own deportment on hers, Joan. There must be no stigma in this marriage with young Montagu. I'll brook no dishonour, no outrage. Get an heir as soon as possible and settle down into married life.'

Closing the pages with a clap that raised yet another cloud of dust, returning the book to the shelf, Edward angled a glance at me, all comfortable intimacy over in the shade of scandal and adultery. 'Should you not be learning suitable texts or setting stitches, or whatever it is young brides do?'

No, I could not tell him of my predicament. Edward could not rescue me. Indeed, unwittingly, Edward had made all things clear to me, as terribly shining as the gilded image of King Arthur, that he had just hidden with some force.

Chapter Three

Early February 1341: St. George's Chapel, Windsor

The Bishop cast his eye over the assembly gathered before God, where the royal blood of England was all-pervading, admonishing them to silence with the mere lift of a finger. Edward and Philippa stood amidst the throng. Returned from Flanders, the Queen had honoured me by attending my marriage, before she would depart to the little manor of King's Langley for her seven-month confinement, closed off from the world until the birth of this child.

All eyes were focused on me. On William Montagu.

A quietness of expectation fell. The Bishop of London beamed at me. Not the Archbishop of Canterbury in spite of my mother's hopes. He was *persona non grata,* not welcome in the royal presence as things stood.

Will turned his head, stiff-necked, to give me the glimmer of a nervous twitch that might have been called a smile, before turning to fix the Bishop with an anxious stare.

I was as cold as death. No smile. No anxiety. Nothing beneath my girdle but a grim certainty.

Indeed, my mind was empty after weeks of maternal

bombardment, Philippa's gift of silk and figured damask chill against my skin, heavy in its weight of gold tissue, eminently suitable to a princess on her wedding day. My lungs were icy as I inhaled every incense-filled breath. The only warmth was William's hand around mine, clammy with nerves. Despite the February damp, I could see perspiration on his brow if I glanced sideways. It had, I surmised, nothing to do with the new liking for sable fur at neck and cuff and hem that gave him a marked resemblance to the monkey, an ill-considered gift from some foreign ambassador to the royal offspring.

I was standing at the altar, hemmed in by the fixed regard of congregation and of the carved saints and martyrs, my hair released into virginal purity, uncovered by veil or coif, rippling magnificently over my shoulders in bright gold, that challenged even the crucifix before which we would take our vows.

The progression of the marriage ceremony wrapped me about, heavy with portent, impossibly different from my first marriage which had been private, personal, secretive. Utterly lacking in any ceremony. Here we were trapped in formal ritual, the Bishop's robes more bejewelled than mine. If I looked to my left Edward and Philippa were resplendent, lacking only their crowns to enhance their regality, both so young and hopeful, yet to reach their thirtieth year. Ned too was burnished beside Isabella, ostentatiously wearing her reliquary which was no more magnificent than the Salisbury livery collar that was a gift from William to me. It rested on my collarbones, the gems glinting as I breathed with hollow foreboding.

Thomas Holland, I recalled, briefly, had given me no gifts of any kind.

My mother was engorged with her success. Lord Wake merely looked threateningly fierce whenever he caught my eye, which tended to stir a note of hysteria within me. When I had made my vows to Thomas our company had also been of the raptor variety, although they had ignored us.

Countess Catherine was supported by Lady Elizabeth, clad in a vast array of ancient gems. The Earl was still absent, still sojourning as unwilling guest of the French king.

At last the Bishop turned to Will. It was as if the congregation held its breath to absorb the holy vows on our behalf.

'William Montagu, *vis accípere Joan, hic præsentem in tuam legítimam uxorem iuxta ritum sanctæ matris Ecclesiæ?*'

I heard Will swallow, but he did not hesitate.

'*Volo.*'

He would not dare.

The space around me grew, leaving me alone and insignificant. This was it. This was the moment for my own declaration of intent.

'*Joan, vis accípere William, hic præsentern in tuum legítimum marítum iuxta ritum sanctæ matris Ecclesiæ?*'

I allowed a slide of eye to my mother's austerity. I saw fear there. I had been declaring my wish to repudiate this marriage since the day she had seized hold of the Montagu proposal.

I lifted my eyes to the Bishop who was nodding encouragingly. My voice was clear and cool. No hesitation. No stammer. Had I not made my decision? I would not go back on it now.

'*Volo.*'

Momentarily I closed my eyes, held my breath, anticipating the bolt of lightning that would strike me down, for surely God would judge my vow and find me wanting. Or some busy person in the congregation would decry me false.

Nothing. No flash of light, no voice raised in condemnation.

Behind me, my mother's sigh was almost audible. Will's hand closed convulsively around mine so that I winced a little as we exchanged an awkward nuptial kiss.

'I wasn't sure you would go through with it,' he whispered, his cheek pressed to mine.

The ceremony continued. The drama had been played out, brought to its glorious, heart-stirring end by the choral offering of glory to God. I imagined most of our companions were now anticipating a warming cup of spiced wine before the overblown festivity of the wedding feast. I was the wife of William Montagu. One day I would be Countess of Salisbury. William and I would be cornerstones in Edward's splendid court, our children securing the Salisbury inheritance for all time.

Why had I abandoned all my professed principles of honour and loyalty to the vows I had made to Thomas, rejecting at the eleventh hour all my fine words that I would never join my hand with that of William Montagu because it would be invalid for me to do so? Many would deem me weak, easily influenced, readily submitting to minds and wills stronger than my own; or to a streak of pure worldly ambition as wide as the River Thames. I could imagine the scorn at my sudden inexplicable change of heart.

Was I driven by an ambition to be Countess of Salisbury in the fullness of time? Surely it was a more advantageous future for a royal daughter to be Countess of Salisbury, rather than the wife of a mere household knight, living on a meagre income? Perhaps it was family pressure, too great to withstand, ultimately being dragged to the altar by a determined mother who issued dire threats of my being forced to take the veil if I continued in my disobedience. Or, in the end, did I just give up hope and submit to the easiest path?

It might be that many a daughter, caught out in the sin of worldly disobedience, would do exactly that.

So why did I abandon my oft-repeated intent with such glib readiness? Because in the closing days of the old year my duty had been made as clear to me as the brilliant glitter of my new collar. Thus I had walked of my own volition to place my hand in Will's. Once more I had taken these new vows without threats.

Let the world judge me, as it doubtless would, the chroniclers dipping their pens in poisonous ink when they discovered what I had done. At best I would be deemed a pawn in the maw of family political intrigue. At worst an ambitious power-seeker, acting with cold and cruel dispassion, abandoning one husband for a better.

I cringed at the worst.

But so be it. I could keep my own counsel. Who would be interested in my reasoning? The deed was done and there was no hand to it but my own.

Let the world judge as it wished. I raised my head to acknowledge Will's faint smile of relief, and later, as we shared a marital cup of wine, our lips matching on the rim to the murmured appreciation of the glittering aristocratic throng, there was only one thought in my mind.

I would have to face the repercussions when Thomas returned to England.

I must be strong enough to bear it.

It might be that I was now the wife of William Montagu in the eyes of God and Man and the King of England. It might be that King Edward's cheerful beneficence was marked by his allowing my distant father-in-law to grant property to Will and myself. It might be that we had an allowance which I was able to spend on the fripperies of life. It might be that we were in possession of the manor and lordship of Mold in North Wales and the eventual reversion of the manor of Marshwood in Devon, where we could establish our household if and when we so chose; both of them too far from court for my liking.

All of that might be true, but there were few changes in my life at this time.

We did not live in our new properties; I did not even visit them. My life, and Will's also, was still fixed at the peripatetic court wherever it decided to travel and put down its temporary roots. I continued my education. Will continued to flourish as a future knight. I could not imagine living alone with my own household, far from the centre of court and the intrigues of government. This was what I had known my whole life. I could not imagine having no one with whom to have an intelligent conversation other than Will, Countess Catherine or Lady Elizabeth.

But then neither could I imagine living in isolation with Thomas Holland on some estate near Upholland in the far distant and drear reaches of Lancashire.

Yet Will and I preserved, in a superficial manner, the appearance of a married couple. We had plenty to say to each other when we met. At meals. At receptions. At embassies. At the hunt. We were the Earl and Countess of Salisbury in waiting. Will made a point of coming to see me every day.

Sometimes he kissed my cheek if no one was watching.

More often than not he made do with a salute to my fingers.

I curtsied and bade him welcome.

The livery collar – for was I not now a Salisbury possession? – was placed in Countess Catherine's jewel coffer for safe keeping while Will and I danced, our steps matching with some exactitude. We had danced together since we were both old enough to stand. We had a lifetime of familiarity between us to give us an ease in each other's company. Seeing us together, my mother, relaxed, decided that she could afford to smile on me. So did Countess Catherine. And Queen Philippa.

Will was my friend. Despite the vows and the priest's solemn words, we lived as we had always lived since we were still considered too young to share a marriage bed. Indeed, Will, his age the same as mine, seemed content to wait. I prayed that he would continue to be so. My mind was full of waiting. I could speak to no one, although I did try.

'What will you do when Thomas returns?' I asked Will.

'I doubt he will ever return now. How long has he been gone?'

'A year.'

'My mother says that he is dead.'

I pursed my lips.

'You don't miss him, do you?' Will sounded anxious.

How could I say yes? It was a strange sort of missing. How could I miss a life I had never experienced? Sometimes it seemed that Thomas was disappearing into a distant void. To my shame, recalling his features was no longer an easy task.

'You are my wife, Joan.' It was the ultimate statement of possession.

'I acknowledge it.'

'And Thomas Holland is assuredly dead.'

Thus Will had it fixed in his mind that Thomas would never return to cast a cat amongst any flock of pigeons. He no longer thought about my promises to another man, or worried over the knowledge that Thomas had known me intimately. For him all had been wiped clean under the holy auspices of the Bishop of London. Will had no fears for the future.

But I had.

Late Summer 1341: The Royal Manor of Havering-atte-Bower

The first intimation that the day was to hold something out of the ordinary was the bounding into our midst of the hounds, pushing and investigating with no thought to royal deference. The second was the glow that spread over the Queen's stolid features as she looked up from the small garment she was stitching. Both were enough to inform us who had arrived. We all, apart from the royal infants, rose to our feet, only to be waved back to what we had been doing.

We were sitting beneath the trees, in a number of artful groups, enjoying the warm days of late summer, with Queen Philippa keeping a watchful eye on her youngest children, John and the baby Edmund who, unbeknown to him beneath his downy thatch, had caused all the trouble between King, Queen and Archbishop. Their nursemaids were in attendance. So was Ned, as well as Will who had journeyed to visit Countess Catherine on some matter of estate affairs, and had come to make his farewell to me before returning with Ned to the manor at Kennington where the Prince's household was established. We were a large and noisy group, which became even noisier when the King arrived with his dogs and the usual parcel of attendant knights, squires and huntsmen.

Without ceremony, Edward kissed Philippa's cheek, patted Isabella's head, cuffed his heir a light blow to his shoulder with a wry comment on the splendour of his new satin-lined cloak, anchored by two uncommonly large gold buttons, before inspecting the two-month-old baby in his crib. Then, all niceties accomplished, taking us all in with a smile and a mock bow, he announced:

'Look who we have here, for our entertainment.'

Edward beckoned.

'Someone for you to welcome, newly returned from brave deeds and doughty fighting. We will be pleased to listen to all he has to say about distant wars.'

I had no premonition of this. Not one shiver of air had touched my senses, not one whisper of warning. Stilling my fingers on the lute I had been playing, I looked across with open interest, a ready smile for a visitor with a tale to tell. As did we all.

My fingers flattened with a discord of strings. I forced my lungs to draw in a steady breath. Thomas Holland was not dead. Thomas

Holland was not severely wounded. Thomas Holland was no longer committed to the religious fervour of a crusade.

Thomas Holland stood in our midst. Six feet tall in his soft boots and thigh-length cote-hardie. Smiling and urbane.

How could my blood run so cold when the sun's heat was so intense? So too was my face cold, where the welcoming expression seemed to have set into place, while my throat was constricted by a turbulence that refused to be brought into order. I could feel Will's eyes snap to mine, but I would not look at him. This was the moment that had been an underlying murmur of trepidation through all the months of our marriage. I had anticipated it, planned for it, but now that it was here, I did not know what to do. For the first time that I could recall I was bereft of thought or decision of what I should do or say. Any memories of the emotion that had driven me into marriage with this knight were effectively obliterated. It was not love that washed over me. It was not physical desire, kept in abeyance for all the months of his absence, but fear. I felt nothing but consternation. I should have been word perfect in this initial meeting with him, particularly in company. I was not prepared, and kept my lips close-pressed as Sir Thomas bowed and made his greeting to the Queen, as one thought returned to me, the obvious one.

Did Thomas know? Had he any knowledge of the passage of events since he had been gone from England? Of course he did not. No one would have seen the need to tell him. The private and essentially intimate development of the life of Princess Joan was of no concern to a knight who did not yet have a reputation or a source of wealth to make him a notable at court. Edward was pleased to see him because here was a source of new tales of war and glory, and because he saw the military potential in him, but Thomas was not yet one of the inner group of knights in Edward's confidence. No one would have seen a need to tell him of my change in circumstances.

No, of course he did not know.

All seemed to be held in suspension, like close-ground herbs in red wine, but that was simply my imagination. All was in fact returned to normality as if every one of my senses had been restored to life so that the scene was in brilliant focus, the scents from the roses heady with musk, the noise of dogs and children clamorous on my ear. Will shuffled at my side, suddenly discomfited since the man he had assured himself was dead quite clearly was not. Edward ordered his huntsmen to collect the hounds and dispatch them to the kennels. Philippa likewise dispatched her babies to the nursery. The older children except for Isabella, whose nose twitched with interest born purely of her own lurid imagination, returned to their own private occupations. I held the lute to my breast like a babe in arms.

And Thomas?

Thomas had all the courtly dignity not to single me out with either look or movement, except for a sleek passage of a glance as he took in those who waited to greet him. We were all acknowledged with the same courtly bow which did not surprise me for he had not spent all his life on a battlefield. No, his inherent grace did not surprise me. Nor did this state of not being dead. I had never thought that he was. But his physical appearance shocked me, so much that my breathing remained compromised.

The King drew him forward into the family group, placing a compassionate hand on his arm.

'We have heard of your exploits, Thomas. And now we see the consequences of being in the thick of battle. How did this come about?'

'It was nothing, sire.'

'Modesty becomes you, but tell us. Here's my son who would dearly have loved to have been fighting beside you.'

Thus summoned, and it had to be said with a bad case of hero-worship for any knight who had enhanced his reputation on the battlefield, Ned took the jewelled cup from Philippa to hand to Thomas. And Thomas, accepting and raising it in a little toast, launched into the tale of his adventures on the field of battle. The battle where evidence told, horrifically, of his wounding.

The battle, the blows, the courage of his fellow knights, the victorious outcome; the King and Prince and Will, as well as my brother, John, hung on every word. And then Thomas was coming to an end with a wry smile.

'I have taken an oath to wear this mark of God's grace in sparing me, until I have fulfilled my duty to His cause. And my duty to yours too, my lord King, on the battlefields of Europe. God spared my life. I will dedicate my sword to Him. And to you. And this badge of my wounding will be seen and noted from one end of Christendom to the next.'

It was a brave speech with all the energy and dedication I recalled which would make him a prime candidate for the King's new order of knights. And I could not take my gaze from him, from his face where he wore a flamboyant strip of white silk to hide the damage to one eye. Here was my knight who had caused me so much trouble, tall and lean and bloodied in battle, his darkly russet hair still curled against his neck, his face fair as ever, his uncovered eye bright with the emotion of his welcome amongst us. He had lost the other in some distant conflict.

Watching him in the centre of the little group of those with whom I had grown up, here was Thomas Holland, a man amongst boys. A knight amongst squires. Thus I studied him, assessing my own reactions to the man I had married against all good sense. A strange mysticism hung about his figure as he came to sit at Philippa's feet, the silken band not a blight, not a disfiguring in my eyes. It was a glamour that he had been hurt so desperately but yet continued to burn with knightly fervour. And how intriguing that he had chosen to enhance the glamour with white silk rather than a common strip of leather. There was much to Thomas Holland that I did not yet know.

And perhaps never would.

'Can you not see?' Ned was asking, kneeling beside him, appalled at the prospect of suffering such a fatal disability for a soldier.

'I see well enough with the eye that God has seen fit to spare, my lord. The infidel who dealt me the blow no longer breathes God's air.'

'But perhaps you can no longer fight.' Ned was frowning. 'With the sight of only one eye.'

Thomas smiled, which stirred my heart a little. 'The King of Bohemia, famed throughout Europe for his courage, has lost his sight completely. He is determined to fight again on the battlefield with his knights leading him into the fray. Why should he not since he can still ride a horse and wield a sword? My state is not so desperate. I will assuredly fight again.'

Filled with awe, Ned reached across to touch the white silk. 'I would be as brave as you.'

'As you will, my lord.'

At my side, Will was as silent as I.

Until Edward led Thomas away, leaving a little hiatus of disappointment now that the excitement was gone. I simply sank to the ground with a mouth as arid as a summer stream, still clutching the lute. Thomas had managed one more fleeting glance in my direction, which might have been a question, or perhaps even a warning that he would in the fullness of time seek me out.

But not before I sought him.

'Are you going to play that?' demanded Isabella who had not been centre of attention for a good half hour. 'If not, give it to me.'

'Take it!' As I handed it over, since playing dulcet melodies on a lute was no longer a priority for me, a hand fastened round my wrist. I looked up at Will who was on his feet, standing over me.

'What are you planning to do?' he asked, *sotto voce*.

'Find some means of speaking with Thomas Holland in private, of course.'

How could he even ask? The three of us could not remain incommunicado, hoping that this problem would simply evaporate in the warm air. What did Will think that I would do?

'I forbid it.'

Exasperation took its toll of my tone. 'You have no authority to forbid it.'

'I have every authority. You are my wife.'

I stared at him until he blushed and released me.

While I was moved by a little compassion; this was not Will's fault. 'I have to see him, Will. He needs to know. I have to discover some means for us to meet alone.'

'So he does need to know, but it is a matter of much interest to me, what exactly you will say to him. And how he will reply.'

It was a matter of much interest to me too.

'I will be sure to tell you,' I said. 'Every word.'

'You will not allow him to kiss you.'

'I doubt that in the circumstances he will discover any desire to kiss me. I expect he will find my behaviour sufficiently incomprehensible to douse any passion!'

Allowing Will to pull me to my feet, I curtsied neatly towards the Queen, and began to walk away in the direction of the departed King and his brave knight.

'In fact,' Will added, keeping pace with me. 'I am coming with you.'

I hurried my steps.

Thomas, my courageous, lamentably absent but heroically wounded husband, met with me in the private chapel, an intimate space much used by the Queen. Set aside to the honour of the Blessed Virgin, Thomas was directed there by a servant I had dispatched, for I could think of no other means of ensuring the lack of an audience at this time of day when the public rooms were full of servants and those who would come to petition the Queen in her abundant mercy. I was waiting for him, offering up a final silent prayer at the little jewelled altar with its benignly smiling Virgin when Thomas, offering a coin to the page, walked in.

I had heard his firm footsteps approaching. This time I was prepared.

'Joan.' For a long moment, as I turned to face him, he stood and looked at me, then held out his hand. 'How could I have forgotten that my wife was beautiful?'

His face, bronzed and a little hardened through campaigning, undoubtedly lit with pleasure, which should have pleased me. And it did, flattering as it was. But once the pleasure had been buried, I knew that this was going to be just as difficult as I had envisioned.

'Thomas.'

I placed my hand in his and angled my cheek for a kiss.

'Can I not claim your lips? You were my wife when I left. Even though the Blessed Virgin had not sanctified our union.'

'You have been gone a long time,' I said, uncertain whether I wished to throw myself into his arms or retreat beyond Philippa's little prie-dieu. My emotions were all awry. He was all I recalled, dominating the little space with his height and his military air of polished competence, but there had been far too much water under this particular bridge to simply take up where we had left off.

'A year,' he said. 'Perhaps a little more.'

The expression on his face had stilled, becoming wary as if he saw a distant troop of horsemen approaching, and he was unsure whether it be friend or foe.

'Which is a long time for a wife not to hear from her husband.'

Startled at my sharpness, Thomas now regarded me with some indecision. 'But you knew where I was. You knew my plans. Have you fallen out of love with me already?'

'No!' I pressed my fingers to my lips. Here was no time for emotion. 'It's not that.'

'Then what? Do you feel to be a neglected wife? There's no one to gossip here. The holy saints won't judge us if I kiss you.' He pulled me nearer as he bent his head to do just that. Then paused as a pair of feet scuffed the stone paving behind the pillar to my left. Thomas looked up, over my shoulder, the kiss postponed. 'Will!' Then back to me. 'I did not know that we were not alone. Why are we not alone?' I could all but see his mind working. 'You arranged this tryst. Why did you bring Will with you?'

Because Will, with a surge of Salisbury authority, had insisted.

'Yes, I did arrange it. There is a complication,' I said, scowling at Will who promptly scowled back.

Catching the tone of this exchange: 'What is it?' Thomas asked. Then turned to Will. 'Do you need to be here? Have you become chaperone in my absence? The lady is quite safe in my company.'

Will redirected his scowl from me to Thomas. 'You should not be kissing her.'

'Why not? It is perfectly acceptable for a knight to kiss a lady's cheek.'

'But not her lips!'

'I have not yet done so. She has not allowed it.' Exasperation was setting in. 'Princess Joan is capable of being her own chaperone. She certainly was when I left. Now, go away, Will.'

At first he had been prepared to smile. But by now, sensing something truly amiss, Thomas's hands had tightened around mine.

'You have no right,' Will said.

'I have every right. What is it to you?'

My hands were released when I was placed firmly to one side. Thomas was fast abandoning discretion, while Will, grabbing at his courage, stepped out of the shadows until he stood beside us, an unholy triumvirate.

'I know that you will say that Joan is your wife,' he challenged.

Thomas's eyes slid to mine, full of questions. 'What if I do?'

'It's a lie. A filthy lie!'

If Thomas was surprised by Will's aggression he chose not to respond in kind. 'You know nothing of what is between this lady and myself.' He punched Will's arm, gently enough. 'If I were you, I'd say nothing that would reflect on her reputation. It would ill-become a knight in the making to sully the good name of a royal lady.'

'I'll say what I like. I'll shout out the truth, even if no one else will.'

'Enough! You have said enough!' Thomas took a step forward.

Immediately I was there between them, a bone between two dogs whose hackles were raised, whose teeth were all but displayed in vicious snarls. I prayed the teeth would not be buried in my flesh.

'Joan?' Thomas's eye had narrowed. 'How much does he know? Have you been indiscreet?'

Whereupon pride stiffened my spine. 'It does you no credit to accuse me of indiscretion until you know what has occurred in your absence.'

'Then tell me. I am lost in a fog of accusation and ignorance.'

Will retaliated with a deal of resentment and a torrent of invective. 'We were all impressed with your fortitude. We lapped up your tales of warfare and courageous deeds, Sir Thomas. But I don't care how brave you were. I don't care how notable a figure you would wish to be with the white silk you wear as a banner. I don't care how many important friends you made on the battlefield. She is not yours to kiss. Joan is my wife.'

'Your wife?' Thomas laughed, disbelieving. 'What nonsense is this?'

But I could see the watchfulness in every muscle braced against what was to come. It had to be said.

'It is true,' I stated. 'I am Will's wife.'

'What?' A harsh growl of a whisper.

And so I explained, all in a voice as sleek as the Virgin's celestial blue robe, which reminded me so sharply of the King's sworn intent to honour his knights in cloaks of similar hue.

'It is true, Thomas. I am Will's wife. We were married by the Bishop of London before the whole court in the chapel at Windsor. Everyone is very pleased. My mother and uncle are delighted at their good fortune in securing this match. The King and Queen promoted it, my royal blood a gift for the loyal Earl of Salisbury, and they smile on us. There is nothing we can do about it. I took my oath. I am Will's wife.'

Thomas absorbed this severely pruned version of what had occurred in his absence without speech, his hands fallen to his sides, his eye on the altar as if calling for heavenly confirmation. Until I heard him inhale, saw the glint of the low light on the buckle of his belt as he moved, as he erupted into a flare of sheer temper.

'By the Rood! Is my hearing compromised, as well as my sight? This cannot be.'

'Most certainly it can be, Sir Thomas.' Will was not slow in driving the knife once again into the wound. 'My marriage to Joan is all signed and sealed with royal witnesses. Who witnessed your travesty of a match? I doubt they even exist. I think there was no legality whatsoever in your supposed union. Your return makes no difference to my legal binding with this woman.' Will almost crowed with the achievement. Perhaps not the most tactful of responses.

Thomas looked at him, the fingers of his right hand now clenching hard on his sword hilt. Then he rounded on me.

'Why did I not know of this?'

'How was I to tell you? I did not know where you were.'

I would not admit that I had thought of sending a courier. And abandoned it as a lost cause.

'How could you allow it to happen?'

Which question I expected. I had no intention of begging for a trite understanding if he chose to heap the blame on my shoulders. But then there was no need for me to find a reason.

'She had no choice,' Will leapt in. 'It was the wish of my family and hers and of the King himself.'

'Ha! The power of the Salisbury faction, of course. How could I withstand that, even if I had been aware of the skulduggery behind my back!' Thomas loomed over me again, so that perforce I must look up. Which I did. 'Does the King know? About our marriage? I presume not, since nothing has been said and he welcomed me back with open arms and promises of friendship. I presume he is as ignorant as I was until two minutes ago.'

No he does not know. What would be the value in bringing royal wrath down on my head. Or on yours. But I would not say it. There was no room for pity here. Instead, once again, I delivered the bare facts.

'My mother, my uncle Wake, and the Countess of Salisbury simply swore everyone in our households to secrecy. In fact no one but our priest knew, so it was easily done.' I hesitated, then carried on, face expressionless: 'They all hoped you would simply not come back.'

'Your mother hoped I was dead.'

My lack of a response was answer enough. Thomas released his sword hilt, taking a moment to marshal his thoughts and his temper while Will and I exchanged a glance that was more fury than despair.

'But this marriage to Montagu here is invalid, Joan.' Thomas had won his battle with pique. 'It cannot stand before the law.'

'No, it is not,' Will continued the flinging down of his gauntlets. 'It is your marriage that is not legal.'

Thomas's hand was clenched into a fist, which I feared he might use, when once again I stepped in, gripping Will's sleeve in a desperation of powerlessness. 'Yes it is legal, Will. You know it is. Even our priest said it was a marriage *per verba de praesenti* and quite binding, even if it is a matter for disapproval. You cannot pretend that it is not. It is we that are pretending, Will.'

'I suppose I should be grateful to hear you admit it,' Thomas said. 'So what do we do now, Mistress Joan? Are you Holland or Montagu? Do we live as a threesome, like hawks in a mews? In secrecy? Or do you and I announce our marriage to the world and defy anyone to question it?'

'Only if you are prepared to include in this little plan a flight across the sea,' I remarked, waspishness rearing its head. I had not meant to say it, but emotion overcame my best endeavours to remain calm. Thomas Holland was past being calm.

'I have a better future in mind, and I refuse to abandon my ambitions. But hear this, Joan. I'll not let you go. I'll not give you up. Not to either the King or the Earl of Salisbury. You are mine by a well-witnessed exchange of vows. Nothing will change that.'

'I will deny it,' Will said.

'You can deny nothing. This is a declaration of war.' And then on a thought that pulled his brows together. 'Has your marriage been consummated?' Thomas demanded.

Will flushed. I said nothing, causing a bark of unkindly laughter from Thomas.

'No,' Will admitted. 'Yet she is still mine.'

'God's Blood! We'll see about that!'

Thomas strode out of the chapel. Will and I were left looking at each other.

'He did not take it well,' Will observed.

'No, he did not. Did you expect him to? You threw down the gauntlet and Thomas picked it up.'

'I wish you hadn't promised him, Joan. I wish you had not got yourself into this mess. Why in heaven's name did you do it, when it is obvious to me that you don't have any deep feelings for the man? If you had, you would not have given your assent to wed me at the eleventh hour. Either that or you are frivolous beyond belief.'

The accusation stung. Did I too wish I had not done it? In that aftermath, in the stillness of the little chapel, I did not know. When I refused to answer his savaging of my motives and my character, Will left me there, striding after Thomas, so that I was once more alone with the Virgin and a terrible sense of disappointment. It would not be shaken away. In despair I knelt before the statue, perhaps hoping for some solace. A little beam of sunshine touched the window, then my coifed hair, the warm dust motes dancing in the still air making me sneeze.

And that was it. There I was, back to that day when I had made my promise to Thomas. Experiencing it again, I was no longer sad. I sparkled with doubt and delight and a magnificent defiance, as I had on that day. It was a glorious moment, vivid with colour, even the scents and sounds intruding as they did on that day to awaken my senses. I sat back on my heels, my hands clasped hard in my lap, my fingers intertwined, and allowed it to sweep over me, all over again.

Spring 1340: Ghent

There was Thomas Holland, waiting for me in the angle of the outer wall where a door opened discreetly into the royal mews.

'Are we alone?' I asked.

It seemed that we were, to all intents and purposes. His page and squire did not count. The royal falconer had been lured away for an hour by the promise of ale and a handful of small coin.

Thomas nodded, offering his hand. 'We have time,' he said.

At his feet, a bundle of armour wrapped in stained cloth, an assortment of swords, and a rough travelling coffer that had seen many campaigns. I noted it, acknowledging that somewhere his horse would be waiting. It all told its own story of how the day would unfurl, but I would not allow the quick slap of loss to mar what we would do together. What we would be together.

The wind whipped around the buttress to ruffle his hair into disarray and shower my veil and cloak with the dead leaves that still caught in corners such as this. Later I thought it might have been an omen but my imagination was too much engaged to look for portents of doom. Every sense was strained. I looked over my shoulder, for I would be missed soon, a servant sent to discover my whereabouts. There was a limit to the lax supervision; I might have been able to snatch more freedom here in Ghent than in Windsor, but princesses of the royal household were not free to wander unescorted.

Or to give their hands and lips where they chose.

Thomas Holland took my hand, his firm as he raised my fingers to his lips and then, drawing me closer, kissed my cheek.

'You are late. I was in two minds to leave,' he admitted.

It was not encouraging, but he opened the door and led me into the dusty warmth, the air redolent of straw and fur and bird droppings, but not unpleasantly so. The royal raptors shifted on their perches. A goshawk hunched its displeasure, mewing sharply at the intrusion.

I sneezed.

'Did you think I would not come?' I asked, recovering.

'I wasn't sure. Perhaps you are still too young to know your own desires.'

'Is procrastination the preserve of youth?' It was a phrase I had often heard Queen Philippa use when her children thwarted her wishes. 'I am old enough to know my own mind.'

He faced me, foursquare, releasing my hand as if he could give me leave to make a bolt for freedom if I so wished.

'Then say it, Joan. Do you wish it?'

I barely paused.

'Yes, Thomas. I do wish it.'

Indecision must still have impaired my expression when he had expected nothing but delight. His brows drew together.

'I am not convinced.'

'Well, you should be. If my answer were no, I would have hidden until I saw you ride out of the gates on your way to war.'

But how could I not be uncertain? What I desired weighed heavily against the consequences that snarled and snapped at the edge of my determination until it was ragged. What we did here today could not be hidden for ever. Thomas's voice fell gruffly, not into chivalric declarations of love, which I might have liked, but into legal niceties, which were certainly more pertinent.

'There is no bar, Joan. There is no impediment to what we will do.'

'But there is no permission either.'

'We do not need permission. Only our own desire to take this step.'

'They would stop us if they knew.'

'So they do not know. Nor will they. Or not yet. Not until I have made a name that cannot be balked at.'

I did not think he was naive, but it seemed to me that his eye was on the immediate fight, not on the vista of the whole battle. Now he was looking over his shoulder, at his page and squire who had entered and occupied the small space with us and the hunting birds, so closely that the page threatened to stand on my hem.

'You two are here to witness what we say. You will not speak of it to anyone, until I give you permission to do so.'

'No, Sir Thomas.' *The squire's reply was trenchant. The page, simply overawed into silence, shook his head.*

'On your honour,' *Thomas demanded.*

'On my honour,' the squire repeated. The page gulped.

He turned back to me.

'A pity you could not bring one of your women with you. She would be a better witness and one not likely to die in battle.'

The page paled.

'I could, of course. But only if you did not mind it being gossiped from one tower to the next within the half-hour.'

Sometimes men, even much admired men, were highly impractical. I hoped Thomas's minions were not given to gossip, or were so afraid of his revenge that they would keep their mouths shut. The page's mouth had fallen open in distress.

Thomas was holding out his palm.

'Let it be done.'

'Let it be done,' I repeated.

I placed my hand in his, palm to palm, my fingers lightly clasped around his wrist, and his closed around mine as he began to speak.

'This is my intent. Today I am your husband. If you want me as your husband.'

The birds rustled, a fragile-seeming merlin beginning to preen with intensity, while I repeated the words.

'This is my intent. Today I am your wife. If you want me as your wife.'

'You have my love and my loyalty and the protection of my body until death claims me.'

'You have my love and my loyalty and my duty as your wife, until death claims me.'

'I am your husband of my own free will.'

'I am your wife, without duress. So I wish it.'

So speaking our intent, we stood and regarded each other. It was not a marriage I had envisioned. Here was no ceremony, no panoply, no festive celebration. My garments were not the lavish extravagance of a bride and Thomas was dressed starkly in wool and leather, fit for travel. No incense, no choir, so flattering candle flames. Here was no royal union, only a simple statement between a man and a woman. If the hawks heard our vows they were entirely unreceptive.

I sneezed again in the close atmosphere. Not the most romantic of gestures.

'So it is done.' Releasing my hand, Thomas signalled with a tilt of his chin to the squire and page who made an exit, leaving us alone. 'It is legal and binding. Except for the consummation.'

Now was no time for hesitation. 'Where?' I asked.

With his shoulder he pushed at an inner door that led into the domain of the falconer, where there was a stool, a coffer, a peg to hold a cloak, and a rough cot.

'It's the best I could manage.'

He made a bow worthy of the most elegant of courtiers, then closed the door at my back.

So the falconer's cot with its musty covers – and some feathers – witnessed the fleeting physical union of a Plantagenet princess and a minor knight from the depths of Lancashire. Hearing tuned for every fall of approaching footstep, I later admitted to not enjoying to any degree the overwhelming passion that I had hoped to experience. Instead it was fast and uncomfortable and undignified. I would not admit to the sharp pain, even though I suspected that Thomas was considerate in his urgency, having all the experience that I lacked. The surroundings were not conducive to lingering kisses, the circumstances not engaging to passion. The falconer's bed with its disreputable mattress made me aware of fleas and mites rather than the culmination of physical longing. Yet my virginity was gently won by a man who said that he loved me.

It had made me his wife.

We set our clothes to rights, which took little time since few had been removed in this briefest of interludes.

'When will I see you again?' I asked.

'When I have made my fortune.'

'When will you tell the King?'

'When he is in the mood to listen. I had hoped immediately.' Thomas, *thoughtful if somewhat inept, was helping me to secure my veil, brow creased in concentration. My firmly plaited hair had barely been disturbed. 'Unfortunately, as it is he'll give me short shrift so I'll not risk a blast of temper.'*

I did not argue. Edward was not in the best frame of mind to listen to anything other than finance and war against the bloody French.

Leaving me to make a better fist with my veil, Thomas fastened the buckle of his belt, stooping to collect the sword that had been placed against the wall. 'Edward admires courage and initiative.' He shrugged a little. 'If I earn a reputation for bold resourcefulness, I don't think he will be slow in giving this marriage his support. And now I must go.'

He kissed me on his way to the door, for that was the truth of it. He was a soldier, with no other means of earning his bread or a reputation. I had known how it would be, but perhaps I had not expected to be abandoned so precipitately almost before I had donned my cloak, with one final word of advice.

'You are not to speak of this, Joan. It is my place to tell the King, not yours. He may be your cousin, but I'll not have his wrath turned against you.' And then, unexpectedly stern: 'I worship the ground that you tread, little princess.'

As if to prove it, he dropped to one knee, lifting my hem and pressing it to his lips.

'You do know what they will say, don't you? That I wed you only because you are the King's cousin. That I shame my knightly calling.' His face uplifted to mine was unexpectedly grave, the lines between his brows savagely wrought.

'I know it. But I know the truth,' I assured him.

'I want you for yourself. Never forget that.'

Then while I was recovering from so unexpected a piece of courtliness, Thomas had risen, bowed with his fist against his heart and made his departure.

What was left for me? I climbed to the tower to watch him ride away to join the King's military force, complete with his armour and weapons and travelling coffer, his page and squire in attendance and a small retinue at his back. I had a husband. I was married to Sir Thomas Holland. I was now Lady Holland. He would go to war and I would return to England with the Queen's household.

I thought that I might weep at this precipitous loss; it had, after all, been an emotional day. But I did not, for there was no grief in me. An exasperation perhaps, a longing, a momentary flash of panic, like the sun against the metal of Thomas's helm, but that was short lived. The household within which I lived would remain in ignorance until a better time. I hoped, all things considered, that I was not carrying his child. If so, the consequences would crash over my head sooner than I expected.

I had no desire to be subject to Edward's wrath.

★★★

In Philippa's chapel at Havering-atte-Bower, the beam of sunlight moved, blinding me for a moment with rainbow brilliance, bringing me back to the present. Deciding that it would be better if I were not discovered here – although it would be easy enough to concoct a reason that would not be questioned – I stood, smoothed my skirts – no feathers here – and walked to the door. Where I paused, looking back at the serenity of the Virgin, all the old questions forcing their way into my thoughts to disturb and destroy my certainties.

Why had I defied my mother and the King to marry a lowly household knight, rejecting some puissant marriage that was planned for me? Never had I been asked that one question, except by Will in a fit of pique, not expecting me to explain. Why had I done something so reprehensible, so contrary to my upbringing, treading a path so shocking that it would set the court into a blaze of malicious chattering? I had wed a man with nothing to recommend him other than a handy sword in battle and a handsome face, a man with neither money nor family nor influence. Why would I be persuaded to throw away a future of pre-eminence as wife of some great magnate or European prince, a foolish step that would seem beyond comprehension?

I walked slowly back to kneel once more before the Blessed Virgin, choosing possibilities as I had so many times before, rejecting most of them as of no account.

Thomas had barely wooed me, possessing no troubadour skills to awaken the yearning of a woman for a lover. The arts of courtly love had passed him by. It had been a soldier's wooing, plain and unembellished. 'Tell me the name of a knight who would not willingly kneel at your feet.' The most dramatic declaration to fall from Thomas's lips. He was not given to flights of fancy or romantic gestures, but it had not mattered. I had not needed them.

I had known that my mother would oppose this union. Was this a true reason, to thwart her dreams in a fit of immature defiance? I thought not, although there was an attraction in such subversion. I could not quite reject the tingle of excitement when I knew that I had stood against my mother, destroying any plans she might have been carefully knitting together for my future.

Did I love Thomas Holland? Was it love, my senses overcome by a youthful infatuation, that drove me to launch myself into so foolhardy an act? Did I know enough about love to give myself into his hands when all about us would cry foul against both of us, and against him, for seducing a young and royal maid? But I had not been seduced. I had not been persuaded against my will. I had not been an unwilling bride. I could never shift the blame to other shoulders than my own wilfulness. A woman growing up in a royal court grew up fast. I knew well my own mind.

I studied the star-crowned Virgin, the grave face that looked down on me with her enigmatic smile, full of compassion, as if I would find an answer there, and indeed I did, although it was already resident in my own heart.

I loved him. Thomas Holland had claimed my heart and I had willingly given it. When he had left me it had hurt my heart, a frenzied fluttering like a moth against a night shutter.

It was undoubtedly love for the man who had taken me out of the confined household of royal children, addressing me as a woman who might have the safekeeping of his own heart, even if he would never use such poetic terms. I was moved to desire his face, his superb stature. I looked with favour on his skills, as I applauded his ambition. He would become a great knight, as famous as Sir Galahad. He would be lauded, hung about with rewards, and I would be his wife. He was a man, experienced and confident, where those around me were still mere youths, untried and without polish. He had stirred my emotions into a flame that lit every corner of my existence.

But there was a canker in the perfect fruit, born of my own experience and my mother's warning. Was Thomas attracted by my royal blood as a path to greater ambitions? I was considered a valuable bride in the Monatgu marriage; I would be doubly valuable to Sir Thomas Holland.

It was not a worthless thought. Those with a cynical turn of mind, or even a worldly one, would say that Thomas Holland had an eye to the future, catching a willing princess as a trout would catch a mayfly. The Earl and Countess of Salisbury had been keen to snatch me up; would not Thomas Holland show equal desire to tie my future to his own self-seeking side? It could be that his plain words spoken in the mews hid the scheming of a man who sought earthly greatness through the blood of his wife, opening many doors for him, or would have if I had gone to him with royal blessing. It could be that Thomas Holland would have wed me had I been the most ill-visaged princess in Europe rather than Joan the Fair. It could be that I had been trapped, against my better judgement. If that was so, then I would be well rid of him if I rejected Thomas in favour of Will. If I allowed my love to wither and die, choking it with bitter recrimination.

But I had not been trapped. I was as much to blame as Thomas for this predicament.

'Is Thomas Holland nothing but a knave?' I asked the Virgin.

Despite her silence, I did not think so. All I saw in him was a grave honesty. What I did think, as I left the Virgin to her tranquillity, was that we would both be in disgrace when this debacle fell at the feet of the King and Queen.

I would be no one's path to greatness.

Chapter Four

What now? The immediate future was a matter for much speculation
for those who knew the truth.

After the clash of wills in Philippa's little chapel, it came as no
surprise to me that Thomas made no effort to publically reclaim
me as his wife. What would he do? Announce it with trumpet and
drum, dragging his squire and page before the King to swear that it
had all taken place? I imagined the scene; the dishonourable knight,
the abandoned wife, the innocent husband, all faced by the infuriated
King who had been made to look a fool by standing witness at a
marriage that was legally void.

So Thomas kept his mouth firmly closed, and as the months limped
past with no ruffling of the surface by errant winds, there was a general
sighing of relief. My mother and uncle were in watchful agreement
that Thomas should fade into the background and the disgraceful little
episode be allowed to fade with him. The Earl of Salisbury, when
he finally returned to our midst on a promise never to fight again
in France, rejoiced at his release and his acquisition of a Plantagenet
daughter-in-law. Will and I continued to pursue the life assigned to
us by custom in the royal household while the King, still happily in

the dark, saw no reason not to continue to take Thomas to his bosom, encouraging his reminiscences of battles and feats of arms.

An edgy acceptance in which we all settled into playing our allotted roles. There were no rumours. Not one word was whispered about that marriage in the royal mews at Ghent. As the months passed, it seemed that it had never happened.

As for the three of us most closely connected: Thomas remained aloof and silent, I kept my counsel; Will, with creditable insouciance, swept the whole event behind the tapestry, having decided that Thomas was no threat.

And I? I watched both Thomas and Will, becoming adept at hiding my true feelings. By this time I was having difficulty in deciding what exactly they were. It all had a dream-like quality, within which I sensed the black clouds of an impending storm. Of one thing I was certain. It could not go on in this tranquil fashion. Eventually the clouds would break and we would all be doused in shame and scandal.

'I am impressed, Joan.' My mother was becoming as complacent as Countess Catherine. 'You have grown into this Montagu marriage. I commend you.'

'Yes, madam.'

We were pacing side by side behind the Queen on our way to early Mass, as was our wont.

'It is all for the best.'

'Indeed it is, madam.'

Her eyes narrowed, as if she could not quite trust my compliance, before adding: 'Reluctantly, I am given cause to admire Holland too.' She inclined her head in the general direction of where he was standing in the little group of knights beside the King, who was awaiting the Queen. 'He has the good sense to realise that to speak out now will harm no one but himself.'

And me, of course. It would do my reputation no good at all.

We did not speak of such things.

Meanwhile Thomas returned to his position as one of the household knights, with aplomb and royal approval. But he had not forgotten. And he did speak of such things.

'I will win you back,' he said in an short aside as we emerged from Mass, our sins duly assuaged for another day, the households of King and Queen mingling. I was not forbidden to speak with him; that would have caught too much attention. Instead we became skilled at seizing strange opportunities.

'How can you win me back?' I handed him my missal to carry, under pretence of inspecting a damaged link in my girdle. 'How can we untie this legal knot? It is pulled so tight that it can never be picked loose.'

'I've never retreated from a battlefield. I'll not retreat now, with right on my side.'

'This is no battlefield,' I returned. 'This is a fully fledged rout. We are all defeated.'

'No rout. No defeat. I see my way ahead.'

Before I could ask him what it might be, I became aware of my mother bearing down on us. Thomas might be undaunted, but I was fast becoming resigned to my fate, for I could think of no ploy to escape one marriage and leap into another. In the last moments of privacy I looked up to find him watching me so that I could not look away. Indeed nor did I wish to. In those few brief seconds the intensity of longing was a shocking thing, filling all the spaces in my heart caused by Thomas's absence. It took every effort of my willpower not to stretch out my hand to touch him, even the lightest of pressures on his sleeve. Which would have been irresponsible, damaging to the myth that we were all intent on believing. Oh, Thomas! Unsettled by the sheer power of my reaction to him, I snatched back my missal and walked away, keeping my fears and my longings to myself. Until the next time…

It was like a sore tooth, a constant annoyance. A permanent worrying that could not be put right by a simple tincture of poppy.

★★★

'I will never give up hope for us, Joan.' Standing together by some slight of foot, we both looked across at the elegant procession of dancers in the Queen's new dancing chamber as if it took all our attention.

'I think that I might have.' What good in not being honest? As I slid a glance, I saw him frown. 'Unless you are prepared to abduct me.' In a moment of true despair, I sank into levity.

Thomas remained afloat in practicality. 'And what would that achieve?'

'Everything, if you want me as you wife.'

Was I serious? Elopement was not for me. I was merely irritated with my inability to see a way through the overgrown thicket of our dilemma.

'I could abduct you, of course.' Thomas was brutally blunt. 'But I'll not condemn myself to skulking around Europe, looking for a handout, with you living in a tent on the tournament field, complaining about the food, the cold and the stains on your best silk – your only silk – gown.'

He knew me remarkably, if unflatteringly, well.

'That's not complimentary.'

'It's not intended to be. I know what will make you happy. Tournament life is not one of them.'

'And you are not motivated by your own ambitions?'

'Of course I am. You know I am. I will fight for King Edward, for England. To run off with you would sabotage that plan.'

'And your ambition is more important to you than I am.'

'At this moment, it is a matter of debate in my mind, Joan. I have not known you so argumentative before.'

'I have never before been faced with the quandary of two husbands at one and the same time!'

As fast as a sparrowhawk's descent on an unsuspecting sparrow, anger flared between us, fortunately masked by a lively carol being played on pipes, crumhorns and drums, accompanied by an energetic group of heavy-footed dancers.

'I did not expect to return to England to find my wife cosily in bed with the Montagu family.'

'Only with one of them. I did not expect you to return at all! And as far as I know you have a wench in every camp between here and the Holy Land.'

'And why not? When I cannot trust my wife in England to remain loyal. Does he pleasure you well in bed? Better than I?'

'As well as the camp followers give you ease at the end of a long day.'

'I have always suspected you of a strong streak of frivolity.'

'I have never been frivolous in my life! And you know full well I do not share Will's bed.'

A heated argument that we abandoned when, the drums and pipes falling silent, heads were turned in our direction.

Did we kiss? We did not.

Was I dragged into a fervent embrace? Never.

Where was the passion, the emotion that had driven me into Thomas's arms?

In winter hibernation.

Until I had had enough. And so had Thomas.

★★★

'If we don't abscond,' he said, as we waited on a cold December morn for the hunt to assemble, 'then we must do it legally.'

I thought about this as one of my women tucked my skirts securely between leg and saddle. And when she had completed the task and moved aside: 'A court case. Is that what you think?'

'Why not?'

I knew why not. 'There's no point in appealing to the English courts. They'll do what Edward tells them. You'll get no justice there.'

'True.' Still standing, fidgeting with his gloves, Thomas signalled for his page to tighten the girth since Edward had arrived, then mounted, pulling his horse level with mine. 'There is another method of besieging this castle, of course.'

I looked across.

'You are not allowed to harm Will!'

'I did not mean a dagger in the heart! God's Blood, Joan! Would I do that? I've nothing against him personally. I'm still thinking legally.'

There was only one route I could think of. 'And what would that be? Do you foresee yourself kneeling at the feet of His Holiness the Pope in Avignon and appealing for justice?'

'Exactly that.'

I looked at him aghast. My comment had been born out of pure cynicism. 'Have you come into a family fortune?'

'There is no family fortune. I make my own way in the world.'

'Then who will speak for you? Who will loan you the money? I have none.'

'Nor would I take it from you.' His tone softened and almost he reached to touch my wrist, before thinking better of it, shortening his reins instead.

'It would cost a small fortune.'

'Which I do not have. Not until I have made a name for myself.'

'And how will you do that?'

But I knew without asking the question. There was only one way for men like Thomas. To fight overseas. To shine on the battlefield where he might take prisoner men of consequence and ransom them for the desired fortune. My heart plummeted.

'And how long do you presume that this planning will take? How old will we be before you ransom enough prisoners and your coffers contain enough gold? I would like to see it before my death bed claims me.' A thought flittered across my mind, and not a pleasant one. 'I would like to be extricated from this morass of our making before Will is considered of an age to take me in physical matrimony and gives me a handful of Montagu children who will tie me to this marriage for ever.'

It had crossed Thomas's mind too.

'A year or two. Three at most.'

'Is that all?'

'It all depends on the campaigns. There will be war again between England and France. And if not there will be others where mercenaries are welcomed.' His expression beneath the white silk was severe as we walked our horses behind that of the King. 'Have you no confidence in me?'

I would have replied but William was approaching on a spritely roan and I saw the necessity to retreat. Of course there would be war, there would be every opportunity. There would also be opportunity for Thomas to be cut down in battle. I had every confidence in his courage but was not the lack of an eye an impairment, whatever he might say to the contrary? I did not think that he would be the man he had once been in the tournament, despite the blind king who was led into battle, his reins tied to those of his entourage. That was no life for a man who was intent on wealth and reputation.

'Yes, I have every confidence,' I said. 'Just don't tell me about the King of Bohemia!'

What I kept tight-held within me was the fear, the dread that the whole complex situation, the whole knotty problem, could be immediately resolved by Thomas's death by a lance through his chest or an arrow through his throat. It was not unknown. It could happen before I tasted married bliss.

And here was Will, drawing rein beside me, his thoughts not on wedded bliss.

'What were you talking about?'

Suspicion was not entirely dead then.

'About Sir Thomas's need to make a living from fighting.'

'So he will be leaving soon.'

'I expect so. When he can find a war to suit his purposes.'

'Good.'

'Why? Do you not like him?'

I regarded him beneath lowered lashes, interested to hear what he would say.

'I do,' Will admitted as if it surprised him. 'My father says he is a good man to have at your side.'

'So you would happily send him off to his death.'

'It would solve my problems!'

I was afraid that it would.

His brows snapping together as he continued the line of thought, Will added: 'And I would no longer feel that I had to consider your loyalty to me, every minute of the day when I was not at your side.'

'You dishonour me, my lord,' I replied with a false smile of great sweetness. 'I know exactly where my loyalty is due.'

'And what does that mean?'

Applying my heel to my mare, I left him to his uneasy deliberations.

The hiatus between myself and Thomas came to a hasty end as the court began to hum with a bustle of preparation. Thomas's hopes were about to be fulfilled, for Edward was collecting an army and preparing to take it into Brittany. Sir Thomas Holland acquired a spring in his step that had nothing to do with me.

'So you are going to Brittany.'

'As soon as I can. Don't expect letters. I am no writer.'

'How will I know if you are well?' Then added: 'If you are alive?'

'You won't. Until I return as victor or on a bier.'

He snatched a kiss, as brief as the one on our wedding day. I sighed. I would find no use for ointment of lily, so well recommended by those who knew, to repair painful fissures of lips, product of too many heated kisses. My lips were destined to suffer only from the cold winds of winter.

Thomas did not return with a victor's wreath or on a bier. He did not return at all but, with the truce, went on to Bayonne with Sir John Hardeshull. Followed by Granada with the Earl of Derby where there was a crusade against the Moors. It was to be more than a year before I saw him again, by which time all my hopes had been dashed.

January 1344: Windsor Castle

The final tournament of the day was well underway, the quintessential skills of a knight on show for us all, à *plaisir* rather than à *outrance* with King Edward's knights making a fine showing in the lists.

The war was in abeyance. Edward was home, summoning all the armed youth of England to Windsor, as well as as many earls, knights and barons as he could lay his hands on. This was the second of his great winter tournaments. Queen Philippa was present with a clutch of royal children.

Thomas was home too. He was not dead. Neither was he rich. His expression was bleak.

'I have not made my fortune,' he announced in passing.

And that was that.

Now we watched, admired. We watched as Edward dislodged his opponents with extravagant ease. We watched as Thomas, white silk a-glimmer in the frosty light, fighting with bold strokes irrespective of his impediment, won the prize. We watched as the Earl of Salisbury, Will's famous father returned to us, full of good humour and authority as Earl Marshall, rode at his opponent. The thunder of hooves, the cries of the supporters, the groans of those who lost their bets on which knight would prevail. We watched and the day was glorious indeed. Then, in a strange little silence, herald of disaster, the attention of the crowd centred on one occurrence.

The Earl of Salisbury was unhorsed.

The Earl lay on the ground while his horse cantered off, to be caught by his page.

The Earl lay pinned like a beetle in its carapace, his face still masked by his tilting helm.

Surely he would rise? Surely he would get to his feet, remount his horse and ride back to receive the commiserations from friends and the women in the royal gallery?

The Earl lay motionless on the ground.

Then his squire, kneeling beside him, struggling to remove his helm, was signalling for help. Signalling with increasing concern.

Edward was the first to be at his side, pushing aside the squire, fast followed by Will who bounded from the ranks of the Montagu retinue where he had been acting as squire. At my side Countess Catherine sat unmoving, chin raised.

'He will be unharmed. He has been unhorsed before.'

But her hands were tight-clasped in her lap, and I felt the beginning of a little fear that unfurled in my chest as the King looked up, scrubbing his palms down his cheeks.

The Earl did not rise.

Heavily unconscious, he did not speak, not even when he was carried inside. And later in the day, with one of the King's doctors frowning over him, a litter was harnessed to six of the King's horses to carry him to the family home at Bisham, the Earl's new manor that he loved so much, because it seemed to the Countess that it was the right thing to do.

Will and I went with them, a dour cavalcade.

The King watched us go, grief and fear engraved on his face.

We were at his bedside when the Earl died at Bisham Manor on the thirtieth day of January, never regaining his senses. We stood by his bed as his laboured breathing faltered and stopped. The priest made the sign of the cross on his brow. We bent our heads in prayer, the whole household in mourning. How tragic that the Earl, restored to family, home and pre-eminence, his reputation as soldier and royal counsellor still glorious, should be struck down by a cheap death on the jousting field.

'There will never be another like him. So great a man, so noble a soldier.' The Countess's eyes were proudly dry but stark with loss. 'The King has lost his truest friend. He can never be replaced. The first and greatest of the Montagu Earls of Salisbury.'

I heard Will inhale sharply, then he turned on his heel and walked out. Sensing his resentment of both the death and his mother's assumption that Will would never be his father's equal, I stretched out a hand.

'Let him go,' the Countess said, demeanour pinched and cold with the waiting. 'My son is old enough to shoulder his responsibilities. He must step into his father's shoes, however unlikely it seems.'

Will's brother and four sisters stood irresolute.

I did not think that I could forgive her. I had seen death approaching, but Will had not expected this. Nor had he expected the immediate reproof from his mother, that he would always live in his father's shadow. I curtsied to the Countess.

'I think that he should not be alone, my lady. There is no need to quite step into those magnificent shoes today. Tomorrow will be soon enough.'

And before she could deny it, I went to find him, discovering him where I knew he would be. Will was not one for prayer, seeking out solace in the chapel. Instead he was in the stables, running his hand down the neck of his father's favourite horse, murmuring some affectionate words I could not hear.

'Will...'

He hesitated, then resumed the stroking of the massive gleaming neck.

'I won't talk about it.'

Instead of arguing the case I went and touched his shoulder. Even when he shrugged me off, I persisted and rubbed the back of his neck gently. When I rested my forehead against his back, at last he turned to me and let me fold him into my arms, the first true embrace born out of affection and compassion in all the years of our marriage. He did not weep, but his body was taut with emotions I could not name. And then he relaxed against me a little as I stroked his hair.

'I am so very sorry, Will.'

It was not unknown for knights to meet death or serious injury in jousts à plaisir, but that was no comfort to Will who had worshipped the great soldier that his father had been. The shock held him silent.

'It was a better end than many,' I tried. Better than execution. Better than the head being severed from the body by an incompetent felon. 'He had his dignity to the end.'

'He was a good father.'

'He was caring and affectionate.'

And then, as if it were an entirely new thought, Will raised his head. 'I am Earl now.'

'So you are.'

'I did not expect it.'

'Of course you did.'

'I didn't mean… But not yet.'

'You will be an exceptional Earl. As good as your father.'

'I will not be the King's great friend.'

'No. There are too many years between you. But you will be one of his most loyal counsellors and soldiers.'

'You have great faith in me. More than my mother has.'

'I have known you all my life.'

'So has my mother.'

We laughed a little at the foolishness of his remark.

'Do you realise, Joan? Today we have both grown into our fate,' Will said, defending his furred collar from the teeth of the huge friendly creature now being ignored, and I looked at him, a query in my gaze. 'Because now you are Countess of Salisbury.'

That was it. Earl and Countess in a stable, nuzzled by a curious animal. I wiped the remnants of tears from Will's cheek.

'You do not weep,' he said, an observation rather than censure.

'He was not my father. I am sure that I have wept for my father too, even though I did not know him.' I could not remember.

Will's hand closed hard round mine. 'I cannot be my father.'

'No. You are yourself. Why should you not be a man of similar renown? And why should Edward not take you as his friend? Friendship is not always a matter of age.'

'So what do I do? To become a King's friend.'

'Talk to him.' I recalled talking to Edward about maps and King Arthur.

'Talk…?' I saw a momentary panic invade Will's expression. 'What do I talk about?'

'About war and… and maps and clocks…'

'Clocks?'

The panic deepened.

'Perhaps not, although Edward has a liking for such things. He finds them intriguing. Go hunting with him. Hawking. You can do that. The King will always have an affection for you because of your father that will stand you in good stead. Now is the time to make it your own.'

It seemed good sense to me. All Will needed was some years under is belt.

'It's easy for you. He is your cousin.'

'Believe me, Will, it will be much easier for you. You are a man, not a mere girl. And you are now Earl of Salisbury.'

Will blinked as if, at last, it had just struck home. 'Thank you for your comfort, my lady. Earl and Countess of Salisbury.' He huffed another little laugh which caught in his throat. 'And so we have much to do. My father made it clear. Let us go and tell my mother what she needs to know about my father's funeral.'

We were Earl and Countess of Salisbury.

William was sixteen years old. So was I.

We interred the Earl with suitable solemnities at Bisham Priory, which he had established and where he had expressed a wish to end his days on earth, after which Will and I returned to the court, leaving behind a lachrymose Dowager Countess who had yet to come to terms with my superseding her, in name if not in actual authority, within the Salisbury household.

The subtle changes within the royal household from that day of deadly celebration in January were immediately apparent but took a little time to absorb in their entirety.

The Queen, despite carrying yet another child, was gravely quiet, acknowledging the King's loss of the friendship he had held most dear. As for Edward, there was no Earl of Salisbury to advise and cajole and laugh with him. Ned, also unnaturally solemn, was too young to take the Earl's place, nor did he try. The King walked and talked and ate with a little space of dark loss around him. More startling, it was as if he had lost heart for his plans to install a body of chivalric and glamorous knights, now that his most famous knight had gone from this life, the man who had ridden at his side the night he took back his throne from Earl Mortimer at Nottingham Castle.

It was hard to believe that before the fatal tournament, flanked by the Earl of Salisbury and the Earl of Derby, Edward, a Bible gripped in his hands, had vowed to begin a new Round Table in the spirit of King Arthur, creating a great round structure to house the three hundred knights who would be invited to join. The building, which he had begun with such hope and joy, was left half-finished, collecting cobwebs.

A bleak sorrow pervaded all.

'Talk to him,' I urged Will when, greeted as the new Earl, yet another shimmer of panic settled over him, 'but don't be too cheerful. Tell him about your new tapestries for Bisham. It won't be difficult.'

'Come with me…'

'How would that help? Go and be a man amongst men.'

I could help him no more. Wishing him well, I went to supervise our occupation of the chambers set aside for the Earl and Countess.

No, it was not difficult. As the biting cold was touched with a hint of spring, the King's spirits lifted and the court began to gleam again. By the time we settled into the austerity of Lent, it was much as I had known it and Will was blossoming with a new confidence.

'Good fortune, Joan.'

Sir Thomas Holland, with the gloom of January still about him, bowed.

'Sir Thomas.' I curtsied stiffly, already sensing an uncomfortable exchange. 'My greetings to you too.'

There was no one to cast more than a glance in our direction at his formal assembly. The past was the past, over and done with, and with it all the doubts and debates. My mother had left the court for one of her own properties of Castle Donington, under the conviction that the tragic death had stitched me even more tightly into the garments of this marriage.

'Countess of Salisbury.' Thomas bowed again. 'I commend you, my lady.'

I stared at him, not enjoying the baleful light in his eye as he continued:

'I imagine it colours your view of our marriage, to my detriment. I can expect no resurgence of loyalty from you now. It is the way of the world.' And when I raised my brows: 'Why would you give this up,' he gestured with a sharply raised chin to the robe and fur and the livery collar and to my regal coronet as consort of an Earl, 'to be wife of a household knight?'

I was dressed to give honour to some foreign dignitary, come to make an alliance with King Edward. I was clad in Montagu magnificence all red and white lozenges and ermine fur, from my head to my feet.

I continued to regard Thomas, oblivious to the casual glamour of his own appearance, the silver lion rampant on the chest of his tunic, as I felt anger begin to beat in my head. Did he consider my loyalty so worthlessly ephemeral that the unexpected acquisition of a noble title would shackle me to Will's side? Clearly, he thought exactly that. Living with the Dowager Countess's resistance and Will's grief had reduced me to a low ebb. Now resentful of such a slur on my integrity, I was in no mood to either deny it or make excuses.

I stoked my hand down the extravagance of the fur, luxuriating in it.

'Why indeed?' I said. 'Yes, Sir Thomas, I have always wanted ownership of ermine and a strawberry-leaved coronet. I have decided that I will cleave to this Salisbury marriage after all. I might even find a true affection for William and rejoice to carry his heirs.'

'Of course you might very well do so.'

Thomas's teeth were all but clenched. My spine was as rigid as a halberd.

'Being a princess in my own right bears absolutely no comparison to being a Countess through marriage,' I added. 'It is what I have always sought. I am surprised that you have not already accepted it. We have no future together, Sir Thomas.'

'With which I concur. Security and rank is not to be sneezed at.' He was as cross as I. 'It's better than anything I can offer you, by God! It is merely that I did not think that you would be so capricious, or quite so brazen, in where and when you offered your affections. The speed with which you have changed horses mid-battle is formidable. I should take lessons from you.'

'But you do not know me at all well.'

'As I am beginning to learn.' He bowed his head curtly. 'You have assuredly made the most prudent decision.'

By now my anger had achieved a heat all if its own. How dare he denounce me as capricious in the giving of my affections. As for brazen…

I forgot to be regally controlled to match my gilded strawberry leaves.

'Am I capricious? I was under the strongest impression that I was married to you. I thought that our hearts were engaged. I have had no indication of your heart being engaged by anything but the good health of your livestock for the next tournament.'

I was in no mood to be soothing. I knew exactly the road along which my acknowledged love's thoughts were travelling. How presumptuous of him, to believe that my sudden change in rank would seduce me. How humiliating. And yet how troubling that I had found myself thinking the same unsettling thoughts. Living as Countess of Salisbury would be far more comfortable than as Lady Holland.

Thomas was scathing.

'Of course I am concerned for the well-being of my horses. What did you expect? Declarations of my love for you at every opportunity?'

'Certainly not.'

'My life depends on the soundness of my horseflesh.'

'Ha! Thus your priorities.'

'Hear me, Joan.' Suddenly he had a fistful of my ermine crushed hard. 'I feel honour-bound not to address you or touch you until our marriage is recognised. I may not be an Earl but I know what honour is. Just at this moment it's like being confined in a…' Thomas was not poetic. '… in a dungeon where all is black and formless and there is no way out. Until I can raise enough coin, you are destined to remain chained there as Countess of Salisbury. You might as well enjoy it.'

It was like trying to follow a cat through a maze.

'I thought you had just agreed that it would be a good thing for me to keep my ermine – for both of us.'

'I did not agree. I stated what I thought might be in your mind.'

'You have no idea what is in my mind.'

'As I know.' The air shivered between us. 'I need another war.'

'Well at least it might relieve me of one husband. Which would be better than having two. And an incomplete relationship with either of them!'

He was preoccupied, and did not respond as I hoped he might, studying his hands where they were now clasped on his sword belt. I smoothed my mistreated fur.

'I need employment of some kind, Joan.'

Fury drove me, unfortunately, to sneer. 'What can you do? Other than fight?'

Here we were trapped, in a complex spider's web of our own making. It might be better if I resigned myself to life with William which would not be unpleasant, but it would not have that spark of exhilaration that had brought me from my bed this morning in anticipation of seeing Thomas, even for a handful of minutes. Life with Will would not have this bright conflict that awoke my senses, even when I was angry with him. Crossing swords with Thomas was heady with possibilities. Arguments with Will were no better than a buffeting with a soft cushion.

I knew which I preferred.

'Is there nothing else you can turn your hand to?' I asked.

'I am a knight. A soldier. A fighting man.'

'I did not presume you would turn to labouring like a peasant.'

He frowned into the middle distance, as if I had sowed some small seed of an idea.

'What are you thinking?'

'Nothing that need concern you.'

'An answer that I dislike.'

'You'll get no explanation from me.' Then he gave a shrug of one shoulder. 'I'll say this. That campaigning gives a man many arrows for his bow.'

Which was no more enlightening.

'I've never seen you use a bow.'

'I am excellent with a bow. I think I see my way to establishing myself.'

'Until the next battle.'

'Of course.' His gaze, suddenly on mine, sharpened. Without warning he pulled me into a corner where there was no discreet shelter whatsoever, looked over his shoulder, then kissed me, full on the mouth. 'I don't like being furtive. It goes against the grain, but how long is it since I have done that?' He kissed me again so that my skin was far too hot within my figured damask. 'What value honour, Joan? I have just destroyed every tenet of chivalrous behaviour I placed before you.'

Before I could answer that it was far too long, and I did not mind at all, even though it was dishonourable, he was striding away, leaving me none the wiser. What was he planning? I had the feeling that I would not like it.

But I had liked his kiss. It had reawakened all I had forgotten.

So what had I been thinking?

Everything of which Thomas had accused me, because the death of the Earl had stirred up the whole order of my life, dropping it into a completely different formation of shapes and patterns, like a child's mosaic. Now I was Countess of Salisbury with the future prospect of vast estates and wealth, an enviable position at court, in the close clique around the King and Queen. Not a position to be cast lightly aside if my mind was set on an influential future.

But then I had always been accepted within the King and Queen's own family. There was no advantage for me in the Salisbury marriage.

I did not need it. It would give me nothing that I did not already have as the daughter of the Earl of Kent. Except perhaps a permanence through Will's foremost rank.

But why would I rank the position of Countess above marriage to the man I loved enough to marry in the face of so much opposition?

There was one supreme advantage, of course. I sighed a little.

'I am Countess of Salisbury,' I spoke the words aloud. 'I am immune from all scandal.'

It made good sense. Take the husband that fate has given you, I advised myself. Cut your garments to suit your cloth. To do otherwise risks untold grief and damage.

All well and good.

Why had I been so angry with Thomas? Because the title and the garments and the coronet did indeed tie me even more securely into this marriage. Escape became unimaginable. And so, being thwarted, my own wishes being overturned, I had aimed my ill humour at my bold knight. Now, in the aftermath, I was full of regret for my selfish attack, forced as I was by that kiss to accept that Thomas still had the power to make me forget myself. To want what I should not.

And what was it that he was planning?

I suspected, recalling his cold plotting, that I might not find it acceptable at all.

'Joan. Joan!'

I yawned and continued to read. I was alone, and enjoying the solitude, losing myself as I rarely did in the romantic exploits of the inestimable Sir Galahad in his search for the Holy Grail when, from Will's chamber there was the unmistakeable sound of his boots being removed, of coffers being opened and slammed shut. My peace would not last long.

Will had found a need to return to Bisham, a brief visit that, so it seemed, had lasted no longer than a week before he was back with me here at Westminster. I would give him five minutes before the door between the two rooms was thrust back.

There. Barely five. He had exchanged his travelling garb for hunting leathers. I thought there was a furtive look about him as he loped across the room, took my hand and kissed my cheek.

'There you are, Joan.'

'How are things at Bisham?' I asked.

'Difficult. My mother thinks I should remain there to become familiar with the running of the estates, even though I do not have full power over them until I am twenty-one. My mother thinks that I should become accustomed. So does my grandmother.'

I watched him as he shuffled from stool to window and back again. His thoughts were entirely suspect.

'And what do you think, Will?'

'I'm not sure.' Then he grinned. 'I feel shackles tightening round my ankles whenever my mother issues instructions to speak with the steward or my father's council or even the cook about what my grandmother can and cannot eat.'

'I know what you think.' Standing, I tucked my hand into his arm. 'You'd far rather take up your sword and join the King in his next campaign.' I knew Will well by now. I knew how he reacted, and I knew how to get him to tell me the worst. 'Come and walk with me. The King is still talking with Philippa.'

Leaving our rooms we strolled slowly towards the royal apartments.

'It is what my father would have done.' For a moment Will grimaced. 'And so would I. But it's not as easy as...'

'Of course it is.' Not that I wanted Will to hotfoot to France to engage in battle, but it was time that he threw off his mother's yoke. 'Who ran the estates when your father was elsewhere? When he was imprisoned in France? I'm sure that the Countess didn't.' My own mother might have her fingers in every estate pie, but not every wife or widow was as driven to oversee every insignificant detail from bedchamber to cellar.

'Our steward,' he said. 'And my father's council of knights and clerics to oversee all matters. My mother has no interest. Or application. Or ambition, even. I suspect she lacks the knowledge for checking ledgers. Not that she doesn't keep an eye on everything that goes on, and if she does not, my grandmother certainly does. Despite appearances to the contrary, my grandmother is an uncomfortably percipient old woman, even if she does refuse to eat roast meats.'

'So why can this not continue?'

'Our steward is old. I think he was appointed by my grandfather. His sight is failing.'

'So appoint another.'

I sensed him looking at me, and returned it. There was a thought in his mind that continued to disturb me. As he blinked, I saw what it was.

'Oh, no,' I said.

'You could do it.'

Of course I could do it. I had the ability. I had the application. I had the education, and could learn soon enough where I was lacking. But like the Dowager Countess I lacked the interest, the ambition to become my own steward. I could overlook the ledgers at regular intervals under the guidance of the steward but I had no intention of spending every day with the minutiae of detail of the Salisbury possessions. The life I saw for myself was at court, in the whirl of government and intrigue and political gossip, not tied up in ordering and supervising every meal the family ate.

'No,' I repeated with some force. 'Employ a steward. You have the money.'

'No, I do not. Nothing like all of it. Not until I reach my majority.'

'Then apply to the King. He will be understanding. He'll not let you live in penury.'

But Will showed more resistance than I expected.

'I can't employ just anyone. I need a man of loyalty and skill, of experience in handling finance and people.' The more he talked the more I saw him persuade himself that this would be the best option. Will had no wish to do it himself. Then, as he remembered his financial state, his eye fell once more on me. 'But why can you not do it while I am away fighting?'

So we had our first real argument. I would not be tied to ink and lists and tally sticks. I would become as morbid as the Dowager Countess.

'And if you think that your mother and grandmother would allow me to take precedence over their wishes at Bisham, then you are a fool!'

'They would if I ordered it.'

Sometimes Will was astonishingly naive, unwilling to let the matter lie, believing that I was the perfect answer to his problems, and selfish not to concur.

'I prefer dancing to accounting.'

By this time we were standing together in the Great Hall.

'Can you not do both? If you would only…'

'If I do that I will be supervising your ageing steward for the rest of my life. Employ another. Someone with life and ambition and foresight in him.'

'But you have the time on your hands. Whereas I have to go and hunt.'

'Hunt? Now there's a valuable occupation! You hunt while I bloody my fingers with quills and tally sticks and endless rent rolls.'

Will looked hurt. 'It was you who told me to find time to be with the King.'

'But not at the expense of the running of your estates. They cannot be neglected.'

'Please Joan… ' he wheedled, his smile a thing of great charm.

'No.'

'My lord – '

We both turned. There, also clad for hunting, a hawk on his gloved wrist, a brace of hounds at his heels together with a couple of enthusiastic pages, stood Sir Thomas Holland.

Will, still preoccupied with my refusal, acknowledged him with a curt nod of his head. I simply stood.

Thomas was solemn, worryingly formal. 'My lord. I would request a word with you before the King arrives.'

I looked from one to the other as Thomas sketched a somewhat dismissive bow in my direction as if he thought I should retreat and leave this discussion to men. Will looked as surprised as I. I returned a suitably bland expression. I was going nowhere.

'I have a proposition, my lord.'

'What sort of proposition?'

I had no thought whatsoever of the thunderbolt Thomas was about to hurl into our midst.

'It is in my mind that my proposition would be of mutual benefit.'

Will now managed to look wary. He might have persuaded himself that Thomas had abandoned his pursuit of me, but the underlying suspicion would take a long time to die completely.

'Of mutual benefit?'

'So I think. Now that you are Earl of Salisbury. We both have soldiering in our sights, but there is none on offer.'

'Well that's true. I'm hoping the King sees a need for a new campaign in France…'

And they were suddenly brothers in arms, discussing warfare. I would leave them to it, and drifted away to where Isabella, clad in a sumptuous array of verdant satin, had come to ride with her father. I had not stepped twenty paces when, behind me, my quick hearing picked up the fact that the merits of this sword against that one, this helm or that one, had been abandoned.

'… my services,' I heard Thomas say. 'It is my understanding that you have need.'

I could not believe what I was hearing. Ignoring Isabella, I marched back again, to hear Will admit: 'Yes I do. I've only just been speaking of it with Joan…'

'I could remedy the problem.'

I saw Will's face brighten. 'Do I understand, Sir Thomas, that you will offer me the use of your wide experience?'

'Yes. I know you'll see the value of it, for both of us.'

Will was looking as if a weight had been taken from his shoulders. Within seconds I was standing beside him.

'As I am aware, you have no talents in this field, Sir Thomas,' I said.

Which Thomas acknowledged, and promptly rejected, his reply addressed uncompromisingly to Will.

'If I can organise a campaign and lead men into battle, my lord, I can supervise the running of the Salisbury estates. I can negotiate with your council. I am in need of an income. You need a steward. I would see it as an honour to serve you, and your family.'

It was quite a declaration, and all of it probably true, but it filled me with a cold dread, even as I admired his gall in seizing the opportunity. And no one looking at Thomas would ever believe that this was anything but a genuine offer; I had not known he was so skilled at dissembling. But was he dissembling? Nothing would persuade me that this would be good policy. Nor did Will seem to think so, regarding me as if I were guilty in inviting Thomas to make the offer.

I lifted my shoulder in a little shrug. I had no wish to live in such a household, maintaining a semblance of seemly co-existence. But first I would wait to see what Will would say.

'As my wife says, you have no experience of stewardship.'

A smile curved Thomas's mouth. 'Campaigning gives a man many arrows for his bow.'

A statement I recognised. So this was what he had been planning. I fixed Thomas with a stare that would leave him in no doubt of my displeasure.

'It might work.' Will rubbed his thumb along the edge of his jaw, an action I recognised when his decision making was compromised, as he avoided my gaze. No, it certainly would not work. I took a breath to suggest that Will should take time to think about this, and consider other alternatives – any alternative – when a hand came down heavily on Will's shoulder and a fourth voice entered the fray.

'An excellent choice, I would say.'

None of us, intent on this negotiation, had heard the King approach. Edward was positively jovial.

'It will give you a helping hand, lad. And you, Thomas, some experience for when your ambitions lead you into land ownership, when you have sufficient prize-money at your disposal. You'll need something to leave to your heirs other than a worn suit of armour and a bundle of weapons.'

By the Virgin! Edward did not know what he was doing.

'We have not considered other stewards yet, sir,' I said.

'Why bother? This can be done in a handshake – and then we can all blow the cobwebs away with a good run after the hounds. If it's a matter of money, Will, I'll arrange a grant until your own resources become free for your own use. There!' He clapped his hand down once again on Will's shoulder. 'All signed and sealed, and you have your new steward.'

The King beamed and moved away, the hounds following in a wave of brindled flesh, leaving Thomas and Will to shake hands, well pleased with the deal.

As the King had said, we had a new steward.

Will was light with relief. 'We must talk further about this, Sir Thomas. Are you going, Joan?'

Why would I stay? To listen to these two men set up a household containing the three of us? I would if I thought for one moment that either would listen to a word I said. Will would see the offer as manna from heaven as long as Thomas did not demand too much in payment. As for Thomas's motives – I could not discern them. And the King, all unwittingly, had put his blessing on the whole procedure.

I smiled with an air of sweet acceptance that challenged my control, and left them to the discussion of terms.

I had no intention of allowing a *ménage à trois* of this strange nature to develop without my hand on the reins, my pride balking at such an outrageous situation. The fact that there were no adverse comments regarding our new household was an irrelevance. If anyone should discover the truth of our marital difficulties, we would all be cast into the mire. I would fight tooth and nail to prevent it.

And what is it that you will do?

My query remained unanswered, since Edward had countenanced the agreement and all Will could see was the relief at being able to shrug off his duties onto broader shoulders than his own. I could see no possible intervention that would make the slightest imprint on this new scheme. But to have all three of us, together with Will's mother and grandmother, under one roof was more than I could tolerate.

Of course it would not happen. Surely at the eleventh hour Will would remember, between the first chase and the second, that Thomas had a legal claim on me as his lawful wife. Surely that would be the strongest argument for him to refuse Thomas as steward.

I was furious with Thomas that he should give me a morning of worry. What was he thinking? There would be nothing immoral in our household, for I did not think that was Thomas's intent. He was a man of strong principle. Of duty and of loyalty. And, it seemed, of exceptional cunning.

'What's wrong?' Isabella asked as she prepared to follow her father.

'Not a thing. I would advise you not to ride to the hunt in that gown. You'll scare the hounds.'

Isabella looked askance. 'I will do as I please. You look as if you would like to give your husband an opinion he might not like.'

'Will is always most accommodating to my desires,' I said with no certainty at all.

The hunt was over. Will returned, plastered in mud and pleasure.

'Will, I have to speak with you.'

My accommodating husband swept aside my desires before I had even voiced them. 'We have a new steward, Joan. Now doesn't that solve all our problems? Sir Thomas is keen. I can continue to live at court, and you don't have to strain your pretty eyes at the ledgers.' He cast himself down on a stool, signalling to one of his pages to pull off his boots.

I was beyond words.

Will sensed my lack of enthusiasm so wisely dismissed the page. 'Well?'

'I am delighted to hear our problem is solved!'

'No, you are not.'

'Of course I am not. How could you do something so... so ridiculous?'

'It seemed eminently sensible. The King agreed.'

'The King doesn't know the complications here. Oh, Will! Are you witless? What if the tale of my first marriage is dropped amongst the gossip mongers at court? And there we will be, the three of us, happily living within the same household.'

'But there is no such talk, Joan. It never was a legal binding between you and Sir Thomas.' I set my teeth at his perennial insouciance. 'You are married to me. Besides, who's to talk of it now, after all these years?'

'Scandal has a way of emerging when least expected. How the court will enjoy this. We will be a general laughing stock. Or you will. Have you even thought about it? The cuckolded husband. I can imagine what will be whispered, that Thomas used blackmail to get this position, threatening you to make him steward or he would broadcast the marriage to all and sundry. Do you want that?'

'It won't happen.' Will poured himself a cup of ale since I made no attempt to do so. 'Holland has given up on the prospect of you as his wife. He sees it as all water under the matrimonial bridge.'

'Did you actually discuss it?'

'No. We did not need to.'

'Such honour amongst men! I don't believe it!'

It was becoming increasingly difficult not to sweep the cup from his hand.

Will's tone dropped to a condescending level. 'This will be a purely business affair. There is no need for you to fear for your reputation, Joan. It would not surprise me if he did not seek another bride within the year.'

'And did you discuss that too?'

'What if we did?'

What could I say? Hardly that I had no belief in Thomas's sanguine acceptance. But neither could I make a fuss. Will had decided and it was done. All I could say: 'Well, as long as my reputation does not suffer. I have no wish to be part of a household drenched in the scarlet of scandal.'

'Nonsense. Of course it won't.' A twinkle graced his eye as he kissed my cheek. 'And my mother and grandmother will be there at Bisham as chaperone. There will be no dishonour or impropriety.' The twinkle became warmer, his voice a little sly. 'Besides, I think that it is time.'

'Time for what?'

Despite his mud and dishevelment, Will's arm curved around my waist.

'I think, dear Joan, that it is time that we consummated this marriage.'

My heart thumped uncomfortably. It was time. It was more than time. I did not want to even contemplate it.

'Not while you are covered with mud,' I said.

'That's easily remedied.' He kissed my cheek again as I turned my head so that he missed my lips.

'And not while we are in mourning, Will,' I added, snatching at reasons. 'It would not be seemly.'

'No, I suppose not.' He looked as if he had forgotten.

I patted his arm. 'Later.'

It was not, naturally, to be expected that this would be my last word on the subject of our new steward. These were addressed to the man in question.

'How could you conceive of something so outrageous?' I wasted no breath.

I cornered Thomas. Sometimes Will was too innocent a target. The King did not know what he had accomplished, but Thomas did. Thomas knew very well what he was about, all carefully planned like a battle campaign. He needed an occupation. He knew that our new household was in need. He could be uncommonly persuasive, as I knew to my cost.

'With uncommon ease.'

'Did you think this… this *debacle* would please me?'

'I don't see it as a debacle. And frankly, Joan, I am no longer certain what will please you.'

'If even the whisper of our marriage escapes, the Salisbury household will become a thing of ridicule.'

'But who will speak of it? Your family won't. Will and his mother have their mouths sewn up. The Earl is dead. You priest is unfortunately – or fortunately – gone to receive his due reward in heaven. Our witnesses are sworn on the threat of God's vengeance that they will not speak until I tell them to do so.'

'I fear that someone will.'

'The hawks in the Ghent mews? They are all dead by now.'

'You have an answer to everything.'

'Well, I don't. I don't yet have an answer to how to get you back. Any ideas?'

'No.'

'Do you wish to come back? I am not even sure.'

'Neither am I. I am no longer sure that you love me. Or that I love you.'

'You are a fool, Joan.'

'I am beleaguered, Thomas.' He simply looked at me with lifted brows. 'You cannot expect it to be easy, living together in such close proximity. Why would you do it?'

'Apart from a need to make a living? It is very simple. I will be able to see my wife. I will be able to talk with her, to serve her, even if I cannot touch her. Even if I can never take her to my bed.'

His honesty touched me, like the soft caress of a dove's feather. Life was becoming more difficult by the moment.

Chapter Five

Thomas Holland took to estate management like a starving rat to old cheese-pairings. The elderly Salisbury steward was retired and Thomas stepped into his shoes in the dark, draughty and sprawling manor of Bisham with capable feet.

I was astonished at the precision with which he undertook every thing that came within his responsibility. There was nothing demeaning in a knight taking office as steward in a great magnate's household. Indeed it would be considered a step of pre-eminence for Sir Thomas Holland to hold such a position. How right he proved to be: if he could lead men into battle, he could win over the serv-ants from high to low and earn their respect, using either a bark of command or choice vocabulary favoured by the soldiering fraternity. When he did not know, he asked. He approached Will's council with dignity. He addressed Will's mother with a cool decorum that she enjoyed, while pandering disgracefully to Will's grandmother with charm. In his dealings with Will he was deferential but firm in his opinions. He had them all eating out of his hand.

Here were unknown depths to this man, a range of skills of which I, in my short acquaintance, had never been aware. Perhaps he had not too, but his growing mastery won my admiration, another layer to add to my discomfiture.

And in his dealings with me? Thomas's behaviour towards me was exemplary. So was mine towards him. There would be no dishonouring of Will.

Dowager Countess Catherine, at first, proved more than suspicious.

'I do not approve. Was this your doing, Joan?'

'It most certainly was not,' I replied lightly, as if it was of no moment to me. 'I would never have considered Sir Thomas to be adept at such a task. Your son was the one who accepted the offer. The King also thought it was a good idea. If you consider that I am a woman willing to discredit my birth by allowing any level of immorality beneath my roof, you do not know me well.'

She stiffened at my claim to have authority at Bisham. We did not speak of it again.

And so we lived, seemly as nuns in a convent. I could not see the future. I knew that this state of calm could not continue for ever. It was certainly the calm before the storm I had first envisaged so many years ago now, but when this tempest would break and how devastating the deluge, I could not imagine.

Sometimes I could feel Thomas's stare, boring into the space between my shoulders. Once the touch of his hand when he passed me a napkin with which to wipe my fingers was like a charge of power between us. It stopped when I dropped the napkin. He placed it, neatly folded, beside my knife at the table.

Nothing overt. Nothing deliberate.

By the end of the first month, when I was wishing for the comforts and luxuries of my cousin Edward's rebuilding at Windsor, Will, in light-hearted mood, began to suggest suitable brides for our steward. Thomas, so it seemed to me, began to listen. I too listened, frozen into displeasure.

But would it not be the best possible of outcomes?

I learned the worst of myself in those days. I could not have Thomas Holland, but I would not willingly hand him over to another woman. Green-eyed jealousy was not an emotion with which I was familiar; never having in my privileged life the need to desire what belonged to another. Now I experienced its discomfort, its piercing fury.

Meanwhile the King, with much enthusiasm that was fast transferred to his household knights and military men, was planning a new campaign in France.

It left me restless, driven by a need to say more, to do more when it became a subject of discussion that, given this opportunity, Thomas might once again take the path to war and never return. Honour said that I should say nothing. Duty said that I should stay as far away from him as I could except in the daily needs of the household. But whether it be romantic yearning or merely thwarted desire, it drove me to find him in the depths of the vast arched cellar where he was occupied in counting barrels and sides of cured meat with one of his minions. My only excuse was...

But I had no excuse, rather a need to be within his self-imposed domain.

'My lady?' He looked up from the list under his hand.

'Sir Thomas.'

'Can I be of assistance?' I detected a lack of enthusiasm.

'I believe you can.'

'I am your servant, my lady.' And to the underling: 'Take this and give it to the cook. He will tell you where there is a lack in our accounting. Ask him if he can explain the whereabouts of six tuns of fine Bordeaux wine.' And when he had gone, 'Now, my lady. I can think of no need for you to be in your cellar at this time of day.'

He was not friendly. He suspected me of playing with fire. There was much truth in it.

'Will you sit?' I requested.

'Where?'

He made no move to do so.

'That barrel will do.'

'Why? It would not be courteous for me to sit while you stand.'

'Just sit down!'

'If you wish, my lady.'

How prosaic. He angled his body to perch on a small barrel of salted fish, while I stood in front of him.

'What do you want, Joan?'

He was no longer my steward but my lover.

'I might never see you again.'

He did not question what I might mean. Perhaps he understood. Or perhaps he trusted me, as he should, to deal circumspectly. And yet when I touched his face, the lightest of touches with my fingertips against his cheek, he flinched a little, and when my fingers travelled on to discover the tied ends of the silk band, his own rose to still them.

'Don't!'

'But I will. I did not think you would be shy of your scars.'

'I am not. But what man would willingly exhibit them to the woman he loves?'

His voice was suddenly harsh, tearing at my heart. I softened mine in compassion.

'Then I will tell you. A man who is proud of their begetting. A man who was courageous in battle. You have both those attributes.'

'Then do as you wish.'

He let his hands fall away, as I loosed the silk.

Jesu!

He was horribly scarred. The eyelid permanently closed now, a scar ran deeply across it from his hairline to just below the arc of his cheek bones. Any deeper and I suspect he would have died. Gently,

I touched the puckering flesh, no longer red and angry after all these years but I could imagine how once it was. He was a brave man to withstand the pain, as were so many of our knights.

I could also understand why he had hidden it from me, for it had destroyed his comeliness and there was a vanity in him after all. Yet how typical of him to draw attention to it in so cavalier a fashion. Under my ministrations Thomas remained perfectly still, as if carved in marble. But when, without warning, I leaned and pressed my lips against his disfigurement, I felt him exhale long and deep, as if he had long held a fear of which he could not speak.

'You do not despise me,' he said. 'You do not find the scar distasteful.'

'I do not.'

I smoothed my fingers over the silk I still held, contemplating his future, and mine, unable to envisage either.

'Will you ever not wear this?' I asked, struggling against the huge well of sadness that seemed to have opened up beneath my heart.

'One day. When I am full satisfied with my fighting for the honour of God and St. George and England. Then I will take it off.' For a moment he hesitated, head tipped back so that he could look at me. 'Does it disgust you?' he asked again.

'No. Did you think that it would?'

'How am I to know what is in a woman's mind? And one with royal blood, that has the power to bestow on a woman inordinate pride. I am only a soldier.' For the first time since Thomas had returned to England and found me wed, I heard regret in his voice as his fingers found mine and pressed down a little. 'I still cannot believe that you were willing to join your name to mine.'

'We haven't made a good fist of it,' I said. 'And I cannot hurt Will. He is my friend, has always been so, and has no ill will towards either of us.'

For a long moment he looked at me as if weighing the words he wished to say.

'Remember this. If I die in battle, so that we never discover an opportunity to be together as man and wife, remember that I never loved anyone but you.'

He touched my cheek with the back of his hand, while I turned my head to press my lips there. It was the most tender of caresses, awakening all I recalled of that youthful love that had afflicted me. I pressed his hand against my cheek, enjoying the moment of unexpectedly breathless affinity.

But not for long. His voice was suddenly as edged as the sword that he did not wear.

'Why did you do it Joan? Why did you allow yourself to be thrust into this marriage? Why not just tell the King that you could not legally take the step? That you were my wife? You wed me in good faith, yet within the year you had entered into a marriage with William Montagu. But why? You are the most headstrong woman I know, yet you let yourself be browbeaten into denying me. How could you do it, to cause so much inconvenience? This chaos is of your making.'

The atmosphere in the cellar swooped into the cold of winter ice. Could he not have acknowledged that I had caused him heartache rather than ripples to the surface of his pond? I pulled away from him, hurt and angry at this sudden steep descent from tenderness to blame, yet knowing that my actions must seem to him bound by nothing but female inconstancy. Why would I compromise my soul by laying my hand to a second vow, when I was bound by a first one? It would seem incomprehensible. But now I was weary, weary of being castigated as shallow and disloyal, driven by self-interest or youthful extravagances to defy my mother and choose my own path. I felt colour creep into my cheeks as I accepted that perhaps I had made the wrong decision in not declaring my inability to wed when I stood before the altar with Will, but it had been done in a true spirit.

If Thomas was going to war, he should know.

'I did it because...'

But I had kept my counsel for so long. What would be gained by my abject confession? I pared it down.

'If I had confessed to what we had done,' I said, 'I was afraid I would burden you with a dangerous notoriety. My intentions were of the best.'

Simplistic as an explanation, but not entirely untrue.

'Then God help us when they are not of the best.'

Which was not helpful.

'Were you forced into it by your mother? By the Countess of Salisbury?'

'Yes.'

It was the easiest confession to make.

'And you agreed to remain silent.'

'Yes.'

'But Edward would have to find out sometime.' Thomas's hands were planted on his knees, the frustration no less. 'If I returned and laid claim to you, all the world would know, as I've no doubt it will, when I do exactly that.' He exhaled sharply as if coming to an unpleasant decision, his hands clenching into fists. 'Better to ride over rough ground as fast as possible.'

'I owe you my heartfelt apologies,' I replied stiffly. 'For making matters worse.'

His scarred brow was still grim. 'You were very young, I suppose, to be left to make these decisions.'

I stiffened again. 'I was quite capable of making them.'

'I expect you were. But my absence did not help matters, did it?'

It was the best apology I could hope for, and when Thomas took my hands in his and smoothed out my fingers, taking the opportunity to press a kiss into the palm of each hand, I allowed it. Then, because I must, I replaced the silk to cover the worst of the scars before touching my lips to it.

'You are very generous,' he murmured.

And Thomas framed my face with his hands, to bring my lips down to his. There in Bisham's cavernous cellar, it was to be the first and the last time that we touched so intimately, in recognition and, if truth be told, perhaps in hopelessness, of what had been between us. The first and the last time that we could be accused by the world of impropriety.

'God keep you safe, Thomas.'

'As I pray that he will keep you, my lady.'

It was as if replacing the mask over his wounds, the removal of which had released so much emotion, had now restored our relationship of lady and steward. Turning quickly, my chest tight, I left him to his allotted task while I returned to my private chamber in utter misery. My choice had been questioned. The inadequacy of my decision laid bare. And I had not told him the truth.

'Where have you been?'

Will passed me in the Hall, seeing me come from the direction of the kitchens.

'Sir Thomas is making lists in the cellars.' I felt that my face was aflame with guilt, but supposed that it was not, since Will made no comment. 'Sir Thomas thinks there will be a new campaign. And he will go, I am sure of that.'

'Does he? Then I will go too.'

So neither one of my husbands might return.

It might have astonished me that Sir Thomas Holland's position as steward to the puissant Earl of Salisbury bore no importance whatsoever as soon as there was a campaign to be fought. It did not. Neither did his responsibilities to wife and mother make much impression on William. As soon as the King began preparations for an expedition to set sail from England in the July of 1346, planning to land in Normandy and once more wage war, the brave knights of England, and of our household, sailed with him.

So began a strange time, that time of waiting that we had experienced so often in recent years, with the Queen in the early throes of yet another physical sign of the King's devotion to her. The celebrations were put aside, the hunting, the exuberant festivities. War was no time for rejoicing until the victory was secure.

We did not speak of defeat.

Couriers were awaited, their news snapped up with relief when we heard there was a safe arrival in the Cotentin, where the King knighted Ned on the spot near where they landed on the beach, as well as knighting my husband Will. It was a magnificent beginning for the campaign and Countess Catherine wept tears of pride. I listened for news of Thomas and my brother John, now enjoying the pre-eminence of being recognised as Earl of Kent on the battlefield. There was none, but no news was good news. My brother might be young but he must make his mark in battle and there, surrounded by so many friends, was the perfect opportunity.

As the army settled in for a long campaign, we settled in for the long wait; Philippa, sanguine, encouraging us all in good spirits. She had a husband and son to lose, and both much loved. We followed her example of straight-backed determination as she complained of her swollen ankles and growing bulk, wishing me better fortune when Will and I began to consider our own family.

'When he returns from this war, that will be a good time to make your marriage a true one,' she said, her nausea abating for a time. 'You are both of an age, and more. I was much younger when Edward and I made our marriage complete. I will persuade the King to grant you both a more substantial allowance to furnish your extended household. Children are an expensive commodity, as I know.'

I curtsied my thanks.

'William will be an exceptional husband,' Philippa observed, fortunately not detecting my silent prayers that my future, as she read it, would never come to pass.

'I can think of none better.' The Dowager Countess, come recently to court, was at my side.

'Neither can I, madam,' I agreed. 'Let us hope that we hear good news of William's success in battle,' I added before she could be eloquent on the complementary talents needed to be an exceptional wife.

News came in droplets. There was a vicious siege of the town of Caen, followed by a battle at a place called Crécy, a great victory where the English knights and archers decimated the flower of the French army, so the heralds proclaimed in their dramatic discourse. There were deaths, so many deaths, both English and French. The blind King of Bohemia met his noble end on the battlefield, cut down in the thick of the battle, his horse tied to those of his entourage.

Would Thomas's compromised sight have a similar tragic outcome?

It was not to be contemplated. I set myself to entertain Philippa and avoid my mother and the Dowager Countess. Meanwhile, the King put in place a siege around the French garrison in Calais, summoning Philippa to join him, to spend Christmas with him in his base at Villeneuve-le-Hardi. I considered travelling with her but decided to remain in England where it would be advantageous for me to keep my eye on Thomas's surrogate steward. I was fast learning the duties of the life of the Countess of Salisbury.

'It will be a burden that never leaves you, for the rest of your life,' my mother observed with more satisfaction than I liked.

'It is a burden I will decry as soon as Will and our steward are back home,' I said.

'Yet you stay in England to shoulder your responsibilities!'

'It is my decision.' I had no wish to spend Christmas in the company of both Thomas and Will in Villeneuve-le-Hardi. It would be exhausting.

My mother might have wished that Thomas had met a glorious end on the battlefield. He did not. We heard that he had excelled at the siege of Caen, that he had proved the quality of his leadership at Crécy, that he had come through the fighting with barely a scratch. No doubt he would tell us all about it over supper at Bisham and Will would be full of admiration as he told his own tales of brave exploits.

We heard that they were coming home.

Relief setting its hand on me, so that I slept without nightmares sitting at my shoulder, I set myself once more to master the art of living with both.

★★★

October 1347: London

The noise began as a rumble, as distant thunder or the approach of a multitude of heavily loaded wagons. Soon it would become shouts and cries of welcome. Of delirious fervour, well fuelled with ale.

England was in jubilant mood to see their King returned from war and from victory. As was the Salisbury family that hemmed me in where we awaited the return of our hero, the young Earl. He had fought bravely. He had been knighted, the young Earl proving himself to be a knight in the mould of his magnificent father. It was a time of rejoicing as the combined Montagu connection looked forward to a glittering future. With the young Earl and his royal wife, the family would see a resurgence. Now it was time for that royal wife to carry a son, the heir for the future.

There were glances in my direction. Queen Philippa's observations, that it was time that I fulfilled my wifely duties, were shared by others, particularly my mother who graced us with her presence.

Where would I be within a year from now? Countess of Salisbury, all good sense remarked, with a babe in arms. That would be the order of things and there was no path for me to tread to Thomas's side. I must thank the Blessed Virgin that Will had proved to be as amenable and affectionate as he had been through his boyhood. There were few wives who could claim as much.

I contemplated the months ahead unfolding.

Would we return to Bisham and live out our lives there, with Thomas as our steward as we all grew into old age? Would Thomas wed again, introducing a new wife into our household? It could not be deemed an onerous future, even when they would both be off at the first opportunity to fight again for England's glory if the peace with France did not hold. Will would insist that we become man and wife in body as well as in soul, of that I was certain, and I could not in all honesty refuse. There would be no doubt of my future, to raise children to take on the great inheritance of Salisbury.

I swallowed hard against the bloom of disappointment. I would have an affectionate husband but must learn to live without that brief experience of love that I had discovered with Thomas. William, for all his excellent qualities, did not move me to forget myself. Which might, of course, be more appropriate for the Countess of Salisbury. I must accept what was placed before me on my gold plate, poured into my gold cup for my enjoyment.

But how much harder it had become since Thomas had infiltrated himself under my nose. It was easier when he was on campaign, except then I worried about his life. Or death. Perhaps he had made a fortune in ransom money at Crécy, enough that he would purchase his own estate. When my spirits were at their lowest ebb, I hoped that it would be so.

But now all must be put aside for this magnificent return.

The procession approached, we awaited them, the palace of Westminster providing a superb backcloth. Glittering in armour, gleaming with polished horseflesh, resplendent with banners and the tabards of the royal heralds, the King and his knights drew near. When the late autumn sun shone to bathe it all in gilded triumph, it was impossible not to be carried along with the sheer glory of it. The crowds cheered their returning monarch who had beaten the French into the ground. And the Queen, with their new baby daughter Margaret, a potent symbol of the longevity of this royal family, stood in our midst with tears in her eyes.

The citizens cheered even louder when it was clear that the procession included French lords, taken prisoner. There were voices that demanded their deaths, but that would not be. Sombre our reluctant guests might be but there would be no ill treatment, rather a cushioned captivity until a hefty ransom was paid by their loving families. Still in possession of their armour and weapons, their colours flying boldly in the light breeze, they knew they would be feted as worthy foes. They even managed to smile a little at the crude suggestions.

Will, his gaze seeking me out when I curtsied a formal greeting as the King's close entourage dismounted, smiled his own personal delight in his achievement of being knighted in the illustrious company of Prince Edward on landing at La Hogue.

Behind in the procession, Sir Thomas Holland was riding, unscathed, all his old glamour intact beneath the blue and silver of his heraldic emblems, looking straight ahead, a curious expression on his face as if he might be debating some difficult step that rid him of any desire to smile. And then, I decided that I was mistaken, for when he had swung down from his mount with all the easy grace I recalled and was come into the Great Hall, he was as spirited as any as cups of wine were brought and greetings exchanged with long-abandoned wives.

I cast a surreptitious glance. Thomas still wore the white silk that had become so recognisable on so many battlefields as he rode against the enemy. I had never seen him in full battle mode, but could not imagine Thomas being anything less than dashing when in the throes of battle-energy, his sword in his hand, riding with verve and panache against the enemy ranged before him. Yet it surprised me a little that he still chose to be masked. Had he not fought bravely enough by his own standards that he might now remove it? I recalled the scars bravely got, bravely borne. I recalled the shattering tenderness of that moment we had spent together in the cellar redolent of cured meat and salt fish. I remembered the overwhelming longing that had gripped me. And that I had rejected. That I must reject again.

When he finally looked in my direction, I inclined my head as I would to the man we employed as steward.

Sir Thomas bowed to me, his employer's wife, unsmiling.

The blood quickened, beating heavily in my wrists.

But then Will was there to kiss my hand before turning to salute his mother, allowing me a little space in which to see the effects of war on my husband. Experience had tempered him. He even appeared to be taller, proud in his achievements. He was no longer the young Earl who had departed to win his spurs. Here was a man with confidence, assurance, maturity, as he released himself from Countess Catherine's warm embrace and took my hand to draw me apart.

'I have returned, dearest Joan, to reclaim my wife.'

He planted kisses on my cheeks with enthusiasm.

'As I see. My prayers were answered,' I said, managing to retrieve my hands when Will showed a desire to keep possession of them.

'You prayed for me?'

'It is my duty to pray for you, as a good wife.'

I smiled at him, strangely enjoying the return of this warm affection which demanded nothing more from me.

'Which you will now become,' he whispered in my ear, jolting me out of what was foolish equanimity. 'As soon as I get out of this armour.'

Will had returned with a purpose, to claim more than warm affection from me.

Any reply was postponed as the King, in regal mode, leapt onto the dais, turning to the festive gathering with arms widespread to draw all attention.

'We have so much to celebrate.'

His face was alight as he held out his hand to Philippa that she might join him in this moment of euphoria, the new child still clasped in her arms.

'So many English knights,' he announced, looking round the throng, 'who risked the fatal spilling of their blood for England, so many who fought until exhaustion beat them to their knees. We have much to thank them for today. Most of all I would commend my most dear son.'

Ned was beckoned to stand before his father, which he did with no sense of humility. His eyes were bright, his stance as regally arrogant as I had ever seen it.

'It was my greatest honour and pleasure to confer a knighthood on him as a symbol of our achievements across the sea. I cannot express my pride that my son should have been in the thick of the battle at Crécy, and so valorous in claiming the victory for us. And so many here.' He swung round towards the Montagu gathering. 'Not least the son of my great friend William Montagu, so sadly missed. He would have gloried in the courage of his son this day if he had lived.' Edward beamed at Will who flushed from chin to hair line.

'And then there is Thomas Holland here, who proved his worth. Here is one image of him that will live in my mind until the day I die, and in the memory of England, for I will see that it is celebrated wherever brave men raise a toast of good English ale.'

There was a general murmur of appreciation from the knights, who obviously knew the reference. Edward's features were aglow with it.

'We were at Rouen, where the bridge had been destroyed so that we could not get at the French. We were thwarted. And what did Thomas do?' The King left the dais to clip his arm around Thomas's shoulders. 'He did what we might all have wished to do. He stood on the edge of that ruined bridge, bellowing across the river at the French army. 'St. George for King Edward', he shouted, again and again. It was a magnificent moment, his voice cracking with the strain. It spurred us all on. And in battle he had the same power with his sword. You have all my thanks, Thomas.'

Thomas bowed. The tension about him, the rigidity in his shoulders, was unquestionable. I had not been mistaken, and there was an air of expectancy too. Surely it was not because he could not accept the King's praise? I glanced at Will, who was merely appreciative of Thomas's exploits.

Meanwhile Thomas, his face flushed, acknowledged the royal commendation. 'Battle moves us in strange ways, Sir. I spoke nothing but the truth. It unsettled the French, if nothing else.'

'And we are grateful.'

The King returned to the dais.

'Before we eat – and you are all invited – we have business to attend to.' In high good humour, the King beckoned to the two French lords. 'Here we have two men of great distinction, who fought well and bravely and deserve our admiration even though they are prisoner. I will introduce you to my court, my lords. The Count of Eu, Constable of France. And here is Lord Tancarville, the Grand Chamberlain of France. Such puissant lords of high renown who will be sadly missed by their families and the King of France. They were forced into surrender at the siege of Caen. Is that not so?'

'It is, my lord King.'

'And you surrendered to Sir Thomas Holland.'

The King's glance at Thomas who still stood on his left was all mischief.

'We did my lord.' The French Constable was gruff but not unappreciative. 'Because we know him and we know his reputation. We have fought against Sir Thomas before and admire his integrity. We know that we will receive fair treatment from him rather than a quick death.'

'As you will receive fair treatment at my hands too,' Edward replied. 'It is my wish, Sir Thomas, to buy the ransoming of these two famous knights from you. Do you accept?'

There was a pronged rumble of comment, of laughter in the chamber. All eyes on Thomas. Was this what Thomas had anticipated?

'It all depends on the sum, my lord. It has to be worth my while. My prisoners will fetch substantial ransoms from their families. Even the King of France might dig deep into his coffers.'

The King gave a grunt of laughter. 'Oh, I will make it worth your while, Thomas. It is my ambition to make a great lord of you, to reward you for your services to me. I can't have you rotting away on a mean patch of land inherited from your father, far away in Leicestershire or even further north. You need to be a knight of merit.' He held out his hand to his page, who placed in it a document, already prepared as if the King had no doubt about the outcome. 'Here is my promise, for the sum I will pay you for the ransom of these French lords.'

Thomas took it, read it.

'Do you agree?'

Without hesitation Thomas refolded the page and placed it in the breast of his tunic.

'I do, my lord. It is more than generous. I am honoured.' And to the two French lords, his expression surprisingly wry. 'My lord the King will arrange your ransoms, my lords. You will be entertained royally at the court until they are paid. You do not need my word on it. You are worth a magnificent sum.'

'The lords are worthy of it.' The King handed a cup of wine to Thomas. 'What will you do with such a sum? Purchase land perhaps. Build yourself a castle. I know there'll be nothing from your family for you to inherit beyond a handful of manors.'

'I will neither purchase land nor build a castle, my lord.'

'Then what? Will you go on pilgrimage to the Jerusalem?'

As Edward looked surprised, light began to dawn for me.

And as it did, every sinew in my body was tense. How much had Edward promised? Enough to give Thomas no hesitation. I knew exactly what he would do with it, if it were enough. And if it were… But what would be the repercussions? For me? For Will and for Thomas? It was as if a black abyss had opened before us, into which we, all three of us, might fall and be consumed. My mother was unaware of the hovering events. My uncle Wake was engaged in some *sotto voce* aside on the King's extravagance with a group of knights. The Dowager Countess was still consumed with glowing pride in her son. The King and Queen had no thought of what Thomas was planning, of the shocking level of deceit that had been practised at the royal court. Perspiration was suddenly a cold finger tracing its path along my spine.

My attention snapped back to Thomas, to hear him saying:

'I have a purpose for this money, sir.'

Surely he would not announce it. Surely he would not inform the massed ranks of the court of what he intended. The black abyss crept nearer to the toes of my shoes like a noxious wave. In that moment I prayed that the sum would not be sufficient, that Thomas could not proceed as he wished. But I had seen his face. I knew it would be enough.

What had the King done, so unwittingly? First to encourage Thomas as our steward. And now this.

'I have a purpose that has been in my mind for seven years but which I have been unable to accomplish. Now I can do so. I have the means.' Patting the document where it was now hid in his tunic breast, Thomas lifted his hands and, much as I had those few months ago, removed the white silk mask. 'I will wear this no more. I have fulfilled my oath to perform deeds of valour in France, for God, England and my King.'

Was that all he would say? The black abyss of scandal receded a little as my breathing eased, but not much. Rejecting his mask would not demand a fortune from royal hands.

He tucked the white silk into his tunic with Edward's promise of money.

'You are not renouncing your sword, I hope?' the King asked, knowing that Thomas would never do that.

'No, my lord. But I renounce my role as steward to the Salisbury household.'

My breathing once again became shallow.

'As you wish.' The King looked faintly surprised. Will stiffened at my side. I stood perfectly still, waiting. 'You no longer need to earn a living, of course, in the house of another man. Unless it is my own.'

There was a whisper of laughter through the court.

'No, my lord. Your money has been most generous, but that is not the reason why I must no longer be employed by the Earl of Salisbury.' He bowed. 'I think that the Earl will have no wish to employ me longer, in any capacity.'

Will looked startled. I had my own expression well in under control. The King was amused.

'Tell us.'

Thomas swept the court with a bold eye, such that I was astonished at his confidence before the eminent throng.

'It is my intent, my lords, my ladies, to reclaim my wife.'

A look of bewilderment touched the King's face, and many others except for my mother and the Dowager Countess. And Will who stiffened again with an intake of breath as if he had been stung by a wasp.

'Your wife? We were not aware that you had taken a wife. Or are you merely affianced? A secret understanding with some lady, forsooth!' Edward was intrigued.

'I have a wife, sir. And now I will speak her name. We were married seven years ago but I did not have the money necessary to prove it. Now I do. And prove it I will.'

'But why do you have to prove it? Who is the lady?' Edward, perplexed now. And then: 'Is there a problem with her family?'

'Her family is exceptional.'

With no further warning Thomas held out his hand, palm up. His gaze on me was uncompromisingly direct.

'This is the lady who is my wife. And has been for seven years.'

The court, to a man, stared at Thomas as if he had taken leave of his senses. As if during the fighting he had suffered a bang on the head that had robbed him of his wits, impairing his judgement.

'No, no. That cannot be.' The King looked at Philippa for help and received none. She was looking at me with an expression of horror.

Thomas was still staring at me.

'Joan.'

It was a command.

What did I want in that fateful moment? I wanted not to be the object of infamy. I wanted to remain in the affections of the King and Queen. I did not want to hurt Will, who was looking at me as if I had a knife in my hand that I might just use to draw his blood. I did not want the court to whip itself into a storm of chatter and criticism, of finger-pointing at me and at my morals.

I almost stepped back. Surrounded by so much confliction, I almost repudiated him.

But Thomas Holland was regarding me with confidence, with diligence. There was also in that gaze a depth of understanding. He had no notion that I might refuse to step with him.

'My lady,' he invited, his hand still outstretched to take mine.

So what did I want? My heart thudded with the immediacy of my desires. I wanted him. I wanted to be with Thomas Holland, acknowledging that all the arguments in the world could not change my mind. I wanted him now as much as I had wanted him seven years ago when I had stood beside him, my raiment covered in feathers and mites from the mews.

'Joan!' It was Will. His voice was harsh with a world of condemnation in it. 'Will you do this to us? To me?'

I looked over my shoulder, curving my lips into a little smile. Since there was only one action I could possibly take, that smile held a world of apology as I placed my hand in that of Thomas and stepped to his side. I would be Joan of Kent. I would make my own choices as much as I was able. I would follow my own destiny.

Thomas said not a word, nor did he have to. I could read the victory in his face as his battle-worn hand closed hard around mine and he led me forward into the little space before the King.

'The Lady Joan is my wife, as she will affirm. Joan and I took oaths *per verba de praesenti*.' How easily the Latin fell from his tongue. 'There were witnesses to that oath-taking who are still alive to speak of it, and there was a physical consummation. Our marriage is as lawful as your own, my lord. Joan's marriage to the Earl of Salisbury is not a legal one, it never was, and never will be. And now I have the money to prove it in a court of law.'

King Edward's face flamed, the lines from nose to mouth dug deep, becoming even deeper when Thomas compared our marriage to his own.

'Do you say?' It was the quietest of queries but virulent withal.

I held Thomas's eyes with my own. Do it. Say it now. Let us claim what is ours to claim. We had come so far; now was not the time to retreat. Even though I trembled at what we were doing.

'I do say it, my lord.'

The King looked at me.

'Is this the truth, cousin?'

'Yes, my lord.'

He rounded on my mother whose expression was as blank as an unwritten parchment.

'Did you know of this?'

Would she deny it? Would she place the blame fully and foursquare on me?

'Yes, my lord. I knew of it.'

'And you said nothing. You told me nothing about it. You allowed me to believe that the marriage to William Montagu was an honest one.' The King's voice deepened to a growl of anger.

'Indeed, sir.' I had to admire my mother's composure under attack, although I could see her swallow before she told the lie. 'I was persuaded by my priest that the marriage was not a true one. That Joan, being young, had been misled. That she had been persuaded against her true will. In which case, if she had been forced by this knight,' her vengeful eye settled on Thomas, ' the marriage could rightfully be ignored.'

'Where is this priest?'

'Dead, my lord.'

'You said nothing about this to me!'

Edward turned again to me, his ire a terrible thing. Thomas's fingers were firm and steady around mine, giving me his whole support, but indeed I did not need it. I had always seen this eventuality. Here it was. And here Thomas and I must make our case to be together.

'And you allowed yourself to be remarried, madam.'

'I was given no choice, sir. My mother and my uncle were very persuasive. I was forbidden to speak of my marriage contract with Sir Thomas. It was not my wish, but I could not defy my mother and uncle.'

How clear my voice. How certain I sounded. How my heart trembled.

The King was not persuaded to any degree, turning a snarl of fury on Thomas. 'You would make of me a fool Holland. In good faith I gave my cousin in marriage to the son of my most loyal friend. You gave me no reason to suppose I could not. You have lived a lie at my side for seven years!'

Nor was he finished.

'Unprincipled. Immoral. Guilty of crude rape and seduction against an innocent maid. You would pretend to be a chivalrous knight. You are a rogue, sir. You would dishonour me and mine!'

It was as bad as I ever thought it could be, yet Thomas remained astonishingly calm. Because, as his stepping into our steward's old shoes, so he had planned this since the French lords had fallen into his hands. His words to the King were forthright.

'I meant no dishonour to you, my lord. I discovered the situation only when I returned from my crusade. Joan was unable to tell me. I returned to find that she was wed to another.'

Which made no impression on Edward. I had never supposed that it would.

'You wed her in secret! You would undermine my choice of husband for her!'

'No, my lord.' Thomas spoke with utter conviction, his hand tight clasped around mine as if I might flee the room. 'There was never that intention. There was no suggestion of another marriage for Joan when I wed her.'

Edward was beyond reasoned argument. All was denial, accusation.

'You wed my cousin without permission. It was *my* permission you should have sought, in the absence of her father. You should have come to me, and yet you deliberately defied me, seeing it as a chance to make your future, to gild your ambitions. A gullible girl who would be swept away by brash glamour and false words of crude adoration, from a man who forsook his knightly calling.'

Well, this is what everyone would think. I felt Thomas inhale slowly, for here was the true ignominy that could destroy his reputation. That he had wanted me only for my royal blood.

'I discovered a love for her,' Thomas said. 'I loved her then and I still do.'

So simple an answer.

'By God, you are ostentatious in the awarding of your so called love!'

'I speak nought but the truth. I knew that you would not give her to me, sir. I am a mere knight, unsuitable to wed a royal princess. You must forgive the effect of love upon us, as you yourself know its power.' He bowed gracefully to the Queen. 'As for defiance, it was not so. I am your true and loyal knight. I have fought for you all my life, and will do so again. But Joan will be at my side as my true wife.'

'And you? Do you have nothing to say for your disgraceful behaviour?' Edward's eyes bored into mine. 'Now that I recall, you were keen to know where Prussia was. By the Rood! You were already wed to him then. You said nothing. What have you to say in your own defence now?'

I looked up at Thomas, then at Edward.

'I took him as my husband. There was no compulsion. It was done of my own free will, because we wished it. We did not speak of it because we knew we would be condemned for it.'

The King's thoughts had taken a different tack. I saw it in his face. I had wondered how long it would be before someone spoke of our household, so now I braced myself.

'But you allowed yourself to become the subject of immoral accusation, of sordid culpability. You agreed to Holland becoming your steward. You lived in a household with both of these men.'

For the first time the King allowed his accusations to touch on Will, which spurred me into sharp retaliation.

'My behaviour within these marriages has been impeccable, my lord. I brought no dishonour to either Sir Thomas or to the Earl, or to yourself and your court. The Queen instilled in me what is due to my name, and I will uphold that until the day of my death. Until I am free of this legal commitment to my lord of Salisbury, I will not to return to Thomas as his wife. It was never my intent to harm the Earl of Salisbury. As long as no one knew, there was no hurt to anyone. All three of us behaved as we should. There was no betrayal, no source of scandal for any man to sneer over. Now all is laid bare, and things must be put right.'

I would defend my honour to the end.

'Put right. Put right? And how do you intend to do that?'

Thomas replied as if all could be put right with one sweep of his sword.

'I will take my case before a court of law.'

Edward's smile was a baring of teeth. 'And which English court, under my jurisdiction, will uphold your clandestine marriage to my cousin, do you suppose?'

'None in England. But I know of one that will. And you have given me the money to achieve it, my lord, for which I will be everlastingly grateful. I will appeal to His Holiness in Avignon.'

Edward's hands were fisted on his hips while the gathering waited, agog with such a momentous conflict being played out before them. From victory celebration to a supreme clash of will, in which the King appeared to be in retreat, within a half hour. Edward began to threaten.

'I could refuse to pay the purchase price!'

Thomas placed his palm against his chest, against Edward's document.

'You could, my lord. I doubt that you would ever be so unjust. Here I have your written promise. I know that the King's word is law in this land to which I have given all my strength and my duty. I even sacrificed an eye to the mighty reputation of England.' His voice softened a little, even if his grip on me was as painful as ever. 'I have seen your compassion towards your enemies in victory. I know that you would not break your promise to a friend who had risked his life in battle for you.'

'I am not so sure, Holland!'

'I am certain of it, my lord.'

The celebration ended when Edward, taking Philippa's arm, ushered her and the now squalling baby out of the chamber without another word. What was there left to celebrate when the King had been so terribly challenged? I had been intended as a bride to honour a longstanding friendship. Instead I had dragged everyone into a hotbed of scandal and predictable innuendo. Nothing I could say would change that. For Edward, it was as if he had opened a much desired gift, to find nothing but dross.

While I had what I had foreseen. The gossip would entertain the court for many days to come. My reputation, I feared, would be the one to suffer. It had been hard to swallow the censure on Philippa's face.

Chapter Six

The retiring of King and Court left a small knot of people, isolated in the middle of the Great Hall. On one side the Montagus, my mother and my uncle Wake, even my young brother of Kent, all gathered together, united by past connivances and for mutual support in the face of Edward's displeasure. On the other, isolated in his aloneness, but confident in the justice of his cause, Sir Thomas Holland.

And I? I stood between them, my hand still firmly held by Thomas.

It became a moment of illumination, of acknowledgement, an acceptance that here my future truly hung in the balance. I had made my preference known before the King, stepping away from Will, and had given my hand to Thomas. I was nineteen years old, old enough to be more than a cipher or a pawn in the battle between these two men for the possession of my person.

A surge of power surprised me. I was no different from the woman I was yesterday, but Thomas had forced me to make a public stand and I had done so, without hesitation.

Will was regarding me in complete disbelief, for what was the logic in my choosing a knight over an earl? But I knew. Once, long ago as it seemed, in the freedom offered me in Ghent, I had given Thomas my hand and, as it seemed to my youthful nature, my heart. Nothing had changed. I would live with Thomas.

Now I must ensure that my wishes continued to be taken into account. It would not be an easy task for I would face rebuttal from all except Thomas. I lifted my chin. Had I not the strength to weather any tempest? I would claim victory in the end, if victory was there for the claiming. I was determined on it.

But I must achieve it with dignity. There would be no more scandal than we had already created. I would not compromise myself further by taking flight and residence with Thomas against all the dictates of society. In the eyes of all I was still Countess of Salisbury and there I must stay until the Pope allowed me to step across that forbidden line to live with Thomas. I knew the value of legality. I knew the value of acceptance. If there was ever any thought of winning back the King's benevolence for myself and Thomas, it would be through prudent and thoroughly legal behaviour.

Thomas was waiting for me to speak.

'I have to go back to William Montagu, my lord,' I said, quite formally.

'I know that you must, my lady.'

Our thoughts were travelling in concert.

'Until we have proved this case beyond all doubt,' I added. 'Then I will come to you.'

He turned my hand and kissed my palm as he had once before in Bisham's cellar. Now he closed my fingers over it, a seal of our intentions. 'I must leave you again,' he said.

'I accept that. It is in my heart that it will not be for ever.'

Allowing me my freedom, he walked from the chamber and I watched him go. For a moment it was as if my world was coming to an end, that I might never see him again. Pushing aside the thought I crossed the space I had created to stand at Will's side. There before him I announced:

'I am your wife until it is proved otherwise.'

I hoped he would be understanding, which was foolish in the circumstances. He was not.

'Were you unfaithful with him? In our own household?' he demanded.

The King's accusations had bit deep, so deep that I took hold of Will's sleeve and pulled him onto the dais where Edward had been so full of joy, and where we had at least some privacy.

'You are a fool!' I responded smartly.

'How can I trust you?'

'You have known from the start, Will, that our marriage was invalid. I told you it was. What use in pretending otherwise now?'

'I did not expect you to be in league with him, bringing him into our household.'

'Did I bring him to Bisham as our steward? You brought him into our household. I warned you against it.'

'You might also have warned me that he still had his eye on you.'

'I might, if I had known. What would you have done?'

'Dismissed him,' he roared.

'Shh!' I could see our respective families straining to pick up every word. 'I recall warning you of the possible scandal, but would you listen? You dismissed it out of hand. This is more your fault than mine, and don't shout at me. It is unbecoming, for both of us. I have no wish to have our tainted linen hung out for public consumption. Besides which it is a disgrace that you accuse me of immoral congress with Sir Thomas within our own household, when you know full well I would never treat you with such disloyalty.'

Bright colour might creep over his face but Will was immovable, his pride severely dented.

'I command you, Joan. You will not speak with Holland. You will not be in his company…'

'Well of course I won't. He is unlikely to hear me in Avignon!'

My patience was fast sliding away.

'Don't mock me Joan.'

The final words I heard from him that day.

Meanwhile, meeting as we must for dinner and supper or even stitching in that lady's chamber as I was summoned to attend on her, Will's mother, a lady of high principle and dislike of failure, blistered me with her tongue. I had encouraged Thomas Holland. I had sent him off to Avignon on a fool's errand which would only drag us further into the mud of common gossip. It was bad enough that I had encouraged Holland to seek authority in our household; it was obviously my doing. I sighed as Will glared at me but forbore to pick up the cudgels again when the Dowager Countess continued: if her family became even more the laughing stock of the court, the fault was mine. My morals and my loyalties were roundly denounced. I might have royal blood in my veins but I was entirely lacking in princely decorum. But why would that be a surprise to anyone? My father was a traitor, a pardoned traitor perhaps, but the stain of betrayal was still there in my blood.

Throughout, I remained impeccably good mannered. To retaliate would achieve no victory. Not even her denouncement of my family and my own morals raised a reaction. Having learned that severe control could win its own battles, my command over my temper occasionally astonished me.

'You are a disgrace to your illustrious name.'

I set another range of stitches in the girdle, with perfect precision.

'Have you nothing to say?'

'I will consider it, my lady.' My smile was also perfect.

The Dowager Countess abandoned her heaping of ignominy on my head since I would not give her the satisfaction of a puerile response upon which she could promptly leap.

Will simply, wisely, made himself scarce.

And the King? For the first time in my life I felt the heavy hand of royal displeasure. The King was mightily displeased. He had promoted this marriage and now two of his most promising young knights had made him an object of interesting ridicule, and the court was laughing at the whole sorry situation. Edward's purchase of the French Constable and Grand Chamberlain had been the *deus ex machina* that enabled Thomas to go hotfoot to Avignon to destroy the marriage that the King himself had promoted. Oh, he could have refused to pay, to have withdrawn the offer, but we all knew the King well. That would have made him appear churlish and sullen and without honour. Which made him even more irritated with the rat's nest of complications. Had he not honoured Will and I at our marriage ceremony? Had he not arranged for an income to allow the happy pair to live in some style? The royal frown was heavy and more than once turned in my direction.

'What value your royal blood?' he demanded. 'You were raised to know what was expected of you. I feel your shame.'

I might be silent under Countess Catherine's slings and arrows, but I would not be so with Edward. My chin was raised, my eyes held his, even though he was my King.

'I feel no shame. I have been ill-used in this whole affair.'

'I still cannot believe that no one saw fit to tell me about this,' he growled, not for the first time.

And then there was Philippa, regretful, but with a hint of unaccustomed steel in her reprimands, which unfortunately echoed those of her husband.

'How could you do it, Joan? How could you be so careless of what was due to your upbringing at my hands? I am ashamed that you have learnt so little.'

So much shame. I too was regretful in that moment. There were tears in the Queen's eyes and I disliked being the cause of them since her love for me had been vast and all-encompassing, but then I cast aside the shame for I felt none of it.

'I loved him,' I said, repeating Thomas's simple avowal. How many times must I make a public avowal of this? Surely Philippa would understand. 'And I still do.' She knew the power of that emotion. She had loved Edward since she had met him at her father's court, and she a young girl when she had wept at his departure, believing that she would never see him again. It was a fine story. Surely she would understand.

The Queen showed no understanding.

'Sometimes love has to be put aside by those of our rank.'

I opened my mouth to reply. She had not put aside love, but then her parents had supported the union with the young heir to the English crown whereas my choice had had nothing to recommend it. In the light of which, I demurred suitably.

'Forgive me if I have disappointed you, madam.'

'It's not that so much as that I can see no happiness for you. How will this be resolved? A satisfactory marriage with either is impossible as it stands. You always were a wilful girl,' she fretted.

There was no arguing against it.

Isabella who now owned a mature fifteen years, eyed me. 'It must have been love, to make you behave so irrationally. You are never irrational, Joan.' She put down the lute she had been playing in a desultory fashion, even if with unconscionable skill, and linked her fingers as she considered. 'Personally, I can't imagine how you could have made such a choice, although he is very attractive and a silk eye-mask can be dashingly romantic. But now that he has taken it off, all there is to see is a scar.' She grimaced prettily. 'I would not have thought that Sir Thomas would even acknowledge the existence of romance. Does he quote poetry to you?'

'No.'

Poetry was not of great importance at this moment, to either Thomas or myself, but true, his tastes did not run to chivalric poems. More to the laying of a successful siege. But then, neither was Will of a dramatic turn of mind.

'Neither does Will,' I admitted.

'You could teach Will to do so. He's far more amenable and good natured.'

'Then you should marry him!'

Out of all patience I sank to the floor beside her in a flurry of silk skirts.

'Oh, no,' she replied seriously. 'William does not stir my blood. Whoever I marry must heat me to a fever.' Her eyes slid to the Queen who clicked her tongue in dismay. 'I will never choose anyone to displease you, *maman*. Or I will try hard not to.' Then she continued, beginning to pluck discordantly at a lute string until I stilled her with my hand on hers: 'Far better to be Countess of Salisbury, Joan. I would not have wed Sir Thomas in a mews. Just think of the dust and vermin.' She had managed to wring the less-than romantic details from me in the past day. 'I never thought you would either. Perhaps you did it because you knew your mother would not approve.'

Isabella's judgement was disconcertingly apposite.

'I did it because I wished to do it,' I said without embellishment.

'And now we all have to bear the consequences,' the Queen added. 'The King is not pleased. He has gone hunting.'

The King always went hunting when his mood was turbulent.

So the cat was out of its bag and nothing would entice it back again. As the Queen had said, we would all have to live with the consequences, which I was already doing: the escort of two burly servants of the Montagu household shadowed my every step on the strict instructions of my Montagu husband that they did not let me out of their sight unless I was enclosed in my own chamber or a room of necessity.

'We are here for your safety, my lady,' they informed me when I decried their presence.

'Am I in danger?'

'Not now, my lady. We will not permit it.'

Did Will expect me to take flight with Thomas? Or indulge in illicit relations? With an elegant shrug I accepted my escort with a smile of some charm, as I accepted that I would tolerate this distasteful supervision, until the day came that I could dismiss the whole of the Montagu household from my thoughts and my presence.

I must hold to the certainty of it. For if I did not, how would I not sink into despair of living forever in this strange uncertain existence?

Helplessness was not a sensation that I enjoyed. The thought of Thomas's failure gnawing at me from morn to night, it drove me to take any step I could, however limited as it might be, to ensure that Thomas would be both impressive and persuasive at the papal court. I admired his tenacity. What he did not have, and who did, other than a trained cleric, was a thorough understanding of the complex workings of the law. Nor did he have the legal training or facility to speak out and present his own case in a hostile environment. It would hammer the nails into the coffin of Thomas's plans if he arrived in Avignon, lacking the necessary legal guile, faltering over his words and his arguments.

'Do you know any lawyers?' I managed to ask him before he set forth for Avignon, certain that he would not. When had Thomas ever communicated with a pre-eminent lawyer?

'No.'

There was little time for conversation. And what there was, was all business.

'This is the man you need.'

And I told him as I handed him a scrap of parchment on which I had scrawled a name. Magister Robert Siglesthorne of Beverley, an astute man with a high-born clientele, one of whom was Queen Philippa when she needed to consider her dower properties or a charitable foundation. Magister Siglesthorne had considerable learning and a reputation.

'He will plead your case for you.'

'How much does he cost?' Thomas asked, single-minded despite the royal windfall.

'Less than you might think, and he wants the experience at the papal court. You have no ability to speak before the Holy Father, but Siglesthorne has the ear of monarchs and would like to extend the scope of his work.'

'Then he's the man I need. So this is farewell, Joan.' We were walking side by side, but with a large gap between us. 'Look for me in the New Year. There's no time to lose. I need an heir, and we can't wait for ever.'

I frowned a little, despite my determination to send Thomas off with soft words as well as encouragement.

'I know the days are passing, Thomas, but I have not yet reached my twentieth year. I am quite capable of bearing a child.'

'So you may be, but I could be killed in battle next year. Or by a footpad on the road to Avignon.'

I admired his forthright thinking. I could accept his less-than-lover-like farewell in the circumstances.

'God go with you, Thomas. I will pray for you and the success of Magister Siglesthorne.'

Stepping across the divide, gripping my shoulders, discouraging my two lurking guard dogs with a scowl: 'One question, Joan.' He held my gaze, his own as unyielding as granite. 'Is this marriage to Salisbury consummated? If it is, it might sway His Holiness to let the Montagu marriage stand, notwithstanding my own claim.'

I shrugged under Thomas's suddenly strong hold. 'No. It is not.'

'You would tell me, wouldn't you?'

'Would you not know? Does not the steward of every noble house know exactly who shares a bed with whom?'

'Yes. I just need to know from you. It will make our case easier if the Salisbury marriage is in name only.'

'Then you can assure His Holiness that within the present alliance I am a virgin.'

'You must keep it that way.'

'Do I fight Will off with a dagger?' I asked, imagining the unlikely scene.

'What need? Will would never harm a hair of your head, and you know it,' Thomas said with grim humour.

Which was probably true.

'One thing, Thomas,' as he turned away.

'What now?'

I grasped his arm. 'Consider this. Relations are not at their best between His Holiness and my cousin Edward.'

Which certainly caught his attention. 'Are they not? How do you know?'

'It is no secret. When the King is disturbed his voice can be heard the length of a jousting field. Or across an audience chamber.'

'How useful to have a wife with her ear close to the closed doors at court.'

'Even if she is banned from your company through artifice, if of a crude sort.' I too regarded my constant companions with disfavour.

'But listen. Edward disapproves of the number of foreigners appointed by His Holiness to the most lucrative of benefices here in England. Edward has complained to Pope Clement that his appointees are poor in carrying out their duties and is in process of taking action to stop any further appointees without his royal permission. It may be that His Holiness will grasp any opportunity to gain victory over our King, particularly as our illustrious Clement is a Frenchman. In which case you may have a more than sympathetic ear in Avignon. Clement might just be prepared to back your argument to put our King's nose out of joint.'

Thomas considered this advice before beaming at me. 'I didn't know what a clever wife I had.'

'No, you wouldn't. You have not lived with her long enough to discover. And this might help.' Surreptitiously, another quick glance over my shoulder, I gave him a jewel, a cabochon ruby set in a heavy gold mount, intended by some master craftsman for a man to pin into his cap. My guard was now too intent on eating a pasty filched from the kitchen to notice and the other had disappeared. 'Sell it if you have to.'

'Salisbury will not approve.'

'Salisbury will not know. Although I have to admit that it does belong to him,' I felt suddenly bereft, floundering in unchartered waters where I purloined from Will to aid my release. 'But we can't be too nice about this. Don't forget me, Thomas.'

'How could I when you are costing me a Constable of France's ransom?'

Which made me ask: 'How much did Edward give you for your captives?'

'Eighty thousand florins were promised. I have some of it; whether I get the rest is in the lap of the gods and the King's temper.'

It was indeed a vast sum. 'I hope that I am worth it.'

Thomas decided that he had time to kiss me again, briefly but enough to make my heart leap in concert. 'Every silver groat of it.' He grimaced over at the guard who, pasty reduced to nothing but crumbs, had moved a warning step closer to me. 'We have survived seven years of this marriage, living like comets that never come within the same sphere. It is my intention that we will come to rest in one and the same place and breathe the same air. Farewell again, Joan.'

Which I considered to be a disconcertingly romantic image, that would have provoked me to embrace Thomas again if my guards had permitted it.

So Thomas left for Avignon with his petition and his lawyer barely a week after he had returned to celebrate the battle at Crécy. I knew not whether to be hopeful or resigned to being kept in the dark of those distant legal debates. William smiled smugly, hoping that the Pope would prove unco-operative and that Thomas, covered with ignominy at his failure, would never return.

Did I believe that Thomas would be successful?

How could he not succeed? Was not justice on our side? The days of my being Countess of Salisbury were truly numbered.

Still, a shiver of apprehension lurked in corners together with my two guards.

I could read Will as easily as I could read my childhood psalter. Even after his experience on the battlefields of France, the thoughts, mirrored in his face, were translucent and not very comfortable. I suspected that his mother had taken him to task since embarrassment had placed a hectic flush on his cheeks beneath the campaigning bronze. As I made my observation I was with my women, laying aside summer clothes and materials into coffers with layers of herbs to keep them sweet and guard them against the moth. Also with a thought to my removal from Westminster to some small manor in the north that was Thomas's inheritance, all he could expect as a younger son.

'Joan.'

'William.'

Standing just within this female domain he cleared his throat, hands clasped behind his back. 'I need to talk with you.'

'Here I am.' I held a length of embroidered silk in my hands, poised between folding and wrapping. 'You may talk with me whenever you wish.'

Will stood, uncertain, frowning.

'Do you wish to speak with me alone?'

'Yes.'

I waved my women to leave us and sat on the bed amidst the silks and satins, the image of amiability. I could see the thought that the Countess had planted even more firmly in his mind, as clearly as if it were stitched with the colours of the girdle I was protecting between layers of fine linen.

And yet…

I surveyed him as he traversed the room with a distinct swagger. Perhaps I could not read him as well as I had thought beneath the newly-won maturity that sat quaintly on his young shoulders. Of course he would be changed after the months spent with the English army. He had fought, been knighted, enjoyed the camaraderie, celebrated the victory. He had returned home to his wife. Only to be challenged on the first occasion that he had taken her hand and whispered his immediate intentions in her ear. Today there was a confidence in his stride that had nothing to do with the commands of his mother, nor, I noted, before I sat, were my eyes any longer on a level with his. William Montagu had grown in height and breadth. Perhaps I had been unwise to dismiss my women so swiftly; perhaps the high colour had nothing to do with embarrassment and all to do with anticipation of a bout of physical lust. Thomas's warning suddenly clanged in my mind like a mourning bell. But if I could not manage William Montagu after all these years, I had misjudged my skills.

The door closing on the last of my women, Will did not pause until he was standing an arm's length from me, his desirable wife. I remained at ease, but every sense was alive.

'I desire to consummate this marriage.' Will eyed me. 'If consummation makes it a valid union, I've a mind to do it now.'

'Now?' I essayed an expression of maidenly astonishment. 'If you wish, my lord. Will you give me time to clear these extremely expensive lengths of silk out of the way?' I had an eye to extravagance which our allowance as Earl and Countess allowed me to foster.

'I didn't mean this exact minute...'

'No, of course not. It would take more than a minute for me to remove my stockings. But I can start now, if you wish.' I sat more comfortably on the bed, leaning back a little, resting my weight on my hands, and waited.

He was not to be abashed.

'You are my wife. I would make you so, in more than name.'

'And why have you not been of a mind to do so before this?' I asked with true solicitousness. 'I swear you are a man full-formed.'

I knew he was. Since he was not beyond a tumble in the straw with one of the serving girls at Bisham, I was surprised that there was no child from his frequent tumbling.

Will cleared his throat again, far from discomfited, making me aware that there was a pride in him, awakening in me the fact that I must step carefully. This was no longer the young boy with whom I had grown up, but a man who might yet surprise me. Sitting upright, I folded my hands neatly together, carefully at rest.

'I am of a mind now,' he said between his teeth. 'It would be good policy.'

'You mean it would be good to get it over and done with?' I laughed softly, to offset the sudden sprightly tension in the room.

'It is no laughing matter!'

But now, as Thomas had warned in his final advice, it would not be good policy at all for me. If Will took me to his bed – or mine, regardless of the costly silks – in a display of masculine power, it would undoubtedly strengthen his hand in keeping me. This would no longer simply be a *de facto* marriage, a matter of signatures on a manuscript. I would have given my permission for it to be far more than that, and if I had not given permission, who would believe it or give it any thought? Many women did not exactly enjoy their marriage bed or give permission for its intimacies.

'You are my wife,' he repeated.

There was a heady resolve in his eye. More unsettlingly, there was desire. I kept my breathing even despite a momentary fear.

'I have been your wife in the eyes of the church for seven years. Our lack of consummation has not troubled you before.'

'Well, it does now. It is long past time. Then we were too young. Now we are not.'

I studied my fingernails.

'Take off your stockings.'

I looked up. I really had not thought that he would. I could have been wrong.

'No,' I said. 'I have changed my mind.'

'You cannot refuse.'

'I do. I do not comply.'

'You cannot *not* comply. You are my wife.'

My observation on this was placatory, well considered. 'But my position as your wife being now under the jurisdiction of His Holiness the Pope, I will not pre-empt his decision.' I watched Will, ready to forestall any attempt to pounce, for then he would be too strong to stop. 'It may be that the Holy Father will decide that I am not your wife at all. And where would that leave us, if I were carrying your child? So, no, Will. I do not give my consent.'

'You do not have to give your consent. All you have to do is submit.' Irritation shimmered around him as Will took a step towards me so that the edge of his short tunic brushed against my skirts. 'This can't go on, Joan. I want my wife. I want a son and heir. The earldom needs an heir. If you are carrying the Salisbury heir, His Interfering Holiness will not judge against me.'

In a faster action than I could predict, he moved and his hand encircled my wrist, pulling me to my feet. His grip was strong, his breath hot on my face. I pushed against his chest, unwilling to admit to a brush of panic.

'And you will force me? Cry shame, Will! What a marvellous layer that will add to the court chatter, if I cry rape.'

'I would look no bigger fool than I do now, squabbling with Holland over you, like two cats over a dead mouse.'

I wrenched my arm away, but he held on, stooping to plant a fairly accurate kiss on my lips, which spurred me into action.

'You would, if you ended up with a knife in your shoulder, courtesy of the mouse who is decidedly not dead.'

I could move as fast as he, and to more effect. Snatching it up from my bed, I held it in my hand. A paring knife that I had been using against my nails, so not sharp, but the only implement I had to hand. It was sharp enough to make the point. Will lunged for it. I held it out of reach. All hung in the balance.

'You would not!' Will was as shocked as I.

'Try me. And if you risk it, the King in the tilt yard will hear my shriek.'

'The King would commend me, for taking what is my own!'

'Are you certain of that?' I grasped the knife hard.

We faced each other.

No, of course I would not use it. Will was far stronger than I and his months of combat had given him a sleek hardness of reaction and response. Nor would I be the cause of any physical harm to him. Just as he would not force me.

I did not think that he would.

'I never thought that you would be so difficult, Joan.'

There was a sadness in his eye, his ardour deflated.

'Nor did I. But these are difficult times, and this was a marriage I never wanted.' I dropped the knife on the bed and turned back to place a hand on his arm as his grip on my wrist loosened. 'You will make someone the kindest of husbands.'

'I am *your* kind husband! Or I would be if you would let me.'

I kissed his cheek in apology.

All we could do was wait, hoping for different outcomes.

I hoped it would be soon. Will would not remain biddable for ever.

We did not have long to wait. Before the end of the year, before the King had donned his festive robes with feather accoutrements to celebrate the Birth of the Christ Child, there was an explosion of temperament in the Salisbury dovecote.

'This is what Holland has done!' Will burned with self-righteous disgust, gripping between two clenched hands the document he had just received, as if he would tear it asunder. 'As if I am at his beck and call.'

A letter had arrived by means of a self-important courier in papal tabard that glittered portentously with the keys of St. Peter, the missive making its way into Will's hands before I could intercept it. He had promptly vanished into close communication with the letter and his mother, leaving me to surmise and ascertain, as I plied the letter-bearer with ale, that he represented one Cardinal Adhémar Robert.

'And who is he?' I asked.

The courier wiped his mouth on his much-gilded sleeve.

'A conceited, hasty cleric who insists that I arrive almost before I have left. He is the Cardinal who, at His Holiness's decree, will look at the state of your marriage, lady.'

'Have you met Sir Thomas Holland?' I asked, since he appeared to be well versed in what was going on.

'I have that. He's as hasty as my master. And he has a tongue on him!'

So events were moving apace. It was with some satisfaction that I responded to the summons from Will, some hours later in the day, to attend him and Countess Catherine in his private chamber. And now here was Will, casting the document to surface of the travelling coffer before me.

'I have just been in receipt of this damnably offensive command!'

If Will was angry then Magister Siglesthorne had indeed made progress, presumably had achieved something to my advantage. For this was a family council of war. Even my mother, returned to patch the rent garment of good relations with the King over Christmas, was present.

I felt a shiver of excitement. I curtsied.

'Do I read it?' I asked Will with limpid grace. 'Or will you explain?'

'Oh, I will explain. Holland's money has got His Holiness sniffing at our marriage like a starving dog. He has graciously ordered our marriage to be looked into by Cardinal Adhémar Robert. The said Cardinal is empowered by His Holiness to summon us to appear before his tribunal.'

'Whom has he summoned?' I asked.

'Me! And you too. As well as your mother and mine.' He waved his arm in an expansive gesture. 'God's Blood! This letter is to summon all four of us to Avignon forthwith. To return as soon as may be with the courier. To give our evidence before this tribunal.'

While Will's face was livid at the presumption, my heart tripped out of its normal beat. If we were to go to Avignon, then the Holy Father wished to hear me as a witness. Silently I thanked Magister Siglesthorne for his silken tongue and erudite knowledge.

'Do I prepare to go, my lord?'

'Did I say that I had any intention of travelling across the sea and the length of France to make a case which is already made?'

'I have no intention of complying,' my mother added. 'I have nothing to add to the debate.'

'You will not go, my son.' The Dowager Countess was adamant. 'And neither will I.'

'But I wish to...' I said, my heart slowing now with sudden fear. Surely we would not disobey so powerful a summons. To do so would effectively silence me.

'No.' Will's denial left me in no doubt at all. 'There is no right to Holland's claim. I will not go to Avignon. You will not go to Avignon. No one will go to Avignon. I will not give you up, Joan, and there's an end to it. Let this Cardinal come to whatever decision he wishes, but it will be without my help. Or yours. And without our co-operation, I doubt he will be able to make any judgement.'

A pure light of defiance shone in his face.

Could he do it? I supposed that he could. And yet I could not meekly accept. There must be a way. If the state of my marriage was to be heard, the opinion of the bride was an essential part. Cardinal Robert must be told the truth.

I picked up the document and read it for myself. Nothing here that Will had not already indicated. Except that the Cardinal wished to speak with me.

I lifted my eyes to Will's furious ones.

'I demand the right to put my opinion on this. The Cardinal demands it. You do not have the power to stop me.'

'Yes, I do. You will not attend.'

'Then do I employ a lawyer to represent me?'

'No. Would you draw attention to yourself in this manner?'

'Yes, I would, if it is the only way in which I can influence the outcome.'

'It will not happen. You will remain here under my eye.'

'I will ensure that Joan has no contact with the Holy See,' the Dowager Countess said with appalling certainty.

But now Will was standing on his dignity. 'I do not need your help to manage my own marriage and my own wife, madam. From either of you.' His enraged stare took in my mother. 'I will dismiss the courier back to Avignon. He can tell the Cardinal and Holland we will not be meeting with them.'

Never had I seen Will so imperious as he strode from the room to deliver his news to the courier, while I curtsied to the remaining council of war and followed in his footsteps but more slowly, the future a dark shadow before me.

There were, of course, repercussions to this show of Salisbury defiance to papal demands. After a second visit from the courier, with an even more heavily weighted document, the multitude of red seals finally making their mark, the Dowager Countess, under protest but as a martyr for her son's cause, took ship en route to Avignon in the final damp days of November, with the support of King Edward (in an equally well-sealed document) to persuade the Cardinal's tribunal to reject the Holland petition. Or if that proved to be impossible, to ask that the case of my marriage be transferred to an amenable English court.

Where Edward could cast his choleric eye over the judges and sway the final judgement.

I was not sorry to find the Dowager Countess, by turns melancholy or bitterly fulminating on my sins, absent from our midst.

At the same time, because it would be an expensive business for Will to defend his rights at a distance, in December, in a fit of teeth-grinding grace, the King granted him monies from his inheritance. A sign of guilt, I thought. The King had unwittingly financed Thomas's petition; the least he could do now was finance Will's response. Litigation was a costly business. Will would need to pay exorbitant sums to present the most persuasive argument his legal men could construct, and so, with money under his hand, Will appointed the inestimable Magister John Holland, taking pride in boasting that this new man of law had a proud name for success in such delicate matters.

And the repercussions for me? I tried every nuance of defiance and persuasion.

'Are you quite sure that you can afford this transaction, Will?'

'I can now that the King sees my need.'

'You will not win.'

'I will!'

I poured him a cup of ale when we had retired to a private chamber after supper. 'Think, Will. If you rid yourself of me, you can have a wife who will be amenable and subservient. There are many aristocratic daughters who would be honoured to be Countess of Salisbury.' I kissed his head where his hair fell in soft waves, as I pushed the cup into his hand. 'The King will agree to our separation if you are dogmatic enough. You could have your new wife, fast followed by your son and heir by the end of next year. Life would be much happier for you.'

He shrugged me off.

'To do so would be to admit my failure. I'll not be persuaded.' He tossed off the cup of ale. 'Set your mind to it. You will remain my wife until the day you – or I – die.'

At that moment I thought disconcertingly of the paring knife I had once threatened him with.

Meanwhile, the Dowager Countess returned, weary from travel, but with fire in her eye and a set jaw. I was not privy to the discussion that ensued. All I could presume was that she had no success in persuading either the Holy Father or pre-eminent Cardinal to drop the case and allow my marriage to stand. Nor, as it would seem since there was no movement in that direction, would Cardinal Robert allow the English courts to get their hands on his legal conflict. Dowager Countess Catherine had left matters in the hands of Magister Holland since there was really no alternative.

But what of me? Will's advocate could not be trusted to extol my views. Magister Holland would be the enemy, as far as I was concerned. I could not let that rest.

'I demand my own advocate,' I said to Will as we broke our fast on the day after Countess Catherine's return.

'Perhaps we might start one day without an argument,' he observed in gloom, continuing to stuff bread and meat into his mouth, speaking round it. 'Appointing advocates is no easy matter, nor is it cheap.' After much chewing, he eyed me over a platter of some unidentifiable chunks of what might have been venison. 'Why would we need two?'

I replied slowly, carefully, any appetite I might have had destroyed by Will's obvious intransigence.

'Because I have to ensure that my own views are placed before His Holiness. If you will not allow me to attend, then you must allow me to appoint a man who will do my bidding. It's not that I don't trust you, Will. It's that I don't trust your advocate to support me as well as you.' I was holding on to my temper. 'I simply need an advocate of my own employ.'

'I'll think about it.'

'Then think quickly, Will. If you do not, I will go to the Queen and ask permission to appoint one of her legal men. I will have an advocate, one way or the other. You will not dictate to me in this.'

Which Will took to heart. Within the day, glowering suitably, with the threat of my going to the Queen hanging over him:

'I have appointed one who will represent you. Magister Nicholas Heath.'

I was suspicious. So soon?

'Never heard of him. Is he an able man?'

'As able as any.'

'How will he know what to say, in my name?'

'I will send him to speak with you.'

Which gave me some satisfaction. Perhaps he would carry a letter for me to Thomas, from whom I had heard not a word since he had left England. All was unnervingly silent, but an advocate to speak for me would be nothing but good. I waited with a lifting of my heart to interview Magister Nicholas Heath.

Instead I discovered Countess Catherine, come to find me when I was in the Queen's solar. The fact that Countess Catherine was smiling ignited a spark of anxiety in my breast.

'Your pardon, my lady.' To Isabella who was gossiping with me. And then to me: 'I have need of you, my dear.'

With no more than a quick glance at Isabella, I accompanied her to my own chamber, where I found the door to be already open and much activity inside. I entered to stand in the midst of it.

'What is this?'

'I have instructed your women to pack your clothes, Joan.'

'Why?'

A foolish leap of hope, of anticipation. Were we to go to Avignon after all? My thoughts ran on, seeing the Cardinal in my mind's eye, the papal court, the solemn judges, inviting me to stand beside

Thomas and give my evidence. And Thomas, tall and impressive, scarred in battle, wealthy and determined, stating his case. We would be victorious...

Until I realised what my companion was saying.

'We are going to Bisham.'

'Bisham.' I repeated, my fingers stretched flat in the folds of my skirts to prevent them curling into fists. I smelt a rat, and one long dead. There was planning here. This would be no short visit, if the number of coffers being filled by my busy women was evidence. 'For how long?'

'A long stay.'

'I did not realise you were intent on leaving court.'

'I have decided that a visit to Bisham would be restful. For both of us.'

'But it is not my wish to go to Bisham.'

And there, behind me, was Will, now hovering in the doorway.

'Your preference, considering your defiance of my son, has no relevance,' Countess Catherine was saying.

It dawned, bright and shiny, like a new gold coin held in my hand.

'You would not.'

'We think it best.'

I turned on him, in a flare of ill-usage. 'But come in, Will. Are you party to this? I did not think you were coward enough to hide behind your mother's skirts.'

Will stepped in, looking uncomfortable. The Dowager Countess merely looked warmly decisive.

'I do not give my permission,' I said.

'We do not need it,' Will replied.

'I will petition the King.'

'You will not get a hearing.' Will was now as rigidly purposeful as his mother. 'It will be better if you acquiesce quietly Joan. In this too I will be obeyed.'

A picture rose in my mind. If I did not acquiesce quietly, would I be dragged, complaining bitterly? Would I have a guard of soldiers with orders to make me comply? I thought not but I had more dignity than to risk such an eventuality.

Anger burned strong and bright as I silently obeyed the commands to don a fur-lined cloak, already laid ready for me, with a velvet hood. I was being given no choice in where I would live, but one day, I vowed, I would have a choice and I would make Will Montagu pay. For the first time in my life I could find nothing good to say of Will Montagu. How could I ever have thought that I would be allowed, through my own advocate, to voice my objections to my present state?

I learned a hard lesson in naivety.

'I will go to Bisham,' I said. When Will smiled and held out his hand to me, expecting me to accept his judgement, I turned my back. I would not offer even the semblance of good manners. It was not appropriate for a woman of royal blood to be hustled to Bisham, to isolate her, to close her mouth in all matters appertaining to her marriage.

I would wager my livery collar that Magister Nicholas Heath would be no visitor to my doorstep.

I could never have believed the depths to which Will and the Dowager Countess were prepared to sink to silence me. I was kept in confinement, in strict seclusion against my will. Not in a dungeon with lock and key but I was not free to travel outside the grounds of Bisham. For the first time in my undoubtedly self-centred life, I could understand my mother's lifelong bitterness. She had suffered imprisonment at Arundel Castle whereas I, a child of two years, had no recollection of it. And my mother with a price on her head and an executed husband had feared for her future if not her life. No wonder it had put its mark on her character, her suspicions of everyone, her need to ensure her position at court. It explained her driven determination to let nothing stand in her way. I had not understood.

But now I saw clearly as in a fair mirror, even though my life was not in danger, simply my freedom. Being a prisoner to all intents and purposes opened my eyes to the ambitions of those around me and my own weakness. It was made impossible for me to contact Thomas or Magister Siglesthorne or even Magister Nicholas Heath to obtain any impartial legal advice. My attempt to find an advocate to speak for me came to an abrupt end for no visitors were allowed. If Magister Nicholas Heath even existed, if he ever spoke for me in Avignon, he did so without my knowledge. He was never allowed past the great door of Bisham. If Thomas's success rested on my participation, he would never achieve his unbiased legal judgement and all his invest-ment in it would be nothing but waste.

Of course I attempted to send a letter to Thomas to explain my incarceration. Another to my mother, for surely she would not accept this imprisonment of her daughter. They were intercepted, returned without comment, the young and impressionable page whom I had bribed dismissed to be replaced by another, more worldly-wise. My guard was doubled when the Dowager Countess returned to court, leaving me at the mercy of Will's vigilant grandmother, Lady Elizabeth.

I heard nothing from the outside world.

'I wish to speak with the Earl of Salisbury,' I said to our steward, a dour individual who had replaced Thomas.

'The Earl is engaged at court. Is there anything I can do for your ladyship's comfort?'

Oh, I was comfortable, allowed my dignity, served with due reverence as Countess of Salisbury. Any visitor, if allowed, would have seen nothing amiss. I suspected that news had been sent out that I was indisposed and needed a time of quiet reflection. Perhaps, it might be hinted that there was a future heir on the near horizon. No one came. To all intents and purposes as I fumed in the seclusion of my own room, I was my husband's captive.

If outrage could have burst the walls of my prison, Bisham would have been no more than a pile of stones.

'Play chess with me, Joan,' Lady Elizabeth invited.

'I will not.'

'Better to take your fury out on my chessmen than let it eat away at you.' Her eyes, encased in fine lines, twinkled. 'And I will tell you of my young days as Elizabeth de Montfort, when I had little more power over my marriage than a chicken in a henhouse when faced with a hungry fox.'

Placing the chessmen on their board with deft precision, she then proceeded, in a series of quick, clever moves, to threaten my King. My mind was not on the game.

'I'll not play with you again, madam!'

'I suspect you have your own games to play, my dearest Joan.'

Yes, I was furious, unable to vent my anger on anyone, for it would have been unworthy of me to make Will's grandmother suffer. Yet anger was better than despair.

I played chess often in those days, enjoying Lady Elizabeth's keen wit, enjoying occasionally demolishing her chess pieces. I even laughed with her. But time hung heavy. My future was being decided far away and I was helpless, a sensation that I did not appreciate. And what was Thomas doing? Nothing, it seemed, to aid my rescue.

And yes, despair set its hand on my heart.

Chapter Seven

The door of the chapel, where I was kneeling in a futile attempt to achieve some heavenly solace and privacy from Lady Elizabeth at one and the same time, was pushed open. I did not stir. I thought it would be my aristocratic governor, come with unerring curiosity to discover where I might be and what I might be doing that she would not like.

'Magister John Vyse, my lady.'

The faceless servant, one of Will's choosing, withdrew, leaving me with a man I recognised, resplendent in clerical garb.

'My lady,' he bowed.

'Sir.' I rose from my knees, every sense alert.

'I am honoured to be allowed to visit you, madam.'

I suspected a gleam in his eye, except that so eminent a man would never stoop to anything as unseemly as a gleam of malice. Quiet, low spoken, radiating priestly authority, Magister John Vyse was the masterful Dean of Salisbury Cathedral, and here in my chapel in full ecclesiastical regalia of his office, his cope gleaming with gold-worked grapes and vine leaves.

'Should you be allowed to be here alone in my company, sir? You are the first visitor I have enjoyed in too many months to count.' I considered his solemn expression. 'You must be aware of my situation.'

'I am indeed. But as you see, I am admitted. A notable man of the church such as I, my lady, has the right to be alone in your company. I said that it was your wish to confess your sins.'

How could I not be suspicious?

'We have a household priest for such matters.'

An acceptable conversation, but all was not as it seemed here. I must have a care. The Dean of Salisbury might be Will's man, sent to spy and report on my behaviour.

In spite of my cool response, Master Vyse, splashed with a myriad of colours from one of the windows, continued.

'I have informed your steward that it is my understanding that you have sins of a nature dangerous to your immortal soul. They require a cleric of some standing to discuss them and absolve you. I have also informed your steward that the Earl has authorised me to set your soul right with God. Given that authority, there was no question of my being refused admittance. How could there be, my dear lady?' He ran his hand down the gleaming stole. 'I thought it befitted the occasion to show some clerical magnificence. Your worthy steward would not dare deny me, representing as I do the cathedral of Salisbury.'

No, he would not. So what was this subterfuge? My spirits began to dance as they had not danced in weeks. I glanced at the door, which was firmly closed.

'It is true that I have need to confess, sir.'

His voice took on an even more respectful key as if addressing the Blessed Virgin herself. 'And I will hear your confession. But all in good time, for I am here on a quite different matter, my lady. Even so it might be pragmatic for you to kneel as if you were unburdening yourself to me and to God.'

Which seemed eminently sensible, but still I would watch my words, even as I knelt. Master Vyse made the sign of the cross over

my head, while I bent over my linked fingers, the crucifix of my
rosary clasped hard between them.

'So let us get to the business in hand, my lady.'

'I understand then that you have not come from the Earl to lecture
me on my disobedience.' Hope was now leaping within me in lively
mood.

'I am not. I am here to represent you, my lady.'

I looked up, eyes wide.

'To what purpose?'

'To the purpose of justice. At Avignon. His Holiness insists that
you have a new attorney.'

'I was of the understanding that I had one, appointed by the Earl.'

'Well you have and you haven't, my lady. His name is Martyn.'

I frowned, without recognition. Was it not Magister Heath? 'I
know no one of the name Martyn.'

'As I thought. I wager that you have been told nothing.'

'I am kept close here, worse than a nun in convent. Do I understand
that you can remedy that?'

Which Magister Vyse proceeded to do, while I became more and
more irate with every twist and turn in this case that should have
restored me as Thomas's wife. But Magister Vyse's voice was so serene,
so full of patience, that eventually my own emotions settled to hear
what had been developing without my knowledge.

'When Sir Thomas heard that you had been kept here against
your will and under strong guard, he saw the need for urgency and
submitted a second petition. Sir Thomas requested His Holiness to
remedy this impediment – your lack of an advocate to speak for you
– to the cause of justice. So His Holiness did exactly that. He sent
an apostolic brief to the Archbishop of Canterbury and commanded
that you be permitted to appoint an attorney of your own, answerable
only to you, to act legally on your behalf.'

'But what happened to Magister Nicholas Heath? And who is this Magister Martyn?

'It is a long story.'

'So tell it to me.' I abandoned my plan to speak circumspectly. Surely this man was my ally. 'Before God. I have nothing better to do.'

I had had enough of kneeling. I stood and beckoned so that we took two of the stools set against the wall, where we sat face to face. And so this was what unfolded for me. Thomas, appearing before Cardinal Robert's Tribunal, had success within his grasp, Magister Siglesthorne presenting the evidence with superb clarity and detail. The two witnesses of our marriage spoke up about what had been seen and done. Magisters John Holland and Nicholas Heath picked apart the evidence and investigated the reliability of Thomas's one-time squire and page, but being now full grown and men of some distinction, nothing detrimental could be discovered to give their evidence even a shadow of untruth.

'So what is the problem?'

'The problem, if you wish to call it that, is the Earl of Salisbury's determination to win, and our King's collusion with him.'

Magister John Holland had been ordered to absent himself from any further proceedings, at the same time as Magister Nicholas Heath was arrested by King Edward for contempt against the Crown.

'A cunning gambit to stop everything before it could go any further. The contempt was, I suspect, a fabrication, another subterfuge to remove your attorney from the scene so that the case must come to a halt. As you know, the King wishes your present marriage to stand.'

Two new attorneys were appointed by Will. Magister James St. Agatha for himself. Magister David Martyn for me.

'Whom I do not know,' I repeated.

'Of course you do not, my dear lady. It is merely another delaying tactic – Magister Martyn, when he approached the Tribunal,

informed Cardinal Robert that he was in no position to submit
any evidence on your behalf. As for Magister James St. Agatha, he
claimed to know nothing whatsoever about the case.' My informa-
tive priest shrugged his vine-strewn shoulders. 'How would he? It
was not intended that he ever should.'

So much legal subterfuge, of which I had been entirely unaware.
The sordid cunning to which Will and my royal cousin Edward
were prepared to stoop astonished me, but perhaps it should not have
done so. Will would hold me to this marriage, whatever the cost.
What better means than ordering his advocate to absent himself or
claim ignorance? I might be surprised at the lack of honour in his
actions, but then, was I not a valuable wife?

'So what happens now?' I asked, trying not to despair utterly.
'Do I try to get my instructions to Magister Martyn? I don't see
the value of that, if, as you say, he is in the Earl's pay and under his
instruction.'

'I agree entirely.' Master Vyse beamed at me, taking one of my
hands between his. 'I will be your attorney. That is why I am here.'

So. Here was an offer I must consider. His air of authority was
without question, as was his status in the Church, his ability to speak
with good logic and power. There was one problem, my cynical
mind informed me.

'But you are not my choice, sir.' Who was to say that this cleric
would be any more honest that the rest? 'How do I know that I
might trust you any more than I could trust Heath or Martyn?'

'But I have been appointed for your comfort, my lady.' There
was undoubted self-satisfaction in his pronouncement. 'I have been
appointed by the Archbishop of Canterbury himself, on the direct
orders of His Holiness.'

A positive banquet for thought.

'But will you tell the truth?'

'I will, my lady. I am appointed to give your side of this sad situation.'

'Do I trust you?'

'Undoubtedly.'

We stared at each other, both, I suspected, assessing the other. What choice did I have? None at all. This was no time for procrastination.

'Then I will tell you, Magister Vyse.'

And I did. All the details I had told so many times before. Finally, I looked at him, hope resurrected when I had almost abandoned it. 'Can you help me?'

'Make clear to me one fact, my lady. Were you forced into this marriage with the present Earl of Salisbury?'

Was I forced against my will? Force had a habit of wearing many different faces. Ultimately I had not been dragged to the altar, nor had I been threatened with retribution beyond what I could bear. But neither had I been free to reject Will.

'The marriage with the Earl of Salisbury was not of my seeking,' I said. 'I did not wish it to take place. I did not willingly make my vows but felt under a compulsion to do so.'

'Then if that is the case, I can help you.' Magister Vyse nodded briskly. 'I will put your complaint honestly and fairly before the Cardinal.' He kissed my fingers. 'Don't let anxiety drag you down if you do not hear from me. It will not be a fast outcome, I fear, but I hope it will be as you would wish.'

'And if you fail?'

He pursed his lips.

'Then you remain Countess of Salisbury. Not a bad life, some would say.'

No, it was not, simply not the one I wanted. I lifted my head, raising my hand, for there were soft footsteps, slightly halting, instantly recognisable, approaching.

By the time Lady Elizabeth entered the chapel, with all the false discretion common to her, I was kneeling before the altar, the Dean of Salisbury pronouncing his blessing on a newly-confessed sinner.

'Would you give a message from me to Sir Thomas, sir?' I whispered under cover of his final benediction.

'Of course.'

'Will you say this to him.' I thought for a moment. 'Tell him this in my words. Joan of Kent says: *I took my vows to you in good faith. I would do the same again tomorrow. Keep me in your heart and mind, as you are in mine. I pray constantly for your success.*'

He smiled making once more the sign of the cross.

'It will be my first task when I arrive in Avignon, my lady.' And then, when Lady Elizabeth had disappeared through the door into an antechamber, he said: 'Might I enquire why you allowed yourself to become party to a marriage that could only be called bigamous?'

I permitted my brows to climb. 'You might indeed enquire, sir. But it is not my intent to inform you.'

His expression became sterner, delivering a warning. 'It is your prerogative, my lady, but I advise you to search your soul and make confession to God. It was not wisely done.'

Wise? No I had not been wise. But it was not in my mind to explain my lack of wisdom for this priest, or any other, to pick over.

April 1349: Windsor Castle

It was April when the Dowager Countess descended on Bisham on an unexpected visit, her lack of accoutrements and her stance in the Great Hall when she sent for me suggesting that she was not intending to stay long. I kept her waiting, just for a little time, before I entered the echoing chamber and imparted what might be interpreted as a hospitable smile to cover my rampant suspicions. Now what was afoot?

'You are right welcome, my lady.' I curtsied. 'Will my lord husband be joining us?'

'No.' Her smile was as false as mine. 'My son is at Windsor. Pack your coffers, Joan. I would leave without delay.'

I did, without more ado, asking nothing about the cause of this sudden release. I would not wager on her changing her mind if she found me dilatory, and indeed, I had a desire to go to Windsor. I did not know why I must, but I longed to see the outside of Bisham. I felt a longing to talk with the Queen again, even if she could see little good in me. I yearned to experience the sharp tongue of Isabella, still unwed and determined to remain so until she had a mate of her own choosing. I needed to speak with Will. I needed to discover the progress made by Magister Vyse.

My coffers were packed within the hour and we were embarked on what was to be a silent journey, for I had more pride than to waste my energies on empty conversation. My companion spent the journey with her eyes clamped to her Book of Hours. At Windsor we were expected, servants arriving to help me alight and escort me to the chambers made ready for our use.

'Are we to dispense with my guards?' I asked, remembering the shadowy pair who had haunted my steps when last at court.

'There is no longer a need for them. I will keep you company.'

I swung round to face her. 'Why am I here?' I demanded.

Which brought a glimmer of a smile to her face for the first time since we had left Bisham.

'Your husband is to be honoured.'

'Ah! Should I ask which one?'

It was unworthy, but my patience was as frayed as an old girdle. The Countess proved to be immune.

'The Earl, of course. It was thought appropriate, by the King and Queen, that you should be present to witness the recognition of my son's service to the Crown.'

'So this freedom is not a permanent situation?'

The smile proved to be short-lived. 'Not until His Holiness has accepted the strength of our arguments.'

'Am I free to visit as I wish? Without restraint?'

'Of course. With a discreet escort, of course, either myself or one of my women.'

Of course. None of my women had accompanied me from Bisham.

It could have been worse. I could have been accommodated with an armed guard at my back. I would make do with whatever stratagems came my way. I had not even asked what the honour was to be, nor did I greatly care. My friendship with Will had suffered a grievous wound when he saw fit to keep me behind locked doors.

And yet curiosity came to my rescue. I was inordinately pleased to be back at Windsor.

Here it was unfolding around me, a royal device to lift the general gloom in England consequent on the effects of the plague and the stalemate in relationships against the despicable French, while at the same time glorifying God, St. George and the King of England. It was a plan entirely familiar to me. The King would create a body of knights, worthy of those who gathered around the famous table with King Arthur, swearing to uphold their oaths of loyalty and chivalry. My thoughts were taken back to that long, distant conversation with Edward in his library, before this upheaval, when he had enthused over this plan, when he had envisioned Thomas Holland being one of the young and honoured knights. Abandoned in the welter of grief at the death of the first Earl of Salisbury, now it would come to pass.

My initial pleasure at being restored to court was swamped in profound regret that Thomas had lost that opportunity, but I was here, which was far better than being at Bisham. I must perforce rejoice with Will who was indeed to be one of the founder members of the order, in recognition by the King for his father's friendship and Will's own undoubted loyalty. A day of festivity was promised, of solemn oath-taking, of magnificence and breathtaking pageantry organised by King Edward in his inimitable style.

I was escorted to St. George's Chapel by Dowager Countess Catherine and my mother, where we stood and watched, suffused with awe and pride, as the procession made its way to the chapel door. Twenty-six chosen men paced behind the King and Prince Edward, resplendent in the celestial blue of the Blessed Virgin, their cloaks enhanced with silver linings, a garter worked in gold proclaiming the motto that they would swear to live by. *Honi Soit Qui Mal Y Pense.* Evil to him who thinks evil. My conversation with Edward had born magnificent fruit.

I watched Will, unable to hold fast to my hostility. Here he was, a fine upholder of the King's Order of the Garter as he stalked slowly with a stately grandeur suitable to an Earl and a King's friend. He did not look in my direction. For once his thoughts were on higher things, the significant honour that had been shown to him and the great families of England.

But as the sea of undulating blue and silver and nodding plumes moved past, my resentment returned in full force. Thomas should have been here...

My breath was driven from my lungs.

There, in the final grouping of knights, was Thomas, his dark hair fluttering against the silver in the light breeze. The scars could not ruin his grandeur that day, his impressive stature, his head raised in honour of the occasion so that all might see the marks of battle, his expression severe in the holy solemnity. He had returned from Avignon to take his rightful place with the rest of these knights of renown.

I made no sign that I had seen him, nor he me, but the Dowager
gripped my mother's arm and they drew closer to me as if I might
shame them all by calling out to demand rescue. Then he was drawing
level with me: I remained motionless. However much I might wish to
speak with him, it was not possible and I had my dignity to uphold,
and his too. Had he seen me? That was not important. I found that I
was smiling into the sunshine, glorying in the splendour, for Edward
had forgiven Thomas sufficiently to make him one of the honoured
number. Edward had decided that he admired Thomas's skills more
than he condemned his personal choices in life.

All I could do was stand and admire. I would draw no attention,
returning to my chamber without fuss even though every one of my
senses had come vibrantly alive. I would not always be so biddable.
Thomas was in England and speak to him I must. If the opportunity
did not present itself, then I must create one. My mind set itself to
the task.

Then it all began, the celebration of England's victories and a sop to
take the country's dolorous and fearful mind off the plague that had
once again scythed its path through the people of England. It was to
be even more spectacular than the solemn procession to the chapel,
to draw the common folk to cheer and sate themselves with food and
drink and forget their woes. The crowds spoke of defiance, of pride, of
England's glory. It fired my defiance too. I had no intention of sitting
next to the Dowager Countess and my mother throughout the long
afternoon to watch the knights compete in the joust and the melee.
I would not be guarded and hemmed in. I needed restoration of my
freedom, to speak with Thomas, and not merely an exchange of a
distant greeting across the tapestried walls of the women's pavilion
from where we would watch the knights belabour each other with
lance and sword.

Under pretext of exchanging seats from one side of the Dowager Countess to the other, to achieve a better view of the combatants, I waved to Isabella who sat beside her mother, an air of boredom about her, a chaplet of flowers on her head denoting that she would be Lady of the Lists to present the prizes to the victor.

She waved back.

I grimaced across the veiled heads of the Queen's ladies.

No longer bored, a smirk of conspiracy curling her lips, Isabella manoeuvred her skirts, pushing past the royal damsels until she stood beside me, whereupon she took my arm, preparing to lead me in the Queen's direction, raising her voice to almost shrill to make all public.

'Look who we have here, *maman*. Returned from the country at last and restored to excellent health. Come and sit with us, dearest cousin.'

Philippa beamed, her previous ill-will towards me forgotten, her heart softened. The Dowager Countess might remain bland as a dish of whey in the face of such royal approval, yet she was still intent on fighting her cause against Isabella.

'My daughter-in-law already has a seat near me, my lady.'

'But she will join us,' Isabelle returned undaunted. 'Royal princesses together, to honour the victors. What could be better?' Her demeanour was as innocent as a new-born lamb.

'Of course you must come,' the Queen said, stretching out her hand.

Which encompassed all I wanted.

So that is where I sat to watch the inaugural tournament of the King's Order of the Garter, my excitement building as if I were a young girl again, as the new Garter knights rode onto the field where there would be a melee. A return to old traditions perhaps, for melees had dropped out of fashion, replaced by more formal combat and jousting, but here the perfect opportunity for all the new Garter knights to show their skills, with blunted weapons but much enthusiasm.

And I grasped my chance with both hands.

'Exchange cloaks with me,' I said, already taking hold of the embroidered velvet garment that Isabella wore against the April chill.

'Why?'

'Because I need it.'

'What's wrong with the one you are wearing?'

'Look about you, Isabella!'

She was wearing, as fate decreed, a cote-hardie and cloak of costly blue and silver damask, richly trimmed with grey vair, while I had been diplomatically clad, against my wishes it had to be said, in the Montagu heraldic colours of red and white that did me no favours. How fortunate that fate could smile on me, when so few were doing so. I nudged Isabella as Thomas rode past, the silver lion on his shield gleaming on its blue background. I could not manage the lion, but the colours would do very well. I tugged again at her cloak.

'Who am I to stand in the path to true love?' Isabella's wits were quick. She shrugged the cloak off her shoulders and we exchanged garments.

Many admiring glances came our way, for the blue and silver enhanced my own fair colouring, while red and white could not dim Isabelle's lively countenance, but those I ignored. Others were increasingly cynical, increasingly shocked, for who could not suspect what I was about, as all became clear on the field of mock-battle that unfolded before us. The two puissant knights who were engaged in legal wrangling for recognition of my hand in marriage were fighting on opposite sides. Will raised his sword for the King. Thomas fought dourly for the royal opponents under Ned's leadership.

I almost laughed at the incongruity of it. Was I to be the prize?

Whispering began in the gallery, growing louder like a gale

through ripe corn as it became obvious to all what I had done, and how deep was the displeasure of Dowager Countess Catherine, too far away in midst of royal ladies to take issue with me. So I would do more. I looked at Isabella.

'Would you be disappointed beyond measure if I were to replace you as Lady of the Lists?'

Isabella did not even hesitate. 'I think that you would actually snatch this wreath from my head if I were to refuse. I see what you are about.' Lifting it from her own head, she placed the coronet of flowers on mine, taking time to centre it and arrange my veil becomingly. Which of course drew even more attention. The victor of this battle would receive his reward from my hands. 'I never thought that this never-ending tournament would prove to be so pleasurable. For whom shall we cheer? Montagu or Holland?'

'Is there any doubt?'

'There might be. Who knows what goes on in your head.' Isabella was in a teasing mood, and a contemplative one as her gaze narrowed on mine. 'Why did you do it, Joan? Why did you accept Will when you knew you must not? Was it only ambition, to undo the foolish whim that made you, stupidly in my opinion, take Thomas in the first place?'

The age-old question that I had refused to answer more than once, nor would I explain it now to Isabella. I had no wish to become an object of pity, sacrificing my initial love for a superb cause. I would be no martyr in shining garments. That was never a role in which I saw myself, glowing with self-righteousness in the choice I had made.

I shook my head in quick denial – but then I was watching the knights taking their places. My eye sought and once again found the bold silver and blue of the Holland lion in the midst of this mighty and august gathering. Suddenly for no reason at all I could no longer

keep silent as the years rolled back to the moment when I stood in
Edward's library, when I had made my decision, for good or ill.

'That is why I did it,' I said.

'What is why?'

Raising my hand I pointed to Thomas, tall and rangy, his armour
well-worn but his place amongst the knights of the realm accepted
and acknowledged by all as one of their own, of equal valour.

'Look at him, Isabella. Sir Thomas Holland, Knight of the Garter.'

'I know. I see him.'

'You see him now, received with unimaginable honour. What you
don't see is that at the time of my marriage to Will, your father was
breathing fire at those who brought scandal to the court.' I lowered
my voice to barely a whisper. 'There was the issue of Philippa and
the birth of Edmund. Edward was furious that the possibility of your
mother's adultery was under open discussion.'

'My mother?' Isabella's brows had snapped together. 'How ridiculous! I knew nothing about that.'

'How would you? You were too young to hear what was being
said, or notice any court atmosphere. Now it is of no importance.
Any issue between Edward and Philippa has been mended and young
Edmund looks as much like Edward as all the rest of you.'

Exasperation taking hold, I realised that I had been deflected, and
that my hands were tight-clasped as I willed her to understand all
that I had never spoken of.

'How would Thomas fare if he lost his reputation as a knight of
true chivalry? Edward would not employ him ever again – or so I
thought. If the King believed that Thomas had denied his right to
give my hand wheresoever he wished – and clearly to Will – there
would be no patronage for him in England. It would be the life of
the paid jouster at the tournament, travelling from one event to the
next, from Prussia to Spain. Would I want that for him?'

'No. I don't suppose you would.'

'Nor would I, the end to all his dreams of fighting for Edward and England.'

There it was, simply spoken, as it had come to me with clarity, like the writing of a clerk on white vellum, in those days after my conversation with Edward, when I had been condemned to reject Thomas for his own good.

Edward regarded Thomas as a gallant and chivalrous knight.

Edward would invite Thomas to be one of his new illustrious order of knights.

Edward detested scandal and marital dishonour and the damage that it could do. I, Princess Joan, must be free from all shame and infamy, as must all his family.

All of which had driven me to the conclusion, albeit flawed, that to announce the legality of my clandestine marriage to Thomas, and my rejection of a marriage which Edward desired to enhance the status of the Earl of Salisbury, would put a permanent blight on the life and ambitions of Thomas Holland. Edward would see it as an outrage of major proportions, Thomas wedding me without permission, without royal approval, without clerical blessing.

'Any knight who dishonours God dishonours me and will be stripped of his knighthood and cast out of the kingdom.'

This would be the future for Thomas, his position precarious indeed, so that out of a strange reversal of honour I had accepted Will, being astute enough to know that, in the balance, Thomas's adoration of my person on one side and his desire to wield sword and lance and win a name of fame and glory on the other, were very evenly weighted. How could I destroy the gilded glory awaiting him on his return to England? I feared that Thomas would never forgive me, however strong his professed love for me might be.

And, in all common sense, what could I have done, ultimately, to escape this Montagu marriage that I did not want? Run from the court? Taken refuge in some leafy glade as a heroine of a courtly romance might do? Taken horse and ship to travel through unknown and probably unfriendly lands to join Thomas in Prussia? I might have had some courage but not for such a venture. I could imagine the horror in Thomas's face when he had seen me arriving at his crusading camp, a travel-stained wife in flight, demanding succour.

'How selfish would I be to destroy Thomas's dream? He deserved better at my hands. So I repudiated our marriage; I made new vows and wed Will Montagu.'

If I had thought that Isabella would engage with my reasoning, I was mistaken.

'Well I would never have thought it of you, Joan. To put another's ambitions before your own is not a common trait in your character.' And when I made no reply, for her observation was less than flattering: 'It didn't work out very well, did it, all in all?'

'No. It was a disaster. The truth was certain to come out, so all has become shame and dishonour. And the best of it is, as you see, Edward has made Thomas a Garter Knight anyway. So you could say that I read it all wrong. All this... this *upset*... has been for nothing.'

Sensing my profound disillusion, Isabella gripped my hand. 'You were very young.'

'My only excuse.'

'A good enough excuse. I would not have been so selfless.' She sighed at the complexity about to be fought out on the battlefield before us, Will on one side, Thomas on the other. 'My advice is to forget it, for the outcome cannot be changed. All we have to do today is enjoy the sight of our brave knights. But who will win? Will there be blood on the field of battle?'

'Only a few cracked skulls, I imagine.'

Isabella's unemotional assessment had had its desired effect. I had been very young. Now all was past and the future was here to unfold before us. We set ourselves with some pleasurable anticipation to watch.

The melee began, the sides evenly matched. For most in the crowd, well fortified with ale, it was of no account which side would win since were they not all King Edward's brave knights? The townsfolk were jubilant, cheering indiscriminately for King and Prince as knights retired with waning energy and painful blows. The individual battles became more desultory. It was clear that the King's side would be victorious and receptive of the prize from my hand. My attention hopped from red and white to blue and silver as they ranged over the field, both men of skill, both still in the affray, both fighting well. I felt no fear for their ultimate safety other than a bruise or scrape, rather a mild enjoyment, an excitement in the charged atmosphere.

Then they ranged over the field no longer.

By the Virgin! My eye became centred when those colours came together to become engaged in personal combat, sword against sword, that showed no signs of waning, but was increasing in pace and ferocity. My enjoyment was transmuted in an instant into a cold dousing of horror. When Isabella's hand fastened on my arm like a merlin's claw, I realised that I had been struggling to my feet. That she had seen what I had seen.

The clash of metal echoed over the field. Both knights were driving at each other with grim determination. Sword clashed against sword.

'By the Virgin!' I breathed it aloud now.

'Has no one told them that this is *à plaisance* rather than *à outrance*?' murmured Isabella.

No one had. Or the two knights had chosen to forget it in the heat of battle. Who had begun this fierce onslaught I had no idea, but there was no reluctance on either side. Will and Thomas were fighting with verve and audacity as if they truly faced an enemy.

'You will have to award the garland to one of them.'

'I hope they both live for us to make a choice,' I managed, with more calm than I felt.

For a deep fear had begun to bloom that there would be real harm done here. How could I not understand the reason behind this fury of blows? They were fighting for me, for the right to claim my hand and my love. They were fighting out of hurt pride, out of lordly possessiveness. Out of a thoroughly male pique that one had thwarted the other. A silent challenge had been issued and neither looked to be prepared to give way. I discovered that I had indeed risen to my feet, hands clenched on the gilded carving of the pavilion before me, all dignity discarded for this had become a true battle. Nor was I alone in my concern, for Isabella, now standing beside me, unpinned her much used reliquary from her bosom and pressed it into my palm.

'You might need to pray, Joan. Be sure it is for the right one.'

'How can I? I don't want either of them dead and on my conscience. What fools men are!'

'It may be foolish, but who cannot admire a brave man who can wield a sword with so much mastery?'

'I am having difficulty.'

This was ridiculous, my fright lively. I did not desire the death of either. Moreover, if either was harmed on this day, the blame would fall on my head. How would I live, knowing that I had inadvertently caused the death of either man? Beneath my robes the perspiration was cold on my skin. Fighting against terror, I damned them for their overweening male conceit.

But I prayed for both as Isabella pulled me back to my seat. On my right the Queen's lips too were moving in silent prayer, while all around me was an aura of fierce apprehension. Even the cheers had died to a muttering of concern. The King's celebration was no place to witness the death of one of the new Garter Knights. This was an occasion of skill, not of blood seeping into the earth.

'Blessed Virgin, come to my aid,' I prayed. 'And theirs.'

By now a frisson of sheer panic rippled across my skin when a blow from Thomas drove Will to his knees.

But it was not the Holy Mother, rather the King, on seeing what was developing to mar his festivities, who strode across to the combatants. Once within distance, he knocked aside the swords with his own, joined by the Prince who added his weight when Thomas and Will were still reluctant to give way. We could not hear the words exchanged, initially sharp, but at last it went down well enough. It was all ended at the King's pleasure when he marched towards us, our brave knights following. If Edward was surprised to see me as Lady of the Lists he made nothing of it.

'Do either of these knights deserve victory?' Edward demanded. 'They've taken everyone's mind off the plague, so I suppose they fulfilled my wishes even though I had not planned for death on my battlefield.'

I had had time to recover, to run my tongue over dry lips, although resentment at the fright still simmered.

'Perhaps they both do, my lord.' I managed a gracious smile that was edged with ice.

He grunted a laugh. 'Perhaps they do. I don't recall quite so tense a combat in a friendly tournament. The sooner you three settle your differences the better.'

Thomas, glancing briefly at Will, wiped blood from his chin as he removed his helm. His breath was short. 'If I have any claim to victory, my lord, I claim a boon.'

Edward, dispensing regality on all sides, was in a mood to be amused. 'What do you claim?'

'The right to hold a conversation with my wife.'

'No, sire!' Will's face registered horror. 'I do not give my consent. It is not appropriate.'

'And without eavesdroppers,' continued Thomas, unperturbed.

It was in my mind to refuse as I felt my face flush at the ignominy of being squabbled over and so publically, and yet both had a claim on my emotions. One demanded my love and my loyalty, the other my public duty.

'I will not have it, sire.' Will would not let go.

'But I am victor and would have my recompense,' Thomas addressed the King. 'Were we not fighting for the favours of the lady? The favour I demand is her attention. For a mere half hour.'

I leapt into the fray.

'And it is a favour I would gladly grant, sire, before I am forced against my will to return to Bisham, to live once again in isolation.' I had no hesitation in announcing my incarceration, my duty to Will compromised by his autocratic treatment of me, ensuring that my voice was cool and clear, without any of the high emotion that had charged my blood when Thomas was under attack. 'Evidence is being given in my name in Avignon. It is my legal right to speak of this with Sir Thomas.'

'Edward.' Philippa leaned over the flagged parapet. 'You can be magnanimous. He is one of your most favoured knights.'

I became aware of my mother pushing between the ranks of the women. Will fisted his hands on his hips. Thomas remained silent, face set in uncompromising lines, as the King looked from one to the other, now torn between amusement and exasperation. Once more I intervened before my mother could arrive with her own deflection in this argument.

'If it pleases you, my dear cousin,' I said, my expression suffused with anxiety as if I feared being snatched away within the minute. 'You would have my undying gratitude if you would grant Sir Thomas a conversation with me.'

'It is an unusual situation.' Edward looked at Philippa.

'He deserves recognition for his bravery,' Philippa replied.

'More than a garland?' The King gestured at the victor's wreath still clutched hard in my hand to the detriment of the foliage.

There was a mass holding of breath while the King deliberated. Then:

'You fought well today, Sir Thomas, and I can never resist courage on the field. Here is your lady, for a half turn of the hour glass. Not enough time for you to compromise her over-much. Make use of my pavilion. But make sure that you use discretion now that you are a Knight of my Order. You wear the garter. May its message be meaningful.'

'I always was a chivalrous knight, sire.'

While Will, flushed and angry, strode off, sword in hand and his squire in tow, I allowed Thomas to take my hand and lead me to King Edward's extravagant pavilion, a royal page delegated by the King to accompany us.

'You are there as witness.'

But witness to what? What would we say to each other now?

We had hardly entered the heated shadows of the pavilion, its silken door looped back to allow some vestige of air to enter, than Thomas addressed the page: 'Turn your back! Stuff your ears. Not a sound out of you.'

'Yes, my lord.'

I barely waited on the lad's obedience, stripping off the blue and silver cloak against the sudden heavy warmth.

'I thought you were going to kill him.'

I was still finding it hard to forgive those moments of sheer terror.

'I thought he was going to kill me!' Thomas cast his helm and his gauntlets to the floor and drew his hands down over his face before eyeing me with what could not be described as affection. 'I can't believe how much trouble you are causing me, Joan.'

Which I thought might be a typical response from a man under pressure.

'I am not trying to cause anyone any trouble. It was not my fault that we were wed in secret. That everyone questions it.'

'No, it was probably mine.' He studied me. 'That chaplet looks ridiculous.'

'It's Isabella's. Becoming Lady of the Lists was the only way I could see to speaking with you. I am not free to do as I wish. I presume that you know.'

I cast it to the floor where it lay, its flowers damaged, on top of Thomas's blood-smeared gauntlets. A sad combination, I thought, for two lovers.

'Yes, I knew. Do they treat you well?'

'Except for the closed door and the key in the lock from the outside, I am my own mistress.'

At last he smiled, if bleakly. 'It's good to see you. And to hear you.'

'It is not the welcome I'd planned.'

I was caustic. It was fear that had made me so, but it was now beginning to leach away. For a long moment we just stood together. We did not touch. It was only our gaze that held, and said all that needed to be said. Was ever a marriage so benighted? I cast a quick glance over my shoulder but the page was surveying the colourful scene beyond the doorflap.

'Is there any hope?' I asked.

'Salisbury's refusal to co-operate puts a dent in any man's armour,' Thomas growled. 'Our main hope is that His Holiness runs out of patience with the lot of us and makes a decision without reference to anyone. I have met your new advocate, Magister Vyse. He seems satisfactory. Are they allowed to lock up a woman of royal blood?'

'Yes. And yes he is more than satisfactory. He is erudite and opinionated and perfect for the task. Our steward did not dare to turn him away when he insisted on hearing my confession. I think he had borrowed the Bishop's robes to impress.' And then, because it was a thought that had much troubled me: 'Have you decided what we will do if our marriage is rejected?'

'No. Are you giving up, Joan, before the final clash of steel?'

'No. But living alone is wearing on the spirits.'

'Then I carry you off across my saddle bow in a well-documented action. Would you come? I can offer you very little in the way of comfort, but I would love you and let you have your own way.'

Which made me smile a little. I doubted it. What man would? We had no experience of married life together. I thought about this, about whether he was serious about snatching me from the hands of family, whether I would give up the comfort and assurance of the Salisbury inheritance for the chancy pay of a tournament knight. But not for long.

'Yes. I would go with you.' And then, 'I am relieved that you did not kill him.'

'It would have cured a major headache.'

'But created an even more major one. You would have been in chains in the dungeons here, forced to answer for Will's death, while Edward considered whether to have you executed or banished.'

Silence settled over us again, strangely when we had so much to say. The distance too remained between us, when it was in my mind to stretch out a hand to touch him.

'Our time is running out,' I said, only too aware of the minutes passing.

'Then let us be practical. Edward is not as hostile as he was. His pride has recovered. He might give me a castle in Europe where you can reign supreme and I can fight. It's the best I can hope for.'

'As long as I have the key to the door.' Then on a thought, 'Have you any money left?'

'Not that you'd notice. I've sold everything but the boots on my feet.'

'But not your armour, I see.'

'You can't expect a man to do that. I will need that to earn us a living. There will always be wars to be fought.'

I tried not to sigh. Whatever happened in the future, I would be in one place and Thomas in another.

'I suppose you are leaving now the tournament is over.'

'I'll return to Avignon. Forgive me. I have no keepsake to give you.'

No, I had nothing to remember him by, to hold fast in my hand in the dark hours of early morning when sleep escaped me. When I heard the King approaching, making an inordinate amount of noise, I was driven to ask what I had promised myself that I would never ask.

'Only give me your word, Thomas. That you will not forget me.'

He stooped and lifted his sword from where it lay on the floor, and thinking that he was preparing to leave I went to lift his helm and gloves, trying not to show disappointment that he had not given me his word because he could not.

'Leave them,' he said. 'Come here.'

I stood before him as he raised the hilt of his sword between us. 'I swear on the Cross. I swear on the body of Christ. I swear on my own reputation that I will not let this travail come between us. And no, I will never forget you. No man who has known you could forget you.'

His hands were clasped around the cross-piece. I placed my hands there too, above his.

'I swear on the Cross that I will remain a true wife to you. Through all adversity. I will not succumb to the demands of William of Salisbury.'

He knew what I meant and his face was stark, but his words and deeds brought joy to my heart.

'We have made a vow. We will exchange a holy kiss that not even the King can question for its integrity.'

And so we did. Cheeks and lips, light and insubstantial.

'We will remain true to each other,' I added.

Not a kiss of lovers but of two people dedicating their lives to being together. We were no holy pair, but the solemnity of the occasion in the deep shadow of the pavilion was unquestionable.

'Adieu, my chivalrous knight.'

'God keep you in his care.'

And there was the King, as Thomas thrust his sword into its scabbard and bent to collect helm and gauntlets, handing me my unfortunate chaplet.

Edward clamped a hand on the page's shoulder. 'Have they been discreet?'

'They only talked, sire.'

'Is that all?'

'They took an oath, my lord.'

'Good. That's good.' He smiled sceptically. 'I should wish you good fortune, Thomas, but it sits ill with me. I just wish the whole thing undone and re-knitted sweetly.'

'I will do my best, as a Knight of the Garter. I have one final word, if you will allow.'

And when Edward retired to the door, Thomas bowed low to me.

'Magister Vyse gave me your message, my dear wife. I would give those words back to you: I took my vows to you in good faith. I would do the same again tomorrow. Keep me in your heart and mind, as you are in mine.'

He bowed again, to me and to the King, and there we parted. Thomas to Avignon. And I, in a flurry of invective, back to Bisham.

Who would have foreseen the future? That the year would pass in sorrow and grief. My parting from Thomas was not the only burden that I was to bear, since death took precedence over all other events. The Garter tournament, a glorious panacea in itself, provided the briefest respite, for nothing could stop the spread of the plague that took young and old. Rich and poor. My mother died from plague in that year, followed rapidly by my uncle Wake. The two people closest to me in blood, and for whom I felt least affection.

Their passing made little impact on my life, even as I acknowledged that I had grown into some measure of compassion for my mother's view of life, bitter as aloes. A woman under threat could be led to do all manner of things. With maturity I became more accepting of her driven nature. Her determination to see me wed to Will was, in the circumstances, understandable. She had died believing that Thomas Holland's attempt to reclaim me had come to naught. There had been no deathbed reconciliation between us.

But that was not to be my only consideration of the frailty of life. My sister Margaret too was stricken. We had spent little time together since our childhood but her absence was like a bruise to the skin, painful when touched. Of the four Kent children, born to carry on the royal blood of our father, only John and I remained. It was a lowering thought.

And then there was Dowager Countess Catherine who faded into a painless death, probably from disappointment when there was no heir to the Salisbury inheritance. Another absence that barely touched my emotions, unless I recalled her kindnesses to me as a child. As an adult I had disappointed her and she had treated me with less than the respect due.

As the year limped through the months of summer, as autumn leapt into winter with frost and high winds, there was no news from Avignon, not even from my most capable Magister Vyse. It would have to be a rescue, with weapons and fast horses and refuge across the sea, yet I could not envisage it. I had no wish to live in disrepute, pointed at, sneered at. The days dragged me down into a melancholy as we observed strict mourning. Will found every excuse not to come near me and my accusatory tongue. My only company was Lady Elizabeth who kept to her rooms, meeting with me only for Mass. When she no longer wished to play chess with me, I felt that I was tainted company.

Thomas, of course, did not write.

'What would it take for you to tell me that at least you still exist?' I asked the silence of my chamber.

November 1349: Bisham Manor

'Be silent!'

I had never raised my voice in this house. It had never been necessary. Now I stood at the top of the stair to observe the affray that had brought me from solar to entrance hall, my voice echoing in my ears.

My command had the desired effect, more out of surprise than due obedience, and the commotion below me came to a halt with all eyes turned up towards me. Behind me I felt the presence of Lady Elizabeth emerging from the shadows, a slight figure swathed in black veils and a heavy cloak. Bisham in November was cold.

'Who is it?' she asked, curiosity rampant.

'Who indeed?'

One fast glance around the little crowd of people who stood in my entrance hall had every sense in my body alert.

'Would someone explain to me the meaning of this disturbance?' I asked, my voice redolent of authority but supremely neutral. 'It is ill-fitting for the house of the Earl of Salisbury.'

I kept my gaze trained on our steward. He was the one I must cow into submission or the edgy confrontation might disintegrate into bloodshed. The hall was awash with a knot of our household knights, boots muddying the tiles, swords already drawn, and my heart was hammering so hard and fast that I thought it must be heard by every man in the room. I allowed none of it to be evident as I trod down the steps, every inch the Countess of Salisbury.

I stopped three steps from the bottom, to claim an advantage of height.

The steward came to stand below me with forbidding mien.

'He is not to be admitted, my lady. My lord the Earl left strict instructions...'

'I will be admitted.' The trenchant voice overrode that of my steward. 'I am already admitted.'

Now I had no choice but to look at him. Nothing so predictable as a letter, a voluble courier. Here he was in the flesh, his hand on his sword hilt but he had yet to draw it in defence or aggression. Sir Thomas Holland, plainly dressed, windswept and muddied, without heraldic advertisement, which explained his presence here in my hall before he was recognised.

A crowd of servants had now gathered to augment the throng.

'My lady.' The steward was anxious. 'Our knights will escort him from the estate, if you will permit.'

'No, she will not permit.' Thomas was unmoving, his sword now half drawn. He eyed my own black veiling, eyes narrowing at what it might mean. 'Who's dead?'

My temper was shorter than I expected.

'I could provide you with a list. But for your immediate consideration, Sir Thomas, Countess Catherine died at the end of April.'

Which brought him up short. Thrusting his sword back into his scabbard he bowed low to me, then to Lady Elizabeth, still hovering at the top of the stair.

'Forgive me. I did not know.' His voice was as brusque as mine. 'You must tell me the rest – but later. What you need to know is that there has been a change in circumstances, my lady.'

He was staring at me, willing me to understand what he was not saying.

'Put up your arms,' I ordered. 'All of you. Let him through. I will brook no defiance here, and neither will your lord the Earl.'

Their lord. Not mine. No longer mine. I read it in Thomas's face, in the tension of his hand still gripping his sword hilt.

When they obeyed, although not readily for Will's dictate was law in this house, Thomas hefted a leather scrip from his shoulder. By the time he found his way to me, he had a fistful of documents in his hand.

'His Holiness is decided,' he announced, snapping the parchment to draw attention to it. 'A papal bull has been dispatched to His Grace the Archbishop of Canterbury for his immediate action.'

'And the result?' I would not be moved. Not yet.

Thomas continued to announce, much in the manner that he had challenged the French army across the river at Crécy. There was to be no doubt in the mind of anyone here present. I might have claimed some privacy but after three years of legal dispute Thomas was intent on announcing with utter clarity the reason for his being here at Bisham.

'Your marriage, my lady, to the Earl of Salisbury is a mere *de facto* union and so is declared null and void. You were never his wife. You are no longer his wife. The marriage never happened. His Holiness instructs that your marriage to me should be celebrated immediately before a priest and as publically as possible *in facie ecclesiae*. That will put all matters right.'

He paused. Then:

'We have done it. At last we have achieved justice.' His eye fell on the steward. 'Any man here who will dispute this may read the documents for himself.'

I trod slowly down the rest of the stairs until I was on a level with Thomas and my household.

'Go about your business,' I said so calmly although my heart leapt and tripped.

'But my lady... ' My steward all but wrung his hands.

'Did you not hear? I am no longer the Countess of Salisbury, but you will obey me in this, the last of my orders under this roof.'

The household melted away, except for Lady Elizabeth who remained a silent observer as Thomas and I stood isolated, a little apart, in the centre of the hall.

'How did you do it?'

'I had little to do with it.' For the first time his voice fell to an acceptable level. 'It was all a matter of lost patience. His Holiness stepped in and appointed Bernard d'Albi, Cardinal Bishop of Porto, a veteran in such cases, to cut through the entanglement with a sword. The Cardinal Bishop lost patience. The Cardinal Bishop, God be praised, closed the case by the plain expedient of issuing a date when he would pronounce the verdict. He would hear no more evidence, no more excuses from the advocates of the Earl of Salisbury. There will be no appeal. His Holiness was pleased to wash his hands of the whole affair, I imagine, after more than two years.'

Two years and more. I was twenty one years old. I had been Thomas's wife for nine years, Will's wife for only a little less. Now all was resolved. It was so hard to take in, that I was no longer under duress from anyone.

Thomas was stuffing the documents back into the bag, regardless of their legal value, before flinging the bag to the floor. There we were. No legal impediment between us. No lock and key. No third person to intervene. What Lady Elizabeth had heard I neither knew nor cared. Thomas had brought my freedom and I would claim it.

Thomas opened his arms.

There was no royal page here to spoil the moment, there never would be again. And yet there was a strange hesitancy between us.

'I have come to reclaim what is mine.'

'And I accept.'

Slowly, I walked forward. His arms closed around me, strong and firm. He kissed my mouth. Then his hand slid down my arm to take mine.

'Show me to your room.'

I turned in a moment of obedience, then all I had learned in the past, all I hoped for in the future, snapped into place.

'No.'

'Why not?'

'We will do nothing that can be interpreted as subterfuge or illegality.'

'We have all the proof we need.' He applied his toe to the leather satchel. 'What more do we want? What more do *you* want? It has taken us a lifetime and a fortune to achieve it. Why cavil now?'

'I accept what you say. But this is what we will do.' I did not release his hand, rather threaded my fingers with his. 'We will go to Windsor where the court will be gathering for Christmas. We will be wed in the Chapel with the Archbishop and the papal bull and the whole court to witness it. We will announce the papal decision with a royal fanfare. And then – only then – when all is achieved in the full light of day – you will take me as your true wife.'

'Before God, Joan!'

His voice had risen again.

'We have waited so long. We will tie the ends, neatly and legally. For the sake of our legitimate children, if not for ourselves.'

'Have I any choice?'

'None. We will do it well and in seemly fashion this time.'

His nose narrowed as he inhaled, but I knew that I had won.

'Then do whatever it is that you need to do to leave this place, madam. There is no time to waste.'

I surveyed my bedchamber at Bisham for the last time, feeling no regret at abandoning the luxury and comfort that had been my prison of sorts for so many months. All my personal belongings had been removed. It was as if I had never been here.

'What will you do?' Lady Elizabeth, at my shoulder.

'Go with Sir Thomas.' My eye was on the prie-dieu where I had spent so many hours of interminable prayer.

'You must make your peace with my grandson.'

I turned to face her. What she saw in my face made her step back.

'Why should I?'

'He did not beat you.'

'He locked me up. He denied me justice.'

Her pressure on my arm was light as if a fragile bird had landed there.

'Make your peace, Joan. Who can see the future?'

'All I see is that your grandson is not in it.'

The grip tightened like a talon. 'It may be that one day you will need an ally. You do not know what you will be called on to face. It may be that one day you will need William's kindness and loyalty.'

It struck a chord, deep within me, so that the worst of my acrimony drained away. So it might be. It would be a foolish woman who turned her back, refusing to mend a broken bridge, however difficult the task. No, I could not foresee the future, but I recognised it for wise advice. I leaned to kiss her dry cheek.

'You have my thanks, Lady Elizabeth. If nothing else you have taught me to play an excellent game of chess.'

Will's grandmother smiled. 'God be with you, Joan,' she said. 'I know that you will follow the straight course to what you see as happiness. But don't forget to keep your friends from the past.'

Thomas and I were wed, again, beneath the austere and no doubt frowning arches in that most holy of holies of St. George's Chapel at Windsor, with no great concern for our garments or untoward festivity. I was clad in the first silk robe that came to hand while Thomas's knee-length cote-hardie had seen better days, although at least its sleeves had an eye to what was fashionable, short in front and trailing gracefully at the back. The only deference to my being a bride was that I wore my hair loose and unbraided beneath my veil. There was no livery collar as a gift in this ceremony, for celebration was not in anyone's mind. At papal insistence, our marriage was solemnised by no less that the Bishops of London and Norwich as well as the Bishop of Comacchio, the papal nuncio himself. No one was to be left in any doubt of my restoration to the bosom of my true husband. It was an event achieved by persistence, King Edward's gold, and the Pope's irritation with every man and woman concerned in the affair.

'And in spite of a certain low cunning to stop us,' Thomas observed *sotto voce* as I placed my hand in his once more, 'who would have thought the noble Montagu family capable of such sleight of hand?'

'Who would have thought them capable of creating so much ill-will?' It would still not be an easy task to forgive Will for his part in the last two years of stalemate.

In the eyes of the whole court we took the conventional vows. No hawks here, but Philippa, resigned and prepared to be sentimentally tearful over a new bride, bestowed her majestic presence on us. Isabella ready with a sly congratulation and at least some envy. My brother John disinterested in fraternal fashion since it affected him not at all. Ned, surprisingly stern in his brief well-wishing, declaiming, rather enigmatically, that it might be impossible for me to achieve all the happiness I was hoping for. And the King, stopping off to honour us in an edgy fashion, en route between Hereford and Calais, managed to give an air of acceptance despite his impatience for he had a vastly important project in mind and resented the delay caused by something so trivial as a marriage, particularly that of a woman who, Edward observed, not *sotto voce*, did not seem capable of making up her mind. Calais was about to come under attack from the French. While Thomas and I exchanged vows and concentrated on the legalities, Edward was plotting ways and means of organising his own invasion of France with a substantial force of archers and cavalry without raising the French alarm. It coloured the whole proceedings, with Edward's instructions to the trio of bishops to hurry it up.

I suspected that Thomas would be riding with him for Calais before the ceremony was over, if the King had his way. My grip on my lord's hand was uncompromising.

And then it was done, the shade of my mother standing at my shoulder, where I shrugged off her dismay with a light heart. This was no poor knight who joined his hand to mine, a knight without land or prospects. This was a Knight of the Garter whose name would be writ in gold. I was certain of it.

'It is still a poor marriage for a princess of the blood, to a man with nothing but his military accoutrements and his annual payment from the King,' I imagined her saying as the Bishop of London, whose jaundiced expression suggested a degree of displeasure with the whole event, announced the final blessing on this troublesome couple.

Was I satisfied?

I felt Thomas's increasingly forceful presence beside me, standing with me before the altar with a commanding air of confidence. When I turned my head to look at him, he looked at me. Yes, I had made the decision that was right for me. Between us were love and acceptance and a strong hope for the future together.

The lines beside Thomas's eye and mouth deepened into a smile, and in that smile, of triumph, of pure male gratification in what he had achieved, I read the strong emotions that had kept him battling for me against all the odds. I discovered that I was returning the smile.

Yes, I was satisfied. As much as I ever was in life.

I knew this interview would be difficult, but I could not avoid it. To do so would be the work of a coward and I was never that, and I had in mind Lady Elizabeth's advice.

'I have come to say farewell.'

It had not been difficult to discover Will. Where would he ever be when he needed time for reflection? He was in the royal stables, not that I would ever believe that he would avoid me. In his quiet way, he had grown into a man of a certain courage. I had not seen him since we had laid his mother to rest beside the old Earl at Bisham Priory. We had had little to say to each other that was seemly on that occasion. We pared it down to commiserations.

Now he simply stood and looked at me, a well-polished bridle in his hands. Anger was there in his stance, but also resignation, the friendly contours of his face finely drawn. It might have been a task more fitting to one of his squires but he had been polishing as if his life had depended on it.

'Your grandmother says I should make my peace with you.'

'And what do you say?'

It would not be easy. This, as I well knew, had been a blow to his pride. He would be forced to accept the sympathy and not a little mockery from his knightly friends that he had been unable to keep a wife. It was not every day that the Earl of Salisbury lost a valuable wife in a legal judgement. My antipathy towards him, that he had dared to manipulate my future, that he had lied to me, that he had kept me in a veritable prison within my own home ebbed like a spring tide. Once I had liked him. Now that I was no longer answerable to him, I could perhaps like him again.

'Farewell, Joan.' His expression was closed to me.

'Is that to be all there is between us?'

I remained distant from him. On this occasion Will clearly did not like me, nor did I blame him. I had rejected him for a mere knight. But I was not disheartened. I knew what was best for him.

'I regret the death of your mother.'

His straight regard was sceptical. 'There was no love lost between you.'

'Growing up as I did under her dominion, she had a hand in making me the woman I am.'

'I think that she would have denied that.' He lifted a shoulder and let it drop. 'She never really recovered from my father's death. She was devoted to him, saw no wrong in him.'

'So much so that she did not see that her son would be a great man too,' I replied with more sharpness than I had intended. 'She was proud of you but was loathe to see the steadfast courage in you.'

'Ha!'

I raised my brows in query.

'I am unused to such fulsome commendations from the woman who was my wife.'

'I can be fulsome, now that I am free.' At last I smiled at him. 'You should marry again, Will. As fast as you can. Enjoy some marital bliss.'

And there at last was an answering gleam in his eye.

'My thanks! Then I should tell you. I already have a new wife in mind.'

He still had the power to surprise me.

'So fast? I should feel slighted.' It was easy to mimic disappointment. Which he did not believe for one moment. 'She'll never be the wife that you were, Joan. Or that you were not. You will know her. Elizabeth. Daughter of Lord Mohun of Dunster.'

An eminently suitable match. I did know her. 'Is she your own choice?'

The harness was cast aside. 'Yes. Her family are willing.'

'Of course they are. Who would not wish to be wed to the Earl of Salisbury.'

'You, for one.'

I laughed and at last approached to grasp his hands that were now free to be grasped. 'You will deal well together. Much better than we ever would.'

'I expect life will be calmer.' He rubbed his fingers over my chin, leaving smears of polish so that I wrinkled my nose. He rubbed it away with his sleeve. It was good to return to this slight intimacy.

'I will always be your friend, Will.'

'I suppose I will be yours too, when my pride has recovered. I regret some of the past years.'

I kissed him on the cheek.

'Some of them it will be better to forget.'

There was a task I needed to carry out. A task the outcome of which I thought might become of importance to me in the future. I was unsure why I should be so concerned, but the need occupied my mind to the exclusion of all else, a constant itch like a louse in a seam. Best to put it right.

'Will you give me something?' I asked.

Our very public marriage thus over in a rush, and before Edward would persuade Thomas to abandon me and join the new adventure to save Calais from French inundations, I made my petition. Thomas was already preoccupied with the details of the forthcoming campaign, even now being recounted to him by Ned and my brother John.

'I need something from you,' I repeated, tugging on Thomas's sleeve.

'You cannot refuse a bride on her wedding day,' Isabella remarked in passing, 'even if it is for the second time. Or even the third...'

I pushed her away. This was important, not to be discussed within hearing distance of anyone but Thomas and myself. I only broached it here because I was unsure what his next move would be under the persuasion of his fellow Garter Knights.

'If it is in my power, you will have it,' Thomas said, walking reluctantly aside with me. 'But if you want jewels or fine clothes, you will have to wait. It has beggared me to get you at last.'

'Such an admission to make to a bride!' On impulse, I touched his cheek, free to do so at last under the quizzical but indulgent eye of the whole court. 'You have all the documents from the Cardinal's decisions,' I said.

'Yes.'

'All of them?'

'Except for the papal bull. Which is somewhere in the Archbishop of Canterbury's keeping.' His brow wrinkled as he pulled his thoughts back from the need to gather archers and retainers. 'Are you afraid that there is still a question over our marriage?'

'No. Not at all.'

But the concern touched me again and made me shiver, like the first hint of rain on a hot day, presaging a summer storm.

'I'll keep them safe, if that troubles you.'

And it did trouble me, although I hid it. 'Would you be willing to give them into my keeping?'

'I will. And be glad of it.'

'Will you do it now?'

'This minute?' And seeing my brows rise. 'If I must.'

Escaping from the audience chamber where we had been gathered, we made our way to Thomas's accommodations in this warren of a palace. Small and cramped as it was, he was forced to riffle through pieces of armour and outer clothing until he produced a small roughly constructed travelling coffer, not at all suited to precious documents. There they were, stuffed in as if of no importance. If it had been a weapon he would have cleaned and wrapped it in linen until it was next needed.

Sighing, I took the coffer from him. 'I will look after them.'

'Why?'

'Why not?' I thought about it, eventually saying, 'I think that they might be more important for me than for you, one day.'

'I can't think why. As long as all is legal for the inheritance of our children.'

'I am not sure why. I just have a need to keep them under my eye. And now come with me.'

'Where?'

'To a more comfortable chamber than this rabbit hutch.'

In the coming days I smoothed out the documents, re-ordered them, and had a coffer made for them with a lock and key. I kept them in my chamber; when I travelled, they travelled too. Why the insecurity? It might be that one day I would need to prove once again which marriage was legal and which was not. I would have the evidence to hand.

Throughout all the careful arrangements I made, I remained fully aware that I had done damage to my reputation. I had heard the whispers when Thomas and I had made our vows before the combined bishops. Royal brides should not indulge in clandestine events which would cast doubts on what was legal and what was not, but on that day when we consummated our marriage in fine style it was far from my thoughts. We had waited long enough. Not a falconers cot or Thomas's hard mattress but a bed, a huge Montagu travelling bed,

brought to Windsor by either Will or the Dowager Countess at some
time in the past, with all its carved posts, its tasselled hangings and
embroidered symbols of Montagu power. I had made use of it when
at court. I would make use of it now.

'This seems strangely inappropriate,' Thomas observed, still fully
clothed, stretched out and looking up at the Montagu motifs on the
tester.

'It has not been used apart from me to sleep in.'

'Time it was!'

'Might I suggest that you remove your boots?'

There we were, alone; two persons legally wed, with all the past
anguishes forgiven, enclosed together in one room with a bed and
privacy as there had not been for so many years.

'I thought of you,' Thomas said, obediently as he sat up to pull
off his boots. 'I thought of you in the rankness of battlefields. In the
long-winded sessions in the courts at Avignon. When I was your
steward.'

'All the time, in fact?' I laughed a little to hide a surprising nerv-
ousness as, clad in my linen shift, I sat on the edge of the bed,
remembering the discomfort of the falconer's cot.

'No,' he admitted, with as much of a sheepish grin as I had ever seen
from him. 'Sometimes I was preoccupied. But you were a beacon in
the darkness, a precious gift that by pure chance I had won for myself
when I had nothing of value to my name other than my sword and
my horse.' He shuffled to sit more closely beside me. 'I should have
been thrashed for taking you as my wife as I did, but how could a
man resist the beauty that you owned as a young girl? And of which
you were fully aware.' His fingers, heavy with sword and rein calluses,
trailed down my cheek. 'Did you think of me at all?'

'Yes,' I admitted promptly. 'I thought of you when I needed to be
rescued from the locked doors at Bisham. Your absence infuriated me.'

He regarded me steadily. 'I swear there is as little romance in you as there is in me. How can so beautiful a woman have so little sentiment in her soul?'

'I have no idea. But my senses are truly engaged.'

'Ha!' His gaze turned speculative.

'Did I not stand beside you when you challenged Edward? Did I not give up all for this?'

I swept a hand to indicate our present surroundings; better than the mews they might be, better than Thomas's accommodations, but the chamber I had been allotted on my arrival, the castle being thronged with important visitors, was not comparable to any of the rooms I had enjoyed at Bisham as Countess of Salisbury. The bed might be impressive but the light through the high windows was meagre, and the tapestries had never seen the hand of a master craftsman. Moreover, who knew where we would spend our future nights?

Then my hands were captured, as were my lips. When Thomas drew my shift from my shoulders I shivered with some apprehension.

'You are as much a virgin as when I left you.'

'Of course.' My breathing was compromised. 'Did you truly have a harlot in every camp?'

'Not quite every one. Did Will never try to bed you?'

His mouth imprinted kisses along my shoulder. Breathing was becoming difficult, but pleasurably so.

'Not with any real enthusiasm. Or success.'

'I will be very successful.'

'I have no doubt of it.'

And he was. Was I disappointed after a lifetime of waiting? Not so. My disquieting memories of the discomforts of the Ghent mews were cast into oblivion, as they deserved.

Chapter Eight

January 1350: The Manor of Yoxall, Staffordshire

I was effectively struck dumb. But not for long

'May the Blessed Virgin preserve me!'

I had not expected quite such a change in my circumstances. This was not naivety as much as lack of experience. But here was a shock that made me pull my mount to a standstill while I took stock. I had informed Isabella that I had no fear of living on a knight's holding in the wilderness of the far north of the country. Raised as I had been with all the comfort and wealth of King Edward's court, I had not known the half of it here in Staffordshire.

Penury. Poverty. Depredation.

The words jostled in my mind. This was to be my experience as Lady of the Manor.

'We are pleased to welcome you, Lady Holland.'

It still surprised me when I was not addressed as Countess of Salisbury.

'It pleases me to be here.'

I smiled around me, and at the youthful steward, warmly because I must. It had to be said that it did not please me at all but I stepped through the door, stopping to look back at the courtyard, the outer buildings, the stable block, with an inner shudder. Then proceeded within to where the rest of my household awaited me.

'You have the ability to dissemble with great ease, Joan.' Thomas took my hand and led me into what passed for a Great Hall. It was no larger than Philippa's personal audience chamber. 'It is a quality I have always admired in you.'

'I have polished it over many years,' I said, still smiling, 'but not under these circumstances. Do you wish to live here? Do you wish me to live here?'

We were at the utterly forgettable manor of Yoxall in Staffordshire. I doubted that I would discover Yoxall on any map in Edward's collection. Small, isolated, if anything it was even more dilapidated than Broughton in Buckinghamshire that we had passed rapidly through. The manors had belonged to Thomas's mother Maud, whom I had never met. On her death she had left them to Thomas, a lifetime interest.

'No. I do not wish to be here.'

But he too smiled on his dependents and accepted the wine cup, drinking manfully of its harsh contents. I sipped with decorous precision, intent on leaving as much as possible.

'At least we have somewhere to live,' he had said with no great enthusiasm when, after greeting his retainers, his cook and his indoor servants, we were left alone.

So this was to be my life, perhaps with an unspoken expectancy that this new royal bride would have the coin in her coffers to put all matters right. As we had travelled north we had been surrounded by evidence of despair and ruin: plague had ravaged those who worked on the manors, lack of investment over the years had done the rest. This was not a wealthy family that I had joined. Thomas merited the promotion to the rank of banneret, but clearly he lacked the two

hundred pounds annual income to support the status. The two manors
I had inspected would never be worth two hundred pounds each year.

Nor did I have the wealth to remedy the lack.

'I have the strongest impression,' I said, placing the wine cup and
its contents on the floor beside the hearth, 'that you regret that our
marriage stepped into the path of your joining Edward in his campaign
to Calais.'

'How can you say that?'

'With ease.'

Thomas had decided not to go.

I made a circuit of the hall. There was very little to inspect. There
was a tapestry but with more holes and damp-induced mould than
stitching. The stools and the tables stacked against the wall showed
evidence of woodworm. I did not like to consider the state of the
bedchambers.

Thomas was watching me. 'We will make of it what we can,' I
said, 'until Edward forgives you and makes you the great man you
ought to be.'

'I hope it is before I die.'

But he took my arm and escorted me around the rest of my new
home while I absorbed a cold dose of reality. I could do nothing but
ensure efficiency and that all under our dominion were fed. The
money at our disposal was astonishingly little so that as I stepped into
what would be my chamber, I had visions of cutting and re-sewing
my gowns. There would be no rebuilding of these two little manors.
Besides, Thomas was not interested in planning anything that did
not involve a charge of cavalry or a siege or a complex campaign. I
knew with some depression of spirits that it would be only a matter of
weeks before he answered the call of duty to fight at Edward's side. I
ran my hand along the soft blue of the bed curtains, over the coverlet
that had once matched but was now faded into a uniform grey.

I grimaced. 'Damp.'

'I'll order a fire to be lit in here.'

I doubted a fire had been lit there since Lady Maud had died. Had she died in this bed?

'What's wrong?'

'Not a thing.' It came into my mind, about the desolate maxim of making beds and lying in them.

And when Thomas found the chance to clip me close and kiss my lips, I was more than resigned. When one has no choice, resignation is a fine thing.

Two months later, when March heralded the first hint of green along the hedges, Thomas left Yoxall for Sandwich where Edward was collecting a fleet to deal with the Castilian navy prowling in the Channel. I remained at Yoxall.

'Are you sure about this?'

'Perfectly.'

I was carrying our first child. Thomas had lost no time in ensuring an heir for his name and to inherit Yoxall. I hoped that the child would appreciate it.

'Just make sure that you return,' I added. 'And if you can win a more suitable inheritance for this infant, I will be delighted.'

So Thomas was there at the Battle of Winchelsea where the Castilian fleet was defeated while I awaited the birth, refusing to shut myself away in self-imposed confinement until my ritual churching, which was the lot of most royal women. Many wives watched the battle from the cliffs, I was told. It did not interest me. I had my own battle to struggle with, in a chamber that still reeked of damp and mould and probably always would. The sheets has been darned and mended beyond further repair.

We called him Thomas. Young Tom.

Thomas, returning from the dangers of battle, still with the light in his eye of an excellent fight well fought, beamed at his son and heir.

'He'll be a good knight. Look at those hands. I'll have to buy him armour and a horse.'

'Not quite yet. I doubt we can afford it.'

Thomas was silent, rubbing a finger over the baby's head which was neatly encased in a white coif. The wisps of hair matched Thomas's own in their dense colour. Thomas's expression was wry.

'Pray to God for good health for this son. I don't think I can afford more children unless there is a war I can fight in.'

I had had much time to consider this. I was not without plans. Shut away in the chilly reaches of Staffordshire had given me much opportunity.

'Is there truly none left of the money Edward paid you for the ransom?' I asked.

'Edward managed not to pay it all, after the first purse,' Thomas admitted, which I had suspected. 'He could hardly demand its return from me without a stain on his own honour. After that he said he could afford no more. The wars were a drain on his purse strings, he said.' He looked across the child's waving arms to where I stood. 'I know what you are thinking.'

'Then I'll say it. Not such a drain that would stop his building projects at Windsor and every castle he possesses. How much is he spending to enhance this and rebuild that? Edward simply did not approve of how you spent the coin you did get. That's the real reason.'

'That may be.' He handed the infant to his nurse who bore him out, leaving us alone. 'And no, there is none left of that.'

Of course. As I had known. The case had beggared him. Beggared us.

'So you will no longer grace my bed?'

'What do you think?'

'I'm not sure. You have shown more interest in your son than you have in me.'

'Then let us remedy it. You are looking amazingly healthy for the deprived life you tell me you are living.'

Since I had been churched and purified after the birth, my votive candles presented to the altar in the Lady Chapel in the Church of St. Peter in thanksgiving for my survival, Thomas proved to be attentive and gratifyingly energetic. For once the damp linens on my bed were not uppermost in my mind.

'It is good to be home,' he murmured in the breathless aftermath.

My concurrence was practical and wifely and made him lose his breath all over again.

As might have been expected, I was soon carrying another child, and since there were no prospects of any notable increase in our income to match that in our family, I decided that I needed to make a demand on some debts and family loyalties.

'We are returning to court,' I announced before the seams of my surcoat needed to be let out.

Thomas made no demur; nor did he show surprise.

'I wondered how long you would be content here.'

'My contentment is at an end. Besides there is an excellent reason to go now.'

At last a marriage had been arranged for Isabella to Bernard, eldest son and heir of the Gascon Lord Albret. It had been arranged that in November a ship would come to carry her across the sea to meet her new husband. It would be accompanied by celebrations and the giving of many gifts. Edward was glowing with the prospect of this well-connected bridegroom. I had no idea of Isabella's thoughts.

I dressed with care, as well as with a degree of artfulness, not enough to dent my pride, but enough to cause comment from at least one influential quarter. I knew on whom I could rely when it came to matters of high fashion and she would have garments in mind since it was her wedding departure to Gascony that I would grace. Thomas did not notice, or if he did, he was wise enough to make no comment. But it was Philippa who embraced me, then inspected me with an air of displeasure after ensuring my excellent state of health and that of my child.

'I have seen that gown at least a dozen times, if not more.'

'And you will see it a dozen more.'

I smoothed my hands over the deep green skirts of the cote-hardie, a colour that had never flattered me. The worn patches flattered me even less.

The Queen examined me more closely, focusing on bodice and hands. 'Where are your jewels?'

I managed a little shrug, an infinitesimal grimace. 'I have none.'

I was grateful that Thomas was nowhere in the vicinity. He could be eloquent on the contents of my jewel coffer.

'Why not?'

'Because I am no longer Countess of Salisbury.'

Isabella, the bride, joined us. 'That does not mean that you must wear a gown more worthy of a kitchen maid to my wedding departure. The fur looks as if it has been chewed.' An exaggeration of course, but she lifted the offending item with a curl of her lip.

'That will be my son. He is acquiring teeth,' I said, not at all discouraged at this turn in the conversation between the pair of them. 'I have come to wish you well. We do not have the money for fripperies. Nor do I need them.' I lied beautifully, smoothly.

'I do not believe that you have been driven to selling your jewels.' Philippa exhibited disgust that I should have been reduced to such extremities.

'I may have.'

'It is unfitting that you should live in hardship.' Isabella was clad in damask and fur with a new jewel pinned to her bodice. Probably a gift from her newly espoused husband.

'I can blame no one but myself. Thomas needs a war,' I said, which was not as inconsequential as it might sound.

'Which he is likely to get,' Philippa confirming my worst fears, 'but in the meantime we will discuss this little matter with the King…'

Philippa was gently outraged. I was demure. Isabella was lively. Edward, when we discovered him in a cluster of his knights, was wary and reluctant as Philippa drew him apart and announced her purpose.

'She looks perfectly presentable to me,' Edward observed, running an experienced eye over my person, ignoring the depredations of time and wear.

'How can you say that? Princess Joan should not look like a poor relation whom we do not wish to acknowledge. It does you no honour, Edward.'

'It's not a matter of honour. I don't have the money to support every one of my knights who marries to disoblige me.'

'Of course not, sir.' I added my own layer of helplessness. 'Sir Thomas understands. He would never petition you.'

'No! But you would.'

'I, my lord? It is beneath my pride to do so. I am here at the behest of your wife and daughter.'

Edward eyed me speculatively. I continued to remain demure.

'I think that you should be magnanimous, Edward, on this most auspicious occasion,' Philippa was warmly soothing.

'Or we could all kneel at your feet,' Isabella warned, with an innocent glance at me.

Edward's reaction was immediate. 'Don't do that! The gossips would be speculating why.'

'You could save the money out of your building schemes, Father, and all that gilding that my mother does not really admire. We could manage with a little less.'

'And we understand why you did not fulfil the whole of the promised payment to Sir Thomas for the French lords, cousin.' I smiled at Edward. 'Many would think you parsimonious but we know that you were merely stretched with other expenditure. And of course you were displeased, as would any proud man be in the circumstances...'

'Joan cannot continue to wear old gowns, Edward!' Philippa added another layer of guilt, while I hammered the final nail into the coffin of Edward's reluctance.

'I am carrying another child, my lord.' I lowered my gaze. 'My children need an inheritance worthy of their royal blood. The manor of Yoxall, in the state it is now, is not fit for a cat to inherit.'

Edward was no match for three determined women. He raised his hand to stop us.

'I will consider a gift to mark the marriage of my dear daughter. And there's an end to it.'

I rejoiced.

But not for long.

In a moment of self-will, astonishing both English and Gascons, Isabella seized the forthcoming marriage in her own hands, at the final hour refusing the much sought-after Bernard. While the ship waited, flags aflutter, to escort her across the sea to Gascony, Isabella shut herself into her chamber. She would not go. She would not wed the noble Bernard. No matter how her father might rail, she would not do it. She would have to be taken aboard with hands and feet bound if that was the royal will. She would go only under such duress.

Isabella fell into disgrace, as would any disobliging daughter. I gave up on any hope for a gift of money to mark the event which did not happen.

'Why?' I asked, admitting to shock as well as disappointment.

'Because I did not wish it.'

'That's no reason.'

'The reverse was a good enough reason for you becoming Lady Holland rather than Countess of Salisbury. I could not live in Yoxall with barely two nobles to rub together and a wardrobe falling into shreds around me. I could not live with Lord Bernard, either. I do not know him. I will not marry a man who does not touch my emotions.'

So that was that. Isabella remained unwed, setting herself with all the confidence of an indulged child to winning her way back into her father's favour while Thomas and I returned to Yoxall, which gave off an even more gloomy air after the bright hues of Windsor.

'I did try,' I told Thomas.

'I thought you would. But with Isabella stabbing Edward's plans in the back, he was in no mood for open handed generosity. The girl is a law unto herself, obviously a Plantagenet trait.' Within a breath, he became serious. 'You must not petition the King again, Joan. Allow me some dignity, to support my own wife without royal handouts.'

'I deserve a royal handout.'

But I gave my word that I would not.

'When I need help,' Thomas warned, as if I were a squire under his command, 'I will bend the knee before him.'

No need. A document followed us, arriving in the New Year. On the grace and goodwill of the King, Thomas and I were granted a royal annuity for the length of my life, a worthy sum of one hundred marks a year. Enough to ease the worst of our ills and allow Thomas to buy a horse and armour for his son. And any future ones. Enough to consign the green gown to where it belonged, a gift to be re-cut and re-stitched with new trimming for one of my women.

26th December 1352: Manor of Yoxall, Staffordshire

The courier was dispatched to the kitchen where he would regale the cook and the two kitchen maids, and anyone else who suddenly found the need to visit there, with the burden of news he carried. They would feed him too, on the remnants of our Christmas feasting. There were no further demands on his time, for there was no one person who needed to know the content of his brief report other than myself. And therein lay the problem. I wondered how our household would receive it. My own mind seemed strangely numb.

'I took the liberty of sending a notice to Calais, my lady,' the courier had said.

Edward had appointed Thomas as Captain of the royal castle at Calais. It meant much travel for him and much separation for both of us but it was a symbol of royal recognition which I would never oppose. The courier's message would be vital for him.

I went to the nursery where Tom, now more than a year old, was finding his feet. When he couldn't walk, he shuffled with uncommon speed. A crow of his laughter greeted me at the door. His shock of dark hair was that of his father, even to the dishevelment. And there was John, a restless child even though still a babe in arms, being rocked in his cradle by a local girl I employed for that specific task. All was comfort with a bright fire and new hangings to dispel draughts. The annuity had made a difference to the state in which we lived.

But nothing compared to the news which had just arrived on our doorstep. That would make all the difference in the world to Tom. He did not know it yet, he would not have any notion of the breadth and width of the effect on his life, but one day he would reap a splendid crop from this new sowing. This child, begotten of our love, heir to a knight's paltry manors, would have a new horizon opening up before him. One day...

I lifted him high in my arms, kissed him, ran my fingers through his hair and returned him to his nursemaid. I did not disturb John who was blessedly asleep.

I could see their father in their long limbs, in the dense hair that grew at all angles. Was there anything of me in them? What would I wish for them? A pride in their blood, an ambition to make their mark on the world. A fierce temper when roused? Perhaps not. A determination not to be thwarted, which I could already read in Tom's demeanour when taken to task by his nursemaid.

I waited for Thomas's return.

'My brother is dead.' My first words as Thomas ran up the steps into the hall. No greeting. No comment on his travel-beaten appearance. Only one thought in my mind. 'John is dead.'

'It's hard to believe. I came as soon as I heard.' Thomas was stripping off gloves, hat and outer clothing, handing them to his squire. 'I've never seen a fighter with such a charmed life in battle as your brother. I've seen him withstand a battering that would have felled a more robust man, and still walk away from it with barely a black eye...'

'Death does not have to come in battle!' A quick anger surged beneath my interruption at what seemed to me an unfairness. 'He died from a fever that took him to his bed at his manor of Woking. He never recovered. He was dead within two days. Twenty-two years is no age to die.'

And, as astonishing to myself as to Thomas, I covered my face with my hands and I wept.

Thomas might not always be attuned to the tears or laughter of those around him, but his care for me was immediate. I was brought into the circle of his arms, even when I resisted, so that at last I leaned and I wept even harder, regardless of dust and grime and the all-pervading aroma of horse and sweat.

'I have never seen you weep before,' he said at last when the flood had abated somewhat.

'I have never had the need.' I swallowed as I recalled the death of my mother and sister. I had not wept for them.

'I am so sorry, Joan.'

'He was all that was left to me.'

Resting his chin on my head, he stroked my shoulder as if I were a distressed mare, while I called my emotions into line. Deciding that I was once more in control, Thomas raised my chin and wiped my face with my own sleeve.

'What a storm. I had no idea that you were so close.'

'We have not been, of recent years. But once we were.' To the sad detriment of my surcoat, I was pulled to sit on the floor near the fireplace where desultory flames consumed green logs with much smoke, Thomas's arms still around me. 'When he was born we were all prisoners of Earl Mortimer in Arundel Castle, our lives at risk. I stood sponsor for him because there was no one else. I was barely two years old, and have no memory of it, but I was told by my mother, and it was important to me. Now everyone is gone. My uncle. My mother...'

'You cannot say that you miss your mother.'

'No.' I punched him lightly in the ribs, fast recovering now. I thought for a moment. 'John's widow will be distraught.'

'I expect she'll marry again. If I recall, she is very young. She has no children to tie her to the family. John had no heir...'

He stopped. He looked at me. I looked at him. The silence that fell between us was thick with realisation as what we had known since first hearing of John's death fell into place, like notes in a well-known tune.

'I respect your grief, Joan. But you do know what this will means for us. For you.'

'Yes.'

'Of course you do.'

I shook my head.

'I'll not think of it yet. I'll not speak of it yet. I will mourn John with grace and due respect.'

'But one day we must.'

Of the same mind, we said no more about it but allowed grief and mourning to run out its full course, attending John's burial at the Church of the Grey Friars in Winchester beside our father the first Earl of Kent. I recalled that my mother had intended to move my father's remains, from a place where he had been executed with such ignominy, to Westminster, but the plan had never come to term, so this is where John's earthly remains would also lie. It proved to be a solemn occasion, with few in the congregation, where Isabel of Jülich, John's young wife, her face blotched with tears, expressed the intention of enclosing herself as a nun until the day that she too died and would be buried next to her dear husband. I had no patience with her, to take the veil and shut herself away. She was younger than I.

'A more maudlin woman I have never met,' I said to Thomas when I could escape her tears. 'She may be a niece of the Queen, but she doesn't possess half her backbone.'

'And I am only thankful that you are not of the same stamp. Will you weep so when I am dead?'

'I will await the occasion and tell you about it.'

His responding smile was sharp and feral. 'I'll postpone it as long as I can.'

As we parted I once again expressed my condolences: 'God keep you, Isabel.'

'As He will.' Already resembling a nun in her widow's weeds. 'I will dedicate my life to Him.' And then with a tinge of unholy bitterness: 'Enjoy your good fortune, Joan. I wish it were not so.'

Not through any dislike of me, I decided, but because of her own lack. She and John had been wed four years, enough time for them to look to the future. And they had not.

'There is no enjoyment in my heart.'

It was all I could say. For here was the consequence of John's death, destroying as it did the whole clear-running line of inheritance for the earldom of Kent. Of my father's children I was the only one to remain alive since John and his wife had no children. I would inherit the Kent lands. I would inherit the Kent title as of right. There was no one to question it.

I was Baroness Wake of Liddell. I was Countess of Kent, *suo jure*.

Thomas and I returned to our manor at Broughton.

'How does it feel to be Countess of Kent?' he asked. 'How does it feel to be one of the wealthiest landowners in England?'

'Little different, when I see the state of our accommodations here at Broughton.' I was unimpressed by the muddy state of the floor as if an army had trampled over it. 'I notice that Isabel still insisted on being addressed as Countess. I expect she'll cling to it like a mite to a greasy head.' I dispatched the children to the nursery, before putting out a hand to stop Thomas disappearing towards the stables. 'It will matter greatly to you, of course.'

Thomas had suddenly the prospect of being a landed lord of significance in the right of my inheritance.

'We are rich beyond my dreams,' he remarked as our possessions were unpacked from the wagons and returned to the appropriate chambers. Thomas was regarding the unloading of the travelling beds, which had seen much travel, with a critical eye. 'Would you like to tell me how many estates and manors you now own, apart from the knight's fees and advowsons?'

I had spoken with John's man of law who had proved to be most enlightening with the result that I knew fairly well what I was worth.

'Forty-three manors,' I said. 'Spread across the length and breadth of England.'

'Which will bring in how much each year?'

'More than three thousand pounds. And that's after Isabel receives a third of John's estates for her dower.'

'So.' Thomas exhaled forcefully through his nose. 'Our bread no longer depends on my selling my sword or capturing French nobles for ransom or your petitioning the King for a charitable handout.'

'None of those. You are a great lord, Thomas, with the right to sit in parliament. As Tom will be so after you. You will be Earl of Kent.'

'Mmn!' Thomas followed the beds into the hall, where he turned to me, brows flat. 'I don't expect for one moment that the King will extend the title to me.'

'Not yet he won't,' I admitted. 'Only when he thinks he has punished you enough. But the inheritance is ours.'

Thomas frowned on a thought. 'I've no mind to tie myself to land management.'

'Nor will you have to tie yourself to it, you ingrate. John has a council of knights and clerks to survey and administer all. We inherit it and use it. Many of the manors are rented out. You can go fighting again, if that is your wish. I wonder if the King will see your new status as a reason to give you more authority than Captain of Calais? It may be so.'

'We'll not hold our breath. The King would consider Captain of Calais enough. Meanwhile, let us go and raise a cup of ale to your new title, my lady. It has been a long day.'

Nor did we hold our breath. As expected, although Edward did not see fit to extend the rank of Earl to Thomas, life changed for us, not least when we moved our whole household to Castle Donington in Leicestershire, a castle overlooking the Trent at the centre of my inheritance with more than a touch of luxury in its buildings and in the woodlands and meadows, not to mention the fisheries and parkland that surrounded it. The deficiencies of life at Yoxall and Broughton were soon forgotten. All those estates that my mother had fought so hard and so long to reclaim were now mine. I bought new gowns. No more frayed sleeves and worn fur, through hard wearing or through artifice.

Yes, I mourned my brother's death even as I enjoyed my own gain. Now we could bide our time until Thomas became Earl, as he should. I would not allow Edward to sweep this matter aside.

I caught Thomas packing for a new campaign, as if he could hide it from me until the day he followed his battle gear through the gate. Or no, there was no campaigning, merely a time of uneasy truce while both sides struggled to find a good reason for a permanent peace between England and France. So if not war, Edward had some other plan for him. Some plan to which I was not privy. Thomas, not adept at dissembling, had an element of guilt overlying his innocent expression.

'Where is it this time?'

'Brittany.'

Thomas continued to place official scrolls into a coffer. This had a legal smack about it. I would wait to see what developed.

'Well at least it's close,' I said, sitting in his chair, as innocent as he. 'It might be a short visit.'

'Yes. Short. And there again – it might not.' He did not quite meet my eye. Nothing new there.

Standing, I tucked my hand within his arm to drag his attention back to me. 'We have spent our whole life not knowing when we would set eyes on each other again. Why did I think this would be any different?' I was resigned more than irritated.

'You knew that when you married a soldier.'

'So what is it that will keep you away for some unspecified length of time? Of which you have not yet told me because you presumed that I would douse your delight with my disapproval.'

Thomas's scarred face broke into a youthful grin. 'The King is sending me to Brittany to run the administration as King's Captain and Lieutenant. He has made me custodian of the young heir to the Duchy until he reaches his majority. I will take up residence at the chateau at Vannes.'

'How old is the boy?'

'Fourteen or thereabouts.'

'So it will not be long before he reaches his majority.'

Thomas's eye could not quite meet mine. 'It's a delicate matter. Brittany is torn apart by civil war. The boy's claim is severely challenged since the King of France supports Charles de Blois, who is claiming the duchy in the right of his wife, the lad's cousin. It's complicated since the young Duke John is King Edward's ward. I'm being sent to hold the balance of power.'

'It sounds to me to be an appointment destined for failure.'

'But I will not fail, my dear wife.'

There was pride here. There was pleasure in the King's recognition of his talents. There was also the knowledge that this would be a lengthy posting, away from England, resulting in a lengthy separation. Thomas's visits to Calais had been intermittent as necessity demanded, but this was of a different nature, heavy with expectation from the King.

I made up my mind. I smiled at Thomas.

'You should have told me earlier.'

'Would it have made any difference?'

'It might.'

'You don't object?'

I took one of the scrolls from him to read its content, before re-rolling it and storing it neatly for the journey. I could see Thomas relax, as if he had won the battle.

'No. But I would have liked a little more time in which to organise my own household.'

Which stopped him mid scroll. He looked up, the unscarred brow crooked.

'I have a fancy to travel,' I continued with airy unconcern, 'and live for a while in Vannes. I have never been to Vannes.'

He relieved me of two more documents that I had picked up. 'You'll come with me?'

'Yes.'

'I will be busy, you understand. You will be alone there when I must travel.'

'Yes. But busy under my eye for much longer than if I were in Castle Donington or Windsor.'

Thomas stopped me at the door as if the small problem had just crossed his mind.

'What about the children?'

'Tom and John will come with us, of course. I believe Vannes to be a healthy place to raise children.'

'Then I'll leave it all to you.'

'As you usually do. And I should tell you. I am pregnant again.'

After which plain and brisk exchange of statements Thomas made no attempt to discourage me. He was pleased, but about my company or about the King's regard I could not say. It was a task that he would do well, while I set myself to travel as required between Vannes and the royal palaces in London and our own manors, much as Philippa had done throughout her younger days. Pregnancy was no obstacle to her, nor would it be to me. I would oversee our estates while Thomas made a name for himself in Europe.

And I would be at his side.

First, I had a visit to make. I had promised that I would not, but such a promise was made to be broken, and Thomas was none the wiser.

'My lord.'

I curtsied before the King who was covered in dust, giving directions for the construction of a new audience chamber at the same time as he discussed the dishes for a great Easter feast with his cook. This was the Palace of Eltham where Edward was in the throes of rebuilding to create a palace fit for himself and his Plantagenet offspring.

'Joan.' He raised me, kissed my cheek. 'I am busy as you see. Not another scandal, I hope.'

'Certainly not, my lord.' I accepted a cup of wine that he beckoned from a passing page and smiled at Philippa who was sitting out of harm's way in a window embrasure. I was sorry to spoil this intimate moment between them. They had so few. But to me this was a necessity. 'I am here to put right a wrong.'

'It sounds like a scandal.' Dismissing page, builder and cook, Edward gulped a mouthful of fine Rhenish. 'I see that you are making the most of your improved financial situation. How much did that embroidery cost you? Were you trying to impress me, perhaps?'

'You see scandal under every stone where I am concerned, Edward. It is unworthy of you since I am now a wife of excellent reputation.' I raised my cup in a little toast, as if already anticipating success. 'This is what I would ask of your kindness and generosity. And your sense of justice.' I smiled winningly over the rim of my cup. 'When are you going to grant the title of Earl of Kent to Thomas?'

It was not an unexpected request. Edward's brows twitched.

'When I decide that he has earned it.'

'You have made him Captain of Calais. Now you have made him custodian of the heir to Brittany and King's Captain. Why not give the title too? It would increase the strength of his arm in your name to be Earl of Kent.'

'You have the title, Joan. That is enough.'

'But it is not enough. It would be most fitting for Thomas to take the title that no other man can lay claim to. My eldest son will inherit it after my death. Why should my husband not enjoy its benefits now? You really are unjust, Edward.'

'I am circumspect.'

Edward was already departing after his cook. Escaping. I raised my voice a little so that it followed him to the door.

'I will not let the matter drop, Edward.'

'I never thought that you would.'

The door closed on his back.

'Sometimes men are impossibly obstinate,' I declared to Philippa.

'Sometimes,' Philippa replied, 'you could try to persuade him rather than beat him about the head.'

'Why?'

'I have found that it works better. Your cousin objects to your trampling on his authority.'

'I do not trample!'

'No?'

I felt a flush rise to my cheeks.

'Persuasion is sweeter than compulsion,' the Queen advised. 'A butterfly rather than a bee.'

I was in no mood to listen. I was no butterfly. I would not admit to Thomas that I had petitioned and failed.

The months, the years, all became a pattern of moves and countermoves, some smooth, some less so, and all underpinned by Thomas's burgeoning reputation as Edward saw fit to bestow office and preferment. We enjoyed the hospitality of the chateau at Vannes when Thomas took up the position of King's Captain with custody of the young fatherless heir to the duchy. Two years later we paid a fast visit to the Channel Isles. Thomas was Keeper, with a mission, helped by his brother Otto to drive the French out of Castle Cornet. Then back to Normandy where we moved into Crocy Castle.

Soon we were on the move again. Thomas grasped the honour of being English Governor of the Harcourt lands in the Cotentin, where we were based in St. Sauveur-le-Vicomte, with custody of the town of Barfleur added in the autumn of the next year. When Thomas was made Edward's Captain and Lieutenant in Normandy and France, it was the greatest of honours, even though I must accept that he would travel further and longer.

We had a young family now, a daughter, Joan, born in the year of 1356 while we were at Vannes, followed by Maud three years later. We lived in some state, which pleased me more than it did Thomas, who was oblivious to the quality of the bed linen or the tapestries that furnished the chambers in which we lived. The exotic spices combined with the culinary exploits of our kitchens that brought distinction to the dishes served to us held little interest to Thomas as long as there was sufficient roast meat to impress our visitors. Life in Yoxall seemed so far away.

The future of our children became important to us, so that we discussed, for some distant time in the future when she was grown, the espousal of Joan to John de Montfort, the young Duke of Brittany, who had proved to be an admirable young man under Thomas's tutelage.

And I? My life was with Thomas, where Thomas was needed, although there was no role for me in the span of his authority.

'Is there nothing I can do?' I asked when I longed to dabble my fingers in the endless negotiations with the lords of Brittany and Normandy.

'I doubt they'll consider a woman's view of any merit or weight.

The office is mine, the royal appointment does not include you, however much you might wish it did.'

It was not a reply I relished. That did not mean that I did not attend the council meetings when I was of a mood to impress these local lords. They must know with whom they dealt. Striking in silks and damasks and family jewels that I had never sold, I played my part, ensuring that it was known that I was Countess of Kent and a Plantagenet princess. Thomas as my lord was a man to be reckoned with.

I was content for the most part. Except when I travelled back to London through a terrible and bleak family necessity, where I discovered that I was not willing to abandon the opportunity to take Edward to task once more.

'When will you allow Thomas to be Earl of Kent?' I asked in passing, without undue deference. My heart wrenched, I was in no mood to be deferential.

'When I see the need.'

My original anger had dissipated over time, but given the present raw place in my heart, I allowed it to fly free. 'I can see no reason why you should not, Edward. His loyalty is superb, and you should reward it. Why will you not be magnanimous?'

But there was no moving him. 'Don't ask again, Joan. You have my compassion at this sad time, but it will not make me change my mind.'

With Edward gone about some important task in which I had no interest because he had inadvertently touched on so personal a hurt, Philippa embraced me, and I allowed it, even though I stood as unyielding as a sack of grain and my cheeks were dry. I had arrived in England escorting a sad little coffin. Our third son, named Edmund for my father, had died after so short a time in this life. I had returned to England to arrange his burial.

'You will always feel the loss, but as time passes it becomes easier.'

Philippa was all compassion, experiencing so many losses in her life, so many of her own young children being taken from her. I could not dwell on it, or respond to her sympathies, which troubled me. I had wept for my brother: why could I not weep for my little son? It was as if the grief had frozen into a knot of ice within my chest, refusing all solace. I paid my last respects with stern observance, paying for Masses for that tiny unfledged soul that I had lost even before I knew it.

After the burial I was relieved to return to Thomas who welcomed me with brisk compassion so different from Philippa's maternal softness.

'You look weary to the bone. Did all go well?'

For a long moment I merely regarded him as he rose from his chair, taking note that he had recently come from some audience, his garments formal, a page clad in blue and silver carrying a banner, now furled. Thomas had learned well how to be visible, how to make an impression on these foreign lords. How assured he was, how poised, every movement governed by an imperturbable view of his work in King Edward's schemes.

'Yes. I am exhausted,' I said. Suddenly, when he smiled at me so that I knew that his sorrow matched mine, was as deep as mine, even without words being spoken between us, there was only one desire within me. 'Take me to bed.'

'I doubt that you have sleep on your mind.'

It was a fierce possession, a worthy homecoming that smoothed away some of the edges.

'And I suppose you asked the King about the title, when you happened by chance to see him?'

'Yes, I did see him. I might have mentioned it.'

'And he said no.'

'In so many words.'

'Leave it alone, Joan. Your stepping in will do no good.'

'My stepping in will remind him that there is no Earl of Kent, and you are the obvious choice. It would be excellent for Tom to see his father as Earl, and to know that one day it will be his.'

We agreed to speak no more about it. His fingers, still rough and calloused although these days he spent as much time in discussion as in fighting, twined in my hair.

'Do you know why I fell in love with you?' Thomas said, catching my interest since he was not one for declarations. 'Apart from being lovely and opinionated and irresistible, you have hair to entice a man into sin.' His fingers tightened a little, to draw me closer. 'Do you ever regret it?' he asked.

'I regret many things,' I replied, hiding my gratification. 'What particularly?'

'You could have been Countess of Salisbury, ensconced in luxury. Instead you have moved from one draughty castle to another. You could have made that choice.'

'To live with Will? I think not.'

'He still admires you. Enough to send you a silver cup last Twelfth Night.'

'He admires me now that I am no longer his wife. And everyone gives me silver cups. How many do we number from Ned over the years? His brother John is following in his footsteps.'

'Enough to furnish all the lords of Normandy when they come to drink my wine and talk about their displeasure over taxation. They particularly like the enamelled ones.'

I laughed a little, my melancholy retreating to no more than a faint ache as I regarded him. 'If I had told you that I wished to remain in the marriage with Will, would you have sanctioned that? Would you have abandoned your case in Avignon?'

Thomas's mouth firmed, twisted in thought.

'Looking back, I don't know. You cost me an unconscionable amount of money and effort.'

'So you did not truly love me enough to fight for me if I proved unwilling?'

'Ah ha! You will never know, my cunning one. Are you satisfied with what we have?'

I thought that I was. What else would I have? I had the title that was mine by right. I had a husband who was noticed when he entered an audience chamber. I had four healthy children, one of them a robust heir for Thomas. We were still young and blessed with good health. It pleased me to hear the distinction of Fair Maid of Kent when I joined Thomas in his discussions even if my role in influencing them was curtailed to wifely exchanges – albeit *opinionated* ones – over a cup of wine or confidences in the marital bed. Age had not dimmed my considerable beauty. What more was there for me?

I allowed my thoughts to drift as we lay in companionable silence, as I gave a passing thought, with some sadness, to Lady Elizabeth Montagu who had finally lost her hold on life. What was it that she had once said to me? *I suspect you have your own games to play.* Lady Elizabeth had had a prescient eye, although I would have not called them games. What would I most want, if I could have it? What would enhance the pattern of my life further?

One word slid into my mind. A seductive word. A dangerous word, perhaps, for a woman.

Power.

I let it lie, savouring it. All very well, but of what manner of power? I had the authority over my own household. I had control over the Kent estates. Was that not more power than most had in a lifetime?

You would desire a hand in affairs at court. You would enjoy the making of policy.

I thought that I would. Philippa was Queen of England but sought no power in her role as consort. If I were in her shoes I would do more. I would stand at Edward's side, whether he liked it or not.

I smiled, turning my face against Thomas's throat.

'What is it?'

'I was wondering what Edward would say if Philippa demanded to be part of his policy-making.'

'I expect he would get another child on her to keep her busily away from matters that are no concern of hers.'

'I expect that he would.'

'I can't see Philippa in that role.'

'Nor can I.'

Nor would it ever be for me. Thomas would never seek further political enhancement, so I must let him be. I had my own royal status, recognition, my family, a husband who had earned a reputation second to none, that Edward would eventually recognise.

'Yes. I am satisfied.'

But I would not let it rest. Thomas would be Earl of Kent. The question was: how would I achieve it?

Chapter Nine

Early January 1361: Palace of Woodstock

The dread day had come. I had anticipated it for so long, through all the years of our marriage. What wife did not, with a husband who lived for long days of dangerous travel and forays into numerous battle-fields? But it was not what I expected when I had clung so tenaciously to the new pattern of my life. I had perhaps grown confident, too confident, assured of the stability of my future, assured that I would live out my days with the man I had wed twenty years before and the children he had given me. And because of my tranquillity, which still had the power to surprise me, when the day came it was stark and brutal and without pity, delivered when I was at Woodstock, where the royal court had repaired for Christmas. The war with France was over and we were clad in festive robes, lengths of green velvet that swept the floor to give the court an ambiance of a summer woodland, our thoughts tuned to minstrels and mummers and to celebration.

But here was despair. Here was the unacceptable.

I read it in his face, a man who stood in the shadows at the edge of the bright, greenery-festooned chamber. I did not know how or why his unspoken word touched me so keenly. I did not need him to speak. Not waiting for him to come to me, I walked towards him, conscious of the soft hush of my trailing skirts, the music of pipe and tabour that seemed to fade into a distance that no longer had any importance for me.

'Where?' I asked him.

He did not question my knowledge.

'In Normandy, my lady. In Rouen.'

It was as if I stood in icy water that was rising, inch by inch, until eventually I would be submerged it it. I forced myself to ask.

'How?'

I recognised him now. He was one of Thomas's own men.

'A great malady, my lady.'

My lips were dry, my throat closed so that I could barely get out the words.

'Did he suffer?'

'No, my lady. It came fast to him. A fever. A sweating sickness. I know not its name. It struck him down three days before the close of the year.'

What had Thomas been doing? I had to imagine it, since there was nothing else for me. I tried to bring the formal audience chambers at Rouen into my mind, where before the turn of the old year Thomas had been given the delicate diplomatic task of carrying out the provisions of the Treaty of Brétigny. I could imagine him presiding over the discussions, the attempts to bring concord after all the years of war and broken truces between England and France. He would be forthright and outspoken, contemptuous of procrastination and flowery terms. He would be strong in precision and a need for speed. His days as King's Captain had given him a forceful turn of phrase when required. I knew that he would be listened to, by men from both sides of the divide, as he would listen to them.

Who would have ever envisioned that the man who had bellowed across the river at the French in a fit of helpless rage should have found such depth of authority, demanding respect from French and English alike? His battle scars were regarded with awe. His experience was admired.

Because the fighting was over, I had lapsed into a false sense of serenity and pride. Beware such falsehood. Peace brought no man safety and long life. Yet Thomas had been, at last – at long last – endowed with the title of Earl, to strengthen his presence at the diplomatic table where he had learned such skills, of patience and calm speaking, of weighing the rights and wrongs of a case, in the presence of the erudite lawyers at Avignon. He had learned the ability to persuade. Edward had seen the gifts he had, and at last rewarded him, his most loyal of knights, in fitting manner. In the end it had taken no badgering from me, nor even sweet persuasion. Finally Thomas had enjoyed the distinction of being Earl of Kent. Perhaps I had appreciated it more than he, but there had been a marvellous dignity in him as he knelt before King Edward to receive the accolade.

I would never forget that moment when Thomas had kissed me and I had rewarded the King with a smile of true gratitude. And now I was rent with desolation, closing my eyes as if I might bring him close into my mind. I could not.

'Where is he?' I asked the reluctant courier who was shuffling before my silence. 'Have you brought him home?'

'No, my lady. He is buried in Rouen.'

'Buried?'

'It was thought best, my lady.'

'But why?'

Who had taken it upon himself to order this? I would never look on his face again. I could not accept that he was already sealed in his tomb, and I not be aware of it or present to witness it.

'It was not my doing, my lady. My lord the Earl was buried with all honour in the cathedral. There was no disrespect.'

'Disrespect!'

The courier had taken a step back, which warned me of the effect of my ire which would achieve nothing. Or perhaps it was my appearance that unsettled him. I thought about this, taking off the mask that I still wore, crushing its golden strings, realising how ridiculous I must have looked receiving such desperate news behind the calm, silvered visage of an angel. I had not even noticed that my voice echoed with emptiness behind the moulded buckram. What had the courier thought of me? But I did not care. My mind seemed to be taken up with trivialities which the terrible news could not pierce. Thomas did not appreciate court games. He preferred the reality of battle. Perhaps he would have enjoyed court life more as old age touched him. Now it never would.

He would have been forty-six years old in this new year of 1361.

I tried to recall the last time I had seen him before bringing the children home to England. It was expected that Thomas would follow soon, when the signatures on the Treaty of Brétigny were dry. I had left him to complete the business alone.

Had I kissed him? Had we confirmed our love together in intimate embrace? I was sure that we had, but I had no sense of it. Perhaps we had merely parted with the brisk farewell engendered by a relationship of long standing, I preoccupied with organising travel with four young children, Thomas summoned by some demanding baron.

How I wish that I had known. But that was not how it happened in life. Death came hard and fast and without warning.

I breathed in, casting the mask from me, where, as it fell at my feet, it was pounced on by a small child, perhaps one of my own. All my thoughts with Thomas, I did not even notice. Yet in that moment it baffled me that I had had no sense of impending loss. How could I with the children noisy around me, but no more boisterous than the courtiers indulging in masked flirtations. But here was the Queen approaching. What had she read in my face now that my mask was removed. What had she seen in the set of my shoulders to bring her to my side?

One thought came clear into my mind as if written in gold, one event that I must set under way. We had been apart for so many years in our marriage. We would not be apart in his death. I must do it before the Queen came to fuss and set free my loss in disproportionate emotion. Now was not the time for uncontrolled outbursts.

My breath caught on what would have been an inappropriate laugh. I had never felt further from tears as I did with the destruction of my life writ large in the words and in the face of the courier. I had been waiting for Thomas to come home. I had been longing to see him again. But not like this.

I addressed the courier with stern orders. 'I wish you to return to Rouen tonight. I wish my husband's body to be disinterred from wherever it rests, however magnificent it might be. I desire his body to be returned to England, with all due honour and respect. He will be buried here in England. I wish you to arrange that for me. I will give you appropriate moneys before you go, and I will meet you when you bring the Earl's body back to England.'

He blinked. I thought it was in his mind to tell me of all the difficulties.

'It is my wish, and my wish is paramount.'

'Yes, my lady.'

He had not expected it. Strangely it pleased me to do something that many might think outrageous. I would have Thomas buried where he would wish. It would not be in Rouen.

'I will furnish you with an escort. I wish it all to be accomplished with grace and dignity, a soldier's entourage and befitting the Earl of Kent. There will be no expense spared.'

How little time he had enjoyed the title. I would ensure that it was acknowledged at his death.

'Yes, my lady. I will see that it is done.' Then as he bowed, and turned, he stopped to open the scrip at his belt and remove a small item that fit in his hand so that I could not see it. 'I have been instructed to give you this, my lady. It was found in the Earl's possessions. We thought that you might wish it to come to you rather than be buried with him.'

He placed it in my hand, bowed, and departed to fulfil my demands.

And I?

I opened my fingers to disclose the silk band, discoloured now through age and use, that Thomas had worn to proclaim his dedication to his cause of England and England's King. It shocked me that something so personal should be returned to me. Enclosing it within my fingers again, I hoped for some essence of him, but there was none.

And there at last, when my power to order my thoughts and my actions was fast waning, was Philippa, her hand on my shoulder, knowing what had happened.

'Come with me. You need solitude for grief.'

I had no grief. This rock lodged in my chest did not allow for grief.

I looked around the festive court, which Thomas would never see again, the declaration of victory after the successful culmination of the French wars. Edward resplendent in a coat of black satin, embroidered in gold and silver thread, a magnificent woodbine enhancing the whole, twining round a support. A recognition of his love and loyalty for the staid woman at my side. How I envied her. There would be no more twining for me.

You did not twine anyway!

I might have done.

Philippa touched my hand with such love and compassion in her face, and I realised that I had not yet spoken to her. I could not. What could I say that would heal this wound that had created a hole where my heart had been.

Solitude?

Yes, I did need solitude, but the grief was far from me. Rather I would curse and rail at what fate had stripped from me. I still could not grasp the sense that he had gone.

It struck my mind that the Queen looked strained, almost anxious. Her fingers wound again and again through the beads of her rosary as if she had some greater worry that compromised her own peace of mind. I put it out of my thoughts. I could not think of her. Later, when I was mistress of my emotions once more, but not now.

I met the body of my husband at Dover and travelled beside the coffin to Stamford. It was in that long cold journey in those final days of January where at last it was brought home to me that it was Thomas's earthly remains that I accompanied, covered with a cloth bearing his own Holland heraldry because that is what he would have wanted. The silver lion proudly rampant against its blue background powdered with lilies. The emblems of the Earl of Kent were too new to do justice to this final journey.

Again my mind took flight from such a grim loss. Instead I forced it to concentrate on what I must arrange. Mourning would be put off until all was done to my satisfaction.

Why Stamford?

Where else? Thomas had no loyalties to any other place. It was a church well-loved by his Holland family and Thomas, in his heart, was never one for magnificence and splendour. There in a chapel adjoining the Greyfriars church, he was laid to rest beneath a plain slab which did no justice to his adventurous life. I watched as the deed was done. I would build a sumptuous chapel there to contain and embellish his tomb, whether he would approve or not. A finer memorial would be created than this plain script. He would be well remembered by all who stopped to read.

I shed not one tear. As the cold hemmed me in I considered how unfeeling, how indifferent, I must appear, if any man was interested enough to note. I had wept at John's death, soaking Thomas's tunic, yet Thomas went to his grave with no weeping from his wife.

Later. Later I would weep when I acknowledged that my world had lost its keystone. I stood, stern-faced, a hand on the shoulders of my two sons who were as silent as I, intimidated by the incense-laden solemnity and a morose King Edward. For at the last, my cousin the King had travelled north to mark the Earl of Kent's passing, standing beside me beneath the grim northern stonework, draughts freezing our feet, his garments adding a touch of royal splendour to the dour occasion. I wondered why he had come.

'Thank you, Edward,' I said. 'My lord the Earl would be honoured.'

I did not feel like praising him overmuch. Thomas had borne the title for a mere three months. Edward eased his weight from one foot to the other under my displeasure, which was no less cold than the stone paving.

'He will always be Holland to me, charging across the field at Crécy,' he said, voice thickening with emotion as the clergy began to disperse. 'The silver lion shining fiercely, always in the thick of the fray. He was one of the most valiant of my knights. We had our differences, of course.'

'It took a long time for you to get over them.' I was not of a mind to forgive Edward.

'I regret his passing. Mortality touches us all.'

An uncomfortable silence that I would not break.

'He made you a fine husband, Joan.'

'I never thought to hear you admit that!' Oh, I was unforgiving of past intolerance.

'I don't wish us to be at odds over this. I doubt Thomas would have wanted it.'

'You should have allowed him the title long before this.'

'You cared about it far more than he did.'

'But it would have been a sign of royal approval. In the cut and thrust of holding together your lands in Normandy it would have been inestimable.'

'Well, I did it, didn't I?' Edward was gruff. I was not won over.

Before I left Stamford, I left money to employ three priests to pray for Thomas in never-ending petition for the progress of his immortal soul. He would need their intercession. A sword would be of no use to him now, but I would ensure that the image on his tomb included a fine example, as well as his armour. There would be no doubt that here lay a knight of renown.

I could not believe that he had left me again.

This time it had not been his choice, and I had no power to stop him.

At the last I had the silk band placed in Thomas's coffin, folded neatly against his heart that no longer beat. It seemed to be the best gesture I could make. I had always understood his dedication even though it had taken him away from me.

Spring 1361

'One day, Joan, you will wed again,' my cousin the King had observed when he escorted me south from Stamford.

'I have no thought of doing so,' I had replied.

I had thought him being ruggedly compassionate, taking my mind from my loss, encouraging me to look ahead to my future life and that of my children.

'It will be good policy,' he had added with callous unconcern, 'for me as well as for you.'

Upon which pronouncement I saw the truth.

When none of the Lenten fair tempted me, this one indisputable fact gave me food for thought; too much food, and little of it pleasant. Much like a surfeit of salted fish, indigestible after the first mouthful.

Returned to Woodstock, because I was not moved to go elsewhere and where I had left my two girls under the Queen's care, I viewed my situation, as if it were a painted image, vivid and detailed, from Philippa's Book of Hours. This is what I saw.

Myself, buffed and polished like a damascened blade, the most valuable of widows.

Of course Edward would see my value, as would many others with an eye to their own ambitions. I was a widow, an influential and undeniably wealthy widow, titled in my own right. My Plantagenet blood in itself was of inestimable value to an ambitious lord. I was thirty-two years old, with proven fertility, and not yet beyond child-bearing years. I had the ear of my cousin the King. Occasionally. And certainly of his wife, the Queen. I had four healthy children, two promising sons to uphold the name of Holland, two daughters to be wed into the aristocratic families of England or Europe.

I was, therefore, a woman of some consequence, an object of desire like a fine jewel without flaw, set in a mount of pure gold.

I inspected my reflection in my mirror. The ivory surround had become worn over the years but the face that looked back at me was little changed. If anything the years had given my features more clarity, more strength. My hair, now in seemly order beneath my mourning veil, was untouched by time. I was still the Fair Maid of my early years.

I put the mirror away.

There should be much to please me here, but there were also, growing strongly through the hard carapace of my daily existence, the seeds of future uncertainty. The path of my life would take an unforeseen direction. I might be a widow of a bare three months, but it had been made known to me that there was already a handful of men close to the King, or who would desire to be so, men who were widowed or unwed, who would seek me out.

I was not so naive that I could not expect this.

So there would be offers for my hand. I had already seen the specu-lative gleam in Edward's eye after we buried Thomas in Stamford. Why wait? he was thinking. I could see it in his mind as he escorted me back to Woodstock. Here is the perfect wife – if one could ignore the taint of past scandals and a wilful disposition behind the beautiful exterior – to tie some influential man to the English throne, or reward a good friend for services rendered. Who will be the fortunate man?

Edward had been generous in his care of me on that journey, considerate of my sadness; I had been forgiven; I was his dear cousin again. Now that I was aware of the tenor of his thoughts I could feel him assessing my worth as a bride on every occasion that our paths crossed. Perhaps a bride to be sent beyond the sea. He might see it as an advantage to remove an uncomfortable presence and make a strong alliance at one and the same time. My new husband, whoever he might be, would not have to wait long to attain the honour of my title, of that I was certain. He would not have to wait well–nigh eight years, as Thomas had. My title and my wealth would be just another jewel to dangle before a mighty foreign lord.

So I must remarry.

Ah, but would I be allowed my own free choice, or indeed any influence at all, in Edward's choice of ally?

More unpalatable food for thought to land on my platter.

Edward would want his own way in this, but, I decided, I would fight against his royal command if that choice proved disagreeable to me. I could fight not to wed at all. Had not my mother remained unwed through all the years after my father's death? Had she ever been sought as a wife, and refused? I did not know.

Yet did I wish to remain isolated, unwed for the rest of my life, a *femme sole*, a nun in everything but life behind walls and locked doors? I had had quite enough of that experience, brief as it had been, at Bisham. There were advantages to having a powerful husband, for a woman who might interest herself in the world beyond her solar. I had ambitions. I had always had ambitions, and I would have them again. But now I was desolate, ground down by what must be a grief I could not express, one that kept me company from sunrise to sunset as well as through the dark hours. Yet I hid it well at court where it was easy to fill the moments of time with the habitual cycle of attendance on the Queen, a daily appearance at Mass, the donning of a fair face for any audience when my presence was demanded and I could make no excuse. I did all this with unyielding demeanour, rejecting any pity, hiding my melancholy until I was behind the closed door of my own chamber, my women banished. Even there, empty of all emotions, tears did not come.

So I sat, spinning out my future like a spider in its web, but my spinning collapsed into a heap of unconnected strands. I could not see my future. My dreams and hopes, once so well structured, were formless.

Attending the Queen with her painted damsels in the hour after Mass, when petitions for her favour were brought and presented by hopeful subjects, in a moment of vulnerability I once more surreptitiously surveyed my face in my looking glass. Perhaps my cheeks were more hollow that usual, my eyes less bright, my lips close knit, but there was no reflection here of the wretchedness that ate at me, only the boredom that yet another request for a favourable trade in sable fur from the lands to the east might engender. There must be more for me to grasp from life than this.

'Your looks will soon return, Madam Joan.'

One of Philippa's damsels come to stand at my side, an impertinent young woman who was not as sympathetic as her soft words might imply, although she was never less than courteous. I had no time for her.

'I expect that they will.'

'Grief does that to a woman. Drains her of beauty, my lady.'

'So I am told. How fortunate then that I have enough beauty and more to withstand such draining.'

'Whereas I have none at all to drain, so they say.' This made me give her more attention. How confident she was, her dark eyes direct, challenging even. 'As a woman grows older it is more difficult for her to keep her looks. And how easy it is for a woman's intentions to be misjudged and laid bare to crude invective. That too, I believe, can engrave hard lines on a woman's face. Unless she is strong enough to reject all criticism of her behaviour.'

Which made me stare at her. What was this damsel's meaning in so enigmatic an appraisal. Was it a criticism of me? Yet tucking the glass away into my sleeve, my mood less than combative, I would not respond. I was too weary.

'I will remember that when age touches me. How kind of you to give me the benefit of your experience, mistress.'

She curtsied. 'I meant no disrespect, my lady. I spoke only from my knowledge of life. Although I accept that it is unnecessary, for your knowledge of such matters is far greater than mine.'

Leaving me to pick apart her response. She was younger than I, and no, she had little beauty. What she had was a strange glamour in her dark hair and dark eyes, her bold smile, her even bolder advice, if that is what it was. Was it jealousy that had laid its unlikely hand on me? Envy of her striking confidence that she would approach me in a manner that was not altogether deferential. I was left alone, which I had intended, but I knew that I had been sharper than I ought to be. I had few friends but this damsel was not one to whom I would give my confidences. This damsel might not be beyond using them to further her own desires.

But here was Philippa come to rescue me, as she had so often in the past.

'You will feel better when the sun shines again, Joan, and we can celebrate at Easter.'

Philippa, missing little, chided gently as the petitioners departed with their promises of royal favour and an agreement to purchase yet more sables. Despite her good intentions, I doubted that I would ever feel better.

'All grief will pass,' she continued, choosing to walk beside me. 'Edward will hold his Garter festivities, and we will see once more his brave knights impressing us with their polished skills, yet still allowing Edward to emerge the victor because they know they must. We will cheer them on, as we always do...' Her words stopped short. The smile of gentle anticipation faded from her lips. 'I should not have said that.'

I tried to smile.

'I cannot expect you never to mention Thomas again. Yes, he would have been there in his Garter robes, and in the tournament. And yes, he would have had the sense to allow Edward to deliver the winning stroke. Others will take his place. Within a decade he will hardly be remembered.'

I was surprised at the harshness of my tone.

'I am so sorry.' She leaned to touch my arm.

'So am I. I do not wish to speak of it.'

'But you must,' Philippa persisted. 'All I see is a hard control.

Your face, your voice, even your posture. You are allowed to weep for him, Joan.'

Yes, Philippa with her soft heart would have wept, but I drew back, turning my face from the interested royal damsels who were quick to gossip and quicker to revel in the misery of others. For in that bright picture created by Philippa's careless words, Thomas's death became real in my heart as it had never been, not even when I stood beside his tomb to witness his body being laid there, promising to create a tomb worthy of him. Thomas would never again fight in a Garter tournament.

With a murmured apology I left the room. I would never weep in public, nor would I allow melancholy to hover like a black cloud. Instead I would hide my misery behind a competent mask. I would not reject company, but would shrug off the malice, denying any hurt. My marriage complications had made me an easy target for the damsels' lightly winged arrows of spite, but I would deflect them with a skilful, if not always pleasant, turn of phrase. As long as I was not over-burdened with compassion I would do very well, and did so until, at the end of the day when Philippa would, in the seclusion of her chamber, have handed me her comb, instead drew me into an embrace, which I thought was for her benefit rather than my comfort. Still I was selfish, my thoughts inward looking.

'What will happen to me now?' I asked, muffled against the broadness of her shoulder, my debilitating fear of the unknown once more firming its grip.

'You have your children.'

Philippa would like nothing better than to spend her days between the disparate needs of her children, even those now full grown. For me there would not be enough to occupy my mind, nor were my sons and daughters of an age to need more than nursemaids and governors.

'And you are so beautiful.' Releasing me, she gave me the comb so that I might begin to loosen her hair from its pleatings and cunningly engraved metal restraints. 'I sometimes think that... .'

I waited. And when her gaze remained on the far distance, I prompted, 'What do you think?' Philippa had worries on her brow, which did not dissipate as I applied the comb with a gentle hand. 'Are you in pain?'

A fall from her horse two years ago when out hunting with Edward had wrenched her shoulder, which had not healed well. Sometimes her discomfort was considerable.

But Philippa shook her head. 'No. Only of the heart. Forgive the megrims of an ageing woman.'

I did not believe her. 'What do you think, dear lady?' I repeated.

She stilled my hand as if she could not bear my touch, but then allowed me to continue with a sad attempt at a smile as she said:

'That life is easier when you are as ugly as I. An unattractive woman is rarely the subject of envy or malicious rumour. You should know the truth in that. I hear what my damsels say, and so must you.'

Which was not what touched her with such hurt, but I allowed her to turn the conversation as she chose. Her homely features were heavy with a grave sadness. No she was not comely, not even handsome, but the strength of her will was formidable, her spirit a thing of beauty.

'But you are not...'

She raised her hand again to still the comb as I worked it through her thinning hair. 'I am no beauty. You can't gainsay it, Joan. But I know that Edward loves me.' She frowned a little, looking in her mirror much as I had done. 'He has always loved me. For myself.' She looked up at me, as if for reassurance.

Which I gave, from my heart. Here was the one woman I had truly loved. The only woman.

'Of course Edward loves you. Do you doubt it? He sees the beauty, both within you and without. What use is a woman with a fair face if she has no beauty in her soul? Edward sees it in you, and loves you for it. In all his years as King, he has never loved anyone else.' I smiled a little. 'Thomas loved me. My soul is not as beautiful as yours, nor ever will be. I am too selfish. But Thomas saw something in me to love.'

'He fought hard enough to get you back.' Philippa lifted her head and allowed me to continue with my appointed task. 'But his life was enclosed in separate coffers from yours. Did Thomas love you more than he loved soldiering?'

A question that surprised me, and one I could not answer.

'All I know is that he said he loved me,' was the best I could do. 'He came back to me after a campaign. Eventually.'

'Did you love him?' Philippa asked.

Another surprise. 'Yes.'

'Did you love him more than you loved getting your own way?'

I felt my brows flatten. Now this one I did not dare answer. There was more truth in it than I liked, although I would never deny my devotion to Thomas.

'I am not questioning what you had together,' Philippa explained, perhaps seeing the tightening of the muscles in my jaw. 'I am just a little morbid with the swift passage of years. You will be happy again. I know it.'

'I expect that I will.' Unsettled under this pertinent questioning, I continued with long sweeping strokes, until she took the comb from me.

'You have a heavy hand tonight.'

'Matched by a heavy heart,' I apologised with an attempt at wry humour. Philippa needed cheering more than I. 'I expect Edward has some plan for me.'

'If he has, he has not told me of it. I doubt that he will give you to someone whom you will dislike. He discovered the perils of that with our daughter Isabella. We need no more scandals of a matrimonial nature. But one thing I would say, if you will listen.' She closed her fingers around my wrist so that I must perforce listen to her advice, her expression serious as if reprimanding one of her children. 'You need to make reparation to your royal blood. You need to remake your reputation. Oh, Joan, my dear girl. You must see that it has suffered a grievous blow, despite His Holiness giving his judgement to make all smooth. It can be done. It must be done. Your future husband does not need to think that he has been offered a bad bargain.'

Which was as much a slap to my hand that the Queen had ever dealt me.

'Do you not realise why Edward travelled all the way to Stamford to stand at your side when Thomas was buried?' She waited for my glance of surprise. 'Oh, it had a purpose. To show the world that he supported you and the marriage you ultimately claimed. It was to cover any remaining comment on your indiscretion with royal approval. To silence the malicious tongues that claim a life of their own. There have been many. There still are. I fear that there always will be those who will point to your poor judgement in agreeing to wed Thomas Holland.'

I recalled the arch comments from Philippa's damsel. Edward had not silenced the gossips with any great degree of success, it seemed.

'But I loved him,' I said simply.

'I know. It was unfortunate. But that is all past, and you must look to the future. Any great magnate,' Philippa's advice continued to roll over me, 'who considers your value as a wife will know that you have been restored to the royal fold and that the King beams on you as much as His Holiness has done. It is vastly important.'

'He did not tell me,' I said.

'Well, he wouldn't, would he? And I suppose that all you could do was harangue him for not creating Thomas Earl of Kent when the title came to you.'

I felt colour rise in my face, which was an admission in itself.

'Now you must do all in your power to build on that royal approval that the King your cousin has offered you. Promise me that you will.'

'I promise.' What more could I say as I acknowledged Edward's generosity? 'I will be the perfect widow. I will be the perfect wife when the day comes.'

'And Edward, I assure you, will find you a husband who will not be unattractive to you.'

'I promise that I will welcome him.'

Easy words. Easy promises.

We parted on a good understanding even though I considered Philippa to be too sanguine. I thought that within the year I would be living out my life in some far distant place with a man for whom I had little tolerance. And then I wondered, far too briefly to my later shame, what it was that troubled her. What was it that afflicted her heart that she could not bear to tell me?

Chapter Ten

Spring 1361: Castle Donington

I was engaged in an exchange of views with my steward after an investigation of our storeroom, depleted in basic supplies over the winter, principally because our household had spent so little time there at Castle Donington. I was not pleased with the situation, nor with my negligent steward.

'How can we be so lacking in ale? Why is there, as far as I can see, only one cured ham in the cellar? There should be half a dozen by your records.'

'I will look into it my lady.'

'And so shall I! And then I will invite you to accompany me to the lower cellar where I hope that I do not discover…'

Memories flooded back, with all the agony of a sword thrust, of Thomas in the cellar at Bisham when I had hunted him down, unfastening the silk band, acknowledging our love. So painful that I turned away from the steward, walking to the door to draw in breaths of air as if that would dispel that sudden vision.

It was there that my chamberlain discovered me.

'Visitors, my lady. A sizeable escort. Can't yet make out their device.'

Relieved to abandon the sudden, shocking, smack of sorrow, with a final lingering glance to my steward to remind him that I would not forget our task, I climbed to the wall walk to look out towards the east where the sun was struggling to break through heavy cloud. I was expecting no one. Irritated, I realised that I was dressed to receive no one, nor was I of an inclination. My melancholy had not lifted. I was tempted to keep my gates closed, but Philippa's advice remained a constant burr against my skin. To repulse visitors was not what a generous and bountiful princess was expected to do. I must remember to be more bountiful to my slippery steward too.

I smote the hard coping with my fist as I considered whether to change my gown.

And then the sun broke through.

My eyes were dazzled by the gold stitching and ostentatious cloth of gold wadding on pennon and flag. And on the tabard of the royal herald who rode next to the man in the lead. As for him, it sparkled on the chased studs of his brigandine, on the hilt of his sword. I could well imagine the jewels in his livery collar and set deep into his belt. A King's ransom, worn without fear of chance robbers.

'It's the Prince, my lady.'

'So I see.'

The light brightened; so did the approaching image.

For a single moment my breath held in my lungs. And then I breathed out again. This was only the creation of the extraordinary light, which would immediately be dimmed if viewed through darkened glass. And yet I felt the prickle of perspiration along my hairline. He had probably come to see the progress of his godsons, rather than me, to assess if they were pursuing their military lessons.

Ned had stood godfather to both Tom and John, which would give him an interest.

The glitter made me shield my eyes.

The darkened glass, I decided, would have been an excellent idea.

'Do I open the gates, my lady?'

'Of course. No need to ask.' Lost in that brilliant moment, I had given no orders. 'The Prince would camp outside, demand to know why we did not and threaten a siege if we did not comply.'

But I would not change my gown or my coif, begrimed as that of any kitchen maid. There was no need to impress.

By the time I had made my way to the courtyard, the royal guest had ridden in, the gilding and glitter even more all-powerful at close quarters, the silver ostrich feathers appliquéd on his breast, that very personal emblem that he had adopted after the Battle of Crécy, to honour the brave death of blind King John of Bohemia so rumour had it, glimmered balefully. He dismounted, handed his hat and gloves to a page, pushed his hands through his matted hair to ruffle the whole and only then walked over to where I had chosen to stand on the second step where my eye would be on a level with his. He bowed. He extended his hand, and when I placed mine there, he kissed my fingers.

'My lady.'

'My lord.'

'I trust you are well.'

'As you see. Is this a courtesy visit or one with a purpose?'

'It is a duty visit, since you are my cousin. And, moreover, I was passing your door, my lady.'

At which point I had had enough. 'We are very formal today. And unnervingly polite. What do you want?'

He grinned. 'I can soon amend that. Can you offer a cup of ale to a weary traveller, Joan?'

'And to the rest.' I nodded to my apologetic steward who was attending at my shoulder. It was no difficulty to be welcoming to the Prince after all. I discovered I had lacked conversation in recent days. I would welcome even his acerbic comments.

Ned's grin transformed into a sly smile. 'You must be bored. You almost look pleased to see me.'

'I am always pleased to enjoy your company, Ned. As you are well aware.'

Of course he was. Ned's confidence was a bright comet in the heavens.

Gently, making nothing of it, I released my hand from his. Ned had been a constant in my life, a friend, an annoying companion, even though in recent years I had seen less of him in my journeying to Brittany. Now it was as if he was still bathed in light, an impressive knight, a royal son, a King in the making, his name the most famous in all of Europe, whereas I was a widow clad in black, as dull as a winter crow while he gleamed in gold and jewels. I noted with some amusement that his hair had fallen into its habitual well-cut lines against his neck, something Thomas had never managed to achieve. Something Thomas had never cared about.

Preserving an unsmiling visage until Ned's brilliance slowly dissipated, I decided that I must be lonely to have been so impressed. I was past the age of hero-worship for a boy I had known from his cradle. It was only Ned. This strange unsettling had been nothing but a trick of the light, a mummer's sleight of hand born of my own isolation and restlessness.

'Joan? Are you going to invite me further than your chilly court-yard?'

I was staring at him. He was regarding me quizzically. 'Forgive me.'

'You are obviously short on company.'

'Which I had just decided. Conversations with Tom and John tend to be brief and admonishing.' Now I smiled slowly, feeling suddenly lighter in sprit, with a warmth that spread beneath my girdle. 'They will be pleased to see you. They will pester you to engage them in some form of hearty weapon-play, but you must watch John, who's inclined to be sly. First you can pander to their mother and indulge her with news of what's happening at court.'

He climbed the steps until he stood beside me, looking down at me with what could only be a frown.

'So why have you shut yourself away here? I swear you were made for court life. Here you look like a good-wife, counting her barrels of ale.'

'And finding them lacking. Along with the hams.'

At least he had not commented on my black raiment, which I knew leached colour from my skin. He plucked at the edge of my sleeve that was plain and held the suspicion of dust while I was leading him into the hall, and through into one of the smaller chambers where it was good to sit, the sun's rays augmenting the heat from a small fire.

'Apart from that,' I added, 'I am following your mother's advice. I have become a new woman.'

'Have you now? Do I detect a spirit of resentment?'

'Certainly not.'

He accepted the ale, which I poured, and a chair where he lounged at ease, and drank.

'Why are you here?' I asked, choosing a low tapestry-cushioned stool, a little distant from his glory. 'What's happening that I should know about?'

'Nothing of any great moment.'

'No war, then, on your particular horizon?'

'Nor any likelihood. I must turn my hand to matters of taxation and appeasing the upholders of local justice. The justices of the peace are demanding more powers to bring transgressors to account. My father is in agreement, so it will happen except for serious cases that will remain the preserve of the royal assize courts. In the new year my father expects me to attend a meeting of parliament with him.'

His voice had become clipped and dry, in a manner that suddenly enlightened me, so that, as if a candle sconce had been lit, I understood the black cloud that sometimes seemed to hover over him. Peace did not suit Ned. Justice and taxes did not compare favourably with wielding a sword on the battlefield. Negotiating with a hostile parliament that increasingly held the purse strings was far more lethal to his spirits than engaging a French army.

'We are still kind hosts to King John of France,' he added. 'The amount of his ransom remains a matter of intense debate. And that's about all I can tell you.'

Ned was morose. I did not know what to say to him, except: 'Well, Ned, it is good to talk of matters other than the shortcomings of my household. I would enjoy exchanging opinion with the King of France rather than detecting the discrepancies in my accounts. Shall we exchange roles? What you have still not told me is why you have come here. And don't say it was on your way, for I know full well that it was not, wherever your journeying was taking you.'

'Isabella told me that you were – melancholy – I think was her word. I said you were probably just petulant.'

'Isabella is blinkered.' I did not wish to be considered melancholy. 'Your flighty sister can see nothing but that flamboyant Frenchman. Whom I would not trust, I might say. He has an eye to her hand in marriage.'

Brought to England as a French prisoner not a year ago, Lord Enguerrand de Coucy had become a shining light in Isabella's eyes. And she it seemed in his. They shadowed each other, Isabella singing songs of love and desire, which Lord Enguerrand returned in a remarkably fine voice.

'And he might get it. My father is fast running out of options that Isabella will even discuss. After the last debacle, he is stepping carefully. Isabella's French suitor is not the man the King would have chosen but Isabella is no longer a young bride.'

'Perhaps he will go back to France with King John and solve all your problems.' A little silence shivered over the tapestries. 'Your father is also planning my next marriage.' The observation escaped before I could stop it.

Ned raised his cup in a grave toast. 'Ah ha. So that's why you took refuge here. But not yet surely. Thomas is barely in his grave.'

'His second grave.' I sipped meditatively. It was time I went back to Stamford to see how the stone masons were progressing to fulfil my expensive directions. Would not that show me to be a virtuous wife? Or widow.

'Do you wish to wed again?'

I looked up, catching another frown on his face. What a strangely desultory conversation this was turning out to be, from which I could get no sense of direction. Unusual for Ned who was inclined to drive headlong for the main point. Still, I addressed the query with honesty.

'I would not be averse to running a nobleman's household. I have discovered a talent for it. I would enjoy a man with a political interest, with an importance. Meanwhile I promised your mother that I would re-gild my image. I would dredge my reputation from the mud at the bottom of the matrimonial pond and thus become virtuous and seemly in all my future actions.'

'It will take much dredging.' Ned settled back, stretching out his legs, crossing his ankles so that the leather of his boots creaked comfortably. As if he were relaxed. And yet I felt that he was not. There was a tension about his posture and his eyes were narrowed and, I thought, even judgemental. 'Before God, Jeanette, you have managed an adventurous life. The chroniclers are keen enough to write about you when there is no one else on whom to sharpen their quills. They are waiting to see which unfortunate man your eye will land on next.'

Which hurt far more than Philippa's gentle criticisms.

'Well, let them wait. It may be that I will not wed again. I may prefer my own authority over my own lands. I can think of no unwed lord who is not over eighty years and past the age of considering marriage, or under ten and more interested in his hounds and his hero in the joust. There may be some I have missed in between, but I am aware of no one who might appear in my dreams as my perfect knight.'

'Was Thomas your perfect knight?'

'Thomas was too belligerent on occasion to be perfect, and too absent on others. But he was nearer than most.' I forgot about the tension that had seemed to be building in the room as I asked something that had crossed my mind, on occasion over the years. 'Why are *you* still not wed?'

He yawned. Too casually, so that I realised that he was wary of my probing. 'Not through want of planning. I'm too busy to take a wife.'

'When has your being busy ever made a difference to anything you wished for?' My frown matched him. 'One day you will be King. You need an heir. Your father will insist on your begetting an heir. Is it not a priority for you? Show me a man who doesn't want a son and heir in his sights? Mistress Willesford might allow you to scratch an itch but something permanent and legal is essential before you become too old. An illegitimate son is no benefit to the realm.'

Ned had a son of almost eleven years old, the result of a well-publicised liaison with Mistress Edith Willesford, a woman of the household of the royal palace at Clarendon. When I had been embarking on my protracted married life with Thomas, Ned had been otherwise occupied.

'Old?' His eyes widened, homing in on the most pertinent point. 'You are older than I.'

'And I have two sons to inherit this place.' As I waved my hand to take in the sumptuous furnishings, embellished with my income as Countess of Kent, the door opened softly, slowly, and in came Maud, sliding unsteadily round the door, beaming when she saw Ned.

'Where is your nurse?' I asked, stretching out my hand.

'I have run away.' She came to stand at my side and leaned against my leg while I tucked her escaping hair into her coif.

'Which one is this?' Ned asked.

'This is Maud. Named for Thomas's mother.'

It had to be said that he had more interest in my sons than my daughters.

She curtsied with deft precision, before disappearing again at a run when voices were raised outside the chamber.

'Thomas was justifiably proud of them. As I will be one day of my own.' Ned reached to lift the flagon and refill his cup. 'My father has four more sons who will be quite capable of giving him his heirs for England. There is no hurry for me to wed.'

I thought about this, about the pressures on inheritance for all powerful families. For once I put myself into the shoes of my cousin Edward. His own inheritance in the days of Mortimer's dominance had been anything but easy. Now he had created a strong family, a strong country. I was certain that Edward was less sanguine about Ned's unmarried state than this son who lounged in my chamber, sipping my ale. One illegitimate son of eleven years was of no value to the King of England. What's more I was certain that Edward had plans for his son. Why had they never come to fruition? There was every urgency as far as I could see.

I voiced my misgivings about there being no hurry.

'But you are his heir, his beloved first-born son who should wear the crown and wield the sceptre,' I said. 'Every time you ride into battle you put yourself in danger of your life. Why has no marriage been contracted? You were to be betrothed to the King of France's daughter when you were one year old. I don't understand why you have been allowed to reach the age of thirty without a wife at your side and half a dozen sons in your nursery at Kennington.'

'You are behind the times,' Ned replied. 'I was promised to Margaret of Brabant when I was nine.'

'I know.'

'And a daughter of the King of Portugal was being mooted when I last heard.'

'Then take her before she is snapped up by another.'

His shrug was all pride. 'When I offer, I will not be refused.'

'Have you met her?'

'Yes.'

'Is she handsome?'

'Not as handsome as you.'

'Flattery, Ned! And empty flattery at that. As long as she is young and well connected and, hopefully, fertile, she will be the perfect bride. You will be very happy together. And so will your father be relieved.'

The sound of Maud's high-pitched voice reached us, from where she had obviously escaped into the courtyard. Ned rose and walked to the window to look down, laughing at what he saw below, which encouraged me to join him. There was Maud, seated on the edge of an ornamental pool, stretching to reach the bright carp, a danger to herself and the fish.

'John!' I called down, seeing help at hand. My younger son, about to disappear into the stables, looked up.

'Take Maud back to the nursery.'

I could see his scowl at a distance but he captured Maud and led her, protesting loudly, back through the door.

'I don't want to!'

Her final words, fading into the distance.

'Perhaps I'll wait for your daughter to grow up.'

'My girls are far too young to consider any marriage for many years. And I already have plans for them.' Ned was leaning against the stonework, looking across the chamber at me as I walked away to retake my stool. There was something on his mind, something gnawing at him, but I replied lightly enough. 'My daughters' marriages, when the day comes, will be without stain. Whiter than snow.'

Slowly Ned recovered the distance between us, his expression was sombre. Once again he sat, fingers laced behind his head.

'What now?' I asked as I reached for the flagon to fill the little hiatus, to pour him more ale if that is what he wished.

Ned's hands dropped as he leaned forward. My hand stilled on the chased flagon.

'Marry me, Jeanette.'

I was not sure when I stopped smiling. I was not smiling now as I withdrew my hand from the vessel, as my hand fell to my lap. This was a travelling jester's joke. Surely this was a mummer's facade. I studied his face, but there were no grooves of amusement, no gentle malice at my expense. His eyes held mine, his mouth held an uncompromising line, while I felt that every thought in my head was suspended, like eels caught in a dish of aspic.

'I'm sorry...?' It was a query.

'Marry me, Joan,' he repeated.

I shook my head, the tiniest movement, in disbelief.

'Well, that's a miracle in itself. Countess Joan without a word to say.' His face was now fixed in lines of authority. 'Wed me Joan. Be my wife and we will give my father his heirs for the future of England. Marry me. Today. Tomorrow.'

I rose to my feet. It was as if a winter gale had blown through the chamber, ridding it of all the previous tensions, scouring the uncertainties, cleansing the air between us so that it rang as if with a sharp frost. Was this why he had come to see me? Or was this a spur of the moment decision? Whatever it was, it had been issued more like a royal command than a request to a much desired lover, which I had never been to him, or he to me.

I knew that I was staring at him.

'You can't have thought about this.'

'Of course I have. Would I have asked you without due consideration?'

'It is a desperately bad policy.'

'Nothing I do is desperately bad.'

His frown had become a scowl.

'It cannot be.'

Of course I could not wed him. There were so many reasons why not, so many reasons why it would be the most unwise marriage of the century. The obstacles raced through my mind and I accepted every one of them as Ned held out his hand, palm raised. The room was gilded with sunshine, bright enough to dispel every negative thought, but this was an invitation I must not accept.

'Wed me, Jeanette, and we will spar and argue for the rest of our days.'

Surely he could see that it was impossible. I would not accept. I could not accept, even though I felt compelled by some unforeseen power to place my hand in his. Once at Westminster, in that tempest after the return from war, at Thomas's request I had placed my hand in his, heralding my true relationship with him.

Now, I put my hands behind my back.

Ned's hand remained extended in a truly royal command.

'God's Blood, Joan! Will you wed me? Will you be my wife? Would you like to answer now rather than next week? You will be Princess of Wales, and in the fullness of time you will be Queen of England. Don't tell me that you cannot see the advantage in that.'

The King, my cousin, would never agree to our marriage.

'We both need to wed.' Ned's words fell like a shower of hail without mercy. 'Neither of us is driven by love for another. We know each other, our faults and failings as well as our virtues. I expect that I will grow to tolerate your wilfulness. Go and order your women to pack your belongings.'

'Why?'

I was being carried along on a fast stream. Too fast. Far too fast.

'To come back to Windsor with me, why else? You'll be expected for the Garter celebrations at Easter. We'll tell my father that you have agreed and we will marry as soon as we can.'

At last I found my voice.

'This is beyond sense, Ned! Can you imagine what the King would say if you rode up to his door with me riding pillion as your prospective bride?'

'You would never ride pillion. You would insist on your own mare, tricked out with scarlet bridle and bells. But he has to know sometime.' His hand might drop away but the assurance in his voice was still there. 'I would never have thought you guilty of cowardice. You have overcome far greater obstacles than my father's temper, which never lasts long.'

Cowardice.

My blood heated a little. Ned had planned this. It would solve all his problems. What need to woo a foreign bride when here was a royal princess who did not need to be wooed? So he was too busy with taxes and recalcitrant justices to undertake a wooing, was he? I could be slotted into his daily routine of travel, in a fast visit on his way back to don his Garter robes in Windsor. He had commanded me. He expected me to comply. He would never accept that there were so many good reasons why I should never agree to this union.

I studied his face. The fiery assertiveness, the certainty. The bloody arrogance.

'Well?' He extended his hand again. 'It can't be so difficult for you to decide, cousin.'

'I have decided.'

'Good. We'll leave at once. Your luggage can follow.'

'I have decided, Ned.' I was as brittle as glass, and twice as sharp. 'My answer is no. I will not marry you.'

'You cannot have considered the advantages.'

'I see none. All I see is a never-ending line of probably ruinous repercussions, for both of us. Nor will I change my mind. I will not marry you.'

'Then there is no more to be said.'

A curt bow and Ned's glittering visit came to a rapid and undoubtedly discourteous end.

'It will take much dredging,' Ned had said.

It would take a bolt of heavenly light to bathe my soul in innocence. I knew my reputation, as did everyone else. There was nothing that Ned could say that I did not already know; I had become a figure of some notoriety, of little truth and many lies. Enough truth to be recognisable, but with the twist of falsehood to make me wanton.

The injustice of it all simmered beneath my skin as I watched him ride away, his mood as sour as mine. I had refused him, and he had left me in a cloud of dust and haughty displeasure.

'Considering my previous fall from grace, I cannot imagine why you would be so unwise as to ask for my hand in marriage.'

Pride had come to my rescue, making me as haughty as he as he had swung into his saddle, ordering his escort to precede him.

'Why would I not? And if I consider you a satisfactory wife, I am astonished that you would refuse me.' His scowl was superb. 'If anyone can restore your tarnished past to future glory, it is I.'

My anger flared like a warning beacon. 'I suppose I should thank you for so demeaning yourself. Your damned self-esteem, Ned, knows no bounds.'

'You need my damned self-esteem if you would walk once more in the path of heavenly-lit respectability.'

I managed to keep my mouth shut against further counter-attack.

My tarnished past kept me close company on the wall-walk as the light continued to glance on the distant gold and metal, like a will-o'-the-wisp over marshland. I could not claim innocence, but by the Virgin I was not as guilty of sin as the holy and despicably self-righteous chroniclers would say. The manner of my first marriage might have been open to legal question but I was neither wanton nor unprincipled. There was no whore in me, but the world was a spiteful one, its words weighted against me. Even Philippa had seen a need to caution me and encourage me to mend my ways, to live a virtuous life.

But had I not earned my reparation in my years as Thomas's true wife? Apparently not. I could stitch a tapestry of all the reasons why I should not wed the Prince of Wales.

I turned to descend the steps, to return to the necessities of my days at Castle Donington. I was not going to think about Ned. I was not going to think about my reputation, or lack thereof. Instead I sought out my steward once more, to his great discomfort, even though my thoughts were far away from taking tally of our stores.

Of what was I accused? What had I heard in the dark corners of court whispering, beneath the false respect and smiling lips? Even after all my decorous years of marriage to Thomas, there were tales of a dark lasciviousness, of slippery ways. Of uncontrolled lust. Anger licked around me now as dusk fell and the accusations flitted through my mind like the bats that emerged from the tower. They were familiar patterns, such as those I frequently transposed to altar cloth or girdle. Or a familiar tune in which I could sing both line and harmony. My marriage to Thomas, it was still claimed, had been an immoral union, without legality, merely a product of my lust to lure a man to my youthful bed. So wilful had I been that I was unable to wait for the sanction of a priest.

But that was not the worst of it. Had not Will ended his marriage to me because he suspected me of an inappropriate liaison with Thomas when he had been steward in our household? When Thomas had been steward, so the damsels said, I had shared the bed of both. I was guilty of the worst disloyalty to my rightful husband, the Earl of Salisbury, who had thus cast me off, back into the arms of my lover.

I was wanton, lascivious, immoral. Debauched. A figure to be gossiped over by pert royal damsels.

Thus I was condemned, when I had shared the bed of neither.

How unfair that so many fingers had been pointed in my direction. All because I had made that unfortunate choice of wedding Thomas Holland when I was twelve years old, yet clear in my own mind. Was that lasciviousness? I swear it was not. It was as fine a love as I could ever imagine. Yet I was coated in the slime of innuendo, while Will's reputation remained as fair as a June day. Thomas was lauded as a great and chivalrous knight to the end. I was the one to bear the brunt of those who would denigrate wicked behaviour in the depths of the royal court.

Did no one have compassion that I was kept in confinement to allow the Salisbury marriage to stand? Did no one accept the honesty of His Holiness's decision? Thomas and I had been married again in the full light of court approval, even Edward managing a snake-like smile for the occasion, yet I was the one to be cast down in the chroniclers' essays as a Daughter of Eve, offering the apple of desire to hapless Adam. I was the one to be smeared in the filth of Sin.

Despite it all, Ned had asked me to become his wife. He had, in true princely style, demanded that I obey, riding roughshod over my unsuitability as a royal bride.

But when did an English prince marry a woman with a questionable marital history and a dark shadow of lasciviousness hanging over her? When did the future King of England not marry a woman of status and rank and European connection to enhance his own prestige, a girl who was a virgin cosseted since childhood in the ways of a princess consort? When did an English prince not set his sights abroad to the high-blooded families of Europe?

Never.

I was no innocent virgin bride to enhance the marriage of a future King. My marriage to Ned would never be accepted. Any noble daughter of high blood would be a better political prospect than the Fair Maid of Kent. To wed me would be seen as a lost political opportunity. A wretched step. An ill-considered project. Ned must look elsewhere, as he would when he recovered from my refusal. When, with some introspection, he detected another, more serious, even darker abyss lurking within a marriage to me.

My Holland children were legitimately born. I had the proof. But, given all that was said, how would England accept that any future son born to me and to the Prince was the true heir of his body? How could any man believe in my absolute morality? My pure integrity? If any mention was made of Ned's son born out of wedlock, it was done in jovial tone, acknowledged and tolerated as a passing youthful *amour* that could be forgiven. Was he not virile? Had this not proved that England would never lack for a potent heir?

But my transgressions as a weak woman would be shouted from the wall-walk at Windsor Castle. If there was any trace of legality clinging to my marriage to William Montagu, then all my children with Ned would be dubbed bastard, unfit to rule. One Pope had effectively severed my legal connection with Will, but his successor to the three-tiered diadem, if he was of a mind, could equally well restore it. And since I had been condemned out of hand as owning a strong streak of immorality, how could any child of mine be accepted as the true child of my husband?

I doubted such thoughts had ever crossed Ned's mind. He would have what he wanted. He always had.

And what's more, I captured a final fleeting thought: Ned and I were too closely related in our Plantagenet blood for the Archbishop of Canterbury to give his blessing.

You could always get a papal dispensation…

Burying the idea deep, I shivered as the sun sulked behind a cloud and disappeared over the horizon as Ned had some minutes ago. Given my tarnished past, why England's glorious Prince of Wales would want to take me into holy wedlock was beyond my understanding. There was every reason not to enter into this marriage, and it would be an ill-advised woman who cast them all asunder.

For a moment I covered my face with my hands.

I had sent him away.

I put yet another signature to yet another document. My days were full. I could never make claim to time hanging heavily on my hands, for the demands of my steward and chamberlain at Castle Donington were many and varied, given the spread of my estates from the northern Scottish border to Suffolk in the east and across to the lush lands of the west. For the first time in my life, realising the true burden taken on by my mother, equally I realised that although the intricacies of estate management might have run deep in her blood, it was a mere trickle in mine.

My steward placed before me yet another list of rents, both paid and in arrears. I ran my eye down the less than fascinating details of a water mill, a fulling mill and a lead mine, all in the manor of Ashford, a manor which, to my knowledge, I had never visited.

My steward departed, taking some of the documents with him. Would that he would take them permanently. Low in energies, I continued to sit, my eyes focused on nothing in particular, until a thin stream of sunshine crept into the tower chamber causing my rings to gleam heavily with gold, the stones to glitter, their shine eclipsing the morning's tedium.

My gaze focused. The pen fell unheeded from my fingers.

In that moment of gilded brightness, in spite of all my certainty of past days, the lure of a quite different future laid its hand on me, beckoning me, as glittering as my rings, a future of power and influence and supreme authority. Had it not been offered to me? Yet I had thrust it aside. A future at Ned's side. In that moment my hands spread wide on the board before me, as if they would flatten all my excellent reasoning for refusing Ned's offer. Who would make him a better wife than I? The sun warmed me like an ermine cloak and I envisioned such a future. Princess of Wales and, in the fullness of time, Queen of England. I would wear that ermine, I would wear the royal crown. I would no longer be concerned with mills and mines and ravaged houses. Instead, all the promise of God-given power would be at my fingertips. All the reality of it.

I rubbed them together; they all but tingled.

But I had refused him. Ned had ridden away with my rejection ringing in his ears. Walking to the window into the full glory of the sun, I lifted the mirror hanging at my belt. I would make a most beautiful Queen, more beautiful than England had ever known. How could I have thrown away, so wantonly, what Ned had offered me?

A new certainty took hold. What I had done could most assuredly be undone. I would undo it.

Within a day I was ordering my women to make ready. One more day of preparation essential to a determined woman and I was on my way to Windsor.

Spring 1361: Windsor Castle

As I alighted from my litter, for I had no intention of arriving wind-swept, I shook out my skirts, lifted my head so that my black veils rippled and climbed the steps to one of the great chambers of Edward's new building, where I was announced. There was Edward, Philippa beside him, presiding over the usual gathering. I curtsied, every sense stretched to assess the reaction in the room to my arrival. The guests continued to eddy in ever changing formations as people talked and laughed and drank the wine dispensed by the pages. No ripples here consequential to what Ned had proposed, but why should there be? His rejection would be the last thing he would have broadcast. I was made welcome, warmed by Edward's smile, my health and that of my children enquired after, invited to sup with them.

My rejected royal prince was not present.

I could wait. My campaign was as well planned as any siege of a recalcitrant town.

Nor was Ned visible for the rest of that day until we knelt for the service of Compline, the solemn ending of the day casting its cloak of peace over all, when he knelt beside his father to accept the priest's blessing. If he saw me, kneeling demurely beside Isabella, my sombre mien cast into relief by her fur-embellished splendour, he gave no recognition.

But I knew that he had. My mourning might be deepest black but the sables were superb, as was the embroidery that enhanced hem and sleeve, my hair plaited into a regal coronet.

Oh, he knew. Hence the lofty angle of his chin.

Compline over, when we must perforce meet, and I had no intention that we would not, Ned was superlatively cool. 'I didn't know you were coming.'

'There is no reason why you should.'

'No, there is none,' he agreed.

'As you advised me, I was expected here.'

He regarded me as if I were a stranger for whom he had little liking. 'You seemed to be dug deep into your steward's failings for the duration, when I left.'

I smiled winsomely. 'I changed my mind, Ned. The right of any woman of good sense. As you see, I am no good wife today.'

The cool regard was transmuted into a frown as he assessed the value of my finery, of the jewels that made a statement of grandeur at throat and breast. 'No. You are all Plantagenet. Your beauty rivals the sun.' The frown deepened. 'You will be delighted to know that there has been an offer for your hand in marriage.'

I raised my brows gently. 'So tell me. I am agog.'

'Sir Bernard Brocas sees you as a future addition to his family. The King might look kindly on the offer.'

'Sir Bernard Brocas?' I could not hide my astonishment.

'A worthy knight. A brave one.'

And a very dull one, as I knew full well. He would send the Angel Gabriel to sleep with his reminiscences of deeds on the battlefield at Poitiers.

'He might suit you very well, since I do not,' Ned added.

I leaned a little closer so that the musk of my perfume, in which my veiling had been steeped, must touch his mind. 'He might suit me very well. I will speak with my cousin the King forthwith.'

Ned left me, striding through the crowd.

I was not dissatisfied, despite Philippa's concerned regard. I had no intention of speaking about a husband with my cousin the King. Not until I had snared the one I wanted.

The days passed as I expected, filled with all the activities much beloved by Edward's court during a time of peace. I avoided Ned. He avoided me. I flirted mildly, as much as it was possible to flirt when in mourning, shrouded in dark veiling and with no true desire to do so, with Sir Bernard Brocas who appeared much enamoured of my company, paying me much attention. Why would he not when I set myself to engage his interest? I did not admire him as much as he obviously admired me, or as much as he admired himself, but he proved to be good company with a multitude of tales of his exploits on the battlefield to pass the time.

When I did not yawn from sheer boredom.

Sir Bernard, most opportunely slid perfectly into my planning.

As for Ned...

Ned might be avoiding me, but I was aware of him.

I had been too precipitate in my refusing him, too quick to acknowledge the obstacles without keen consideration of the advantages. Knowing Ned as well as I did, his pride had suffered a severe blow. He would not approach me again, without persuasion. Or would he? Would he perhaps, in his pride, refuse to accept my denial, continuing his campaign to force my acceptance? Ned was quite capable of making his warhorse leap either to right or to left to outwit the enemy and grasp victory.

For once I was uncertain, but I had no intention of leaving the outcome to chance. What had taken my day of preparation in the fastness of Castle Donington? I knew little or nothing of cures for suffering and such ailments as afflicted my household. That was for my

women and physician. What I did know was a fistful of applications
for a woman to enhance her beauty.

Anointing my hair with a thick concoction of white wine and
honey to bring out the gold, I progressed to whitening my skin with
ground lily root mixed with half a goose egg, to be applied overnight.
Juice of wormwood to preserve my lips from the ravages of sun and
wind. Teeth whitened and breath refreshed with fennel and lovage.

I was pleased with the results.

Edward of Woodstock was under attack.

'You are watching me,' I accused him, patting his arm.

'Of course I am,' he said, stepping away. 'You would be disappointed if I did not. It's a woman's ploy. I suppose that I should tell
you that you are looking very beautiful today, although I don't see
why I should. A woman does not refuse a prince with impunity.'

So Ned was giving nothing away, except for a bad case of disgrun-
tlement. Well, we would see. 'This one does,' I replied, my expression
as sunny as my mourning allowed.

We had joined a small party of courtiers, tempted out into the
pale sunshine to loose arrows at the butts set up for us in the practice
yard. Edward had joined us and Isabelle with her ever-present French
swain. The laughter was light-hearted, the contest keen, as men and
women paired up to pit their skills.

'You will partner me.' Ned at his most officious.

I smiled with a shake of my head. 'I am invited to partner Sir
Bernard. He is proving most attentive.'

I indicated my waiting admirer.

'I will make your excuses.' With an interesting grimness about
him, Ned was already selecting my bow, measuring it against my
person, frowning then selecting another. Ned did not brook refusal.
'Sir Bernard would not appreciate your glowing looks. They would
be wasted on him.'

'Your royal and all-powerful father is scowling at you,' I suggested amiably, taking the bow from him. 'And at me. Which explains perfectly why I regretfully refused your kind offer to join my hand with yours. The King would never allow it.'

'Regretfully refused? You rejected it out of hand. And no, he is not scowling since he knows nothing of what passed between us at Donington. It's your imagination. He is suffering from a griping of the guts after overeating last night.' Ned handed me an arrow before taking up his own bow. 'You are my dear cousin and we will match each other in a happy spirit of competition.'

I complied with gentle grace, noting the combative light in his eye. It would work very well for me.

'Would you consider Sir Bernard a good match for me?' I asked without preamble.

Ned's brows climbed as he notched the arrow and loosed it at the butt. It hit dead centre. Of course it would.

'No.'

'No?' I followed his example, but lacked the dexterity and the eye. The arrow lodged in the outer rim.

'That was a poor shot.'

'I'll do better next time.' I glanced to my left where a solitary figure was watching. 'I think Sir Bernard is hunting in earnest.'

'I know he is.'

'Really?'

'He approached me,' Ned said through what appeared to be gritted teeth, which pleased me inordinately. 'He's looking for a wife and aims high. He has asked me to pursue an alliance between him and yourself.'

'And what did you say?'

'I said I would plead his cause.'

'Would you?'

'No, of course I would not. Would you wish to be lady of his trifling manors in Berkshire and Hampshire?'

'I might. He is a man of ambition and not a little wealth.'

'He's also a good soldier. He fought alongside me at Poitiers to some effect. But that does not make him a suitable match for you.'

Another royal arrow sped to its mark with fluid ease. Carefully, thoughtfully, I selected my second arrow. I notched, stretched, aimed. The arrow buried itself in the very centre beside Ned's.

'Better! You've been practising.' Ned was still scowling. 'Don't tell me that you would consider Sir Bernard Brocas as a husband before me?'

'Why not? The King would support it.'

'I'll not allow it.'

'You have no power to allow or not allow, dear cousin.'

'You don't care for him.'

'Do I have to?'

We stood face to face while arrogance and self-will waged their own war between us. Ned regarded me, plucking at the feathers until the flight of his next arrow was useless.

'Does your heart belong to any man, Joan?'

'My heart, if I ever had one, is encased in a tomb in Stamford.'

'If you say so.'

He tossed the ill-used arrow to the ground while I swung away from him, disturbed at this deliberate stirring of my past grief, so that I aimed badly and missed the butt completely.

'You are not concentrating,' Isabella called over from where she and Enguerrand were engaged in more arch conversation than archery.

'I am being undermined by your brother,' I replied with a bright smile that was entirely false.

Ned leaned on his bow in exasperation. 'Our cousin is being as infuriating as ever!' Then stood, contemplating my far-flung arrow, now disappeared into the grass. I stood beside him, doing likewise as if the fate of that arrow was all important when it was not important at all. Now was the time to make my move.

'So will you inform Sir Bernard that I am not averse?' I asked.

He spun round, casting the ill-used bow to the ground, waving away a page who leapt to retrieve it.

'By God I will not!'

'Must I remain unwed?'

'No, you will not.' In a movement as slick as the dive of a kingfisher into a carp pond, his hand snapped round my wrist. 'You will wed me.'

Ah. At last.

'Why?' All dulcet enquiry, I withstood his fierce stare.

'Because I want to wed you, and unless I am very much mistaken you want me, or why all this magnificent posturing? I don't know why you refused me the first time. Nor why you spent any time in luring poor Sir Bernard into your toils, although I have my suspicions.' A wry smile touched his mouth. 'You will wed me. Do you agree now?'

A long moment. I kept him waiting.

'Before God, Jeanette!'

Why wait?

'I agree,' I said.

'That's it then. You will be my wife.'

As brief a wooing as any woman could have as the contest was winding down, leaving us as the only pair still at the butts. Looking back over my shoulder at him as I readied my final arrow I asked, because it was not a matter that could be avoided, by either of us: 'What will you do about your father? He has such plans for you.'

'None of which have come to fruition in the thirty years of my lifespan. I am old enough to make up my own mind.'

'How true. But he won't want me, Ned.'

'Yes he will. You can win him round.'

'I will not even try. He regards me with deep suspicion. And who can blame him?' I lowered the arrow, casting it and the bow to lie with Ned's on the grass, for after all the contest was over. Had I not won? Except for the final, crucial, most important step, and I could see no firm ground in this morass. 'My lamentable past attests to my failure to win the King round to anything. I know what will happen. You will be sent hot-foot to Gascony to put you out of harm's way, a foreign bride hastily conjured from somewhere, while I am married off to Sir Bernard or to some northern lord who never comes to court and keeps me shut away in the fastnesses of the border country, leaving the King to rub his hands together in ultimate triumph.'

'Well, he might.' Ned contemplated this, picking at a loose thread of gold that marred the perfection of the cuff of his archery glove, before fixing me with a regard that suddenly awakened within me a feather-edge of worry, although his question was innocent enough. 'So what do you suggest, Madam Joan?'

I took a breath as the past fell over my head, shrouding me like a beekeeper's net. Had I not already considered this? I would not travel that route again, too full of legal complications as it had proved to be. Surely Ned would choose to approach his father in time-honoured fashion and ask a royal blessing on our head. Did not Edward love his son enough to ultimately give way? Since there would be no need to repeat past mistakes, and since I had learned enough to reject such an outrageous route out of hand, I stood in silence, until I became aware that Ned had turned to face me foursquare.

I tilted my head, expecting, perhaps, some declaration of admiration.

'I know a way,' he said. 'So do you. If you have the courage to embark on this particular well-travelled ship.'

I simply stared at him, aghast. He stared back.

'Do you mean what I think you mean?

'Yes.'

'But no. I cannot.'

'Why not?' His hands were a vice around mine when I might have withdrawn them, as if he would force the decision from me. The certainty behind his invitation hammered in my head, but it was as if a ball of ice had lodged in my stomach.

'Look what happened last time.'

Ned shook his head. 'Last time was nothing like this time. You are hardly going to wed Sir Bernard next week and complicate the whole issue. If we do it in this manner, we face the King with a *fait accompli*. Nothing simpler.'

'There's nothing simple about it! I can't do it!'

'God's Blood, Joan! What can my father do, but accept what is already done? Think about it.'

So I thought. No, it would not be my choice, but it would achieve the desired end. And how typical of Ned to take this decision with little thought for its repercussions.

'Are you going to honour me with a reply?' he asked, fast running out of patience. 'You have had more than enough time to decide about our marriage, as well as the imminence of the Second Coming. Do you agree?'

I looked up, to find him smiling at me, if the fierce command in it could be called a smile.

'Will you wed me, Joan?'

Could I do it? Could I take ship with Ned in this fashion and weather the resulting storm of disapprobation once more? It would outmanoeuvre the King's opposition, but in truth I could not accept that this was the best path to take.

'Yes,' I said, in a hurry before I could change my mind. 'I'll do it. But not in a mews.'

'Why would we wed in a mews? And what's wrong with a mews anyway? I didn't know you disliked falcons.'

'I don't,' I remembered vividly. 'The dust makes me sneeze.'

As if under some compulsion, as if the outcome would clarify the fateful decision we had just made, Ned took up my bow and the rejected arrow, loosing it at the butt with casual accuracy, once more hitting the centre.

'Then that's what we'll do.'

'I would like a wooing.' I was surprised at the wistfulness of my tone, embarrassed by it. I had never needed a wooing when my mind was firm-set.

'No time for that.' He took my arm. 'Do what I tell you and all will be well.'

It was unusual being ordered what to do. And agreeing to do it, without argument.

For a little time we sat together on a bench in the *plaisance*, dust motes dancing, the daily life of the castle echoing from the open windows of the rooms behind us. Gloves discarded, my hands, softened and whitened with deer tallow boiled in water, were enfolded once more within Ned's large ones. He took them without my permission.

'I knew you would accept in the end.'

'You knew no such thing. You were entirely put out.'

I had forgotten the height and breadth of his confidence. Or how his regard could become astonishingly sly.

'Would you turn down the chance to be Queen of England? That would not be the Jeanette that I know and admire.' He lifted one hand to his lips, then the other, disregarding the grime from an afternoon of archery, before enfolding them again. 'I have always had a liking for you. You must know that.'

'I know no such thing. I have no recollection of our exchanging compliments.'

'We can now remedy such an omission.' He kissed my cheek, which made my heart flutter, just a little. 'Do you like me?'

This was acceptable. This was within my encompassing.

'Yes, I like you. I always have, when you were not boasting of your prowess.'

'I never boasted.'

'Yes, you did. You had your own pavilion and a complete suit of armour with spare helmet and sword when you were eight years old. You wanted nothing more than your sisters to admire your skills. I remember sitting in a windswept practice yard while you belaboured my brother who had much less skill than you. You spent much less time in the mud.'

'So you do like me.'

'Yes.'

'And might love me.'

My answering smile, all I would give, was enigmatic as I considered the extent of my lessons for that day. I had learned the value of female guile that a woman might use to bring a man to her heel. I had learned the value of careful planning. I had learned the extent of my ambition. Had I learned more about love? I thought not. It shamed me that such a wayward emotion had had no bearing on my decision to become wife of the Prince of Wales, but then I doubted that it had played any role in Ned's planning either.

'You seemed to be in close communion with my brother.' Isabella of course, come to discover our absence.

'Not particularly.' I had no intention of telling her, so would say as little as I could, but then there was no need to deflect her questioning.

'Tell me how you enhance the colour of your hair.'

'With your dark hair, you need a green lizard, topped and tailed and cooked in oil.' I ignored her grimace. Better that than a further demand as to what Ned and I might be discussing. 'Anoint your hair with the concoction. My women swear on its efficacy to improve its thickness and lustre if your hair is darker than mine.'

Her glance was not one of conviction but she nodded. 'If it will persuade Enguerrand to approach my father over marriage, I'll try even that. What do you think?'

'I think that marriage has no importance for me.'

I thought that she believed me.

I did not like to contemplate the Queen's reaction when she learned what Ned and I were planning to do.

Chapter Eleven

Spring 1361: Kennington Palace

The sense of *déjà vu* was overwhelming, but then I had expected no less. Where did we plight our troth? Not in the mews but in the chapel at Kennington, a favourite manor of Ned's, built by him on the triangle of land given to him by the King as a gift to the son of his heart. Edward would not have approved of the use of this gift. We both travelled, separately, on some pretence that I cannot now recall, not that it was necessary, for who would take account of our actions? No priest, no incense, no drama, no banns – so much a mirror image of my first union – but the witnesses, two of Ned's squires, were not sworn to secrecy. It was Ned's intention to tell his father immediately.

I made no attempt to persuade him otherwise, knowing that I would fail. Ned was not a man to be turned when in pursuit of the hare. The sooner the King knew, the sooner we could face and withstand the royal blast. Besides, what could Edward do, once we were wed? The King had learned from bitter experience that it was not a status that could readily be overturned. His Holiness could not be relied upon when vows had been exchanged and the union consummated, however irregular the proceedings. Ned and I would marry with the legalities in place; the fripperies of priest and festivity could come later. Along with the King's displeasure.

I stood at Ned's side in the silent and all-but-empty chapel at Kennington. It felt right as Ned spoke a simple soldier's vow, *per verba de praesenti* as I had experienced once before although the atmosphere was very different. Rich, sumptuous in its gilded carving, it breathed its blessing on us. I did not sneeze. No shiver passed over my skin. No presentiment of future difficulties. The last time had caused such trouble but what could trouble us now? What indeed. We would weather the storm to set sail on fair seas.

Ned's confidence was such that he was aware of no storm, merely a slight breeze to ruffle the waves that would be fast calmed. His vows were forthright, more suitable to a commander of men than a man engaged in taking a wife.

'On this day I wed you, Joan.'

'On this day I wed you, Edward,' I repeated.

'You are my wife.'

'You are my husband.'

There was a pause.

'Do we need to say more?' Ned asked. 'I think that's all we need for the legalities.'

I felt strangely empty, as if there should have been some thunderclap or lightning bolt to mark this occasion which would change my life so completely.

'You could attempt a little emotion,' I suggested.

He grinned, the familiar brightening of his features. 'Then I would say this, if you want emotion. I have always admired you. I would honour my admiration with marriage. So on this day I marry you, my dear Jeanette. I expect that we will come to love each other.'

No bride, I accepted, could ask for more.

'You have been my friend and, in childhood, my companion. I

honour your decision and accept that from this day I am your wife.'
He was looking at me. Perhaps he hoped for more too, but Ned as
always was difficult to read.

He kissed me on my lips. 'So I make my vow.'

'As I make mine.'

It was done. I was no longer Countess of Kent. I was *per verba de
praesenti* Princess of Wales.

I felt that I was standing on the edge of a chasm so deep that I could
not detect the bottom of it, yet all was not without its gratification.
We had avoided the discussion of emotions. A sensible decision in
the circumstances.

We consummated our marriage, *per verba de praesenti*, as a legal necessity since there was to be no legal loophole through which the King
might climb. Here was a circumstance I had never foreseen, sharing
a bed with the boy with whom I had been raised from childhood,
with whom I had competed, argued, shared lessons, danced. We were
children no longer yet our disrobing was a matter of practicality, not in
the heat of physical passion. Here was no flirtation, no overwhelming
desire to submerge the necessity of the deed in poetic nonsense. And
yet it was not unpleasant. We were both experienced, both practical
in giving and receiving pleasure. Ned, if nothing else, was thorough
in awakening all my senses, as I seemed to awaken his.

He lay on his side when the deed was done, looking at me, one
hand planted firmly on my hip as I looked at him.

'Do you suppose that you are carrying my heir?' he asked.

'Already?' I discovered that laughter was not far from us, a blessing
that warded off any embarrassment.

'My son Roger was got with great rapidity.'

'I admire Mistress Willesford,' I remarked. 'Where is she, by the
way?'

He caught the dryness of my tone. 'Edith is settled happily in the household at Clarendon with an annuity for her care of the child. She need not trouble you.'

'She does not trouble me...'

'As for my heir,' Ned interrupted, his fingertips against my lips, 'we, my charming wife, will try again. A marriage *per verb de praesenti* has, as I am aware, no restriction on the number of consummations.'

I was engulfed in caresses and kisses that may indeed have resulted in a royal heir for England. Yet as I kissed Ned, who had made this so easy for me, I thought that I was disappointed. What right I had to be so, I could not determine. I could expect no more from a union which was one of sheer pragmatism, for both of us, I suspected. It was time that I abandoned all those immature dreams of love and romance, which indeed had never moved me overmuch. This was acceptable enough for a mature woman.

What I did feel for Ned in our physical union was an intense gratitude. I had been left no time to even think about Thomas. Ned's enthusiasm rolled everything before it so any reluctance in me was overcome, subsumed in speed and precision. It was all undertaken, I surmised, with the same competency as the campaign at Poitiers against our French enemy.

I watched him as he slept, his face buried in the pillow, dark hair springing with its usual exuberance. He was very dear to me. I could envisage what the future would hold with regard to my royal status, now so much enhanced. What it would mean for Ned and I, two individuals now shackled together, I had no very clear idea at all.

Nuptials complete, we returned to Windsor to face the King and Queen, except that Edward and Philippa had moved their joint households to Havering-atte-Bower, and so we travelled on to what was more hunting lodge than palace. We rode side by side, Ned allowing his mind to be taken up with what would happen next.

'I could take my father hunting. And break the news to him when he's feeling sated with a good run and kill.'

I glanced across. 'Are you admitting to a desire to fall into a retreat?'

He returned my glance, his brows twitching at my disparagement of such a scheme. 'Certainly not.' And then: 'What would you do? I know you'll give me your opinion anyway. Why break the habit of a lifetime?'

'Just tell him. We have done the deed. No need to wrap it in ceremonial or gold trappings or even blood and guts. He won't like it, however it's done.'

'Deliver it like a thrust of a lance.' He gestured as if he held such an effective weapon.

'If you wish. Then we stand back and wait for the blast of temper that will shake the roof.'

Reaching across the space, he took my gloved hand in his, so that our horses must walk closer together.

'I expect that you will be a managing wife.'

He did not seem to be inordinately worried by the prospect. I had forgotten how well he knew me. 'I will try to be.'

He laughed, his spirits high. 'Second thoughts?'

'No. None at all.'

Second thoughts? Regrets? I had none. I had made my decision that day at Castle Donington when all the reasons why I should not wed him had paled into insignificance beside the overriding reason why I should. Marriage to a man of my own choosing, to a man of future power, pre-eminent throughout all of Europe. To a man of reputation and acclaim who would effectively mend my reputation as soon as our marital oaths were exchanged.

Nor would I be the only one to gain in this blessed union. Would

I not make a most exceptional Princess of Wales? Would I not be the most impressive and capable Queen of England? I had all the gifts to be Ned's consort. I would bear him children. I would enhance my beauty to impress those who needed to be impressed, using my knowledge of men and the royal court to make his rule strong and successful. I would prove a better Queen Consort than Margaret of Brabant, or any Valois daughter of the King of France. Could I withstand the opprobrium of those who would cast clods of earth at my morality? I could. I had done so all my life. Would I flinch under the King's disparagement? I would not. I was Plantagenet, and Ned would restore me to ultimate respectability.

As for the legalities, we could overcome the legal barrier to our marriage with no difficulty it all. Popes were open to persuasion if the purse of gold was heavy enough, even if the ban against us was two-fold within the degrees of the forbidden union. If Thomas and I could win against the weight of the Montagu name, what could not be achieved with the whole power of English diplomacy and England's wealth behind us? Were we not wed? It would be merely giving legal sanction to what was already done, with no complication of a second marriage to stand in our way.

No, there was no room for regret.

Better to be Queen of England than the wife of a slavering lord who was pleased to have royal blood between his sheets. I would be princess and queen, the dark pall of past treasons neatly obliterated, my reputation restored. Putting aside my black garments, I would take my place at court at Ned's side, the insecurities of my youth, which still had the power to discomfit me when I lay abed with my mind not at ease, erased by the authoritative hand of the Prince of Wales. No one would question my right or my talent to pursue my new role.

Ned still held my hand, unaware of any sidelong smirks from our entourage. I felt the warmth of his grip through the fine leather. There were no regrets, I would swear, beneath the gold-applique of the damask cote-hardie that he wore, regardless of dust and sweat of travel.

Love.

We had not spoken of it, skirting round it with careful feet, like ducks on a frozen pond, conscious of their balance. Admiration, yes. Affection too. Did I love him? I did not know. Like and love. Affection and love. Were they not leagues apart?

I had loved Thomas.

I thought about the two men to whom I had been wed: Thomas and Ned. Both soldiers, both men of action rather than books and music. Both happier on a battlefield or in negotiation with an enemy. How similar, yet there were differences. Of course there were. Ned had the gloss of the court ingrained into every inch of his royal-born skin. The assurance was his, the assertiveness instilled there from his youth. Ned would never question his position in society, his future, the direction that fate had chosen for him. He was gilded and sublimely dispassionate whereas Thomas had been forced to earn his reputation, to build his own confidence and his assurance, which he had done until they presented a bulwark against the world. For Ned, arrogant self-reliance, with no need of any bulwark, had crowned him on the day of his birth.

I must remember that salient fact in this marriage. Ned was a conqueror, a commander, a man who brooked no opposition. I must indeed cut my cloth to suit this new garment.

'We will tell the King together,' Ned announced as the disparate towers and uneven roof-lines of Havering came into view above the trees. 'That we are bound by love. Is that not the truth?'

His question startled me. How closely his thoughts had been running together with mine. I became aware that he was waiting for my reply, so I gave one, of sorts.

'Is it?' I asked.

'I love you as much as I love any woman. And more than most.'

'But not as much as planning a military campaign in France.'

He laughed aloud, dislodging a pair of roosting pigeons that clapped through the branches overhead, making my mare shy. 'That would be too much to ask of me. As it would be too much to ask of you to put love before ambition.'

'True.'

But I had to hide a quick frown. Were we both so self-serving? No, there was no love between us, if that was the overriding passion of the troubadours, the love that counted all things lost for its own sake. I would accept what I had achieved. Successful marriages could be built on far less than we had between us. Love? I did not think so, and was glad. It made a woman too vulnerable.

'You have done what?'

Despite the low growl, so low that it barely touched the ears of the courtiers present, the question throbbed through the air of the Great Hall. We will announce it publically, Ned had decreed. I had agreed, encouraged even. And so we did, with all Ned's unshakeable belief in himself that what was done must be acceptable.

I had been less sanguine. It was soon proved that I had the right of it.

The King waited, as if we would refute it. Explain. Deny. We did none of those things.

'Joan is my wife,' Ned repeated.

The King's gauntlets and royal hat were dropped to the floor where a page scurried to collect them, brushing dust from the velvet folds, which to me seemed to be an irrelevance given the developing clash of will. 'And you come here asking for my blessing?'

The muscles in the royal jaw were rigid, the eyes bright with a terrible passion. I had expected an outburst of anger, a raging storm such as he had showered on Thomas in similar circumstances; not this cold rage that was a rumble of approaching thunder. It was directed at Ned rather than at me, but for certain Edward would soon turn his eye in my direction. And who could blame him? Any plans he had envisaged for a European alliance had been magnificently, comprehensively, cut off at the knees.

'I see no regret in you. In either of you.'

Here in this vast space was much disparate emotion. The King's icy disgust. Philippa tremulously emotional. Isabella frankly curious, face aglow. The household wavering between shock and glorious intrigue.

The King my cousin proceeded to icy eloquence. 'Where is the value to you, to England, in this union? My heir was raised to seek, through his marriage, the need for political gain, for supremacy. We would have an heiress from one of the foremost European families.' Edward's eyes were as implacably feral as those of his hawk which he had hastily handed to his falconer. 'What have you to say?'

'Only that I desired Joan as my wife and she agreed.'

'Does a prince marry for personal desire? He marries for dynastic grandeur. It is not well done. Do I need to extol the lack of virtues in your chosen bride?'

We all waited to see if he would.

I considered that there was much disappointment when he did not. Instead: 'This marriage will be annulled.'

'It will not,' Ned replied, as imperturbable and his father was glacially furious. 'It is done, *per verba de praesenti*, and it is consummated. There are witnesses. It is legal.'

'As we know through bitter experience.'

Edward's regard now encompassed me, while Ned's hand stretched for mine and he drew me to his side in protection, as if we were truly indivisible.

'Would you repeat the mistakes of twenty years ago, cousin? With the heir to the Crown? Have you so enslaved him that he could not resist you? Then, you were young. It might be argued in your favour that you knew no better. Now you know exactly what you have done. I swear, Joan, that your family has been a thorn in my flesh for too long.'

Breathing softly, ignoring the habitual slight, I remained calm. I would not look at Philippa's face.

'There is no enslavement, my lord. I have used no dark powers.'

'I swear there was no such thought in my son's mind until you were conveniently widowed.'

Ned came to my rescue. 'You dishonour me, father. You dishonour my wife.'

'Dishonour? Is your behaviour that of an honourable man? No heir to the throne has married into the English nobility since… since God knows when. We marry into the best blood of the highest families. Your mother is the finest example and…'

'Joan is our own royal blood,' Ned interrupted. 'Joan is your first cousin, daughter of your own father's brother.'

'Tainted blood!'

'You yourself removed the charge of treason. She is no more guilty of treason than I. She was raised at your own court under the aegis of my mother.'

A superb point that Edward chose to slide around.

'It is an illicit match. It is invalid. You are bound within the four degrees of consanguinity. And compaternity as well, by God, since you stood godfather to two of her children! Which, the last I heard could be punishable by excommunication.' Edward's temper was beginning to acquire some heat. 'Is that what you want? The English heir to be the talk of Europe because he is excommunicate?'

'Then we need a dispensation, sir.'

'And you expect me to do it? To go to the Pope, cap in hand, and beg for a dispensation for a marriage that has already taken place in some appalling secrecy, for a woman who has already come to his attention through a previous unfortunate liaison. And for which, if he is inclined to be difficult, you could both be excommunicated. And what will that say of the legitimacy of a son of your loins? Is she already carrying a child by you? By God, Ned! You ask a lot of me. I don't want this. I don't...'

Philippa's hand on his arm stopped him. The first time she had spoken. The first time she had moved. Until now she had stood, unyieldingly calm as a statue of the Blessed Virgin.

'You must do it, Edward.'

He almost shook her off, but did not. I could see the level of control he must exert.

'Why must I do it?'

'Because to refuse would create a worse scandal than to accept. It is the last thing that you want. We don't need more scandal at court.'

More scandal? I thought that there was an edge to her tone, an unusual astringency now that she allowed it, as if there was some difference of opinion between them. Not the question of Edmund's birth that had been laid to rest, so long ago now. This was something new, and Philippa was stern in her advice.

'No, I do not want scandal.' The low growl had returned, brows meeting in a bar. 'But I'll not be driven into this like a boar whipped into a trap to face the dogs.'

Edward strode out, his hounds and his huntsmen following.

'Will you at least consider it?' Ned's voice, now as angry as his father's, followed him.

'I will not retract.'

'Neither will I.'

An impasse.

The matter was left to simmer, both men adamant as by now the grist had been well-ground and the court, occupying the rabbit warren of corridors of Havering, knew exactly what was afoot. I collected a variety of stares. Some condemning. Some malignantly joyful. Some merely assessing. Rumours flying, my reputation was once more ground into the mud of the forest beyond our doors.

'I admire you, *sister*,' Isabella said, her only comment. 'I hope that I would have dared to do it.'

She remained my friend. She did not ask me if I loved her brother or if this had been an occasion of political ambition.

Meanwhile King and Heir were at daggers drawn, polite but barely so. Philippa was awash with anxiety, and something else drew a disfiguring line between her brows. For the first time in my life the Queen did not wish to speak to me, and it hurt. There was no way forward, our marriage remaining in a strange limbo.

Returned to Westminster, for no other reason than that the King insisted, there was no respite for me as my new ennoblement became a subject of unfortunate debate in the streets of the capital. I became weary of pretending that I did not hear, until I could pretend no more, when riding beside Philippa on the short distance from Westminster to the Tower. The voice to my left from the dense crowd, which always gathered when royalty passed, was disastrously raucous.

'Here comes the Whore of Kent. How are you this fine day, m'lady?'

I allowed my eye to travel over the throng before latching onto an artful expression, whose owner may or may not have been guilty. It mattered not. If this was what I must face, then I would do so with all the Plantagenet aplomb I could harness.

'The Fair Whore of Kent, if it pleases you,' I replied with a winsome smile.

There was a guffaw and much jostling.

'Does the Prince enjoy you warming his bed, lady — and many another, so we hear?'

'He has not complained yet.'

There was a brief pause, Philippa refraining with regal dignity from clutching at my arm.

'Does he measure up, my lady?'

'The Prince measures up superbly. And he'll have your head on a pike if he hears any lack of respect from you, sir!'

A cheer went up. Philippa clicked her tongue against her teeth. I was heartened. It did not shut them up, but the crowd and the household learned to be circumspect and to beware my sharp tongue. It pleased me that much of the laughter at the end had been appreciative.

So Ned and I fell into a familiar routine, enforced by the day to day affairs of the royal household. Separate chambers, separate daily existence.

'I feel like a child again, my movements proscribed by servants who report back to my father.' Ned was irritable. 'We could go back to Kennington and wedded bliss.'

'Except that we are still under a cloud.'

'I have to believe that he will relent when he grows tired of growling at me. Meanwhile we will have to snatch kisses behind tapestries.'

'So I will get my wooing after all.'

'Briefly!' The kiss was snatched, the irritation for a moment soothed.

Not for long.

Not permitted to sit together at meals, I was requested to take my stool beside Philippa and her ladies, which was no hardship, except that it drew attention to Edward's mighty disapproval. What Ned and his father talked of when they hunted I did not know. In the middle of the tension was Philippa, obviously intensely unhappy.

'Come and sit with me.'

Directing her damsels to the far side of the room, she drew me beside her, in the solar where we spent our chilly Lenten days, so that I took the book I had been perusing and sank to a cushion at her knee, close to the fire, relieved that she had relented and would speak with me. It seemed to me that she wished to be private.

'I regret that you are in low spirits, my lady. Do you wish me to read to you?'

'No. Is it so obvious? But hardly surprising as things are.' She was fretful, plucking at the embroidered altar cloth at which she was making no progress. 'Edward is preparing arrangements for a celebration. We are all to be dressed as birds – pheasants I think. I am in no mood for it.'

At such close quarters, her hair severely curtailed by her veil and gold filet, her complexion almost grey, I thought she looked close to exhaustion. At least she was in no mood to take me to task too harshly.

'I have always called you daughter. Now it is legally so. Or almost. Oh, Joan! Why did you have to go about it in this fashion? Did you not learn the first time that it only brings heartache and division?' She turned my face to the light with fingers that trembled. 'I think my son has always had an affection for you. What youth would not admire so beautiful a girl who shared his young life? But do you love him?'

And as I was forced to assess my emotional state, one that would satisfy her and at least have a vestige of honesty, she continued.

'The rumours, spread by my foolish damsels, are that you were more than childhood friends, separated from declaring your love by birth and destiny. But now you have decided to seize the day and make that love a legal thing. Is it true?'

'No.'

'I never thought it was.'

I spoke the truth to her, because it was impossible to lie. 'I never saw Ned as my lover. We were too young, and he younger than I. His thoughts were all on warfare and fighting. And mine...' The truth dried a little.

'You had eyes only for Thomas Holland. You were precocious and he was already a knight and gallant enough. Of course you would be drawn by him. How would a youth of ten years compete, even if he was a prince with the promise of the crown? Royal blood had no attraction for you. Or at least not then.' Her regard was shrewd behind the pain. 'It was always Thomas.'

'To my cost,' I admitted ruefully.

'To your cost.'

I looked up again. Something more than weariness lurked there, something unpleasant, until she guarded her expression, and I asked the question that had always troubled me.

'But you said nothing. You did nothing to thwart what was fool-hardy – as I see now. Should you have stopped me?'

'I should. But we were in Ghent and I suppose, looking back, I was preoccupied with the birth of my son John. I don't think I was very well. If I thought about it, I would have said that it was a youthful extravagance that would die a normal death, and to oppose you would drive you into defiance. I always saw that in you, Joan. Perhaps I should have kept a closer eye on you, but I did not think that you would go so far and take such an extreme step.' She stared at me and gripped my hand. 'Have you told Ned that you don't love him? Don't tell him. It will break his heart. You have always been his Jeanette.'

I shook my head. This was a caring mother speaking. I thought Ned's heart was stronger than that.

'And what about your heart, Madam Joan. Do you have a heart to break?'

'I will not hurt Ned,' I said when the silence had spread out between us against the backdrop of chatter. 'He knows. He knows that I loved Thomas. He would wait, until the affection between us becomes love. He believes that it is within his power to ensure that one day I will love him, and perhaps it is. Ned has a self-belief greater than any man I know.'

'Men have the ability to pretend all manner of things that are not so.'

As I knew. Will had always believed that I would stay with him when I came to my senses. I almost told her that, to lighten her spirits, but it was then that I saw the tears in Philippa's eyes. Guilt struck me, as it sometimes must. This woman had given me so much. No, she was not well, not at all, and I noticed how stiffly she was holding herself. Perhaps she had been suffering for some time, her infirmity disguised by the formality of her garments, for indeed the years were weighing on her, and I had not realised. I had not thought of her as much as I ought, even when I had seen her distress.

'I will be a good wife,' I assured to make her smile again. 'I will be everything you want me to be.'

But now it was clear that she did not wish to speak of her son. Her glance was towards the ladies in the window. Full of remorse, I took her hands that trembled. 'I know that your shoulder pains you. Do you wish for me to call one of your damsels?' The shadow of panic in her eyes astonished me. 'But that is not all, is it?'

'No, it is not all. Can I tell you? I can tell no one else.' Her voice fell, presuming my compliance as she poured out the hurt, the despair, that she had kept hidden for so long. 'Edward thinks it will not hurt me, if he is circumspect. And I, in my self-delusion, have led him to believe that it will not, because I know that I can no longer give him pleasure. My joints are on fire. How can I give him physical fulfilment when every move is agony for me? But the agony in my mind is greater than that in my body.'

I saw it in her eyes, where I read what she had not said, what it was beyond her to say.

'He has a mistress?'

I breathed out slowly, disbelieving. Was this indeed the unacceptable, the unutterable sin, come to pass? The sound marriage of Edward and Philippa based on love and loyalty over so many years, come in the end to the King taking a mistress under his wife's nose, and she concurring with it? In all the years I had known him, there had been no breath of scandal that Edward had been false to his beloved wife. Was this what Philippa feared?

'Yes,' she breathed. 'He has taken a mistress.'

'Who?' Our voices were now lowered to a collusive whisper, our heads together as if pouring over the open text still on my knee, an illustration of Sir Galahad riding off on some hopeless knight-errantry. I was still of a mind to deny any such disfiguring grub in the heart of the fair fruit of their marriage. 'A woman of the court? Someone we know?'

She laughed, a harsh note in that usually melodic voice. 'One of my own household, no less. And with my consent. Even with my contrivance.' She indicated the women. 'The dark girl. If you are going to look at her, don't stare. I'll not draw more attention than I must.'

Carefully, as if merely taking account of who was present in the little knot of damsels, I glanced across to meet the eye of a woman with dark hair and well-marked brows, not beautiful but a striking woman. And she was very young. I knew her, of course.

Mistress Alice Perrers.

A low-born damsel who had caught the Queen's eye for her intelligence, brought into the royal domain, one who had already crossed my path with her absurdly direct observations on my own situation. I stared, regardless of Philippa's warning, my own concerns buried, when I saw no circumspection in this young woman, more a confident sleekness. She simply stared back, as if sensing the direction of my thoughts, before going back to her allotted tasks, and yet there had been no challenge in her stare. Because of that I believed Philippa. Mistress Perrers was confident in her role as royal mistress.

'I have acquiesced,' Philippa was explaining remorselessly, unaware of the tears that had begun to slide down her cheeks. 'You could say I have arranged it. Rather a woman I know, and a servant, than a woman at court who will smirk and condescend. She is my creature as well as the King's. She will obey me too. She will be discreet and not crow her victory over me.'

But my thoughts were centred on Edward.

'Where is his loyalty, after all the children you have given him, all the love you have bestowed on him? I despise him for it.'

'You must not. It is better this way. He is still virile, while I am in decline.'

'Oh, no, my dear lady…' The depth of her sorrow wrung my heart.

'It is true. I see my death. I already envisage my tomb.'

I held her hands in futile attempt to absorb her pain.

'I could not do that. I could not employ his mistress as one of my damsels. Knowing it. Accepting it.'

No, I could not do that. It was beyond any consideration. Accepting that I must be blind to what happened on campaign, Thomas had had no mistress to my knowledge within the years we had been together. Nor had Will. Would Ned ever share his bed with another woman if he grew weary of me? Mistress Willesford was a woman from his past, consigned to remain there. Oh, no. I would make sure he had no mistress but me.

'I don't suppose you could.' Philippa rallied, as she must have done so often before. 'But I can. I must. That is not a matter for us now, and you must not meddle.' Her level stare was as implacable as that of her first-born son. 'You will say and do nothing. Indeed I should not have told you but sometimes weariness weighs down on me.' She touched my cheek, the tears already drying on hers. 'I will speak with the King about this marriage of yours,' she promised, her shoulders straight again, her chin lifted. 'But I promise nothing.'

That spring and summer the court fell into gloom such as I had never seen, not even after the death of the old Earl of Salisbury. Edward was sunk deep in a pool of dark distress. Even as early as February, before I had made my vows with Ned, the heavens had seemed to presage the disasters that now befell us. Burning lights were seen streaking across the night skies. The sun was shadowed so that at noon it appeared to be nightfall. The young corn withered, young fruit fell from the trees. Some claimed to see visions, hosts of soldiers garbed in black and white, issuing from two castles in the clouds, to wage war. All these signs and portents spoke to the chroniclers of calamity.

At least it turned their thoughts from me for a short time.

And then we felt the cold hand of death, irrespective of age or status. So many at the court succumbed. Five empty seats were counted when the King's Order of the Garter met in April. One of them Thomas, of course, the rest Edward's closest comrades in arms: the Earl of Northampton, Sir John Beauchamp, the young Earl of March, while in March, the most painful blow of all, the

Earl of Lancaster had departed this life, that most trusted friend of King Edward. Death hovered on all sides with its noisome breath. And as it claimed its allotted toll, Edward fell further and further into despair, unable to clamber out of it, the constant problem of our marriage overlaid with further loss and desolation. He would not speak of the future. Even when spring blossomed into early May and we might have thought of a lightening of spirits, the plague came. It hit children hard.

'My reign is blighted. It is God's judgement.'

In the past Edward had held the Garter tournament to lift England's spirits. There was no tournament. Hunting gave Edward little respite. Philippa retired into her pain and anxiety behind closed doors. Alice Perrers continued to be an efficient damsel, a quiet, respectful presence, presumably giving what comfort she could to a grieving monarch. I vowed my revenge for the pain she was causing when my own situation had been put to rights. Mistress Perrers would reign no more.

'What do you say when you go hunting together?' I asked Ned.

Ned gave my query short shrift. 'Very little. When I pursue the subject, he clams up. His new goshawk has more to say for itself. We need acknowledgement from the Pope, Joan. Who would have thought that my father would be so stubborn?' Ned was brittle with anger. 'It must be settled. My son must be born in the full glare of legitimacy.'

'If I were carrying your son.'

'If there were a chance of your carrying my son! I am tired of waiting.' His eye, turned on me, was inviting. I did not resist when he guided me to his chamber and proceeded to divest me of my raiment. 'At least let us enjoy the moment despite the presentiment of gloom and doom.'

And we did, Ned's restless impatience driving him to action that left me breathless and him sated. Ned had the power to make me forget my present woes and my past loss. It seemed that I could do the same for him. Laughter returned to us at least for a short time after we had bemoaned the intransigence of the King.

Chapter Twelve

I went to the King. I had no thought that I could break this unyielding, but no one else was trying and I knew full well that it was my reputation that was causing the problem. I was not afraid to beard the lion in his den. I did not tell Ned, who might have stopped me. In the store of garments and masks, readily to hand for a festivity, Edward sat in misery.

'Go away, Joan.' As soon as he turned his head, hearing my footsteps and saw who it was. 'I haven't the time for this. You know what I think. Nothing you say will make me change my mind.'

'I will go if you send me away. If you consider the provision of a court masque more mind-consuming than the happiness of your son. I can understand that it might be so, since the Garter tournament is so important to you. I understand that it is essential that the King's subjects see him attired in the robes of a Saracen, covered with indecipherable mystical symbols.'

I kicked lightly at a box of such materials, my skirts raising a cloud of dust and a clatter of buckram pheasants' wings as they fell to the floor. It seemed frivolous to discuss my future surrounded by feathers and spangles but so be it.

'Enough, Joan. There will be no court masque. Not now. Not ever.'

Elbows on knees, he regarded me from beneath brows that seemed not to have lifted from a scowl for a se'enight.

I resisted the desire to ask him why he was hiding amidst this tawdry glory if he had no intention of using it. 'I am here as your cousin,' I said.

'Or as a daughter by law I don't want.'

'I want you to reconsider.'

'Reconsider?' His cheeks achieved a wash of high colour. 'What are they saying in the streets? Have you not heard?'

'I have.'

'You have overreached yourself! Virgin of Kent, if you are lucky, although the implication is clear. Whore of Kent if you are not, by God!' Breath hissed between my teeth, as he seemed to find some perverse pleasure is saying it. 'They laugh over their cups in the alehouses. They toss your name around as if you were some tavern harlot. Is that what I want for the Princess of Wales? I am not the only man in this realm to consider you unsuitable as wife to the future King. To carry the future heir.'

I held my temper. 'I have never been adulterous.'

'You are bigamous, adulterous and profligate.' His eyes narrowed on my tight-fitting sleeves. 'Extravagant too. If I am not mistaken those buttons are diamonds. What did they cost?'

I accepted the challenge and returned it.

'Two hundred pounds. Are they not beautiful? Shall I tell you how much this ring cost? These two fine brooches cost your son one hundred and thirty pounds. Do you also wish to know the cost of this gown? Far less, I wager, than Philippa's sables.'

'They are outrageous! There is ruin in your blood. It is not from your father, I swear.' Edward was peevish, drawing the fine length of a peacock feather through his fingers, again and again, so that the the triviality of it all caused me to loose the reins on my temper a little. Surprising him, astounding him, I snatched the feather from his fingers, broke it and tossed it aside, letting emotion colour my voice for the first time, for it would do no harm in this vicious atmosphere.

'Listen to me, Edward. This marriage is legal. We both know that it is. If you refuse to recognise our marriage, if you will not help to set all to rights with His Holiness, you will create a rift with your son that will never be healed. He worships you. You are the hero he admired as a boy, and still admires. It will be a blight worse than the plague if you cleave this path of dissension between the two of you.'

Edward plucked out another feather. Twice he pulled it through his fingers, as if daring me to snatch it again. So I would not.

'Was it your idea to exchange vows in this chancy manner?'

'No. It was none of my doing.'

For a moment he looked baffled. 'It was Ned.'

'Yes.' I might drop to my knees beside him, but there was no softening of petition in my voice. 'You know your son. When his mind is made up he will not be turned. If you do not make this marriage fully legal, the scandal will be far greater than it is now. It is in all our interests.'

'And yours more than most. You see yourself as Queen.'

'Yes, I do.' It was the first time that I had ever put it into words. Now it had a life of its own. 'And I see my children as legitimate inheritors of your crown.'

'He should never have done it.' Edward cast aside the mangled feather.

'Will you answer me honestly?'

He grunted an assent of sorts.

'Would you have wed Philippa, if it had been forbidden by your mother? You married her because you loved her. Is it not true that you needed a papal dispensation because Philippa is your cousin? I know it was so. You can hardly condemn me for actions which have simply replicated your own. The manner of our marriage was regrettable, perhaps, but my blood is as good as any. As good as Ned's as you full well know. I may not be a woman of European status but I am a princess of England. You may argue against it but not with any weight, however hard you try.'

Which effectively silenced him. I stood, taking a step back.

'I will leave you to contemplate the future. And no, Ned did not send me. I came here to place before you a reasoned argument. Even if you reject it, at least you have now seen the truth.'

He looked up at me. 'Are you breeding?' he asked with a crudity unusual for Edward.

'No.' I walked to the door amidst all the foolish festive decorations, turning at the last. 'Not yet.'

'Thank God for one blessing.'

'If you stand in our way, I will not work to heal the rift with your son.'

A threat that I immediately regretted. Nor did I think that I had won the argument, but who was Edward to condemn my morals when the harlot Alice occupied his bed under the eye of his so loyal wife? I bore down hard on that sudden burst of fury. That was no way forward for any of us, nor must I make life any harder than it already was for the Queen. So I set myself a new task, with new skills demanded of me. I would show him that I could be a worthy daughter, a formidable support for England and for the Prince of Wales. I would leave him in no doubt at all that I could be a wife of great value.

Resisting my inclination to leave him to his miserable contemplations, I pulled up a stool and sat opposite, waiting, my hands folded neatly in my lap. I was learning that confrontation with an obdurate man did not always achieve victory. Some would say that I should have learned it long before now.

'You look troubled,' I said. 'I am willing to listen.'

'I don't trust you.'

'What is not to trust? I recall days when we could talk without dissent poisoning the air between us.'

I tried not to show the sharp stab of Edward's thrust at my heart. I had never been disloyal. Perhaps careless of my status, certainly wilful, but I had never deliberately cast a shadow of scandal over the Crown. Had I not always done what I could to put matters right? Returning to Thomas had been right. Yes, this marriage to Ned was a turbulent river which I must step across, but not now. Edward must be made to accept that I was more than a receptacle for gossip and mischief. I would give good counsel, if Edward would cast aside his scorn, but Edward remained caught up in some inner turmoil that refused to be broken apart.

Still I waited. Then, slowly, he began to speak, a trickle of thought, as if a dam had been breached by the smallest crack. He had forgotten his animosity towards me.

'Do you know, Joan? I am within sight of the fiftieth year of my life. I have spent most of that life fighting enemies in England, in Scotland and against France, and now we are at peace, to God's great blessing. My reign is secure. My country is secure from enemies. I have an exemplary wife and enough sons to carry on my name. But what now? How do I bring further glory to my reign?' His brow furrowed with concern, as if he were in a labyrinth and could see no way forward, only high hedges on both sides, blocked pathways ahead. 'We are beset with death and disease, by dread signs in the heavens, for which I have no remedy. My wife suffers, may the Virgin bring her respite in her travails. The friends of my youth are dead. My heir is entangled...'

He scowled at me.

'Your son is entangled with me,' I prompted.

'Yes. I would not have had this marriage. It brings England no value. Only scandal and rumour, France laughing up its sanctimonious sleeve. You are a source of disaffection.'

I felt the muscles in my jaw tighten but I preserved the benign demeanour. 'I will repair the rumours. There will be no scandal. When I carry your son's child, the potency of England will be fulfilled. That is, when I carry your son's legitimate child, received into the bosom of the Church.' My voiced acquired an intimate note, a deliberately seductive note beneath a businesslike approach. I had thought long and hard about how to reach Edward in his dark thoughts. 'How would you wish to be remembered, Edward?'

His brows flattened as he stared at me, redolent of suspicion.

'You have brought peace to this land. You have made the name of England feared and respected. That would make you a great King when tales are told in history. Will you not pursue this greatness?'

'But how would I pursue greatness now? I have no heart for it, any of it.' He was cold, drawn down by loss and isolation. 'My brave Garter knights are decimated. All the hopes I had for them. There are no more wars for me to fight.'

I had not realised quite the depths to which he had sunk.

'Shall I tell you what I would do?' I asked.

'How would you see inside the mind of a King?'

'No, I cannot. But think about this, cousin. Can you not replenish your Garter knights? Fill the empty ranks so that those who have gone before have brave men to step into their shoes, to continue the glory that they created.'

'Who do I choose to be men of the same calibre to stand with me?'

I felt my heart settling, my advice becoming smoother. 'You choose your sons. They are of an age to sit with your knights.'

'But it should be a celebration. I am in no mood for a celebration.'

'Then create your new knights as a memorial to those who have served you well.' At last he was listening to me. 'There are women who would also serve you well, even if not on the battlefield. Why should a wellborn woman not be a Garter lady?'

'My wife is already Lady of the Garter,' Edward growled. 'Hoping for promotion Joan?'

His tone had turned cynical. The despair had receded but he was not better inclined to my advice. With a smile I changed direction.

'Only if it pleases you, Edward. Why not turn your mind to something that will speak your name to future generations, when wars and battles are forgotten and England blossoms into peace and prosperity?'

'What? Do you suggest that I become a merchant and bargain for trade?' Edward retaliated in what was almost a sneer.

Oh, I knew what would forge this miserable King's name in gold.

'Building,' I said. 'Why not spend your time and your money on building for the future? That is how you will be remembered. When men see the product of your energies they will praise you for your foresight.'

Once I had taken Edward to task for spending so flagrantly in this manner rather than recognising my own need. Now I had to use whatever came to hand to drive away the demon of melancholia. I saw a slide of light in Edward's dull eye, and thanked the Blessed Virgin. But all was not won yet.

'Do I need new castles?'

'Why not? Or replenish those you have. Give your Queen and family accommodations worthy of them, hung with cloth of gold if you wish.'

The cloth of gold, the furnishings, did not yet interest him.

'It might be good policy to build a new castle or two to keep the French from eyeing my shores.' I saw the light begin to brighten.

'You could always name a new castle for the Queen. She would like that.'

I was sorely tempted to say: *Dismiss your mistress. She would like that even more.* But not now. Not yet.

'And where do I get the money for this venture, Madam Joan?'

'What you don't spend on war, you spend on peace. Do you not have the money from the King of France's ransom? I understand the full amount has been decided and I doubt you've spent it all on feathers and masks.'

I watched as the emotions sped across his face. It had fired him. I had thought it impossible, but he was renewed, his mind thinking ahead once more rather than sinking in a morass of wretchedness.

'And if the taxes are lower because of the peace,' he agreed, 'then my parliaments will welcome me with respectful greetings that do not cover a snarling face.'

'What a venture for your days of peace, Edward.' I chanced a touch on his hand, as I might in the old days, from which he did not flinch, and I took a breath, hoping that I did not go too far in gilding this particular lily. A little interpretation of the signs and portents by a clever woman would do no harm. 'There is so much that you can do, Edward. The heavenly portents are not necessarily a sign of punishment for England, but one of God's support in a time of difficulty. Who else would send a flaming star across the heavens, but God as a sign of his blessing on this realm? One of the armies was dressed in pure white. Do you recall? That surely was your own army. You will vanquish the black-robed foe. Perhaps it means that we will overcome the black powers of the plague itself.'

Edward stood and, taking my hand, drew me to my feet.

'You are an astute woman, Joan.'

I thought he might say cunning. I would not wish to be seen as guileful, although many would say that I was. How useful a smile and a soft word of advice had proved, directing his thoughts into different tracks, encouraging him to look ahead and use the powers that he had been blessed with. He was renewed and I was pleased to see it.

'If you had been born a man, I would have had you at my side as one of my counsellors.'

'If I were a man, we would not be in this marital predicament, my lord.'

But I acknowledged the compliment with a curtsey.

At the door, I delivered a final parting gesture, because it seemed to me to be good sense. 'The people of England would like to see you, Edward. You are their hero. Don't shut yourself away here, when you bring them strength and hope. Did you not defeat France? Have you not given them a magnificent heir? The people love you and they love the Prince of Wales. Don't leave them to feel bereft in your absence.'

It was as if he had grown taller, reclaiming all the glory that he had laid aside.

'I will take your advice, Madam Joan.' Until the quick frown. 'Why has no one else sought to give me any before?'

'Perhaps because they do not dare, because they do not wish to gain your enmity. Your opinion of me is low, Edward. It will not get any lower for my advice.'

And, at last, Edward laughed, a rusty sound as if it had been little used of late.

I opened the door, then paused, looking back to see him standing amidst the detritus of peacock feathers. 'The Queen is frail today. She would like to see you.' And then, because I could not resist, and felt no pity for him. 'It would raise her spirits even more, Edward, if you would banish Alice Perrers to the most distant castle that you possess.'

I closed the door on his astonished face with a sharp snap. What had possessed me to say that? And yet I did not regret it. It needed saying and I would risk the consequences.

I did not keep my promise to Philippa. How could I? I could not ignore a grievous situation that brought such hurt to her. She might accept it with all graciousness; I could not, when I discovered the royal harlot walking towards me along the upper gallery, clearly treading her immoral path towards the King's chambers. After my recent depressing exchange with Edward I was in a mood to be combative rather than charitable.

'Mistress Perrers.'

Quite deliberately, I stepped in front of her to make her halt.

'My lady,' she replied. Her curtsey and downcast eyes were the essence of demure womanhood. All skin-deep, I presumed, now that I knew the truth. I wasted no soft words on her.

'Your position here brings distress to the Queen.'

'But it brings comfort to the King. The Queen and I understand each other very well, my lady.'

'You would place yourself on a level with the Queen of England?'

'Not so. But better a royal mistress who serves the Queen with all humility than one who would laud her victory over her husband. I know my place. My discretion is renowned, my lady.' Her eyes lifted slowly to my face. 'While yours, if I may advise, is not.'

It was a reply worthy of any one of my own. Her dark eyes offered an indubitable challenge. Was that what disturbed me in this woman? That she too had the courage to make her own path in life, despite those who would condemn and vilify? My heart raced with the thought that we were not much different in what we had done, flouting convention and gainsaying courtly behaviour.

I made the only reply that was possible.

'One step, Mistress Perrers, only one step of your pretty but ambitious feet that brings the Queen to tears, and I will see your dismissal.'

Mistress Perrers' smile lit her face, making her unremarkable features quite lovely.

'Unless you have the ear of the King, my lady, I doubt you will achieve it. Edward's ear is mine and mine alone. I understand you have no success in winning his liking for your unfortunate marriage to the Prince.'

Her accuracy touched a nerve. 'You are remarkably indecorous.'

'I have need to be. As do you, my lady. Do we not both enjoy power for its own sake?' She must have read my reaction to this unexpected reply from a mere damsel. Her words were as finely drawn as her beautifully ached brows. 'I expect you will deny it, but there is much that is similar between us. Royal whores are not the only court women to spark the fire of gossip.'

'I see no similarity. And you are impertinent.'

'I am also in a hurry, my lady, if you will allow me to pass. The King has need of me.' *And no need of you.* The implication was clear as day as she stepped round me. For a moment I thought she would say more, but she did not, continuing on her path to the King's door. There she stopped, looking over her shoulder.

'I know that you will use every means to ensure my dismissal, my lady. You will not succeed now, but one day you will, for is not all power finite? One day I will lose the security of Edward's desire for me, or death will cut the final thread. But until then, my position is sacrosanct.' Once more she smiled. 'It may be that you could find some value in that, if you were prepared to step beyond your prejudices against a woman of no birth.'

The door closed softly at her back. The battle lines were drawn.

What had she implied? I considered that she might have the temerity to offer to put my case before Edward, to win his support for me, in the aftermath of a tumble on the royal bed. She had not, which was wise. What a worthy adversary she was proving to be, but I would win this battle. One day I would see the dismissal of Mistress Alice Perrers. I would accept no similarity between us, and yet, if I admitted to honesty, I discovered, to my irritation, that I enjoyed the cut and thrust of battle with this undoubtedly intelligent woman.

We were spending the morning inspecting the site of the new building, a castle at Queensborough on the Isle of Sheppey, accompanying Edward at his invitation to give an appreciative audience to his new scheme, product of my prompting. It was a bright, windy day, the cool air from the west sufficient to raise the spirits if they were downcast. Philippa appeared more content than of late, even though Alice was present. Isabella and de Coucy were in decorative attendance while I was hot in my all-enveloping robes that might just suggest a burgeoning body. Ned's hand was beneath my arm, as I had instructed him.

'Why?' He took his attention from the stonework that would eventually develop into two huge towers overlooking the gates that gave access to a passage that would act as a barbican, trapping any invaders. As he cast an eye over me, I knew what he saw. His gaze, appreciative of the luxury of heavy velvet, sharpened at the voluminous cote-hardie and cloak I had chosen to wear. 'Are you perhaps carrying my heir?'

My smile became brighter at his quick wit. 'No. But it won't come amiss if you are solicitous of my health.'

His brows rose a little, before his eyes were warmed by a sly smile unworthy in a future King, but perfectly worthy of me.

'What a duplicitous mind you have, Jeanette.'

'It will help if you look delighted with me.'

'I am always delighted with you.'

He patted my hand, asked if I wished to sit, then departed to find me a cup of ale. The Queen, standing beside me, surveyed the scene before us, where Edward was busy with plans and builders.

'You are a source of never-ending amusement, Joan. If I was a suspicious woman I would think you involved in subterfuge. And if that is a pregnancy, I wager it will be the longest in history.'

Philippa was engaged with the scene before her, encouraged by a morbid interest in the effigy that would grace her tomb. Merely smiling, as if holding a secret close to my heart, I set myself to amuse, sipping occasionally at the ale. She might doubt my veracity but I knew that, in her gratitude, she would not betray me.

A wind of change had blown though the chambers and antechambers of the royal palaces, a veritable storm that swept and renewed. Did the King take my advice? It has to be said that he did. The vacant seats, unoccupied when the Garter Knights assembled, were filled with the most royal of blood. Lionel, John and Edmund, royal sons, took their places, clad in their blue robes. But the King had an eye for the occasion, as a memorial. Lavish lengths of scarlet and black were ordered so that the jousts, festive in themselves, were also deeply respectful, the living knights in red pitted in skill against the mourners of the dead in black. Garter emblems and brooches were handed out, furs lavishly bestowed. Edward commemorated his dead with superb aplomb rather than retiring to sigh and bewail. The people who flocked to enjoy the spectacle appreciated seeing their King and cheered when ale and food were dispensed with a liberal hand.

Yes, he had taken my advice. In the days that followed, Edward made himself evident whenever he could, spending much time on this new town and castle at Sheppey which he had called in honour of the Queen. He met with parliament whose members were pleased. He went out and about, making use of royal occasions to remind England who was their King. The marriage of the royal daughter Mary to John de Montfort, who claimed the duchy of Brittany, a marriage that Thomas and I had considered for our own daughter Joan, was one to raise hearts cast down by so much death. Edward almost smiled on Isabella and her French lover.

He almost smiled on me.

There was nothing the King could do about the plague which

continued to rage unchecked, but I had done all I could. I practised great forbearance when he did not address himself to my own predicament. Now Edward came to join us, waving aside the builders, to take up a position foursquare in front of Ned who was unrolling one of the charts showing a detailed fine-drawn plan of Edward's building.

'You give me no choice, sir.'

'I have expressed no opinion on the building. But I can if you wish,' Ned replied, a little chillier than usual, a little more formal, but looking perplexed. 'It is your decision to make, sir. It would seem to be an excellent site for a castle to protect our shores and I have to admire the design with the encircling walls without towers...'

'Not the castle,' Edward interrupted. 'This... this situation between the two of you. I have consulted my men of law and the Archbishop.' There was no softness beneath the frowning visage. 'They tell me there is a way out of this whole tangle of matrimonial threads, without causing too much of an upheaval or drawing too much attention. We will petition Innocent VI for a papal dispensation.'

Which you could have done weeks ago, if you had been willing to take advice.

I beamed at Edward.

'Thank you, my lord,' I said, glancing at Ned who preserved a stoical exterior as, taking a document from the breast of his tunic, Edward thrust it towards his son.

'We have to be clever here. This is our proposition. Your marriage, inadvisable as it was, was not in contempt of church law, or disregarding of the displeasure of His Holiness for two people too closely related for comfort, but with the intention of subsequently obtaining the necessary authorisation.' Edward's own displeasure was still more than evident. 'Two young people, unable to wait, charged by lust, carried away in the heat of the moment. We will rest on papal compassion for your youth and foolishness – though both of you are hardly immature striplings – to free you from threat of excommunication, and issue a dispensation so that you might have a valid public betrothal and wedding. That should put an end to all subterfuge.' He looked from Ned to me, expecting some reaction. 'We will send a royal herald…'

I nudged Ned.

'There is no need,' he said. 'We already have it in hand, sir.'

Edward cocked his head. I left the explanation to Ned.

'We could wait no longer. My esquire Nicholas Bond has been sent to Avignon to obtain the licence for our marriage.'

A cloud hovered on the horizon as if to threaten the sun.

'Indeed, my lord,' I said quickly, 'we could not wait.'

'So you pre-empted my decision.'

'I have applied with all legal arguments,' Ned said, 'as heir to the throne.'

'I am sure that you have. And enough gold coin to sink one of my ships on the journey over there.' Edward grunted with a slide of his eye towards me and my robes. 'So be it. No time for bewailing the spilling of milk. If my cousin does indeed carry a child, the sooner this is put right the better. I'll send my own legal men after your squire since I doubt his voice will be enough. It's complicated. Confraternity of course because you are related in the third degree through your common great grandfather Edward the First. But then there is compaternity too, since you stood godfather to the two Holland boys.'

It was as if he were holding a royal audience, Edward informing us of matters which we knew full well without the legal explanation. Edward's heart was not in it but he would support our claim. But would the Pope see fit to absolve our sin, or would I once again be suspended between a shadowy and a legal marriage?

'This is no position for you to be in, *if* you were to be carrying a child.' His gaze wafted over me, holding as much suspicion as Philippa's had. Edward had never been obtuse. 'I am outmanoeuvred by my own son and you, madam. I recommend abstention until we have settled this and untied all the knots. You will see the sense in it. There must be no breath of illegitimacy over my grandson. I trust you will make my son a good wife, a loyal wife.'

He snatched back one of the rolls that contained the plan for his new castle, walking a few steps away, before having second thoughts, swinging back towards us.

'We need no more gossip over this than already exists.' There was the faintest brush of colour along his cheekbones, as if Edward was aware of his own misconduct. 'I have considered this. One thing we must be absolutely certain of. Your marriage to Holland is over, without argument, through his demise, but there is the annulment of your second marriage to Salisbury, since he is still very much alive. I want no suggestion that you might still be wed to Salisbury. When you carry the heir to the English throne, it was be a legitimate birth. It is necessary that all be made clear within the law.'

I curtsied low. It was very necessary. 'We are both aware of how much we owe to your forbearance,' I said, eyes lowered as a good wife should. 'There will be no child until we are wed in the full light of day.'

Edward grimaced, a twist of his mouth, so often seen when Ned was faced with unsurmountable obstacles. 'Better you than me, Ned, taking her as your wife.'

Edward and Ned clasped hands in a fair pretence at reconciliation. Edward kissed my cheek. Unsure that he would ever be reconciled to me, I felt a huge sense of relief that at last our precipitate action would receive royal and papal blessing.

'Well?' I realised that Edward's expression held an interesting speculation as he drew me a little distance from the party.

'Well what, my lord?' I realised that his support was not going to be without its cost. Edward was about to take advantage of my relief.

'You could show your gratitude, cousin.'

'And how would I do that?'

'A loan,' he said promptly. 'This drains my finances inordinately.' He waved towards the building operations which swarmed with stonemasons and labourers. 'The French King's ransom is slow in materialising, despite his being sent home with all my good will. It was your idea, and it failed.' Edward was predisposed to whine. 'You are a wealthy woman. My legal men can travel to Avignon with great speed, if I give the order.'

Admiring his pragmatism – Edward's recognition and swift inter-vention in exchange for a loan – I also saw the value to me in having the King in debt for my good offices. Who knew when it would be of value to me? It was a business transaction close to my heart.

'Here's what I'll do, cousin. I will pledge you some of my jewels. You may sell them if you wish or raise money on their value. Will that be sufficient to show my gratitude?'

'It depends on how many jewels and their value.'

'Oh, I will make sure that it is a truly royal gift, from the Princess of Wales to the King of England.' I leaned close. 'But if I see them adorning Mistress Perrers' bosom, I'll make it known the length and breadth of the country. And demand their return in a blink of an eye, with a recourse to law if necessary.'

'Would I do that? You have my word that I will not.'

Again there was a flush of hot colour along his cheekbones that matched the fire in his eye. Did I trust him? I thought that he might very well bestow them on Mistress Perrers, but not yet. Edward was a man who kept his word. We had come to terms after all.

'I'll hold you to that word,' I said.

As Edward, in a fair mood at having achieved a victory against overwhelming odds, ushered the party closer to the massive building works, I was halted by a hand on my cloak.

'You should be congratulated, my lady.'

'Still here Mistress Perrers?'

'As you see, my lady.'

'I thought you might have found a ready excuse to be elsewhere.'

'No my lady. I received an invitation from the Queen.'

I studied her, again intrigued by this woman, in spite of my hostility towards her.

'What does the King see in you?'

I thought she would be flippant in her reply. Instead her face became solemn.

'The King tolerates me – even loves me – because I do what none of his household is prepared to do.'

'And what is that?' I was curious.

'I tell him the truth.' A smile touched her mouth, coloured her pale skin. 'As perhaps do you, my lady.' Her eye travelled over my robes, as had many that day. 'Except perhaps on this occasion when it might be useful to be furtive.'

She was too percipient by half. 'Stay out of my path, Mistress Perrers.'

'I will. Your doings have nought to do with me. I wish you well.' She stepped around me, as she had once before, as bright-eyed as my pet monkey. 'You might ask yourself, my lady, why the King changed his mind. Was it your voice of persuasion or mine?'

She was a clever woman. Had she added her soft voice? I did not believe that she would since I was no friend of hers. Perhaps she hoped that I would become such a one.

No, she was cleverer than that.

'Was it yours?' I asked. 'I would wager that chain of sapphires it was not.'

'I would not wager with these gems, my lady. Their value is too great for me to risk my loss of them. One day, when Edward is dead, my place here will come to an end. I must make provision for that day, as you make provision for your future. For one day your power too will die a death. But no, I did not persuade Edward. It will please you that it was his own choice.'

She went to stand beside him, taking an interest as he pointed out where the great walls would be built.

'I despise that woman.' Isabella at my shoulder, venom in her regard.

I almost responded in agreement, that I too detested her, her confidence, her self-assurance. But I admired Mistress Perrers' reading of an unstable situation, the sheer transience of it, a weakness in effect that I would do all in my power to exploit. It made me uncomfortable that she should read mine so clearly.

The contingent of royal legal men set off, laden with scrolls, gold and fine arguments, but neither they nor Ned's squire returned soon from Avignon. A situation I recognised all too well. My mind began to plot and plan.

'How long?' Ned groaned, impatient with a situation he could not change.

'You will have to wait with patience.'

'I have no patience.'

'We could pre-empt the decision.'

'And do what?'

'Let me tell you.'

He listened as I outlined my thoughts.

'Will we find a bishop who will do it, and risk my father's wrath?'

'Are you not the Prince of Wales?'

'But this is not a battle. Or perhaps...' his eyes were opaque, unseeing of the stretch of the Thames as he considered the matter, then they fell onto me. 'I think that it is undoubtedly a battle. And since we have come this far, we must drive the charge on to the end.'

★★★

On a day of calm, early autumnal warmth most fitting for our journey, Ned and I arrived at Lambeth Palace, and there, before a not entirely pleased Archbishop Islip of Canterbury, the most pre-eminent cleric that Ned could get his hands on at short notice, we explained what it was that we wanted. His Grace was reluctant, coldly eloquent, despite Ned's frown that grew heavier by the second after we had kissed the episcopal ring and shown him every honour.

'We do not have the dispensation, my lord.' The Archbishop's final summing up. 'We have had no word from His Holiness. Thus it would be unwise for us to proceed along the lines that you envisage.'

'But we will. We will do more than envisage. This lady and I wish to take this step, in anticipation of the papal decision.'

Although I left him to use his authority, spending the time standing before the Archbishop's prie-dieu, turning the pages of the missal, my mind was not on the vivid pictures or holy words. I was willing Ned to remain calm, even though I knew it was a lost cause. He might be seated, as invited to do so, but the tension in him shimmered across the room.

'But we cannot pre-empt it, my lord. That would merely layer another sin on top of the initial one.' I felt the cleric's glance touch on me. 'You are not yet permitted to wed this lady. Why would you wish to take this step, when it is only a matter of waiting?'

'Because I wish it.' Ned's voice was hardening by the minute. 'We can pre-empt it, Your Grace, because it is my will.'

'But I am not empowered, my lord…'

I abandoned the missal to stand at Ned's side, a hand on his shoulder, pressing hard. I smiled at the Archbishop but my question was for Ned, knowing exactly how I could take a hand in what was fast becoming a heated dispute.

'Do you not think,' I asked Ned, 'that we should apply to the Bishop of London instead, if it does not sit easily with His Grace of Canterbury's conscience? It matters not whether the heir to the throne plights his troth before Canterbury or London.'

Without hesitation Ned stood. 'Excellent! And plight it we will.'

The mention of London, an unexpected swipe at ecclesiastical protocol, was more than persuasive. That same evening, as the autumn shades gathered, Ned and I took our marital oaths before the suddenly co-operative Archbishop who gave us his blessing with a thin semblance of acceptance.

Ned smiled at me. 'I would have given you a ring to mark this occasion. I forgot to bring it. Wear this instead.'

He took a ring from his own hand and pushed it onto my finger where it spun, large and loose, but I clenched my fist over it. There it was, the single amethyst catching the light with costly allure. The first step to true legality. All we needed now was the ceremonial, the royal acceptance, the full marriage, in Windsor.

'I want it fast,' Ned announced as we prepared to leave.

'I really cannot publish the bans yet, my lord,' the cleric was nervous. 'Not until the Pope has pronounced. I should not have allowed you to plight your troth with such speed. You should consider arranging the ceremony perhaps at the beginning of next month. His Holiness should have made his decision by then...'

Ned considered this, and I nodded when he looked at me. Within a month would be acceptable. Time and enough for my women to sew a new gown in which I would become Princess of Wales. There were some blessings.

So we returned to Kennington with a degree of satisfaction and much planning, only to be summoned back the following day by a page in Canterbury livery, all our complacency undermined when we were ushered in to find the Archbishop in some state of anxiety, as was I although I was more adept at hiding it. Had we been refused after all this? Was everything Ned and I had done to fall to pieces at the last because, in spite of all my hopes, the Pope saw an advantage in putting some malign political pressure on the King of England?

'Do we have the dispensation?' Ned demanded without waiting for the formal greeting. No bending of the royal knee or kissing of the episcopal ring today.

'No, my lord. It is not as easy as that.'

Fear leapt within me now, fully fledged. All my ambitions, all Ned's autocratic demands, were to be ground under the heel of the papal slipper.

'I have received a papal document, my lord.' His Grace was severe, which did nothing to settle the hectic beat in my throat. 'It is necessary that you know the contents, and consider them.'

'Why? What do I need to consider? I know what I want.'

'There are terms, my lord…'

Ned waved him to begin as we took our seats.

'Make all plain, man, so that we can get on with it.'

The Archbishop, resigned to being hurried along, no matter the importance of the document with its papal seals, placed his hands face downwards on either side of the missive.

'I think that the conditions are not insuperable, my lord. His Holiness is pleased to smooth your future path together. He has cast the papal eye over the previous situation, my lady, between you and your two husbands.' He read painstakingly. 'The marriage between you and the Earl of Salisbury was declared null and void by the papal bull of 1349. His Holiness recognises that this declaration is quite legal.'

'There was no question of it, Your Grace,' I said.

As I knew. Did I not have the documents safe in my keeping?

He glance took in both of us. 'There is the matter of the clandestine marriages that have been a feature of your marital state. The first, my lady, is cancelled with the death of Sir Thomas Holland, Earl of Kent. The second is more problematical – the one undertaken in the spring of this year between yourself, my lord, and the lady here present. Such a marriage without holy approval is open to punishment by excommunication.'

'But His Holiness would not consider excommunicating me,' Ned said. He was without fear, although I shivered at the underlying threat.

'No, my lord. His Holiness consents that this marriage too shall be declared null and void. It was an unfortunate aberration on your part, but it will not be a hindrance to any future step you take. Thus you are both declared to be at this present time unmarried, and so free to marry again under the blessing of Holy Mother Church.' He cleared his throat. 'But I must ask you. You are both required, under oath, to promise that you – that neither of you – will ever again enter into a clandestine marriage. Any such marriages must be foresworn, in my presence.'

Ned's brows rose. I thought he might refuse, his royal dignity impaired.

'Do you so promise?'

'Yes.' I said. 'We will make such a promise.' I closed my hand over Ned's arm. 'Both of us.'

It was easily done to make a promise, sanctified by the Archbishop's own golden crucifix, lifted from around his neck and handed first to Ned and then to me. So few words needed to destroy the mistakes of the past and set our feet on a righteous path. We kissed the jewel-encrusted gold and all was made well, our sin wiped clean. Ned's oath might be dragged from him, but I knew the value of this acquiescence.

So we promised. No more clandestine marriages. But then why would we? This is what we had wanted.

'Good. Good.' The Archbishop reclaimed his crucifix, replacing it so that it gleamed, a reminder of what we had just done. 'You are now both released from the penalty of excommunication.'

'Is that it?'

'Not quite my lord. Do you now agree, as a symbol of your repentance of so thoughtless a deed...'

I felt Ned stiffen again and closed my hand tighter.

'... to build and endow two chapels to the glory of God?'

I thought it was in Ned's mind to refuse, but I slid my hand down to take his, linking our fingers.

'We do so swear,' I said. 'We will endow two chapels.'

'We do so swear,' repeated Ned.

'Then it is done. There is no remaining impediment to your marrying this lady, publicly and legally in a seemly manner.'

'How soon?'

'We must publish the bans, my lord.'

'Then do it now.'

As we left, 'I wish for a copy of the papal instructions,' I informed the relieved cleric. 'Can it be arranged?'

'Most certainly, my lady. I will send them to you forthwith.'

I was amassing a collection. I would not be parted from them.

It was on the tenth day of October, less than a year after the death of Thomas, that I achieved the true fulfilment of the ambitions that had dogged me since childhood. When I had dreamed of escaping the taint of treason, it had never been in this manner. Now my status before all was confirmed, my less than spotless past wiped clean. I was protected from criticism and disgrace, becoming Ned's legal wife and Princess of Wales in the eyes of the world in the chapel at Windsor.

The chroniclers recorded, along with less than subtle comments on my being the Virgin of Kent, against which all present turned a discreet blind eye, that the match greatly surprised many people.

No. It surprised very few, for, by the time we stood side by side in St. George's Chapel at Windsor before the combined weight of the Archbishop of Canterbury, the bishops of Salisbury, Lincoln and Worcester, as well as the abbot of Westminster, it had been the subject of court gossip for as many months as I had fingers on one hand. By the time the bans had been called with disgraceful speed within four days, most there-present regarded this union as a *fait accompli*, and, to avoid any further acrimony from the pens of the chroniclers, merely wished us to complete it.

The weight of the Church dignitaries would add verisimilitude to the proceedings.

If some thought that the King would continue to show his disfavour, they were to be disappointed. No scandal here. When I stood beside Ned at the altar to exchange our vows, our promises were duly witnessed by Edward and Philippa, a handful of their royal children and a vast gathering of court notables and clergy. Nothing clandestine about this marriage. Edward was gruff when we knelt before him for his blessing, but he did not stint on the acceptance of our union, raising me to kiss my hand and my cheek. His ill-will had faded with the aura of holiness and legality. We were restored.

And so I was Princess of Wales, the legal entanglements of the past untied and retied in this act of public witness. One day I would be Queen of England.

Ned turned to smile at me as he held my hand in his to present me to the court.

I smiled back. It was no hardship. This time he had remembered the ring, one that I knew he had had made for me so the fitting was perfect, a piece of worked gold to offset the fine ruby at its heart.

Was my heart engaged? Perhaps it was a little.

And yet my satisfaction was spoiled. Is it not a fact that the germ of discontent lies at the heart of even the most perfect of fruit? Here was a grub, tiny and insubstantial yet still a blemish, at the centre of this peach, even though I had to accept the King's cold reasoning.

I had expected a celebration of vast proportion. For the heir to the throne to take a new bride who would carry his heir, the future King of England, was it not of major importance for the event to be feted? Would we not celebrate that we were legally conjoined? I had enough experience of royal marriages to know what I might expect of masques and dancing, of mummers and tournaments, of foreign ambassadors by the dozen with their heraldic achievements to the fore. Of show and festivity and the shaking out of the coffers of the costumes so beloved of Edward and his court, even down to the peacock feathers. Why would I not expect the same? This was one of the most important marriages of the decade. The English heir, the famous knight of Crécy and Poitiers, wed at last.

Nothing. There was not one ripple in court life to mark our holy wedlock. There was no splendour. The peacock feathers remained packed away. No celebration, no tournament at which Ned could shine, no foreign ambassadors. If Edward had filled his coffers from the ransoming of the French King John, or from my loan, none of it was spent on our union. There was a meal set out for those who attended our wedding. Nothing more.

I looked at the tables with the array of dishes, all quite adequate for a court repast, but hardly for the marriage of the Prince of Wales. Not a stuffed peacock, not a roasted swan, not a Pike in Galentyne in sight. There was no expensive outlay on dramatic subtleties to proclaim our union with heraldic achievements and mythical beasts.

King Edward made all clear.

'Better if you settle into married life away from the public eye. Until they get used to the idea. An heir would be a good thing, too.'

Since there was no arguing against the King's decision, we retired to Ned's manor at Berkhamsted to settle into married life together in luxury befitting our station, discovering anew the shared pleasure in spending the vast sums of money at our disposal. The manor became a treasure house of furnishings for the rooms which we traversed in robes stitched from the finest tissue and fur. The jewels Ned gave me to replace those I had loaned to the King were of inestimable value and quality. Our affection was strong, our enjoyment in each other's company a delight to discover.

All that was needed to fill our cup to overflowing was that I should quicken. An heir for England would call forth an angelic throng to laud the achievements of King Edward and his family. My future would be secure for all time through our children.

What of my memories of Thomas? They would never fade. But with Ned my mourning could be put aside.

I did not tell Ned. One of those strange incidents to intrude on my pleasure. Not that I believed it. It caused me no anxiety for were we not awash with heavenly signs? But, irritatingly, that moment at Westminster continued to haunt me, casting a blight over the bright days when we enjoyed the fruits of our extravagance at Berkhamsted. It had been Sir Bartholomew Burghersh, one of the ageing knights of Edward's court, sitting on a bench in the sunshine, entertaining Philippa's damsels with tales of his past exploits, of ghosts and demons and all such nonsense.

'We have a book...' he was saying, enjoying the moment when they sat and listened. 'It is believed to be the prophecy of Merlin. And do you know what it says?'

There was a chorus of ignorance. Of laughter. They were not

beyond encouraging a foolish old man, and the mention of Merlin always drew a crowd. I made to walk on.

'The King should be wary of it. And the Prince his son. It may be old magic, but it is a grave prediction for the future.'

Which caught my attention like the snap of a trout to gobble up a mayfly. I stopped.

'The Crown of England will not pass to the Prince of Wales.' His eyes travelled round the group, now suitably intrigued, but did not rest on me. 'Nor will it rest on the head of his brothers, even though they are princes of the blood royal and the sons of Kings.'

'So who will rule England?' I asked.

'Merlin predicted that it will pass to the House of Lancaster, my lady.'

Which side-stepped a number who might think that they had a stronger claim to the throne than John, Duke of Lancaster.

'Do you say that some yet unborn son of Duke John will rule?'

'Not I, my lady. Merlin himself so decrees.' His eye sharpened in recognition. 'It will have a bearing on your life, my lady.'

'Only if we believe in such nonsense. You should know better than to tease the damsels, Sir Bartholomew.'

I walked on. It was disturbing, but not unduly so. I had no thought for portents. I looked back over my shoulder.

'Perhaps you should tell him my lord the King, Sir Bartholomew.'

'Perhaps I should, my lady. But I doubt he'll wish to hear it.'

No, there was no truth in it. Merely an old man, meandering in his memories. What possible truth could there be? Or from the mythical Merlin with his magical powers in the reign of the long-distant King Arthur. What need to burden this bright morning with myths and legends, as empty as the birdsong that filled my ears with silly chir-rupings that suddenly irritated me beyond words. Ned would rule, followed by our sons.

Ignore the scribblers, the self-important soothsayers. Ignore the gossips too.

It worried me that I did not quicken. It was becoming imperative that I did.

Chapter Thirteen

August 1363: The Bishop's Palace in Bordeaux

We had settled into the Bishop's palace at Bordeaux, where we were breaking our fast as was our wont in the airy chamber that gave views out over town and harbour. Ned, stretching as if he had been confined in a cage for far too long, was in expansive mood. I saw the change in him since the day when we had disembarked, an excitement about him, a new energy, while I was struggling to keep abreast of his line of thought. Dressed in my customary damasks and linen, I found the layers of my garments oppressive, even so early in the day when the heat had not yet built to its full power. On that morning I was not as appreciative of the southern delights of Bordeaux as I might have been.

But Ned was more than appreciative.

For therein had lain the problem of our new life together at Kennington and at Berkhamsted, as Prince and Princess of Wales. There was, to his mind, so little for Ned to which he could set his hand. There was no war for Ned to descend on, full of enthusiasms and planning and military fervour. True, the Treaty of Brétigny had run into difficulties since the King of France had still not formally renounced his claim over the territories agreed on in the original discussion of the Treaty. On the strength of this being decided, Edward agreed to relinquish his claim to the French throne, in return for complete sovereignty over all the territories he had inherited as a vassal as well as those he had obtained by conquest. It remained a festering sore between England and France, which Thomas might have taken the trouble to heal, but such negotiation to set the wound to rights was not to Ned's taste. Nor did I think he would excel at such affairs. Ned was short on patience when arguments did not go his way.

For a number of months, back in England, he had ploughed his energies into the rebuilding at Kennington, adding a great vaulted hall with pantry, buttery, kitchens and other chambers necessary to the lifestyle to which we both aspired. Carved fireplaces, painted floor tiles, glowing tapestries were bought and enjoyed.

But such cosmetic enhancement could not satisfy for long.

We would, I supposed, travel round Ned's manors and my own, taking on matters of government that Edward saw fit to delegate. These would increase as the years passed, but the King's hold on the width and depth of his authority was as strong as ever in his fiftieth year. And so the future had held a strange incompleteness, without structure, without form. After the energy of campaigning years Ned had no specific task, being above the routine affairs of state except as a member of the King's Council. Yet retiring to the country, as a great magnate might do to lavish attention on his estates, was not in his character or demanding of his talents.

And my own restlessness? I had no role either, in all those months in England, and thus there was as much of a disappointment in me as there was in Ned. I had advised a morose King Edward, to draw him out of his melancholy. What would I suggest for Ned and myself? The building of the new rooms at Kennington was almost complete. Another palace to rebuild, to add glamour suited to our status and wealth? I did not think that it would keep his interest for long.

'If I have to mediate between another two barons who lay claim the same stretch of river, I'll take a club to their heads.'

'There is at our gate,' I warned, 'a deputation of merchants from the town who are angry at —'

Ned had grimaced, not stopping to hear the cause, but marched off to deal with the matter.

It was my cousin Edward who had come to our rescue in true Plantagenet style, with grace and wide-ranging power. So we had sailed from Plymouth on the ninth day of June in the year of 1363, leaving behind us one of the chapels we had vowed to build to repent of our sin almost complete in the crypt of Canterbury Cathedral. A blessing from Edward and Philippa had been given, Edward proud, Philippa resigned but unstinting in her love. I gave a brisk kiss and much maternal wisdom to my Holland sons Tom and John, who were to remain in England to continue their education under royal care. The first they accepted reluctantly as in the manner of adolescent youths, and the second probably ignored, while Ned was embraced by his brother John of Lancaster, whose family ambitions had come under my scrutiny after Sir Bartholomew Burghersh's questionable delving into Merlin's prophesies.

'If you face any opposition, I'll come and rescue you,' John offered.

'I need no rescue from you, little brother.'

'I am consumed with jealousy, you know. To have a principality all of your own.'

How alike they were despite there being ten years between them. Both tall with the agile but well-muscled build of a jouster and swordsman. Both with the pride of Lucifer. Both intolerant of fools, but John made enemies faster than friends, perhaps a symptom of youth. I was willing to give him the benefit of the doubt, won over by his abundance of easy charm when he was prepared to use it.

'Don't cause too much havoc while we are away,' I advised.

'I will not, if you take pity on the Gascon lords who have not been under the thumb of an English ruler living among them. I dare swear they will not enjoy the experience.' There was an unusual seriousness behind John's cynicism.

'They will soon learn,' I said, for why would they not?

I was given a fraternal hug.

'Take care of my sons,' I added.

'I'll teach them a few good passes with a sword and lance. You won't know them when you see them next.'

'Well, don't spill too much blood. Don't teach them rabid intolerance. And keep an eye on Mistress Perrers.'

I was reluctant to leave the woman in her increasingly avaricious role but had no power to rectify it. While I was away in distant Aquitaine, doubtless the rat would play.

John shrugged as if his father's mistress was of no account. Sometimes I found it difficult to trust the Duke of Lancaster.

Before us stretched a new beginning, a new province to rule. For Ned had paid homage to his father for this new principality over which we, on the strength of the Treaty of Brétigny, had complete autonomy. We were Prince and Princess of Aquitaine, rulers of the provinces of Aquitaine, Gascony and Guienne, for the token payment of one ounce of gold as tribute to my cousin Edward each Easter. Our power was supreme, without restriction from England or France. It was exactly what Ned wanted, what he needed.

'Next week it is my thought to make a progress to Angouleme,' Ned was now explaining, placing one document on top of the next with one hand as he drank from a fine gold cup embellished with a geometric pattern of gems, held in the other. 'I'll hold court there and take the oaths of fealty to bind these Gascon lords to me and then...'

Sipping ale from a similar cup, both of them parting gifts to us from John of Lancaster, I could find no enthusiasm for this plan. As the newly styled Princess of Aquitaine I should have been aglow, my anticipation of witnessing our power in action matching Ned's, rather than drawn down into a dark sea of unease.

'We will make a splash of gold and patronage,' Ned explained. 'That should bring any rebels, who still feel an allegiance to the French King, to heel.'

Ned was exhilarated, while all I could think of was that, around me, our household was awash with chatter. So had been the court in England before we left. I had absorbed it with disfavour, but what could I do? The Prince was being sent to Aquitaine by his father, the King, as a punishment for a marriage which was a misalliance, ruining all the royal plans for a brilliant foreign connection. The Prince and I were being dispatched to Aquitaine to remove me from the court so that rumours could die down and we could remake our lives far from the public eye. We were an embarrassment. I was an embarrassment. I was the wrong wife and the King, accepting of me in public, in private would never forgive his son. Just as there had been no celebrations after our marriage, so the King was expressing his continuing displeasure by sending us to a distant province.

Out of royal sight, out of mind. Out of England.

Thus wrote the chroniclers, their words dripping with their perennial poison.

'Do you hear what they are saying?' I interrupted Ned.

Ned swept the matter away with an admirable lift of his chin: 'What do they know? They have not been privy to what has been spoken between my father and me. My ruling this province was being discussed long before we shocked everyone by our nuptials.'

'It is difficult to be sanguine,' I said, 'when conversations halt when I appear in doorways.'

'Well, don't listen. Ignore them. There is no truth in it. I was destined to be Prince of Aquitaine when you were still wed to Holland.'

Which I knew, but found it difficult to rise above those dark lapping waves of innuendo. Where once I would have done with ease, on that morning I was drowning under their weight. I pushed the cup of ale and the plate of fine wheat bread aside.

Ned continued unabashed, striding to the window and back, his concentration wholly on Aquitaine. 'That's my plan – unless there is any outbreak of dissention to hamper our royal progress – and then we'll simply change our route and I'll bring some force to bear.'

I gripped the edge of the table at which we sat, marvelling at the light in his face. He was enjoying every moment of this, in spite of the attendant frustrations of rebel lords and an uncertain situation in France where King John, the most chivalrous man I could imagine, who had been released from his captivity in England on payment of the first instalment of his ransom, had dutifully returned to his captivity in England when the rest of it could not be raised by his stricken country. The French had still to renounce their claim on Aquitaine, even though we were sitting here in Bordeaux as de facto rulers. Ned was not deterred. Were we not in possession? Meanwhile I kept my gaze far from the dish of glazed fowl that he was now eating his way through when not expounding on his plans. Or perhaps it was rabbit, for which the Gascons appeared to have an inordinate fondness, which I did not. I must speak with my cook about it.

'If you will order your women to start the packing of your coffers, I thought that we would complete a circuit of Poitiers and Périgueux, then on to Saintes and perhaps Agen for Christmas. Unless we decide to return here to Bordeaux. I can take homage of the Gascon nobles and they can bow to you. And then after Christmas –'

I stood.

'Jeanette…?'

'If you will excuse me for moment. There is something that I need to do…'

His brows arched. 'You don't have to start quite yet. You have women to do that for you.'

I turned from the table and walked with measured footsteps towards the door, governed by a determination to preserve my dignity.

'Joan...?'

'One moment,' I managed. 'I will not be gone long.'

'It was not my intent to leave before next week... !'

I heard no more. All my senses were turned inwards, as was my self-control. It had become imperative, urgent, that I take refuge in my chamber. I spent an uncomfortable hour there during which my women fluttered and commiserated and smiled with sly enjoyment.

After a cup of wine laced with honey and soothing lemon balm, returning to the chamber two hours later with a more spritely step and a clearer mind, the poison of the gossip effectively banished and the dark sea in fast retreat so that I was more myself, it was to discover Ned was long gone, the remains of his meal and mine fortunately removed.

'Where is the Prince?' I asked a passing servant.

'In conference with his goldsmiths, my lady. In the treasury.'

They were, as I knew they would be, discussing coinage, when I joined them there in the chamber that contained chests and coffers. On the workbench before Ned were tools and moulds, a scattering of bright coin.

'Come and look at this.' He had forgotten my hasty departure. 'Tell me what you think. It is like my father's, so I can say no more in praise, but what do you think of this as a motto?'

I took the coin, weighing it in my hand, admiring the craftsmanship, the words that ran around the rim.

God is a righteous judge, strong and patient.

I decided it was necessary to look closely at the small coin to make out the lettering.

'It is quite small. Could it not be bigger? If you wish to impress.' I picked up a larger coin that lay gleaming importantly on the black cloth. 'Now this one is superb. It is a true symbol of your authority.'

'Yes, I agree.' There was a tinge of regret as Ned, frowning, took it from me, tossing it so that it caught the sun along its rim, before turning back to the goldsmith whose work it was. 'It's good. They both are of the best quality, but I choose this one.' Discarding the large coin, he once more picked up the smaller one, rubbing the image with his forefinger. 'I need to do this rapidly, and with less gold. Do you agree?'

He did not wait for my agreement or for the goldsmith's. That was what he wanted, that is what he would have. It was one way to get his own way I supposed, to ride over any opposition with whip and spur. I felt a hush of irritation stealing in to undermine the return of my good mood, like a cool breeze to rob a spring day of its promise.

The goldsmith bowed his way out.

'A good morning's work.' Ned leaned back against the bench, testing the edge of one of the tools against his thumb.

'Yes.'

The heat in the room pressing down on me, I found a need to sit on the nearest stool.

'Are you quite well?'

'I am perfectly well.'

He frowned. 'Did you eat? I don't recall you eating anything this morning. I don't recall you saying much either...' He was tossing the two coins in his hands as if still torn between the two. 'Perhaps I should have chosen the larger one after all.'

His total preoccupation sharpened by temper, unsettled as it was.

'I'm surprised you recall anything. You were too taken up in your plans to go to Angouleme and after that a circuit of the whole of Gascony.'

A quick step and Ned was standing in front of me.

'What's wrong, Joan?'

'Nothing's wrong.'

'Tell me the truth.'

'The truth is that I will not be going to Angouleme with you.'

'Why not?' His frown was quick to descend as I shattered his vision of how we would proceed. 'I need you with me. It is what we had envisaged when the Gascon lords convene in their Assembly.'

I was cool and measured in my explanation, despite the furious stare.

'Our planning must come to naught because I find myself *enceinte*, and until I can be quite certain that I do not have to stop to vomit into every bush and ravine en route, I do not travel. I stay here where I can hide my mortification.'

The frown vanished, the light back in his face, enhanced twofold, and with it a joy that could not be measured.

'Are you certain?'

The coins were tossed down so that he could lift me to my feet. This was his heir, an event much anticipated by both of us. More important than any new coinage.

'Of course I am certain. My belly reminds me every morning. And sometimes at noon. And occasionally at any time during the day.'

'But it will pass. Won't it?' At last a hint of concern, his kiss on my lips warm with a flattering foreboding of the dangerous days to come. 'You must have experience of this.'

'No, I have none. This malaise never struck me with my previous children.'

I had carried them with ease. I had been proud of it. But now I was stricken.

'Poor Jeanette. Can you stand a cup of wine?'

'I hope so. But don't complain if I can't.'

The wine had no ill effect, but we were both muted in our celebration. This was the longed for heir, but we would wait until the child was born to make much of the event. Children lost in pregnancy or in their earliest days were common, as Ned knew for his own brothers and sisters, as I knew from my son Edmund's death. 'When this child is born, we will drench Aquitaine in gold,' Ned said.

The atmosphere in the vast, high-roofed chamber of the ducal palace at Poitiers was stretched to breaking point, so much so that I was taken aback. It pulsed from one tapestried wall to the other, the clash of opinion virulent enough to destroy any complacency, as well as my immediate pleasure in being reunited with Ned. I had not expected this.

Ned leaving precipitately on his progress, refusing to let grass grow under his feet, my own sojourn in Bordeaux had not been of long duration. With my good health soon prevailing, I was more than ready to be restored to Ned who sent an escort to fetch me, whose commander was quick to impart, and with some pride in Ned's doings that, as Ned had predicted, the Gascon lords were gritting their combined teeth to bow their heads before their new sovereign overlord. There were many sharp smiles and empty promises of perpetual loyalty, but no open insurrection. No devious Gascon lord had as yet absented himself from the homage ceremonies.

So a concern was awoken within me when, at Poitiers, I walked into the palace to a clamour of heated altercation. The tension in the vast hall, which could be carved with a knife, was made instantly plain to me by the cacophony of raised voices.

I did not think that Ned even noticed my presence as I stopped to listen to the complaints. Was it right that the Gascon clergy should be asked to swear homage to the Prince of Aquitaine? They had never had to do so before. As servants of God and the Pope and the heavenly realms, their earthly service was not to be questioned by any man. They were not lords temporal.

'I question it, my lords ecclesiastical,' Ned, standing on the dais and very much the Prince, was announcing as I entered the chamber. His voice struck the walls and rebounded, a sure sign of his heated temper. 'I will have your obeisance, sirs, as your temporal ruler.'

'It is not the local custom, my lord.' One of the bishops took it upon himself to challenge his new Prince.

'Then I will change local custom, my lord.' Ned addressed the Bishop, whose regalia in crimson and gold did not impress my husband one jot. 'It is my right as Prince of Aquitaine.'

'His Holiness in Avignon will not approve.'

Ned's reply proved more belligerent than princely. 'It is not a matter for His Holiness. I will inform His Holiness in Avignon of my desires. You will be obedient to me, here in Poitiers, Your Grace. You and your cohorts of worthy priests will kneel before me, until I give you permission to rise.'

He looked superb, of course, although I doubted that the clerics were of a mood to admire. The gems he wore on breast and hands would pay the taxes of the Gascon lords for a year and more. His pride crowned him as surely as his golden coronel. He would not be thwarted in this, his first discussion with his clergy. It was, I realised, the first time that I had seen him in the heady role of ruler.

The clerics hesitated.

'Do I wait until His Holiness presents himself here, to give his permission? Kneel, sirs!'

The lords temporal knelt; the lords ecclesiastical still remained stubbornly on their holy and self-righteous feet.

What were my thoughts as I remained on the periphery, awaiting the outcome? That my cousin King Edward would not have done this. Edward would have been firm, yes, demanding obedience, but he would have persuaded with softer words. Also I knew that he would have invited the wives of the lords temporal to be present, to calm the atmosphere in this austere chamber. He would have invited the clerics to sit and talk of his visions for Gascony, his iron fist sumptuously encased in a velvet glove.

Ned owned no velvet gloves. The iron fist thumped down onto the arm of the throne he had just vacated.

And neither would Thomas have been quite so heavy-handed, I suddenly realised. Thomas would have talked man to man, soldier to soldier, lord to lord, as I had seen him do in Normandy. He would not have heaped this cold judgement on their heads. He would not have threatened to keep them on their knees until he read their compliance in their bowed necks.

The Gascon lords, both ecclesiastical and temporal, by now had bent the knee, with no good grace. Only then did Ned notice me, but there was no welcome, only a remnant of temper as if I interrupted his audience. Such was his stare that I found myself curtseying, which smoothed the anger from his face. He strode from the dais to take my hand.

'You are right welcome, my lady.'

'I am honoured to be invited.'

'We will talk.'

I surveyed the kneeling throng.

'You may wish to speak your farewell to your subjects,' I suggested.

'Of course.' Ned dispatched them with a wave of his hand.

'I see that you are taking matters in hand.'

'They have enjoyed their independence for too long.'

'Don't be too harsh on them.' Seeing the discontent on the faces of the lords as they left the chamber, bowing to me, it struck me even more forcibly that patience with these proud men could be a better policy. I had read hatred there.

'The sooner they accept my rule, the better for all.' Then, at last, all traces of past discontents vanished and there was the true delight at seeing me. 'Let me show you to your chambers. I have had them furnished and hung with tapestries that I know you would like. And there are new robes for you. You look restored to health.'

'I am.' But still I felt a need to say: 'Don't be too impatient. They have been under French rule for many years, and that a distant one rather than on their doorstep.'

'Then they must learn new ways.'

I sighed a little. It would be no easy task to push Ned in the direction of leniency and patience, but then any concerns were pushed aside in our reuniting. It astonished me how my emotions had reacted to seeing him again after the weeks of my absence. A deep longing had filled me with joy.

Our reuniting became a physical pleasure that kept the Prince occupied for the rest of the day, allowing his harassed household some degree of leisure. At least I had saved the clerical knees from too long an acquaintance with the unyielding floor.

'What will you do, here in Aquitaine?' I asked at length, curious to know Ned's vision. We had been wed so little time; now we would live and work together. I had imagined our holding court in Aquitaine in princely style, in Bordeaux or Angouleme. I had imagined settling into a perambulatory life where we would establish good government after the years of upheaval. Ned would establish his reputation and I would stand at his side as his most trusted counsellor. He would learn to enjoy the toils of government as much as he did the blood-stirring clash of the battlefield. He would learn to manage men and win them to his side with fair judgement and open-handed patronage. It would be a good time. Could we not achieve all of this before we must, as is the way of all things, return to take up the power in England? These years in Aquitaine would provide Ned with the perfect blank page on which to write his own name, his own style of ruling, until his reputation for government gleamed as brightly as that of battle hero at Crécy.

'I will make my own kingdom,' Ned stated.

'It is your own.'

'But the distances are vast and the lords used to their own powers over justice and government.' Wrapping a sheet around me, he drew me to a window so that we could look out as if we would see the whole stretched before us rather than the rooftops of Poitiers. 'There is no system, so I must travel and impose my presence. You will come with me. We will make a grand gesture with wealth and splendour so there will be no doubting who rules.'

I nodded, approving his vision. 'What will you do for money?'

'What a prince must always do. Raise taxes. And since they are so keen on tradition, I will impose a traditional tax. A *fouage* – a hearth tax. That will help to put down the rebels too. The French are regretting putting their hand to the treaty of Brétigny and, my spies inform me, there are French lords already stirring disaffection along our eastern boundaries.' He grimaced, his chin resting against my hair in intimate fashion, although his talk was all caustic business. 'It may be that the tax will be higher than they like, at twenty five sous per hearth, but they can afford it. If they will rebel against me, they must be prepared to pay the cost of my troops to put them down. And to buy a jewel or two to enhance the beauty of my wife. Look at this.' Suddenly I was released as he stooped to delve into the purse that he had dropped on the floor in his previous hurry.

One of Ned's new coins, now minted in quantity, which I took and inspected. But I recalled the glowering looks in the audience chamber when I had arrived. The symbolic message of a gold coin, the first actions of a conqueror to impose his will on a country, might express Ned's ambitions but they would not necessarily win him more friends. Although *God is a righteous judge, strong and patient* must be acceptable to all.

I looked at him as he stared out at the province that would make his name. There had been no friendship or even hearty respect in the audience chamber into which I had so unsuspectingly stepped. Perhaps Ned should have taken more time, to take with one hand, certainly, but give patronage and recognition with the other. And something I had noticed when we had first settled in Bordeaux. His circle of friends, those with whom he spent time, was English to a man. I would hazard a guess, knowing Ned, that he had made no changes here in Angouleme.

'Well?' he asked, his attention eventually returning to me and my introspection.

'Go hunting with the Gascon lords,' I suggested.

'And have them stab me in the back?'

'You will make friends of them.'

'Why should I? They must accept me as their prince. They have all sworn their oaths.'

He did not understand. Here, still as strong as ever, was the wilful driving force that I had known from his childhood when he would have his own way, with no thought that his will should be questioned. He had not grown out of it; I doubted that he ever would. And whereas it might play its role on a battlefield, in a new and difficult state it might not be to Ned's best advantage.

'I think that you should take them into your confidence.'

'I see no reason why I should.'

I left it, seeing the set of his jaw. I was beginning to see the ripples on our particular pond here in Aquitaine, caused by Ned being dropped into it. Somehow I must make him see them too.

But then my participation in Ned's ruling was, of necessity, curtailed.

Early March 1364: Angouleme

The birth of my son was easier than the carrying of him. A joy, more intense than the Angouleme sun that bathed the walls of the chateau, engulfed me as I held the child in my arms in the moments after his birth, an infant no different from the children I had birthed before. But he was different. Here was Ned's heir, much desired. He would be baptised Edward and one day he would be King of England.

There was no doubt in my mind. This child would one day rule, and in so doing would restore my reputation until I shone with righteous glory. I swept aside the empty words of Sir Bartholomew Burghersh as the child cried with lusty life. The Crown of England would be worn by Ned and then by his son and his son too as the years unfolded. The line of Plantagenet monarchs would be continued through my blood. Here, fists waving, his eyes clenched fretfully against the bright light, face still flushed with the effort of it all, was the future King, without question.

I sent him out, wrapped in Ned's heraldic cloth, in the arms of one of my ladies, to his father. And waited.

The child was delivered back to me without a message. But wrapped in his coverings, to be discovered when he was placed in the crib with its gilding and royal devices, was a gift. Which was brought to me.

'Madam.'

My woman placed it on my bed cover. A coin larger than any I had seen, far more impressive than the one I had last admired. And weary as I was from a woman's travails, I picked it up, turning it in my palm. It was the one I had originally wanted, the weighty *pavillon*. There was the Prince of Aquitaine with the badge of his ostrich feathers, standing under an ornately depicted arch, wearing a prince's crown of roses and carrying a sword in his right hand, on the reverse a *fleur de lys* twined with leopards. All true symbols of power and wealth.

I approved the symbols. And the motto.

The Lord is my strength and my shield and my heart hath trusted him.

And the note of explanation that came with it.

Do you approve, my dearest Joan? Copied from the coins struck by the King of France. I cannot let the King of France outshine me in such matters.

So typical of Ned that it made me laugh. In the weeks of my confinement, Ned had had the *pavillon* made for me, for his son, as a telling message to the lords of Gascony and Prince of Aquitaine. The Duke of Aquitaine's rule was now secured, a match for the King of France, now and for the future. I could ask for nothing more, and so I fell asleep, the coin beneath my pillow. Doubtless I smiled. I too had secured my place with this child, sanctified and beyond reproach, beyond criticism. I had fulfilled my role for King Edward and for England.

And the nobles of Aquitaine and Gascony? They would grow used to Ned. They would grow used to me. We would rule Aquitaine with a firm hand but we would bring peace and prosperity.

Oh, but it was a wearisome thing. My child might be born but, still separated from Ned and my new court, time hung heavy on my hands, for I must of necessity remain incarcerated, away from the world of men and their affairs until I was churched. So, while couriers were sent off to England and France bearing the good news, and Ned planned a celebration, I must set my mind to what I could to hurry the hours of each day.

I had thought that I might escape the need to retire for the customary period. I had not been so rigid in my observance when giving birth to Thomas's children, but had been forced to acknowledge that this royal child must be born with all tradition and care. Rigid seclusion in my final weeks of pregnancy and beyond could not be avoided. It was enough that its mother had not been virginal on her marriage, and one of her husbands still very much alive. Ned did not say it, but there were many who would.

Thus I adopted my seclusion in the comfortable chateau at Angouleme with what was becoming a well-practised serenity, even though my ambitions were far beyond these chambers with their locked doors, the shaded windows, and their amiable guards to deter visitors. And as women do, we turned inward, to the essential details of fashionable pleasure. To the skill of hands with lute and needle. To the pleasures of minds with books and songs of love. A female world of children, of gossip. And of course, of praise and censure of our men folk.

'And is the Prince as gallant a lover as your two previous husbands, my lady?'

My English women were well versed in my past. My newly-come Gascon ladies less so, essentially curious, and enjoying the novelty of a princess thrice married. I allowed them the liberties. Boredom takes its toll on pride.

'Sir Thomas, my first husband, had great energy, but much absence. The Prince has energy and skill.' I noted their avid eyes, and so added: 'And much presence.'

'And the Earl of Salisbury?'

'I know not. Both or neither. William and I did not share a bed.'

'Never?'

'It was difficult to enjoy the demands of the flesh when His Holiness was peering over our marital shoulder,' I admitted, remembering, enjoying my women's responses.

'I would like three husbands.'

'For variety.'

'For experience.'

'I could wish that mine had more absence!'

There was much laughter. And since I could detect no censorship, I found myself participating, saying:

'I enjoyed the variety and experience. But now I am satisfied with the one I have. I love a knight whose prowess knows no peer.'

The words came of their own volition. What had I said? It took my breath, as if the air in the room was suddenly too laden with an intensity of feeling to be breathed in. But before I could hold the thought close, my attention was drawn aside, and perhaps I was not reluctant to let it go. As a judgement on my relationship with Ned it was far too portentous for some light consideration. Strangely unsettled, I was pleased to guide the conversation in the direction of jewels and gowns and fashioning of hair, all dear to a woman's heart. The searing heat of Aquitaine in the summer months promised that my English under and over gowns would be heavily oppressive. Anything more than a light veil to cover my hair would be impossible to bear. Already a warmth was building in the room, not compatible with layers of rich silk and figured damask.

I looked around at the women who shared my confinement.

'Stand up, if you will,' I said to a Gascon woman, a young wife of one of Ned's new subjects who had joined my household, younger than I and with a distinct appearance. I had not noticed, but now that she lived with me every day, it struck me that with the advent of spring her garments had undergone a change.

'Turn around.' As she did, I heard a murmur from my English woman. 'I like what I see,' I said.

What I saw was flattering. It was a statement of femininity. But there was some disfavour expressed in English voices as being inappropriate for women of their status.

'So it may,' I agreed as I considered the drift of the material around the lady's figure. 'But some might admire it as the new fashion. And how comfortable.'

'I think it is practical, my lady.' My Gascon lady looked anxious, as if I would insist that she muffle herself to the chin.

I absorbed the complexities of pleasure, of concern, of censure around me. Perhaps it was the monotony that gave impetus to my decision. I stood, monotony banished.

'Send for the sempstresses,' I ordered. 'What the Princess of Aquitaine wears cannot be inappropriate. While our gallant knights are negotiating or fighting or drinking too much ale, we will array ourselves for our emergence into their society. It will pass the hours, and give the court something to talk about that is not taxation and the predations of the French raptors on our borders.'

We engaged my sempstresses, the embroiderers, the furriers. The weather might be warm as the weeks passed into April but a garment without fur would be no fashion statement at all. We combed and pinned and laughed. The Prince's court would be the most powerful, the most notable, the most talked about. The court of the Princess would be as a jewel in the Prince's crown. Together, we would cast the Valois court, and the ageing English court of Edward and Philippa into the shade.

Did we not have the wealth and the power to achieve the vision that filled my mind in those days? My spirits soared at the prospect of my release. My churching and the christening of my son in the cathedral at Angouleme by the Bishop of Limoges would be the talk of Europe. What I did not achieve in magnificence, I knew that Ned would. There would be none of his new golden coins spared to make this a splash of glory.

I could not wait to be with him again after so many weeks apart.

I clad myself in my fine feathers for my churching. Was there no heavy-footed bird to walk over my grave with warnings of what I might have done?

None. Not one, as I allowed myself to be arrayed by my women.

Oh, I suspected that Philippa would be quietly horrified, but Philippa was not here, and Philippa was not known for her elegance.

Isabella would approve the silk that swathed me from low-cut bodice to sleeves that trailed in sumptuous folds, to skirts that swept the floor regardless of the soft Gascon dust. As the new wife of Enguerrand de Coucy, which she had finally achieved in face of all the family opposition, Isabella would dress as she pleased. My sleeves were trimmed with coveted fur, with royal ermine, my neckline, deeper than I would once have worn, was stitched with jewels. I smoothed my hands where the cloth skimmed my breast and hips, more opulent than when I was a young woman but Ned had no complaint about my curves. An over tunic, open-sided, fluttered in the breeze, giving glimpses of the embroidered under tunic, gold fringing drawing attention to the apertures and my figure beneath. Interwoven with pearls and jewels, my hair was plaited and pleated, the diaphanous veil in no manner disguising the bright colour for it was anchored with nothing more than jewelled pins.

Thus, regally clad as Princess of Aquitaine and mother of the future heir to the English crown, I made my procession to my churching, escorted to the cathedral by twenty-four lords and twenty-four knights. My ladies, a phalanx of gem-like colours, were likewise enhanced with the product of our industriousness. It was everything I hoped that it would be.

I curtsied before the Prince, enjoying the open admiration in his face as he offered his hand. The strength of his grasp told me that he had missed me as deeply as I had missed him. But I was not to be distracted. I made my thanks before the Virgin for my safe delivery with a true heart.

Afterwards I heard the voices raised against us. It was excessive of course, the whole deliberate immoderation of it, but it was not every day that a new King was born and received into the church, and the safe delivery of the Princess of Aquitaine celebrated. Ned spent as lavishly as it was possible to spend, without restraint, to impress English, Gascon and Breton alike. Ned had been liberal in his invitations to any lord who might owe him fealty or friendship. The banquet was magnificent, all that my marriage banquet was not.

And then that fatal aside, that no one could pretend to mishear.

'I know nought of such affairs as women's raiment, but I would not wish my wife to be dressed in such a fashion as the women of this English Plantagenet court.'

The declaration issued by a man conversing in a little group of Gascon and Breton lords to my right. My ears sharpened. My head turned.

'The Princess of Aquitaine is pleased to draw undue attention.' The same voice.

'The Princess of Aquitaine most certainly wishes to draw attention to herself,' I spoke gently. 'And to the Prince who rules this land. To whom you have sworn your loyalty, my lord.'

If he was disturbed by my directness, he hid it fast enough, managing a stiff bow. An important Breton lord, Jean de Beaumanoir, Marshal of Brittany, was a man to be wooed to our side, but I detected an immediate dislike in the flat stare that appraised my person. But what did men know of robes and veils? I would speak for myself as Princess of Aquitaine.

'Would you not allow your wife to adopt our fashions, sir?'

'I would not.'

'But you have only to look at the women of my court. Are they not superbly decorative? And this is a celebration. Do you disapprove of fur and silk to mark so notable occasion as the birth of a new prince?'

'I have no liking for it.'

He looked at my household, he looked at me. I liked neither his comment nor his manner, and certainly not the slide of his eye over my raiment, yet I refrained from provocation, this being neither time nor place.

'I am sorry for it, sir.'

There was no such restraint in the Marshal's response. 'If it is a matter of fur, my lady, of which you are wearing much, then I will provide my wife with such. What I will not do is have her dress as if she were the mistress of some Languedoc brigand, flaunting herself in unseemly manner before her guests in garments more fitting for a whore.'

I experienced a species of shock, that I should be denounced in such a fashion, while a silence fell, that could be tasted on the tongue.

'I would have her dressed as an honest woman, with or without fur,' he added.

I felt my spine stiffen, my skin heat as I considered a sharp response to this lord who dare to be critical, but my tone remained even. 'Are we not all honest women, sir?'

'That may be so, but to my mind honesty has to be exhibited. I would not have my wife follow your example, my lady, into excess.'

'You are unwarrantably discourteous, my lord.'

Anger bloomed beneath the light silk of my bodice that had caused all the trouble when my lord of Beaumanoir looked me up and down.

'Your face is as fair as your repute, my lady, but you lack the propriety due to your position, and I have no hesitation in telling you so. If you wish to be honoured as Lady of Aquitaine then you will not do it by this show of excess. Tunics slit from neck to hem. Closefitting garments that reveal what only a husband should see. Hair all but naked. I will not have my wife dressed as a *bonne amie* of a pirate.'

I allowed the attack on my virtue to hang in the air, unexpected as it was, while around me I could hear the continuing silence, heavy as an approaching storm, but I knew it behoved me, impeccably gracious, to control this situation.

'Is that what I am, sir?'

His face was flushed, perhaps knowing that, in his ire, he had gone too far. 'I did not say that, my lady. But your appearance suggests a decadence of which I cannot approve.'

I smiled, allowing the despised fur-enhanced silk of my sleeves to brush his tunic.

'My thanks, my Lord Jean. I like my appearance very well. I like it even better now, for I consider you to be no judge of female raiment. I know that the Prince does not see me in the light of a thief's mistress, but as a royal consort of some distinction.'

Delighted and scandalised in equal measure, the court divided to let me pass as I walked through to Ned's side.

'Did I detect an exchange of some heat with Beaumanoir?' Ned asked.

Although I shivered with my anger: 'A little, but of no moment.'

There was nothing with which to trouble him. All was as it should be. I had made an enemy perhaps, but my control had been exemplary.

Do they not say that pride comes before a fall from grace? Not for me. I would not allow it to do so. Was I not above such overt criticism?

And yet it sowed that tiny seed of anxiety that I could not quite slap away. Would Queen Philippa have allowed herself to be held up to such censure by one of her subjects? I could not imagine it. But since I was not Philippa, I had long accepted the difference in our character. We were both extravagant, but Philippa, the only measuring stick I had, always trod a careful line, to be accepted, to be a stalwart support for her beleaguered husband in the early years of their marriage. Nor had she ever changed, remaining loyal even in these days of her distress with Edward's betrayal of her love. It was not in my nature to be so self-effacing. The Lord of Beaumanoir's observations had brought my temper to life. What's more it strengthened my resolve to create a new court, a new style. The lords of Aquitaine must become accustomed to it.

'If I might have a moment to speak with you, my lady.'

Sir John Harewell bowed himself into my presence.

Here was a man whose ability I admired, a man of proven friend-ship and loyalty to Ned, one of the group into whose hands Ned left the affairs of day to day administration in Aquitaine. Sir John Chandos proved to be a most efficient Constable; Thomas Felton, the Seneschal. John Harewell was Chancellor and Constable of Bordeaux, a profes-sional administrator of considerable worth. I had a liking for him, for his quiet demeanour that gave no indication of the organisational abilities beneath a smiling appearance.

'Certainly, Sir John.' We sat. 'Is it a matter of importance?'

It was rare that Sir John had need to speak with me rather than with Ned. It intrigued me that he should find such a need.

Sir John was not smiling today. Formally severe, he did not hold back, his hands planted on his knees, his face drawn in austere lines as if about to administer some fatherly advice to a child caught out in some mischief. 'Considerable importance. We are losing the loyalty and allegiance of the Gascon lords, my lady.'

'And why is that? Other than that they resent English governance, which was to be expected.'

'It is the profligacy of the court, my lady. It is stirring up a fury of resentment.'

Profligacy. Dramatic words from Sir John, for whom diplomacy was second nature. Was this a personal criticism? After the Beaumanoir clash, I was in no mind to be so censured, thus I permitted my brows to climb.

'Do I dress as a beggar, sir, to please them?'

'No, my lady. Nor should you. But there is resentment at the size and style of the household you keep.'

'In what manner?'

'Have you ever considered the cost?'

'No. How should I? Are our coffers empty?'

Which he chose not to answer. Instead: 'We feed four score knights and four times as many pages at our table – sometimes up to four hundred people in one day. You are aware of the huge retinue that you employ, of course.'

Yes I was, of course I was. Squires, pages, valets, stewards, clerks, falconers and huntsmen: all considered essential by the Prince and Princess of Aquitaine to administer a princely household.

'The food is extravagant, my lady.'

'It is suitable to our estate,' I replied. 'We need to feed the household, Sir John.'

'It is too costly.'

'Do we not have the money?' I repeated.

Our exchange was becoming sharper. I was conscious of the edge developing in my replies as I resented the reproof from my own Chancellor.

'Money is lavished on the work of goldsmiths and embroiderers, my lady, at the same time as we lack coin to expand our administration to all corners of the province.'

For a moment I looked down at my lap. I was clad in the most costly silk embellished with the infamous six diamond buttons which had cost Ned all of two hundred pounds. The embroidery on my gown had been produced by a master embroiderer who had earned more than seven hundred pounds for his skills.

'It is expected that a princess should use her appearance for the purpose of enhancing the regal image.'

I was sure of my ground: Philippa spent far more than I on personal adornment.

'It is not my place to comment on your appearance, my lady,' Sir John said with what I could only interpret as a grave concern. 'But it may be that the hunting parties, the banquets and tournaments give the wrong impression. And it has to be admitted that your garments have given cause for adverse comment in some quarters. It is not my intention to offend. I have come to ask if you might speak with the Prince? He might consider moderation, if you advised it.'

'I will consider it, Sir John.' And as he was opening the door: 'Why did you not broach this with the Prince himself?'

'He will not listen, my lady.'

And so I considered it, for if Sir John showed an element of concern, it behoved me to give more than a passing thought to the matter.

Too much. Too wasteful. Was that the truth of it? But what would we do? Practice dull abstemiousness, living in rags, entertaining our vassals with plain fare? Would it be in any manner advantageous to us if they could sneer, claiming to eat better at home? I did not think so. We were rulers of Aquitaine. Our Gascon subjects must accept their new rulers and what was due to their rank as heirs to the throne of England.

But then, my convictions wavered as I recalled some of Sir John's concerns. Did we truly feed four score knights and so vast a number of pages? Did we need them? Perhaps it would be advisable to be more circumspect in our show of wealth. Only a foolish woman would be blind to the undercurrent of dissatisfaction I had seen, the whispers of revolt. I spoke with Ned about our state.

'Do we spend too much?'

'No.'

'Do we need to feed so many at our table?'

'Yes.'

I abandoned the attempt and Ned dismissed Sir John as a perennial worrier who would be better keeping his mind on the raising of taxes, while I considered it fortunate that Sir John had as yet no notion of the grandiose expenditure that Ned had lavished on the betrothal of three of my Holland children, for Ned was nothing if not thorough. With Tom allied to the FitzAlan Earls of Arundel through a marriage to daughter Alice, Maud was to wed Hugh Courtenay, the Earl of Devon's grandson and heir. Joan's hand was matched with that of the widowed John de Montfort, Duke of Brittany, as Thomas and I had once envisaged. Such prestigious marriages, such a bulwark against insecurity, they warmed my heart although the girls were still too young, even younger than I when I wed Thomas, so that they must remain with me until maturity allowed them to formalise the betrothals.

'You have honoured Thomas greatly,' I said, fully aware of Ned's commitment to the negotiations with these powerful families, with its endless discussion of dowers and settlements of land.

'Why would I not? Such alliances can only strengthen Plantagenet rule in England.'

'So you had no thought of the happiness of my children?'

'As much as you did, I imagine.'

Who knew better than I that happiness in such affairs was never of foremost consideration, even though I knew John of Brittany to be a fine young man, but Ned's callous dispatch of the matter rankled.

'I just thought that I should thank you for your care of my children,' I remarked, infusing the warm air with winter-chill, 'even if it was a cold-blooded means towards an end.'

Which earned me a passing kiss to my brow, and a smile that confirmed all I knew of Ned's affection for them and for me.

Chapter Fourteen

What did the quality and style of my raiment and my hair have to bear on any matter of importance, or the number of knights who sat at our table? Within a handful of months we were dragged into war and bloodshed, a war that Ned felt he could not ignore, involving the little kingdom of Castile on our southern border. King Pedro of Castile came under attack from his half brother, the illegitimate Enrique of Trastamara who, ousting King Pedro, had an eye to the throne for himself.

'Why does it involve us?' I asked, not at all certain that we should be involved.

I was breeding again, queasy with the heat and inclined to be fretful, but fast learning the importance of the alliances gathering strength around us. Ned, still struggling to command the loyalty of his new subjects, was burning with a desire to make his mark once more on a battlefield.

'Trastamara is in alliance with France, against King Pedro,' he said between issuing orders to a relay of pages. 'Pedro has asked me for aid. For troops, in effect, to destroy his bastard brother and put him back where he belongs on the throne of Castile.' He put a signature to one document, snatching at another. 'If I refuse, Pedro himself might go cap in hand to France, to offer them more incentives than the bastard can, and I don't want France involved to any degree in Castile. It would not be to our benefit. In effect we would be trapped like an English nut between two French stones, and I'm in no mind to give the King of France the opportunity to crush us. A King of Castile who is a friend of France is a danger to England and Aquitaine. So I have agreed.' He scowled. 'And had to pay a ten thousand pound weight in gold to tempt Pedro away from France, from the English treasury. My father consented with ill-grace.'

Which I could well imagine.

'So you will take an army.'

'Yes. Easy enough but we will need to travel through Navarre.' He was already halfway to the door of our chamber, handing the pile of documents to yet another waiting page. 'King Charles of Navarre, crafty monarch that he is, won't allow me to march through his lands without maximum payment for his consent. I can pay it, but I'll not trust him. The King of Navarre is as slippery as an eel, but if my brother John can make haste with troops from England we should make a good account of ourselves. I would not be averse to having Navarre and Castile as allies against France.'

So he was already knee-deep in warm preparations. I could see the old vigour beginning to bubble beneath his skin as if a fire had been lit beneath a pot of soup that had long lain still and cold.

'I can see a way to make this to my and England's advantage. In return for my army, I can demand from Pedro the surrender to me of towns along the Castilian north coast. He won't like it but he'll do it if it keeps his crown out of the clutches of his brother. It will give my father something to crow about as well so the gold he finally agreed to dole out will have some recompense.'

'You are enjoying this, aren't you?'

'No. It's a nuisance. And will be a drain on my expenses.' Then he grinned. 'But is marching into battle more appealing than sitting at a negotiating table? By God it is!'

I was resigned.

And so the plans were made with no help from me to become an ally of the King of Castile in war against his chancy brother Enrique in alliance with France, with only the slightest interruption, which Ned made a show of accepting with good grace when he stood outside my bedchamber and held his second child.

'Another fine son. He will be called Richard.'

So it was reported to me by a proud nursemaid who returned the child to me with no gift to mark the occasion. Ned had no time for gifts. It was Twelfth Night, a time of great joy and rejoicing. On that day three Kings honoured us and the child with a visit to Bordeaux where we had returned for the birth. There were festivities in the streets when the Kings of Majorca, Armenia and Castile stood godfather to Richard.

Yet despite my pleasure in my son and the honour shown to him by these august visitors, it was, for me, a time of some trepidation. Ned left Bordeaux on a Sunday of biting winds before the middle of January when I was still in seemly seclusion. Despite my safe delivery and the strength of the new child, I was uneasy. Past memories would not let me be. I remembered Thomas leaving me to go to war. So had Will. And now Ned was gone to his campaign. My life was following the same pattern.

I dropped the cloth I was stitching onto my lap with a sigh of impatience at my own weakness, my lack of faith. Why was I thrown into this anxiety? There was no need. Neither Thomas nor Will had died in battle. Ned had conducted himself with glory through the campaigns of Crécy and Poitiers as well as innumerable sieges. There was no reason why I should fear that Ned should come to grief. The worst that had happened in my past experience was that Thomas had lost an eye, which had been no great loss to him, allowing him to make the most of it in rakish fashion for the next dozen years.

I must wait and hope for news. I had no hope of letters. Ned would send couriers if he remembered. I must rest on my knowledge of his strength and skill in battle.

God be with you. That was the message I had sent him on his departure.

Assuredly He will, as He will keep you, the reply.

So why was I beset by nerves?

'What is it, my lady?'

Instantly one of my women was there to fulfil any desire I might have.

'Merely a melancholy when I have no good reason to have one.'

I ordered her to pick up the lute and sing something cheerful. I had had enough of portents. I did not believe in portents. I would not believe.

But when I lay on my bed the prophesy was reborn, it loomed in all its horror before me. Not the one that put descendents of Lancaster on the throne, Merlin's magical offerings, gossiped over by Sir Bartholomew for the entertainment of young women who knew no better. I had long since consigned that mischief-making, as it deserved, to the cesspit, but this one was far more particular, far more immediate, that it troubled my sleep.

Rising from my bed I went softly to the nursery chambers, to look down at the infant who snuffled in his sleep as I lit a candle, motioning to the watchful nursemaid that there was nothing amiss. A corona of fair hair that gleamed in my suddenly fanciful imagination like a true crown of gold. If that was so, if this babe became King after my cousin, then Ned would be dead, and also the child who was his namesake. I moved to stare down into the second crib. Our first born. Strong and healthy. He kicked at his coverings, awoken by the light.

'They are both well, my lady.'

The nursemaid had caught some element of my concern.

Of course they were for they were innocent and unaware; I was the one to be troubled. I went back to my own bed, where the words came back to me, as if they had lain in ambush until I was alone and vulnerable, yet it was not a prediction that I could ever share with Ned. Sir Richard Pontchardon, one of Ned's knights, was no purveyor of Merlin's myths, but had a sound reputation as an astrologer. His reading of the signs was dire, all because my little son had been born on the sixth day of January, the Epiphany, commemorating the coming of the Magi to visit the Christ Child. And on that day the three Kings of Armenia, Majorca and Castile had come to visit Richard. A portent of biblical proportions. But why had it disturbed me so?

'It is a grave prophesy,' Sir Richard intoned. 'The Magi came to visit the Christ Child who would be King of all the world.' His gaze on mine was unwavering. 'So three Kings visit this child at his birth. It bears heavily on my mind that this child will rule next as King of England.

'I refute it.' My voice sounded hollow to my ears.

'You cannot refute it, Lady. It is written. My reading of the stars confirms it.'

It was stated with a conviction from which nothing would sway him, so it more than disturbed me. The prediction that Richard, this tiny child who had barely drawn breath, would be the next King of England after his grandfather.

I would continue to deny it, of course, rejecting it as mindless nonsense, for were they not an unlikely Magi, since two of our kingly visitors, those of Majorca and Castile, were in exile and so had no power to speak of, indeed might never wear their crowns again. Yet, if it were so, if Sir Richard's prediction proved true, I would lose Ned to an untimely death. I would also lose my first-born royal son.

The enormity of it exerted a painful hold on what must be my heart. Was this love? This sense of impending loss, so strong that I thought I could not bear it.

I turned my mind from it, fearful of the vulnerability that came with admitting to love and prophesies. Instead I would concentrate on what I could do, to kneel before the Blessed Virgin and pray that there would be no battles. That Ned would return.

But what was a war without conflict?

I would watch over my son Edward. But how could I guard against the chance ailments that fate cast in the way of the very young?

There was no peace in me. Moreover Ned would enjoy the campaigning. He would enjoy his brother's company. For a little while his thoughts would be turned away from me, but I would keep mine with him as I picked up fragments of news, of gossip. Intense cold, snow and frost hemming in the Pyrenees, it had not prevented Ned from reaching Pamplona, capital of Navarre. Skirmishes abounded and with them inevitable casualties, but there had been no major conflicts. Nothing to drop me into a well of despair.

And then nothing. No news either good or bad.

My anxieties over distant conflict trebled, for Ned had been joined by his brother of Lancaster and my eldest son Thomas, now a soldier in Lancaster's retinue. John was still at court in England, under the guardianship of John de la Haye, appointed by Ned, but Tom at seventeen years was old enough and capable enough to wield a sword in battle.

There was no reason for me to be cast into despair, I told myself. I would hear if there had been a major battle.

In Bordeaux my two little sons thrived.

How long before I heard? Or saw a return of the courageous knights, full of tales of triumph and victory? I set myself to the lot of all women, to pray and keep the faith. To have an ear to any undercurrent of insurrection at court. There was nothing. I should be at ease but my mind was fixed on what was happening in the south.

It was the second week into the spring warmth of April. A letter. My thanks to the Blessed Virgin who had heard enough petitions from me to finally answer a prayer. I saw the inscription on the cover as I snatched it without apology from the courier's hand. Ned's hand, which was unusual in itself. This I had not expected.

I ripped it apart. Then abandoned pride, because I knew he would not write about his own state.

'Is my lord safe?' I asked.

'Yes, my lady.'

'And my son, the Earl of Kent?'

'He too is well, my lady. And my lord of Lancaster.' The courier, frequently in Ned's employ, smiled with some compassion. 'Your son, my lady, was knighted by the Prince at Vitoria for his valour shown with the army.'

Fear drained from me at last, pride in Tom, relief for Ned, leaving me light-headed in the glitter from the courier's armour. My worries had been for nothing. Sir Richard's reading of the stars and the purpose of the three monarchs had been flawed.

I settled to read, yet was soon dismayed by the lack of content. It was news of a battle, on the third day of April when I had had no thoughts of such distant clashes. That was the day that we had taken the children down to the port where ships had begun to arrive, tempted out on the trade routes by the calmer seas. While we had enjoyed the busy scene, the snap of sails, the curious catches of the fishermen, a great battle against Enrique of Trastamara had been fought at Nájera. I did not even know where it was.

How much falsehood is there in the thought that a wife would know when her husband was in danger? I had not even known that Thomas was dead until the courier arrived. If Ned had died, would I have had a sense of so great a disaster?

We have engaged the Bastard of Spain, Ned had scrawled, *and defeated him.*

The hand was hurried, as if his brother John had suggested that it would be a kindly thought to tell me of the outcome, and Ned had reluctantly concurred between removing his armour and visiting his weary troops who would be his first concern. My eye ran down the single page. A list of those French commanders in the enemy army that lay dead on the field. Two thousand noble prisoners taken. Nothing of a personal comment. I had to presume that Tom and John of Lancaster were indeed unharmed.

I have sent one of Enrique's horses to London to my father as a symbol of our mighty victory.

Well, I supposed that was good. A time indeed for rejoicing. A true soldier's letter.

You will want to know that... .

I wanted to know that he was well. Unharmed. In good health and spirits.

You will want to know, dearest companion, that we, our brother of Lancaster, your son Thomas Holland, and all the noble men of our army are in good heart, thank God, except only Sir John Ferrers... .

Lancaster was safe. My son was safe. Nothing about the future except that they were marching on Burgos.

I stood and walked towards where the courier waited by the door.

'Does my lord return?'

'He goes to gain payment for the use of his army from King Pedro, my lady. The sum must be negotiated.'

'Which should not take long.'

Why should it? Ned had fulfilled his part of this alliance. Pedro would be quick to dip his grateful hand into his purse, but I did not like the sceptical slide of the courier's eye, the lack of a reply.

And so I put in hand a celebration to mark the Prince of Aquitaine's triumphant return. It would not go unnoticed by the Gascon lords who should know the calibre of the man who ruled them. But what was the most important and the most touching for me? The beginning of that letter from Ned.

My dearest and truest sweetheart and beloved companion...

What wife could ask for a better commendation?

I did not think that he had ever spoken the words. How strange that he should write them when writing was not his metier.

If I were of a romantic nature I would have kept it in my bodice, close to my heart. Instead I folded the note and placed it in the coffer that contained the rest of the documents which were vital to my peace of mind and from which I would never be parted.

The battle of Nájera was in April. It was September before the victorious Prince of Aquitaine returned to where I stood on the steps of the great cathedral in Bordeaux, my eldest son's hand in mine, waiting for him. The heat was still oppressive but we would remain there until the vanguard of the army arrived. I had timed it well. Small Edward did not have the patience to wait long, but I had talked to him and given him a pair of his father's best gloves to hold which he did with self-importance. For me it was vital that the child should be here to greet his father.

Distantly I became aware of the noise, the clamour of an approaching army displacing the familiar noise of the crowd and the city around us.

'Here they are,' I said. 'Here is your father.'

Small Edward hopped, red tunic with golden lions gleaming as Plantagenet lions ought to gleam, fair hair curling in the humidity from beneath his little hat.

Then here was triumphant victory in our midst. The blast of

trumpets, war-torn, sun-bleached banners unfurled and lifting on the still air, the weary march of feet, both men and horses. The overpowering stench of sweat and horse and unwashed bodies that in no manner quenched the cheering to bring the army home to joyous acclaim. And, leading all, Ned, mounted in battle array. How long had they spent in putting together this impression of military power and magnificence? The gleam of the morning sun on armour and horseflesh, on banners and helms, was surely a symbol of God's blessing on our venture.

I saw the royal colours of John of Lancaster: there was the silver lion of my own son Tom, who in his maturity bore such a resemblance to his father it was as if Thomas again rode from battle. To my discomfort – and my astonishment – tears stung my eyes and with them a realisation. I had never wept for Thomas. I had never honoured him with such palpable grief, but on that morning my heart was full of a sense of his loss, and his son's glory. For a time I allowed those tears to fall unchecked, as a mark of respect to the Thomas I had lost and the one that was returning to me, then I wiped the tears away.

Ned drew rein. I waited. Today it was my place to wait. Here was the Prince returned to his own, to be acclaimed by all, the predictions of Sir Richard Pontchardon smashed into pieces. Ned was safe and returned to take up his power once more. The voice of the crowd surrounded us, enveloped us, but for that one prolonged moment it was as if we were alone together as our gaze caught and held firm. Even the child's hand in mine was an ephemeral thing. This Prince sitting negligently on his proud bay was the centre of my world, that he had never been before. It seemed to me that it was a mirror image of that day at Castle Donington when I had been blinded by his brilliance. Yet far more than a reflection. Today I was not only blinded but chained by it.

Ned saluted with a smile, then a bow of his head, in recognition that our meeting must become a public thing.

Dismounted he climbed the steps to my side, removing his helm to hand to his squire. He lifted Edward high. Then he kissed my cheeks that were once again wet with tears I could not control; I, who never wept in public. The words I had inadvertently spoken to the women of my household flooded back. I, who never spoke without cause.

I repeated them back to Ned as we stood together because I knew it to be true.

'I love a knight, whose prowess knows no peer.'

His reply was all I could have asked for.

'As I love a princess whose beauty is incomparable. Come, my wife.'

Turning, my heart thudding, every inch of my skin sensitive to the soft air, we walked into the shadowy depths of the cathedral, where we knelt to give thanks for the victory and for God's safekeeping.

And then, I would have let him walk ahead of me to receive the adulation of the populace. He would not allow it.

'Walk with me, my most beloved companion.'

Ned took my hand in his and, without any thought of what might appear seemly between Prince and Princess of Aquitaine, we walked together into the Bishop's palace where all was made ready to receive him.

My heart was full, too full to express what had taken root deep within me. It was unexpected. It was devastating. It was a tolling bell, heralding a new vista in my life.

Was it a triumph? Was the Castilian campaign to aid King Pedro and the great battle at Nájera the victory that Ned had recorded for me? As the light filtered through the high windows in the Bishop's hall it touched on Ned's face, undermining for me the miraculous joy of his return. There were lines of strain there, imprints that I had not seen before, the firm compression of his mouth undoubtedly grim. Nor, almost as soon as we passed beneath the carved archway, away from immediate public gaze, did he hide his disillusion.

'We are bankrupt.'

So bald a statement of failure. His hand tightened around mine, for he still led me with gracious acclaim.

'I had to dismiss my mercenaries because I could no longer afford to keep them.' Ned grimaced through a mouthful of wine, the cup presented by a bowing page, as the banquet was prepared around us. 'A great victory on the battlefield, I swear it, but at what cost?'

He would say no more, the disgrace of his inability to preserve his battle-force sitting sneering on his shoulder like a malevolent imp. And that was not all that troubled him beneath the gilded armour as his attention was requested by Constable Sir John Chandos. I could see the anger that lived within every movement, every reply, even as he considered the comfort of his own men who had returned with him. Hovering for a moment beside him, then unable to wait to learn more, I embraced Tom, who slid like an eel from my grasp with an apologetic grin, before I sought out my brother by marriage who had even more of a name for plain speaking than my husband. By this time a painful anxiety was lodged beneath my chest.

'Tell me what Ned has not yet told me,' I demanded. I was sufficiently concerned to be brusque to the point of ill-manners.

John's expression was more amenable than Ned's but still saturnine. 'What do you wish to know?'

'Why Ned is dispirited. And more.'

John shrugged and proceeded to enlighten me. 'The English position was untenable in the end. Ned did not trust any of his allies, nor do I blame him. A massive armed presence was needed when the deeds of obligation – the amount of money owed to us – were exchanged with the wily Pedro at a ceremony in Burgos. We felt a need to have five hundred men at arms, as well as a company of troops to occupy one of the gates of the city and one of the main squares, to guard us from our so-called friends.' His disgust was self-evident as he inhaled. 'The calculation of what was owed to us took a month, and still it is not paid. As for Charles of Navarre, no one on this earth would trust him to keep a God-given oath. All the promises of remuneration – not worth a flea bite. And I've plenty of those!'

I nodded. 'It explains much.'

And indeed Ned explained even more, when we sat together at the feast and another cup of wine had smoothed away the heat of his fury.

'I swear the Devil himself dragged me into that war. Pedro will escape paying by any means he can. "I owe you much gratitude for the glorious day which you have won for me," he said. Fulsome praise, but I swear that's all I'll get from him. His gratitude for the glorious day will not be paid in gold coin, by God! I presented him with an account for service rendered. Not a trifling sum, and larger than we first agreed but I would have accepted less if he had made it up with a score or so of Castilian castles or the province of Biscay. So I accepted Pedro's oath in the cathedral at Burgos, that he would soon fulfil his obligations, because I had to, or we would still be sitting there like carrion waiting to pick over a dying carcase, but I hold out little hope. Pedro announced that he would not pay a foreign army standing on his own land, which was, in effect, an invitation to get out and not return.' He considered the lees in his cup, his hand white-knuckled around the stem. 'I thought about looting, but it's not the way a Prince should conduct himself. Perhaps I should have done it. It might have been the only recompense I get.'

'But now you are returned, and with honour.'

'I'd rather have the promised gold.' He pushed the cup away, flattening his hands palm down, frowning at some distant scene that disturbed him. 'And then my forces were laid low from the bloody

flux and the sweating sickness. I needed to come home. And here I
am, complaining to you when I should be giving you my full attention, or even taking the time to kiss you. Which I haven't yet done
to my satisfaction.'

As he turned to look at me, my attention once again was drawn
to the dual lines between his brows, the grooves in his cheeks where
he had lost flesh, not unusual in itself through a fierce campaign, but
enough to put its mark on him.

'Kisses can wait. Did you suffer from the flux?' I asked.

'I had a dose or two before I shook it off.' He shook his head,
making it of no account, and the scowl was gone. 'It's good to see
you.' His hand covered one of mine, his face softened but he was
more weary than I had ever see him. I could read it in the set of his
head, in the rigidity of his shoulders. 'All is still unresolved. But it
was a superb battle.'

'Forget battles. You need to rest before the next one. First you
will eat. Then I will arrange for my women to fill a bath with heated
water and scented herbs when this interminable feast is over.' The
pages were bringing in the dishes that proclaimed our cook's artistry
with sauces and marvellous subtleties, the castles and heraldic devices
proclaiming Ned's victory over Enrique of Trastamara. 'It will restore
you to health and good humour.'

'Women's work!' But he smiled, the old lines of laughter dispelling
the new of disillusion. 'I'd prefer to hunt.'

I sighed. 'So we will go hunting. But tomorrow, not today.'

He lifted his cup in a salute to me. 'Tonight will be our own.'

Before we retired: 'Has Ned been ill?' I asked John.

'Yes, gravely, and he has taken long to recover. But we were all
affected with the flux. He will soon be restored to health. I've already
forgotten about it.' John grimaced. 'Except for the ignominy of
constant vomiting and uncontrollable voiding of bowels.'

'Thank you, John,' I said. 'Very graphic.'

'Well, you did ask. It was nothing more than any of our men suf-fered. Just the penalty we pay for poor food and rank water.'

Which suggested that all was indeed well. John saw no need for concern over his brother, thus I need not worry either.

Cleansed, scented against his wishes but not against mine, now lacking the fevered tension that had held him in thrall since he rode into Bordeaux, and perhaps had held him for the whole of the past campaign, Ned took me to his bed, or I took him to mine. We neither of us had a clear memory of how we reached that point in our reuniting. There was born, between the roast meats and the subtleties, an urgency. A desire that flamed and took command. A sort of madness born out of absence, awakening a physical longing to be clasped close in each other's arms.

'Do you know how much I have missed you?' he asked, his face buried in my hair which lay fragrantly loose on his shoulder. Had I not been preparing for this moment? 'You remained anchored in my mind, even when I wished you would not, even when I was trying to come to some sort of terms with King Pedro. There you were, and the thought that I would soon be returned to you. Did you miss me?'

I missed you, and missed you, and missed you...

'A little.'

His kisses were becoming heated along the line of my throat.

'Only a little?'

'More than a little.'

My breath caught as I felt his mouth smile against my skin.

'Are you admitting at last that you love me, dearest wife?'

'I believe that I am.'

'Say it, Joan. You are allowed to say it.'

He was stern. He was the Prince. So I did.

'I love you.'

'Say it again.'

'I love you, Ned.'

I meant it too, every short word of it.

'There, that was not difficult. You should know that I love you too. Let us give credence to it between those magnificently clean linens. Not a louse to be seen.'

'You missed the clean linen more than you missed me?'

There was no need of a response in words. Action was everything. Hunger was everything. The desires of the flesh ruled us both.

We knew each other well. Had we not had two children together? But that night we came to know each other with an intimacy that we could never have guessed at. A tenderness shook him when he disrobed me. He shivered when I touched his skin. I shivered too. It was a night of all the passion and desire that I might have dreamed of.

The bells of the churches of Bordeaux rang to celebrate Ned's return but we were deaf to them. The stars gleamed on naked flesh but we were blind to them. We were not deaf and blind to each other. It was a banquet of touch and sensation and miraculous taste.

While Ned finally slept the sleep of the dead, I took a more leisurely survey of the man who had fought and come home because he needed to. The exhaustion I accepted after a strenuous campaign. His face was leaner, a touch of hollowness here beneath his eyes, and there in the hollow of his throat, a dullness rather than the usual sheen of his hair. He had lost flesh too, as I had initially thought, his ribs more prominent beneath the skin, but all would soon be remedied with rest and good food under my care. No, there was no need for undue concern. His energies had been incomparable; now he would be restored and so would his spirits.

My dearest Ned. My exceptional Prince. My heart unsteady in its beat with this unexpected lesson that he had taught me, I could not resist touching my fingers to his hair, his cheek, lightly so that he would not wake. I allowed the thoughts to come to me.

I had no experience of courtly love, where all was well lost for it, where troubadours and minstrels sang of its glory, more powerful than any other human emotion. In my life it seemed that love, declared so passionately, was more often a means to an end, although my mother would have denied it, and so would the Queen. They would never deny the power of love in their marriages. And indeed had I not felt its heated breath against my nape? Had I not been carried away by the enchantment of it, the intrinsic glamour of being desired as a woman as I pledged my oath to Thomas Holland, a famous knight in the making?

Without doubt it existed, my love for Thomas; a true emotion, the love of a young girl, full of flirtation and excitement, my first experience of a longing, a sheer physical thrill when a man already of repute kissed my fingers and asked me to wed him. I was wooed and courted, secretively, determinedly, all so appealing to my youth, by a suitor of charm and good looks even if he was short on romantic declarations. How could I resist falling in love with him? And I had chosen to stay with him when I could have denied him, our attraction deepening with our life together and our children.

But Ned. Ah, Ned, as he rode through the streets of Bordeaux, glorious, heart-wrenching in his brilliance as conqueror and Prince. What was this emotion that made my heart rap like the tuck of a drum in his military entourage? This love had taken me aback. Here was no youthful frippery, no flirtation, no succumbing to glamour. I had known Ned all my life, for better or worse with all his faults as well as his imperious skills. This emotion was mature and deep, accepting of duties and demands, accepting of his faults, as he accepted mine. As I waited on the steps, holding our son's hand, it had been a bittersweet strike of power at heart and mind. I suspected that it would never leave me.

So what was this that had struck me down, with the heat of a summer fever? A bond that had arisen from nowhere as Ned returned from battle, a desire to own and be owned. A physical longing to be claimed by him. A fear that I would be alone and despairing if he died by a blow from some faceless knight's sword.

I had loved Thomas.

I suspected that I had yet to experience the full might of this emotion that Ned had so inexplicably ignited in me. I feared it. I desired it.

I leaned and kissed his brow. He was home and he was mine. He would not be averse to my lavishing love and care on him. Or, at least until the next battle.

My eyes were opened. The ever-circling pleasures of love were pushed aside as difficulties crammed their way into my thoughts to the detriment of all else. Not before time, Sir John Harewell, meticulous and careful Chancellor, would have said, except that his politeness was legendary. I should have seen the way of things, but I did not, until now.

The triumph at Nájera was as untrue as a false dawn. All was not right with us. Nothing could take away the magnificence of that victory, but, by the end of the year King Pedro of Castile was dead by assassination, his debts to us unpaid and his bastard brother Enrique of Trastamara ensconced in Castile. So all Ned's negotiations and battles were for nothing, only disaffection in Aquitaine and an impossible drain on our finances. Our alliance with Castile was over; with Enrique at the helm they were rapidly hand in military glove with France, where King John had died a tragic death still in captivity in England, his ransom unpaid. His successor King Charles the Fifth, had no intention of giving up the French claims to Aquitaine. To him

the Treaty of Brétigny meant nothing. Although not strong enough
to engage us in outright battle, he was quick to encourage treachery
amongst the already restless Gascon lords who had returned from the
Castilian campaign empty-handed, thus stretching their allegiance to
their English and ever-present overlord to the limit.

As we all knew, one day, when he was strong enough, King Charles
of France would make a forceful bid for Aquitaine. It was a matter of
when, not if. The Treaty of Brétigny was in effect dead.

How facile were our Gascon lords, how treacherous in their smiles,
kneeling before us while they sent off their couriers to Paris with
offers of allegiance in return for their debts being paid by France to
win them over. I should have understood. Ned too. The lords had
been drained dry by war and taxation. But we were unable to give
succour. Our coffers were as empty as theirs. France reaped the crop
of our weakness.

I had envisioned Aquitaine, had I not, as a blank page, on which
Ned would write a future for a new principality in his own hand,
without interference from England. It was a blank page on which Ned
would assert his independence as a Prince in his own right. It was not
a perfect blank page at all. Aquitaine was a state full of dangers and
turmoil, unexpected undercurrents. Ned's writing on that page was,
to my grief, becoming more and more ineffective. I could see it so
clearly. There could be no denial despite my confessed love for him.

Was it Ned's fault? Was the blame to be laid at his door? Perhaps
it was, but the underlying problems were not of his making, that I
would swear.

On a battlefield the Prince was all raw courage and insightful
decision-making. He led his men with charismatic brilliance so
that none would deny the glamour of Edward of Woodstock. His
victories legendary, all clamoured to fight at his side and win glory,
his reputation was second to none despite his autocracy in affairs of

discipline. Would not a commander of such merit be determined on obedience? I thought so.

But in affairs of government Ned lacked the essential patience. Lacked understanding. Lacked the willingness to listen and judge and wait. He had no tolerance for those who questioned his right to rule. Arrogance? I supposed that it was. He did not always see the complexities that lurked below the surface, only the brute resistance to his rule.

'Listen to them,' I advised. 'Take heed of what it is that troubles them and drives them to insurrection.'

But Ned could not acknowledge that the Gascon nobles would rather shuffle off to renew their allegiance to France than give up their prized independence to a despised English prince. Ned would never allow his Gascon lords the autonomy they had enjoyed in the past, as he made perfectly plain in hard words that worried me. I could only hope that experience would show him the clear path to winning his subjects to his vision of Aquitaine, rather than dismissing their complaints when they demurred at some new project of which they had no experience.

Higher and higher taxation was not the way to win their loyalty. Yet how would he pay for the troops necessary to hold this state in some degree of security? France, we soon learned, was fast recovering from her defeat, fast encouraging rebellion amongst our disaffected nobility which Ned was slow to see, and could not always remedy. There were too many Gascon lords prepared to be disaffected.

And I? Did I see?

My eyes were opened at last. Now, at last, I could acknowledge what was happening but could do nothing to staunch the flow of blood from the wound. Oh, I could give advice, I could soothe and persuade, but Ned was a man with a mind of his own and a will to have his way. I was his beloved Jeanette but I was not his counsellor and never would be. I tried, but sometimes even I did not see the the crevasse that was opening at our feet until we tottered on the edge. The expense of our government, the extravagance of our household was as much my fault as Ned's. And yet, in my bleakest moments, I was driven to admit that there was no future for us here in this province, that our future here would be nothing more than a terrible unravelling, like the hem of a silk gown dragged too many times along the uneven flags of a floor. We had had such hopes of Aquitaine emerging as the jewel in Ned's crown until he could assume the more magnificent one of England. Now all was falling apart before our eyes.

I tried again.

'Why not allow the Gascon lords a voice in your councils? Summon their representatives and at least listen to them. It might dissuade them from absenting themselves to give their homage to the French King at every opportunity.'

Ned's reply showed no desire to discuss the matter with me or anyone. 'And allow them to interfere in my affairs? I want no parliament with its grip on finance here in Aquitaine. I've seen what damage a parliament can do in England when it holds the purse strings!'

No, all was not right in Aquitaine. Nor was it right in England or with our far-flung family. It was difficult to know which news affected Ned most strongly. In October of the year 1368 news had come to us from England of the death of Lionel, Ned's brother, the one closest in age. Travelled to Milan to wed the wealthy Violante Visconti, daughter of the Duke, he had submitted to some mystery fever, induced, some were quick to say, by judicially administered poison. Ned mourned, but not as heart-wrenchingly as he did when, almost in the same breath we were told that Philippa was ailing, sufficiently for there to be a real concern for her life. We held a High Mass for Lionel's soul and Philippa's comfort, which was all we could do. Never had the distance seemed so great. How long couriers took to travel the miles with their sad news. Nor did Ned have John's company that they might mourn together, for he had returned home.

If our financial state was as bad as Ned had calculated, for me to ascertain where our money was lost, and without his knowledge, which was easy enough to do since he had no liking for finance other that the striking of impressive coins, I had the ledgers and tallies brought before me. Should I have done this before when Sir John challenged me to consider the extravagance of our way of life? Most assuredly I should, but better now than not at all. I spent a morning, following the pointing fingers of clever clerk.

It was a slap to the senses, open-handedly sharp.

I saw what we had done for the celebration for my churching after Edward's birth, spending without restraint. All who were of a mind to be critical had only to point to the stabling of eighteen thousand horses, all at Ned's expense. The tourneying and jousting lasted for ten days. Imagine the money spent by Ned's generous hand to entertain the knights who flocked to enjoy our hospitality. The candles alone cost over four hundred pounds. The great feast of oysters and peacock, veal and venison and suckling pig. Nor was that all. The new hangings and tapestries for my chambers were a shock even to my love of outward show, as were the hangings of tapestry to clothe the walls of the banqueting chamber, eight pieces a side and an ornate dosser to hang behind Ned's chair. All lit as bright as day by those inordinately costly wax candles.

Too much. Too wasteful. There were the figures before me, black on the page so that there could be no denial. It could be construed as vulgar ostentation. I had never sought vulgarity.

One of the banquets had been cooked over wax candles.

I remembered what I had said to Sir John. What would we do? Practice dull abstemiousness? Our Aquitainian subjects must accept their new rulers.

But it would have been better to be more prudent in the impression we wished to make. To rule more considerately. So much wasted on empty show that could never win the loyalty of these subjects. And then Ned had returned from Castile burdened with a debt that could not be paid. I shuddered at the pounds in gold that Ned had paid into Pedro of Castile's greedy hands.

But what could I say? How could I put this burden on Ned's shoulders? I had been as guilty as he. I had enjoyed the diamond buttons that now afflicted my conscience. Thus I assumed a calm exterior, without judgement, when Ned made his decision, because I could see no other way out of our extremity. But I tried to reason, as a clever woman must reason with an opinionated man.

'We must tax them again,' he said.

It came at the end of a tiring day when Compline had brought neither of us peace in our hearts, only a wearing anxiety that we both hid.

'It will not be well received, Ned. Is there no other way?' I knew that there was not.

'Well received? I am grown tired of their empty promises behind sour expressions. Here's what it must be. Another hearth tax. They are used to hearth taxes.'

'Do we not have enough coin?' I knew the answer.

'No, we do not.' The words were bitten off. 'If you expect to eat off the gold plate with the vine leaves when we next receive guests, you will be disappointed. I have had to break up some of our plate to pay our soldiers. If this continues we will be eating off common clay. A hearth tax is the only way.'

That might be so. They might be well used to hearth taxes, but not as frequently as Ned was demanding them, nor at such high rates. And so it proved. The Assembly of the estates of Gascony, sullen in its sitting when Ned summoned them to give their consent, was more than reluctant, granting such a tax at the extortionate rate of twenty four pence because Ned demanded it, but only on condition that he agreed to a charter of rights which they drew up to confirm their independence. They would no longer be automatically obedient to their English rulers who were dabbling in every one of their Gascon pies.

'I would still advise against the tax,' I said.

'Why? They have agreed to it.'

'They might agree now but are they plotting insurrection at the same time? I think you have pushed them too hard.'

Ned managed a thin smile. 'I'll push them harder.'

What we did not expect was a response from England, even as Ned's clerks were amassing the coin. Ned erupted into the private walled garden where I sat in the shade with my women and the baby, waving a letter in my direction.

'I do not deserve this. Before God I do not!'

At a nod of my head, my women, carrying the baby, retired behind the distant lavender hedges.

'Let me read.' I held out my hand.

But he would not, screwing it in his fist.

'This is a letter from my father. A rebuke, without doubt. He warns me against – what was the word? – novelties in administration. Novelties, By the Rood! I swear that my father would have discovered far more novel means of wringing money from this Gascon stone than ever I could! I know they detest a government working in their midst. I know they prefer their ruler to be many leagues distant so that they can pull the wool over his eyes. But that is not how it will be.'

I had risen to place a hand on his shoulder, which he shrugged off, later being stirred enough to write a reply, which he did not allow me to see. I think he expected me to advise moderation in his relations with his father.

Ned was beyond moderation.

But worse. Far worse. A formal summons from King Charles of France for Ned to appear in Paris to discuss the hearth tax which, King Charles opined, was against all tradition since it appeared to be becoming an annual occurrence rather than an infrequent appeal for help. So our subjects had indeed gone en masse to complain to their previous liege lord and here was the consequence, enough to rouse Ned to burning ire.

'What is this? A demand from a liege lord to his inferior? The French King is no suzerain of mine.'

If it had not been clear before, it was now. The Treaty of Brétigny was long dead and gone, buried deep in its coffin. King Charles, with no intention of abiding by it, would reclaim Aquitaine as his own, and until he achieved it, he would stir up our subjects by any means he saw fit, even summoning Ned to Paris as an underling. All Thomas's hard work to hammer out an agreement from two hostile sides destroyed by a French King with his mind on re-conquest. It made me consider the effect on Edward, faced with his wife's suffering and now the destruction of his famed peace. The end of all his dreams.

Here in Aquitaine, an explosion of Plantagenet temper rent the air of Ned's chambers, to which I added fuel to the flames, for I could no longer remain silent. The still-new bright love did not blind me to Ned's refusal to see the truth.

'I think your father was well-informed. The tax was too much a novelty for them to accept. Certainly it was too frequent.'

'Well-informed?'

'I warned you.'

'So you warned me.' His gesture was dismissive. 'I do not want your warning. Where is your wifely loyalty?'

I withstood the hard stare.

'Loyalty weighs nought against crude reality. Do you know the state of our coffers?'

'Do I know? Of course I know. Why would I levy another tax if they were full to the brim? I suppose you would blame me for going to the aid of thrice-damned Pedro? Or of being unable to wring the promised gold from him?'

'No. But the tax was too much. You must woo them, Ned, not beggar them.'

'And you so experienced in the government of states.'

The cynicism coated me from head to foot.

'I am experienced in the handling of men,' I replied, thinking of all the occasions on which I had negotiated, persuaded, taken to task.

'I had not noticed. You appear to be singularly maladroit at managing the men in your life.'

I felt my own temper begin to match Ned's.

'I wooed you,' I said, remembering the archery contest that seemed so far away in a different world.

'I did not require the wooing. I wanted you. And your advice? What is it? Let me guess. Cancel the tax?'

'We cannot do that,' I agreed, but our voices had begun to fill the chamber, fortunately empty apart from ourselves and a brace of hounds. 'We are too much in debt. And much of it our fault. Our extravagance has become the source of anger.'

'As is your taste for unsuitable garments.'

'I have not heard you complain.'

'I am complaining now. That veil is not suitable for a married woman, flaunting your hair. What has happened to a seemly covering?'

'Do you wish me to adopt a full veil and wimple, as would your mother?'

'You are unreasonable, Joan. I merely ask you to be discreet.'

'As you were discreet in entertaining every knight and his horse in Aquitaine at appalling expense.'

'And you know why I did it. An impression of power is based on a flood of gold. Nor do I recall your complaining. It was to celebrate your churching!'

Which of course led to an abrupt end to our conversation. Which lasted the rest of the day. And the next, Ned unforgiving, seething with righteous anger, discovering a need to be anywhere but where I might be. I accepted that I was not the problem, rather the blow delivered to Ned's pride from his father, accepting at the same time that it would be wrong of me to increase the burden on him while he wrestled with this wound to his self-esteem from the one man who claimed his love and his admiration. The peace must be of my making. I steeled myself as I walked into his chamber.

'I have come to negotiate terms,' I said baldly.

I found myself regarded as if I were an invading force. 'I am not open to negotiation if you are still of a mind to put the treachery of our unruly subjects on my shoulders.'

I stood before him so that he had no choice but to look at me. 'I do not blame you. We are both to blame. I think we have not always been very wise. You notice I include myself in this.'

'Thank you. Should I be grateful that you accept your own part in this monstrosity?'

I set my teeth. This was going to be more difficult than I had envisaged. Ned's expression was shuttered.

'I have not come to fight with you. I am relying on your generosity of spirit.'

'At this moment, I have none.'

'I agree. I see none at all. You are still slouched in that chair while I am standing here. I have made the effort and I think that you might too. If you were truly the chivalrous knight you claim to be, of course.'

He regarded me, at last the beginnings of a smile lurking.

'It must have taken a lot to bring you here to make that admission that you too were in the wrong.'

'Yes. It did. Are you going to banish me or will you come to terms?'

'How can I refuse such an effusive offer?'

The reconciliation was one of a handclasp, as if we were ambassadors of warring states. Except that it was followed by a kiss that became an embrace.

'What will you do?' I asked pouring wine, dreading the reply. 'About King Charles' invitation.'

'I'll accept the summons. By God I will! But I'm no supplicant to this French King. I'll appear before him – with helm and sword and sixty thousand men at my back. Then we will see who holds the power here. Then we will see who rules Aquitaine.'

He looked at me to assess my response to such a provocative policy.

I would not stir another wasps' nest into life.

'Then that is what you will do, if you so wish. And I will support you in it.'

But he would not. He could not. Although the courier was sent with this less than tactful response, I knew that Ned would never be in Paris at the head of an army, however ill-used he felt. For underlying every strain and stress within our domain was the decline in Ned's health. It could no longer be avoided or ignored. Draining, debilitating, one attack followed fast after another, a weakening flux that struck him down. I was afraid, and for more reasons than I could talk of.

Too unwell to travel, as the months passed Ned barely left the palace. Never did he trouble the Gascon lords as he had in the first days when a progress had been the order of his days. There were some days now when he was too ill to stir from his bed. The best of physicians could work no magical cure. And while we remained in

Bordeaux, French King Charles, seizing his opportunity, began to infiltrate his troops into the eastern reaches of Aquitaine, Gascon lords flocking to his banner.

Ned was too ill to be more than fretful, dragging himself between the bed and the privy.

'I can do nothing to stop them.'

I could not even advise him to send out his loyal captains, to enforce obedience in his name. There had been many deaths of his most reliable men, Sir James Audley and Sir John Chandos, his closest friends. He would not speak of this loss, and I dare not, for anger brought him even lower.

When I could see no way forward, I wrote to my cousin Edward, braving Ned's wrath if he should ever discover what I was doing.

Your son is unwell, I wrote. *The King of France drains our strength with attacks on our borders. We need help. I ask it in your son's name, when he will not.*

Ned became more unapproachable by the day while I was fuelled by fear. I became a mistress of the art of concealment. Meanwhile I prayed that Ned be restored to health and the burden of stark fear, that could find no relief in such facile emotions as tears, be taken from me.

Chapter Fifteen

Blessed Jesu!

Aid came to us in our beleaguered state in Angouleme, and with it a relief that lit Ned's face with joy, although that only served to enhance his wasted cheeks, the long bones of his face sharp beneath the skin. In July his brother, John of Lancaster, once again arrived, full of rude good health, accompanied by a force sufficient to bolster our defences. A force that once again brought my son Tom who had grown beyond all my memories. I received John without explanation or excuses or even warning, simply leading him into Ned's chamber. John stopped me before we reached the door.

'Is he so ill that you must write?'

'As you will see. And has been so for many days.'

I opened the door, on a light knock to warn the occupants. John's greeting to his brother was masterly in its self-control.

They talked, Ned supported by a bank of pillows, the servants who had been caring for Ned's bodily needs dismissed. They discussed the deceased Treaty of Brétigny, the untrustworthy King of France, the recalcitrant Gascons. John's visit did far more good than I could ever do at this time. Ned's thoughts were dominated by his sense of failure which John was able to direct into a different path, a more wholesome one, with plans for the future. It was only when I took John out to allow Ned to rest – a high flush along his cheekbones had presaged the return of a fever – that John sighed and let his true thoughts flow.

'I did not know. I had no idea that things had come to this pass. You did not say.'

My reply was cool, disliking the accusation that I had not seen fit to pass on bad news. 'As I knew nothing of Philippa's passing. News, even tragic news, travels slowly.'

John himself had brought the news with him, unable to keep it from Ned that his mother, much-beloved Philippa, had died at Windsor, bringing to an end many months of suffering. I had not yet acknowledged it for myself, this great loss. I would think of Philippa's passing later. Now all I could do was hold my sorrow at bay.

'No. I suppose you would not.' It was as close to an apology as I would get from Ned's brother. Knowing that he would have been stricken by his mother's death, I allowed myself to mellow somewhat.

'I could not worry my cousin the King,' I said. 'I knew your mother suffered. As for Ned, he forbids me to trouble anyone with his ailments. You have seen him on one of his better days. He hides it – you know how proud his is. But it can no longer be hidden.' I hesitated. 'He won't return to England, even though we have talked of it.'

Looking out from the height of one of the towers to which we had made our way, we talked, and it was for me a small lessening of the load. How long I had borne by fears in silence, with no one to whom I could speak freely. And so we talked about Ned of course. About John's own thoughts of a new wife from Castile, an exiled daughter of the troublesome King Pedro, now dead.

'Do you have an eye to the crown of Castile for yourself?' I asked, remembering some past anxieties. If John of Lancaster had an interest in Castile it would remove his ambitions from England. We talked of the future for Aquitaine. Of Alice Perrers who had sunk her claws even more strongly into Edward's deteriorating mind, and would continue to do so since there was no one able to stop her. And then:

'How do you fair?' John asked.

For a moment it robbed me of an immediate answer. I could not recall when anyone had asked after my situation. Not that I would reply with any degree of honesty. Better to keep my own counsel, even with a man I would perhaps call friend, despite his youth. I had little experience of friends, but he was as close as I would come to one. My response was light.

'As you see. As self-willed as ever.' I swept the silken layers of my skirts, still extravagant, with an expert hand. Anything to cover up the distress which would never release me.

'As beautiful as ever.'

'You know how to flatter a woman.'

He took my hand from where it rested on the coping stones and kissed my fingers.

'I see below the surface, Joan.'

'Once Ned did. But now he is too ill, too beleaguered with what, in his eyes, he has failed to do.'

Which hurt so much. We had been together for such a little time to enjoy the love that had finally touched me with its cruel hand, before threatening to snatch away the object of that love. And I wept, shocked to find myself enclosed in a brotherly embrace.

'When did you last weep?'

I pushed away from him, turning away. 'I have no idea.' The storm was soon over. I could not afford weakness. 'I do not weep for myself, or for Ned. But when I am alone, I will weep for Philippa.'

'You don't have to be in control of your emotions all the time.'

'Sometimes it is better that I am. What value are tears? They'll not heal Ned. In truth I think nothing will. I think there is more amiss than the flux.' I turned back, despite the temporary ruin of my beauty. 'Do you believe in divination, John?'

'No more than any man. Why?'

I explained the grievous prediction with the advent of the three kings in Angouleme. That Richard would rule next in England after his grandfather.

'Three kings, two of whom no longer had the power to claim their thrones, one of them dead,' John sneered. 'For shame, Joan, that you should even listen to such falsehood.'

He was as sceptical as I. And yet I could not so easily sweep aside the fear that hedged me about. Who dare be brave enough to cast aside the power of divination? I would not in my heart, however much I might decry it with cynical words.

I had no mind to broach the warnings of Sir Bartholomew Burghersh, calling on the authority of Merlin that the Crown would pass to the House of Lancaster. One day I might, but today there was too much emotion to allow me to take the risk of angering him. Yes, it might be an advantage to have him settled as King of Castile rather than a lurking power in England. Accepting him as a friend did not blind me to the breadth of his ambitions.

John took my arm to lead me back down to the sun-filled inner courtyard. 'We will take care of him. We will bring him back to health.' He smiled with dry appreciation, a man who had enjoyed the happiest of marriages before losing his beloved Blanche only a year ago. 'I think that you have come to love my brother at last.'

'I think I have come to love someone more than myself.'

'Don't berate yourself Joan. We come from a prideful family.'

'I know. And now we have to destroy Ned's pride if we are to force him to accept our help!'

We would care for him if Ned would let us. But, in his inimitable style, he would not.

'I'm not dead yet.'

'No you are not. But you may be if you do not preserve your strength. You are not yet strong enough to lead an army onto a battlefield,' I said. I had stopped being placatory even though my heart was wrung within me. 'Drink this!'

Amaranthus, commonly known as Prince's Feather, which seemed entirely appropriate. Dried and powdered, drunk in wine, it would, with God's grace, heal and ameliorate the debilitating effects of the bloody flux. Not asking what the contents might be, Ned swallowed it, handing me the cup with a glower as if I had attempted a poisoned draft.

'Do I stay here in my bed and let this damned bishop deny the oath he made?'

At his side, occupying the one comfortable chair, John sat unmoving, fingers tented against his lips. I remained silent beside the bed, assessing the strength of the man in it. Of course Ned could never turn a blind eye to this development, nor had we been able to keep the news from him. The French army had infiltrated the region of Limoges; consequently its bishop, with preservation of his ecclesiastical skin in mind, had defected to the enemy. Ned was justifiably furious.

'I made this bishop godfather to my eldest son. Is that not a signal honour? Do I accept his treachery? I will impose my will on this principality if I die in the attempt.'

I dare not look at John as I prayed to God that he would not.

On the following morning I entered his chamber to discover that Ned, against all good advice and with John in reluctant but solicitous attendance, had risen from his sick bed and was in process of donning his armour. Perhaps I was not entirely surprised, but that did not prevent the fear that lodged in my throat.

'You will not.' I was astonishingly calm.

'I must.' His head was turned away as he and John, acting as squire as he must have done on some many felicitous occasions, buckled another piece of armour in place.

'Could you not stop him?' I was perhaps less calm when addressing John.

'No.'

I walked out. I could not stay to watch the determination with which they both prepared to leave once more for war. What did I expect? It was the same pride that was in my own blood. They were Plantagenet princes and no bishop could be allowed to break his oath of loyalty.

But I was there when Ned took his place at the head of his and John's troops.

'Keep safe,' I said.

'I will. Keep my sons safe.'

'You know that I will.'

He leaned to touch his hand to mine. There was no apology in his gaze, which was firmer, more confident, than it had been of late.

'God shower you with His blessing and bring you victory.'

So he made his first journey out of Bordeaux for two years, clad bravely, rallied to his former strength, as he rode one of his war horses.

'I will yet ride into battle.'

But I knew the litter travelled with them.

Pray God that John would bolster Ned's body and spirits and curtail his ambition that would drain his strength before the end of the campaign. Pray God that Ned would come home to me. I could not bear to lose him.

★★★

I had been warned.

Even so, I halted beside the open door, reluctant to move further into the chamber. It was difficult to see, to make out forms and shadows apart from the glimmer of the linen on the little bed, the windows being shuttered to bring some semblance of cool and dignity to this room of pain and tragedy. All was quiet, the servants dispatched despite their reluctance; Richard, not understanding, sent elsewhere in the palace for safety.

I had sat in this chamber, watchful, only an hour ago. I had no premonition when I left for the briefest time to deal with some demand in the household that I should have ignored.

I had no thought of what would happen in this chamber in my absence. How could it come so soon? How could it come at all? All my worries were centred on the city where Ned and John waged war and I knew not what the outcome would be. But while the two royal brothers besieged Limoges, took the treacherous bishop prisoner and razed the town to the ground, I had no sense of the loss that would strike at me. At Ned too.

Slowly I walked forward, suddenly feeling every year of my age, dragged down by the weight of it. And yet I had lived long and adventurously with much complacency in my endeavours. The child would never do that. This child, in spite of all our care, was dead.

How is it that a boy, so full of noise and energy one moment, can lie in his bed and pass from this life, robbed of all colour and movement within a handful of hours? It was assuredly not plague, nor some bite of a noxious creature. Now I was standing next to the bed. His hair gleaming, newly combed, his clothing set to rights after the heated pain of those few hours, he looked as if he was merely sleeping, and would wake to run and shout until the rooms of the palace echoed with his games.

Our son, our hope, Ned's pride. A precocious son, now at five years able to ride a horse, able to carry a little sword with some haughty mien. Ned was already planning a suit of armour for him. Ned had

been seven when such a suit had been made for him. I remembered it.
I remembered Ned's fierce delight in it. So would our son be trained
in his father's famous shoes.

How would Ned respond to this death? I could not imagine it.
Desolation and pain filled me so that I felt the need to howl my grief.

Keep my sons safe he had said. And I had failed him, and them.

However ill Ned might have been, he always had time to speak
with his sons, to laugh with them, to allow them to lift his sword, to
wear his great helm in which they became lost, their voices echoing
so that they laughed with joy. And now this child was dead, a fever
that had swept through his body, draining it so fast that I had barely
taken him into my arms before his spirit had gone.

My thoughts flittered away, to my surprise, back to England, to
my own loss many years ago now and an infant burial in Winchester.
I had had a son called Edmund who had died at such a young age,
even younger, just as this one. But Edmund had ailed and finally been
struck with a contagion of the lungs so that he gasped and choked. The
grief was my own; Thomas had barely known him, merely mourning
him as a father would mourn any son. But Ned loved this boy who
should have inherited his titles and his authority in the order of things.

I loved him too. My beloved Edward.

I had not been able to keep him safe.

I touched his hand with my finger, where his flesh was already
cooling.

I could not weep. My heart was a stone, a fist of ice. I could not
accept this loss, yet I must mourn as the rest of my household would
mourn. I had failed Ned. I had lost my son.

Ned had returned. When he had returned from Castile I had been
there to meet him on the steps of the cathedral, our son's hand in
mine, heady with elation. Now I waited for him in the chapel where

our son's body lay. I knew our steward would send him here and so I waited in the shadows, not knowing what to say when I sensed that he had walked in to accompany me in my hopeless vigil. I could not even turn my head to look at him, afraid of the grief I would see in his face. Afraid of what he would see in mine.

There was a long silence behind me. Then:

'I had to come home.'

The timbre of his voice made me look up and back over my shoulder. Then I turned completely at what I saw.

'When did he die?' Ned asked, walking slowly towards the little bier.

'Two days ago, before the sun rose. A fever touched him during the night. We tried but could not cure it.'

'I wish with all my heart that I had been here.'

'You could do nothing. We could do nothing. Ned!' Now I was on my feet to grasp his arm as he came to a halt at my side. 'How long have you been like this?'

'A few weeks.'

'The same?'

'Yes.'

'Worse?'

He grimaced. 'Yes. I had to come home,' he repeated.

In spite of his own weakness, he stooped and gathered his son's body into his arms.

'I am so sorry,' I said. What empty words. How trite and meaningless. The walls of the chapel seemed to weep around us in their grief.

'Where is Richard?'

'He is well. He is with his nurses. The fever did not touch him.'

Releasing his son, neatening the coverlet that displayed the Plantagenet symbols of power and majesty, he faced me across the wilderness of the little body.

'Do you know?' he said as if beginning a conversation about music or some tale he has heard from a minstrel, 'I cannot even ride into battle. When I led the attack at Limoges, I was carried in a litter.'

I had guessed, but gave no intimation of my past fears. There were too many present ones to unman him and destroy me.

'The degradation smites at my soul, Joan.'

Not Jeanette today. His love was compromised by loss and suffering and the ultimate degradation of being unable to fulfil his destiny as a prince and a knight. I stretched out my hand to touch his cheek that seemed so wasted and pale despite the hot sun that had been beating down on him through the past months.

'Your soul is strong enough to recover.'

'How can I have faith when God takes away my son?'

I lowered my hand so that he could interlock his fingers with mine. 'What do you want to do now?' I asked softly.

I knew in my heart what he should do but I would not pre-empt his decision. Not today. For a long moment he looked towards the altar with cross and candles and the image of the suffering Christ. No more suffering than Ned's present agony. Then he looked back at me, eyes wide and fathomless, yet I could see that he had come to a hard-won decision.

'Go home. I have to go back to England. I am no use in battle here. My mother is dead, my father's hold on England wanes. Perhaps on English shores I will regain my strength. And then, maybe, one day, we will return.'

Our clasp tightened, as I admitted to a relief that weakened me.

'Then we will go.'

Perhaps his health would be restored. He would recover from this monstrous debilitation and stand proudly beside his father in King Edward's final years with Richard as his heir. Perhaps matters were not as desperate as I had thought. I was not too old to carry another royal son. Yes, to return to England was the decision that Ned had needed to make.

'We must stay for the boy's burial,' Ned said. 'We are not yet free to go.'

But now I took matters in hand. I did not even wait to hear him ask what I might think or want. It was, it seemed to me in that chapel, a necessity for his health, both body and soul, that we leave Aquitaine with all its pain and failure. I would make plans.

'No,' I said, drawing him with me to the door where John was now waiting for us, head bent in utter respect. 'We will not wait. You need to go home soon. Your council will take control here...'

'I cannot leave Edward unburied.'

'Your health is of paramount importance. John will undertake the burial. He will do it well, here in the cathedral.'

John nodded. I swallowed. It seemed a sad abandonment, but I knew what must be done. As testimony to his weakness, Ned did not argue. Evidence enough of the state of his body and the uncertainty of his mind.

Returning briefly I kissed my son, as if to reassure him that he was not forgotten, then led Ned from the holy place.

'We will go home. You will be stronger in England and your father needs you.'

He looked at me. 'Yes, we will go home.'

The winds were set fair as we left Bordeaux, leaving the burial of our little son in the care of John of Lancaster. The victory at Limoges which should have been a shining star in Ned's firmament was a bitter farewell, Ned defeated by his own physical weakness. He could no longer rule. He no longer had the strength.

What would await us in England? I did not know, and I was afraid.

Suddenly we could not return to England fast enough. While Ned rested, with freedom to be myself without anyone to watch or make comment, I wept for Philippa, whose death still seemed impossible to grasp. How would it be to return to court where Philippa's benevolent presence and overarching love was absent? I wept for her as I should have wept for my mother, but never did. I wept for young Edward and for Ned; a whole lifetime of unshed tears catching up with me.

Enough! I could weep no more.

I thought it would be a thorny path for both me and Ned when we set foot once again on English soil. Ned must face his failure. I must take hold of my reputation. How difficult either would be I had no idea, but I turned my face to England with courage and a strong resolve as I held tightly to Richard's hand. This was the proof of my value. This child who would reign after his grandfather and father.

April 1371: England

All would be well when we set foot once more in England.

Were those not the puissant words of the gifted anchoress, Julian of Norwich, who, enclosed in her solitary cell, saw truth in the world? I was to read her *Revelations* in later years, as I damned her for her interpretation of God's love for mankind.

All shall be well, and all shall be well and all manner of thing shall be well.

Oh, but she was wrong. I would not sing her praises. How unutterably misjudged her endless optimism. Only the most gullible, the most blind, the most grief-stricken, would believe that it could be so, yet I clasped the hope to my heart, even when I knew that my life with Ned would never be well again. Ned was fractious, lacking tolerance for his own weakness as well as for anyone in his vicinity.

I must be protective. I must be tolerant of his fears. I had learned much in those final days in Aquitaine. I had learned even more since love had settled its presence on me, like a raptor's claws into its prey. Love was a delight but also a great burden.

The lines of the troubadour's song revolved again and again in my mind.

Love is soft and love is sweet, and speaks in accents fair;
Love is mighty agony, and love is mighty care;
Love is utmost ecstasy and love is keen to dare;
Love is wretched misery. To live with, it's despair.

Too late, too late, I had learned what mature love could be. I had learned its power to destroy and harm all peace of mind. I had learned the true glory of it. All the agony and the ecstasy that was almost beyond the strength of the human soul to bear when the one person in whom that love was centred was brought low, to the level of base earth. What could I do to preserve Ned in the face of his suffering?

Nothing. I could do nothing but encourage and show my love in every point on the scale of his battle to live and take on the role for which he had been born.

'I need to regain my strength,' Ned declared. 'I'll not be carried into my father's presence on a litter.'

'Then we will wait until you are strong enough,' I said.

We had sailed for England in a cold January, a fair crossing that caused him no discomfort, but we found a need to settle at Plympton Priory for more weeks than either of us had foreseen, for Ned to be strong enough to continue the journey. It clawed at his patience but it was April before we arrived in London, welcomed by mayor, citizens and a band of minstrels, and not least the gift of a complete dining service of gold plate. That is to say that it was promised but not yet complete. Ned, now able to ride a horse into the city while I was able to smile with more sincerity than I might otherwise have done, accepted it with a fine grace that vanished as soon as we were out of their hearing.

'A pity they could not have sent the gold plate out to me in Aquitaine. I could have sold it in bits to pay my troops.'

It did not bode well for the coming reunion, but I was encouraged that his health had become a manageable thing. Perhaps returning to England would indeed restore him. With the reuniting in my vision, I did what I could.

'You must make peace with your father. Don't forget that he is an old man and will be lost without your mother. Whatever has been between the two of you, he will rejoice at your return.'

'We'll soon find out.'

'And you will clothe yourself as the Prince of Aquitaine,' I said.

As John had done in Bordeaux, so did I act as Ned's squire, lacing the fashionably short cote-hardie, smoothing the nap of the rich cloth, helping him to pull on soft boots, exhibiting no compassion, which he would have detested.

'Do stand still,' I suggested, 'unless you wish to appear before the King as if you had been dragged to Westminster through the gutters.'

'I will if you could manage to hurry up!'

When all was complete, Ned looked suitably princely.

So Ned met with his father.

It was eight years since they had been in each other's presence, and many of them acrimonious ones. The King had not been reticent in his criticism of Ned's administration in Aquitaine. Even more contentious, he had countermanded the hearth tax that had caused such ill feeling, to Ned's fury. But the devotion of father and son still shone as bright as the promised gold plate as they stood together in the audience chamber at the Savoy Palace, John of Lancaster's London home, where we were staying temporarily.

King of England. Prince of Aquitaine.

And, between them stood the heir to the throne, a tiny child at four years old.

I looked on with some species of horror lurking behind my smiling countenance at what I could not deny when Ned knelt in formal fealty before the King. My hopes so quickly raised with the promise of the gold plate were dashed into pieces as effectively as a clay platter dropped onto the painted tiles.

God ensure that neither King nor Prince die soon.

Richard was no age to be King. A regency presaged all sorts of problems, not least the question of who would hold the reins of power while Richard grew. Unaware of my fears, father and son looked at each other, accepting what each saw in the other as Ned rose to his feet and embraced his father, while I could do nothing but stand as support to both. Philippa was no longer a willing helpmeet. It was as if her spirit lingered at my shoulder, her mourning pre-empting my own.

For death lurked in that sumptuous chamber, peering over the shoulder of both father and son. Edward was ill, careworn, his face lined, his eyes faded and deep in their sockets as old age had indeed galloped into his presence. Ned could barely walk into the chamber. I saw the tension in his jaw as he pushed himself from knees to feet to kiss his father on both cheeks. I saw the effort it demanded from him to stand straight and tall as a son should before his father.

'I leave government on your shoulders, my son. It has become too burdensome for me.'

Even Edward's voice had dwindled from its regal tones into almost obscurity, little more than a weak whisper, and beside him, standing not quite in his shadow, was Mistress Alice Perrers, only stepping back when father and son sat to talk more intimately. Seeing me she did not hesitate but made her way in my direction. I watched her with interest, and with displeasure, even perhaps a frisson of true fear. Mistress Alice had acquired an authority, a presence, even as she curtsied before me. How much power did she wield? Was it enough to harm me? To harm Ned? I did not think so but complacency would be a mistake. No longer a royal damsel, she was royal mistress, without question.

'You have done well for yourself,' I remarked, unwilling to exhibit any concern.

'I have, my lady. The King needs help and companionship. I answer that need.'

Again, as before, I could not fault the respect in her obeisance. Age had touched her, but lightly, perhaps even endowing her strong features with a mature charm.

I looked across to where Edward had lowered himself onto a chair, Ned's hand beneath his arm. 'What will you do, Mistress Perrers, when you and your bastards are driven out?'

Her reply was phlegmatic. 'When I no longer have a place here, I have enough to keep me and my children in some comfort. Your cousin, my lady, has been generous.'

'It will be soon.' And when her eyes flew to mine. 'The time when your place at this court is closed to you.'

'Perhaps not as soon as you think. I know that you see me as a threat to your power at court, my lady, as Princess of Wales.'

'And, one day, Queen of England.'

Her glance fastened on Ned. 'If you believe that it will come to pass, I wish you well. I would not wager these rubies that the Prince will ever see that day.'

I looked to see what she saw in Ned that was so imminent. Then I looked at the rubies, where her hand rested on the bodice of her embroidered gown. They were Philippa's. What had we come to, when the mistress wore the gems of the dead wife? Fury raged within me, against all my good intent.

'I am solicitous to your impending loss, my lady,' Mistress Perrers said, her eyes bright but not without feeling.

I could not return it. All my thoughts were bound up with King Edward's foolish weakness in rewarding this woman with his wife's personal gems.

'You have lined your purse and coffers with gold and precious stones,' I accused.

'And that is not all I have in my purse and coffers.' Her pride was a thing to behold, perhaps making her careless for the first time. 'I have bought land and pretty manors. Why would I not? It behoves every woman to make provision for an uncertain future. I have also made plans for my future of which you know nothing. My consideration for the uncertainties that lie ahead has been most successful.' Her lips closed as if she had said too much, then: 'As I have remarked before, we are not so dissimilar, my lady. I advise you to do likewise.'

Once again the accuracy of her comment, like an arrow loosed at its target by a master archer, shivered through me with such pain that I swore my revenge.

I have made plans for my future of which you know nothing.

I would make it my own priority to discover just what it was that Mistress Perrers had been doing in my absence, and if it was of use to me, then I would not hesitate to use it.

For the first time in my privileged life I put the wishes of others before my own. It had taken long in coming. Centred on my own desires, my own vision of my future, I had failed too often, unable to see the truth before me, making me the most selfish of women. King Edward and his own need to solidify his power had not made me tolerant of him. It had not been an easy start for him in his experience of kingship, a mere boy, at the hands of Earl Mortimer and his less than maternal mother. Of course he valued his friends, those who had stood by him. Of course he would wish to reward them, to mourn their passing. I had been less than sympathetic.

There was Philippa in her pain and her anxieties, her isolation when Edward took a woman of her own household to her bed. Why did she not dismiss the woman, and have done with it? But Philippa was overcome with a need to preserve her dignity as well as her fear that she had lost his love. It was everything to her. Did I not now know that?

Even my mother in all her driven need to wipe out uncertainties and ignominy. The past had put a cold hand on her heart. The only warmth came from ensuring the succession of her children to their father's honours.

Now I knew the burden of fear and grief for myself. Ned's needs were paramount. Nothing must disturb the serenity of his mind if it was in my power to prevent it. I would smooth his path. I would put aside my own concerns. I almost wept. Philippa would be astonished at my transformation. I might even allow Edward the comfort of Alice's presence for a little while.

Later, much later, when I had both time and inclination to look back, the years that followed became for me much like the tiny illuminated pictures in my missal. Bright. Vivid. Intense in their detail and life force, with Ned at the centre of each one. Ned grasping all the power and the strength that he could summon to fulfil the role that his father had abrogated and expected his glorious son to fulfil. I was beside him, encouraging, supporting, when I could, exhausted with words. Drained with a permanent anguish that was never allowed to see the light of day.

Some of the images that remained in my mind were astonishingly full of renewed hope. False hope, but still there had been room for a level of contentment. We could not mourn for all of five years. I took them out, these vivid pictures, as if they were jewels in my casket, to examine them and enjoy what could be enjoyed.

Ned presiding over the Royal Council in his father's stead, discussing taxes and matters of the realm, more cautious in his approach than he had ever been in Aquitaine.

Ned riding out through the cheering populace of London, at ease in the saddle, to welcome brother John home to England, to dispense costly gifts to John's young bride, the exiled Constanza of Castile, celebrating with him in his ambition that one day John would be King of Castile in his wife's name.

Ned attending the Garter feasts, resplendent in his robes, in appearance the most impressive of all the knights.

Ned receiving petitions, again with more grace than he had applied in Bordeaux, because King Edward was no longer able to recall the names of his petitioners.

Ned standing beside the King at the opening of the Good Parliament of 1376, aware of the need for conciliation with this body of powerful men who held the purse strings.

Ned at his father's shoulder, standing bold on the aft deck of ship that would take them once again to war, Plantagenet banners flying bravely, to drive the French out of La Rochelle and remake England's reputation and fortunes in Europe.

And then there was Ned, teaching Richard to sit a horse and hold a sword, a young monarch in the making at his father's hands.

And the most poignant of all? Most heart-rending of all? Ned with the restored power to take me to his bed, with all the mastery of our early days, all the clever caresses to rob me of truth of those cautious days, but not with the power to get another child on me.

'My most dearly beloved wife. I could not have chosen better, not if all the princesses of Europe and beyond had been paraded before me.'

For a short time, it rekindled all my hopes that we would live out a long life together.

And for myself, there was the remaking of my own reputation, for had I not been restored, renewed, my earlier notoriety wiped clean? I was once more Joan, the Fair Maid, Plantagenet princess. Our years in Aquitaine had done me no harm, neither at the English court nor with the populace, where out of sight, out of mind, had proved a true maxim. It seemed that my extravagance in spending and unconventional raiment had done me no lasting harm here in England, where even the diamond buttons were admired. I was cheered in genuine affection when I smiled on the crowds. I knew well how to smile. I could not afford to destroy what I had achieved. For Ned's sake, for Richard's, and for my own.

Now I adopted the demeanour of an honourable woman, adding to my renown with generous acts of largesse and almsgiving, undertaken with courtesy, enhanced by a smooth coating of humility to wipe away the shame of my past. The dark lasciviousness, hinted at in some of the rumours, was burnished in gold. And so I rode at Ned's side, raising my hand to acknowledge the acclaim of the Princess of Wales, Queen in waiting.

What was there to trouble me in all of this? What was there to cast me into a creeping blackness of despair, from which there was no escape.

Everything.

There was everything to numb my emotions, because this was nothing but a painted facade. This was a mockery of Ned as the glittering heir, for there, alongside my bright images of my imagined illuminations were those painted in sombre colour, too many of them dragging at my spirits as they dragged at the resilience of Ned's body. This was the truth of it; the weeks when we did not travel from either Berkhamsted or Kennington because Ned could barely stir from his bed. The days when he drove his body servants into a fright because his demeanour was one of imminent death. The days when the pain was so great that he did not wish to see me, when I was barred from his chamber and did not dare countermand that order. The evidence of his agony behind the closed door was beyond acceptance, and beyond his pride to allow me to witness it.

I did what I could to ease his conscience when the lethargy attacked his sense of duty, so that it was I who took on the symbols of power such as a Prince would wield. It was I, not Ned, who attended Philippa's annual memorial service at Marlborough, to honour both the late Queen and King Edward, who led the mourning. It was I who received the gift of the gold plate when it was finally complete, the whole impressive lot of cups and basins and lavers, a working service for a man constantly on the move, a soldier or administrator. Ned would be neither. It was I who received the givers of the gift with such grace, who later wrote to thank them for their kindness, knowing that the dishes would never be used as they were intended, nor would they ever be broken up to pay an army for Ned's use. Ned would never lead an army again.

The Good Parliament, flexing its financial muscles to encroach on royal power, enforcing the dismissal of trusted royal officials for embezzlement and dubious financial dealings, neither the King nor Ned was strong enough to hamper this parliamentary undermining of royal power. My only consolation was that the vengeance of the Speaker of the Commons also fell on Mistress Perrers and her extraordinary acquisition of wealth. When she was discovered to be wantonly and secretly married to a ruthless politician as driven and devious as she, one William de Windsor, her downfall was inevitable. How effortless it had been to discover and supply such information to Speaker de la Mare. How satisfying it was when Alice was peremptorily dismissed from court under threat of imprisonment, which she only avoided by promising to leave court and never visit with Edward again. Parliament, with some neat contrivance by me, had relieved me of Alice's presence at last. If I had not been so absorbed in Ned's concerns, I would have rejoiced more than was seemly. As it was, both Ned and I were reading the writing plain on the horrifyingly decreasing pages of our future.

And the most desperate image of all, bright and bitter that lodged in my mind, leaping into my thoughts, sliding furtively into my dreams. Ned, rising from his couch on a day when he was able to do so, when a bundle of correspondence had arrived from his Council in Aquitaine. He took it, dismissed the courier with calm courtesy, then cast the letters onto the bed before seizing my hands in a grip that showed a strength that soon waned.

'There is something I must tell you, Joan. Although I think there is no need.'

I willed my own strength into him. No, there was no need, but I knew that he must be allowed to speak it. To acknowledge his acceptance of what he could and could not do.

'Then say it, and be assured that I will accept your decision.'

'Without argument?' He smiled slightly. 'Then here it is. We will never return to Aquitaine.'

What need to say more? Ned would never lead an army against the French or the rebellious Gascon lords. He would never hold sway over that distant province. He simply had not the energy, the bodily strength, to set out on another campaign. It was all he could do to travel between Kennington and Windsor, at ease in a royal barge on the River Thames.

'No, we will not,' I agreed.

I could no longer lie or encourage where there was no encouragement to be given, pretending that all would be well when it would not. Ned gave up his claim to the principality of Aquitaine in parliament in November of that year of 1372, less than two years after we returned to England.

He turned from me to look out over the land that was his by right of inheritance.

'We will have no more sons together.'

What had it taken for him to admit that? The love still held firm between us, the affection deep, the desire still aflame. The physical ability was lost in a trough of pain and weakness.

'It is of no importance. Richard grows strongly and he will wear the Crown. He will make an acclaimed King of England, with all the majestic bearing of his father and grandfather. I will ensure that it is so.'

Walking lightly, I touched his shoulder, leaning a little against him, his hand covering mine against his chest where I could feel that his breathing was compromised. It was an intimacy of delicate acceptance of the brief time left, and it was a promise I made with a heavy heart. I would keep it. I would do everything in my power to keep it. It was as if I were touched anew by a burning brand of ambition, not for myself but for my son. Our son.

It was a terrible day. There were many more to follow.

'Will you tell your father?' When Ned was once more stricken.

'No.'

'I think that you should.'

'No need to worry him.'

So Ned would drag himself to the opening of the Good Parliament, and then onto the deck of the warship that would carry them to La Rochelle, perhaps to prove to himself that there was the smallest hope for a future, only to return to Kennington within the week in dismay, when the ship for La Rochelle never sailed. The losses abroad were out of his control. His despair was a thing of terror that haunted him, waking and sleeping, snapping at his heels.

'Jeanette!'

I looked back.

'You must not tell my father either.'

It was in my mind to do so, and he saw it.

'Promise me! On your honour as a Plantagenet, that you hold so dear.'

It was an appeal could not be rejected.

'I promise.'

Chapter Sixteen

The Year of Our Lord 1376: Kennington Palace

In my own chamber, I sat in silence. Ned was dying, not as a warrior or a celebrated King but wasted by a base disease, his glory long past, his ambitions unfulfilled. England had once glittered and chimed to the deeds of his prowess; now it seemed to me that it was sour and sullen, divided and dark with a fast-fading King, a dying heir and a rapacious mistress.

I cast aside the Book of Hours that I had picked up for solace, angry at my own impotence, as I allowed my thoughts to return to another death. When Thomas died he was far away from me. I did not experience the last hours, the harsh clinging to life, the wish to be shriven, the disposition of goods and the desire to make peace with family and friends that made the deathbed of a great lord such a public place. I knew nothing of it until it was all over and Thomas buried. I wished I had been with him. I resented that he had died without me.

I had heard of those who, fast caught in a net of love, knew to the day, to the minute, even to the second, when their lover breathed his

last. I did not know that Thomas had departed this world. I had no
sense of doom of a distant leave-taking.

Even if I had stood at his shoulder, knelt at his side, there would
have been little for me to do. Thomas's death would change my
standing and rank not at all since the title was mine by right. Our
children who carried their father's name so proudly would inherit
his property and his honour as was their right too, through me. All
I would have needed to do in my absolute love for him, and my
total irritation, was to give witness to his passing into the hands of a
compassionate God.

Had Thomas missed my presence in those final hours? His suffering had been short. Had he known that he was dying? I did not
know. All I had been given were the usual platitudes by the priest to
comfort the grieving widow, by the courier whose task it was merely
to deliver the sad news. And I, bereft, had felt no desire to question it
further. I had been willing to be comforted, praying with the cleric
that Thomas had died in peace and under God's care.

How different was this leave-taking?

This was fought against as it was anticipated, as it was feared. I
would lose him, and all the love that had bloomed over the years since
he insisted that we wed against all good advice. And here was the
difference that blighted my soul. My own position as a Plantagenet
daughter and widow would not be undermined, but that of my son
Richard, the child-heir, might well be considered untenable in this
dangerous atmosphere when parliament clamoured for its right to
speak and decide, and all was disaster abroad as France regained her
strength. Who would want a royal heir of only nine years old when
King Edward would so obviously follow his son into his grave within
the year? Sometimes it was difficult to decide who would die first,
King or Prince. King Edward waned before our eyes despite the firm
hand of Alice Perrers, whom I had been driven through necessity to

accept after her triumphant return to the court. Defying parliament and the judgements against her, she cared for the King with a tenacity that I could not deny, even as I despised her for her desire to grasp all the wealth she could.

Meanwhile I fought for Ned's life, not with any knowledge of potions and tinctures, for I had none, leaving such mundane tasks to Ned's physicians, but with my will. I prayed with him. I talked with him. I poured my strength into him. I would not let him go. He had a mere forty-five years of life; no age for a man of Ned's calibre to die of so crippling and humiliating a disease. It was not right. It was not just.

I showed none of my desolation, cloaking my compassion for, before God, Ned wanted no pity. Instead I preserved a tranquillity, my joy in his presence a genuine yearning, for Ned's company was beyond value in anticipation of the many years that I must soon sustain alone. And we would remain at Kennington, the palace he had built for himself and furnished for me in the first months of our marriage. He loved Kennington best of all; even more than Berkhamsted. He would die in his chamber surrounded by his household. With me. And with Richard.

I was informed by my people that the King had arrived. It was late and the Prince was resting as the June day sank into a magnificent evening, the dying sun setting the trees and water aflame. What had driven the man to make the journey from London that could not wait until the morrow? The Prince was always stronger in the mornings.

Not best pleased, I put my raiment to rights, ordered wine to be brought, and descended to the entrance hall to time my arrival with his, viciously hoping that he had not brought the Perrers woman with him. I was prepared to be coolly condescending, even denying him the right to visit his son, but what I saw thrust aside all my resentment that the King should come to disturb us. How much he had aged, even in the few months since I had last seen him, such that he had needed the arm of a servant to help him to climb the shallow steps.

I curtsied low. He was still my King as well as my cousin.

'You are welcome, my lord.'

Edward blinked at me. Then, the servant still in close attendance, he shuffled across the floor as if he had not the strength to pick up one foot and then the other.

'My lord.' I took his arm, motioning away his servant, who would have done the same.

He looked at me as if arranging his thoughts. 'I need to sit a moment.'

I drew him to a stool set against the wall.

'What has happened?' His grey pallor was worse than the Prince's.

'It is parliament,' he said, his voice without inflection as if he could not believe the words he spoke. 'I have heard that they seek my deposition.'

'No!' I too could not accept. 'They would not. How do you know this calumny?'

'One of my knights told me of it. They will do to me what they did to my father, stripping away the crown that is mine, as they took what was his. They will attack Alice too. I must speak with my son.'

I had not enough sympathy for two men so afflicted. All mine was centred on the Prince who lay gasping for his next breath in his chamber, and yet this man who had supported me, who had taken me in when my family was attainted, deserved better. In that moment I feared for him. This was no longer the great leader who had led England to battle and glory, building for the future and for his family. Where was the grandeur of the past? This was an old man who feared dishonour more than death. I signalled for wine, and waited until his eyes cleared and the planes of his cheeks firmed once more.

'How can I help?'

'Where is my son? I wish to see him.'

'He is in his chamber. He is resting.'

'I have business to discuss.'

'I think today would not be the best of days.'

Edward's glance became surprisingly keen. 'Is he rallying?'

Did I lie? Did I fill this old man's heart with hope in this moment of lucidity, to allow him to believe that his son would give him advice and stand at his side while he fought his battles with parliament to retain the Crown, if indeed there was any truth in his fears?

'I need him to be with me.'

And as Edward's voice rose into a full-throated command, as it would have done every day of his life in past years, I could no longer mask the truth. The King would read it as soon as he saw his son. Better to warn him now. I broke my promise to Ned, gently but inexorably, for it must be done.

'No, the Prince will not be with you. He cannot stand at your side again, my lord. You will have to fight your own battles, calling on your other sons.'

It was the hardest most painful advice I had ever given, the first time that I had put it into words, that once spoken into the still air of the chamber could never be recalled. Cruel? Yes, perhaps it was, but entirely necessary. We had hidden the truth for far too long. And still it was difficult to believe that the magnificent Prince was ending the term of his earthly days.

'No. No. He is stronger than that.'

Edward struggled to his feet, stretching out his hand to me, commanding me.

'He is not. His weakness is a burden to him and to those who serve him.'

'He will outlive me.'

'No, Edward,' I said softly. 'I think that he will not.'

He rubbed his hand across his brow then stood, as tall and straight as it was possible for him to do.

'I have buried seven children. I will not bury the eighth.'

I could not reply, however much I knew that I ought to say: 'Ned will be the eighth.' It would be wrong for the King to believe that there was any hope. He must put his own house in order, with the help of his three living sons. I doubted that Ned would ever rise from his bed again. The physicians were not sanguine, speaking of weeks.

'I wish to see him. I will see him.'

I dare not refuse longer.

It was a terrible reuniting. The Prince lay flat on his bed when his body did not writhe in agony. His physicians were in attendance, hastily casting a cloth over the bloody basin at the bedside. Nor could the burning incense mask the reek of disease and death. The King almost staggered at the door, then straightened and walked forward to take Ned's hand. I hovered. There would be no lies spoken now, no denials when Ned's face was as gaunt as his father's.

'I will not say that you look well, my son.'

'I am dying.'

The King had not believed me, but he could not deny Ned or the evidence of his own eyes, in which there were now tears.

No business was discussed on that night. All that mattered was the affection, the loyalty, the admiration, one for the other. They were truly father and son in their deep understanding of each other so that I wished that I had known my own father. Their emotion filled the room, stiflingly hot, so that I made to leave them, indicating that a servant should remain within call but far enough so that he was no eavesdropper on what they might say together. Until the King's words to Ned as I opened the door.

'I want you to come with me to Westminster.'

I strode back to stand beside Ned, a barrier between the two, my gaze commandingly on the King, all compassion lost. 'No.'

The King ignored this. I might not have been in the room. 'I want you to travel back with me. Tomorrow.'

I did not even stay to choose my words with care so that Ned would not be wounded more. 'That will not be. He is too ill. He is in too much pain. Can you not see?'

Edward turned on me, temper flaring like an ill-lit torch, gesturing that I should leave them alone. 'We do not need you.'

Oh, but they did. Both proud men but in need of all the help they could get.

'It is not advisable,' I tried, tempering my language.

'My son rode into battle in a litter against the town of Limoges. And won the battle.' As I well knew. 'He has the strength of an eagle.'

'He is comfortable here.' I looked across at Ned, who managed only a grimace that might have been an attempt at a smile.

'What she means is that I might not have the strength to survive the journey. I might die between Kennington and Westminster.'

Yes I had. I also knew that once at Westminster the control would be stripped from me. Ned would be surrounded by the royal household, cosseted and nurtured by the King's own physicians and servants. I would stand on the edges and wait. I did not want that. He was mine and I would be with him until he no longer needed me.

'I want him at Westminster.'

'But I don't think...'

'He will travel by river. There will be no added strain on him.'

I made to argue, furious with the King that he should at this moment recover his determination. Then I heard the breath that Ned drew from deep in his lungs.

'Don't worry Jeanette. I'll not die on the road. Or the river.' And to his father: 'I will go with you to Westminster. It is right that I should die there.'

'Is that what you want?' I asked, for how could I refuse him?

'It is what I want.' He sought my hand and held on as if it would save him from all the horrors that assailed his mind. 'And you will be with me. To the end.'

He read me very well, as he had always done. Thus it was settled, but I would remain at his side where I had not been for so much of our life together. He was mine and he would die under my aegis.

It was not to be. Of course it was not. Did I expect that it would be? What fools women can sometimes be, expecting to order their days and the days of those they love. Ned was laid to rest on his bed in his own chamber at Westminster, cold and cheerless as it was through lack of use, despite the fine furnishings, of which Ned was now unaware. It was as if the life had departed from these rooms that we had not used since the early days of our marriage. But when I might have expected Ned to rest and recover his strength to some degree, he wrapped his willpower around him like a metal chain and prepared to leave this life with authority and utmost dignity. Nothing was to be left undone. I stood beside him in despair, which he must have sensed as, at the first opportunity he dictated his will. He gripped my hand as he did it. Who was giving comfort to whom here?

'There is time and enough to make my peace with God. I'll not die today. There is much to be settled. And first you should know that I will be buried in Canterbury.'

'Why not here?' I could imagine Edward resisting.

'Near the Chapel of the Blessed St. Thomas the Martyr. It is my command. And it will be done to my ordering.'

There was no moving him, the old self-will unwavering. The Prince would have it so.

And then, even when his breath was short and his energies waning, all the depositions were made with an increasing urgency, to friends and family and servants who had been with him throughout his whole life. No one was forgotten as the clerk scribbled furiously. He would make a fair copy.

And finally:

'Now I will see Richard.'

I could have said that Richard was too young to understand, too young for all the emotional burden of a deathbed, but I did not. I knew what must be done.

Sent for, Richard was almost as pale as his father. Regarding him as he halted in the doorway I considered the rich blue damask of his tunic with its gold stitching suitable for a royal audience, certainly too ostentatious for this occasion, but it would have been of his own choosing, demanded of his servants as they clothed him, and now was no time to offer a reprimand. Instead I beckoned for him to approach and drew him close, Ned stretching out his hand to touch Richard's sleeve. I felt the child flinch as if already touched by a corpse, but I held him still. There were some lessons that Richard must learn, the most important in regal composure.

'When I am dead, you will stand by the bequests I have made, Richard.'

'Yes, Father.' It was barely a whisper.

'I cannot hear you.'

'I will stand by the bequests,' he repeated, hesitating on the word.

'You will remain true to your duty, as my heir.'

'Yes, Father.'

'You will be a wise and good King when the time comes.'

Richard had the look of a hunted rabbit, but held firm with my hands on his shoulders. 'Yes, Father.'

'You will obey your mother.'

'Yes, Father.'

'Kiss me.'

He did after only the smallest hesitation; a formal salutation on Ned's lips. And then:

'What will *I* get, when you are dead, sir?'

My fingers closed tightly into Richard's flesh, so that my son looked up into my face with some astonishment.

'The Crown of England will be yours,' Ned said with admirable calm, whereas I was wondering at our son's avaricious nature. 'You are my heir. Do you understand?'

Richard's face fell. 'But my grandfather has it. What will I have that is mine?'

'What would you wish?'

'The blue gypon that you wore in Bordeaux. The one covered with gold roses and ostrich plumes.'

'It is too big for you.' Ned's patience was a thing of wonder.

'He will grow into it,' I said as I felt Richard stiffen under my hands at being denied. Now was no time for untoward emotions.

'Then it is yours,' Ned agreed. 'And my two best beds and their hangings.'

'The one with gold angels sewn all over it?'

'Yes. The gold angels are yours. Now you may go.'

At the door Richard stopped on some thought that caught on the seriousness of the moment, looked back. 'Will I see you again, Father?'

'Yes. You will see me again. Are you not my son?'

'Yes.'

Richard ran from the room. I could hear his voice triumphant in his release, while I moved to smooth the coverlet with the embroidered ostrich feathers that covered Ned's wasted flesh, my heart weeping for him as he made provision for his end, for Richard who did not understand, but I smiled and touched Ned's cheek, trying for a little lightness in the charged atmosphere.

'And what will you give me, my dear lord?'

I watched as he gathered his strength, pushing himself upright against the pillows. He could barely form the words.

'I leave you all my love. You have always had it. Never forget, even when you wed again.'

'I will never wed again. How could any man replace you? You are my soul.' And I meant it, every word. 'But you must leave me something tangible too. If you do not, the world will record that you despised me and wished we had never wed. That even at the point of death you had given me nothing to commemorate our marriage.'

He was hanging on to consciousness.

'Then I will give you the hangings that you love so much. All those eagles and griffins with their claws and fierce eyes.'

My own eyes were blinded. A gift that had no meaning compared with the loss I would suffer and it was as if Ned sensed my grief for he roused.

'My dearest and truest sweetheart and beloved companion. I give you my son. I leave you my son to nurture and raise as a King must be raised. What more could a man give his wife?'

My cheeks were wet with tears that he could not see.

'You can give me no finer gift, my lord. I will honour it.'

I had my own concerns that were becoming more urgent by the day. When we had travelled to Westminster a small travelling coffer had come with me, as it accompanied me whatever my destination. It was rarely out of my sight and never out of my mind.

Leaving Ned to sleep, with no one to see me but the stitched figures of the eagles and griffins that were now my property, I lowered myself to kneel beside the little coffer. A jewel coffer, to keep safe my wealth of gold-set gems? Many would consider it to be so, knowing my love of outward show. I applied the key at my belt and lifted the domed lid, setting it gently back as the gems on my fingers absorbed the light. Here, contained within this carved box, inlaid with fragrant sandalwood, was the source of all my nightmares, of all my hopes. Not jewels at all, but layers of parchment, of documents.

I lifted out the first one but did not need to unfold it to know its content. Here was the letter, the only letter Ned had ever written to me, after the battle of Nájera, before returning to claim me with such love. But this was not what I sought so I laid it carefully aside. Then I took hold of the rest of the contents, holding them flat against my breast with both hands, as if their weight was enough to strengthen my will, before placing them back into their safekeeping.

Why did I need to do this? I did not need to inspect what was within. The folded sheets of old documents were as familiar to me as the famous contents of my jewellery coffer, and just as well handled. I knew exactly what I would find in that pile of carefully stacked documents. I knew the seals, the signatures and the sequence of them. I recalled with sharp acknowledgement the highs and lows of my emotions as I had received them. Such happiness. Such despair. Here in this little coffer was a map of my life, but now it was more than my own life that would come under the picking of nimble minds and destructive fingers.

Touching the frayed ribbon and chipped wax of the top document, my fear became a swollen river, all but choking me. All the choices I had made in the past threatened to come home to roost like a flock of carrion-eaters. I regretted none of them but the shadow they cast was dark and full of danger. My reputation was much mended but still, in some quarters, the subject of gossip and tainted innuendo. My spine was strong enough, my shoulders firm enough to bear the insinuations; but what of Richard? What a terrible legacy I had given my son to carry. Richard would be a King of renown, but only if he was allowed to inherit as was his right on the death of his grandfather, as long as he was allowed to grow into his power.

Was there any doubt? Not in my mind, but there were those who might look elsewhere. There were those who might not wish a child of ten years to wear the crown, who would look for a man of age and substance and reputation for leadership, with the ability to lead an army. My son was the unquestionable heir to King Edward, only son of the eldest son, but lacking all such qualities; there were men in this kingdom who might make a claim against him that would not be without support. Had not the portents warned me? I had not forgotten them.

So many with royal claims. They marched before me, bold in their demands to be considered.

John of Lancaster would be the choice of some, followed by his son Henry, as the next surviving son of King Edward. But that was not all. There were the offspring of Philippa, daughter and heiress of Ned's deceased brother Lionel of Clarence. Older than Lancaster, Lionel's descendents would take precedence. Philippa, wed to Edmund Mortimer, Earl of March, had a promising family. And there was the worry that assailed me. If this female line was considered to be acceptable, there would be an adult Mortimer claimant clamouring for recognition as the future King instead of boy with a tainted birth.

Tainted. Therein lay the problem.

For I had, wilfully, selfishly, provided these ambitious claimants with the perfect weapon. And then there were the prophecies that were still whispered behind locked doors.

My thoughts interrupted by an insubstantial knock, I closed the little domed lid. No place for prying eyes here.

'Enter.'

My heart thudded that it might be news of Ned.

But it was only Richard, his fair face flushed, his tunic's gold-stitched appliqué dimmed with a thin coating of dust. He had been riding with his governor.

'I have come to tell you, *maman* ...'

I turned the key to lock the contents away, so that Richard was distracted from what he might tell me, running forward to fall on his knees beside the little box. Snatching off his cap to cast it on the floor, he ran his fingers over the coffer, leaning close to peer at the decoration inlaid in gold and ivory, trying to open the lid.

'Look, there is a hart with a chain around its neck. And a gold crown.' He traced it with his finger.

'So there is,' as I smoothed his ruffled hair with my hand. 'It is my own device. One day you may use it too.'

'What is inside? Do you have a key?'

'I do.'

'Can I look?'

I thought about it. But to what purpose? I would not impart my own worries to him.

'When you come of age,' I said, 'I will give you the coffer for your own. It is very precious. You will keep its contents safe.'

'I wish to look now!' And when I shook my head: 'Can I look inside when it is mine?'

'Of course. The contents are very important for you. You will understand when you are older.'

'I will understand now.'

I recognised his father's will, the obstinacy in his jaw when he was refused something he desired, but I would not be swayed.

'Not yet.' I stood, lifting him to his feet, bushing the dust from the azure damask of his tunic. 'But come and look at this. I have a gift for you.'

I was not unaware that Richard would need clear guidance when he became King. I could no longer pretend that it would be Ned.

Watching Richard turn the pages of the book I gave to him, I began to plan with a sure clarity of thought. I needed an ally. A conspirator. Someone as capable of hard-headed political manoeuvrings as I. A guiding hand would be required, and it would be mine, of course; I would ensure that it was so. But then I considered death, that could strike so fast, so unexpectedly, as with Thomas. Or slow and agonisingly, with Ned. I could die tomorrow. How could I ensure Richard's safety? One woman, alone, was no answer to the weakness of my son's position. How could this boy, this child, hold fast to power if he became King within a month, within a year? I could not hold his hand for ever, nor did I necessarily trust the men who would undoubtedly be appointed to the Royal Council to guide the young King, reading naked ambition in so many of their faces. If I did not have a care, I would be pushed aside as a woman of no moment in a man's world. I would be neatly nudged to live out my days as a widow, worthy of all royal recognition, but with no influence on the life and progress of my son.

I found myself staring at one of Ned's much praised tapestries, not the eagles and griffins but one of a woman sitting alone in a garden. She was rich and beautiful, her surroundings perfect, her garments exquisite, but she was alone except for the birds and flowers, and she was powerless. That would be me.

I would not allow it.

Turning my head, I sought out a different scene, a crowned woman from some mythical tale who was directing her servants in her garden, to prune shrubs and pick fruit. What's more, the servants obeyed, their backs bent, their hands busy to fulfil her demands. That was more to my taste.

And so I considered. I might not need a husband, but I most certainly needed a man at my side whom I could trust with my innermost fears and who would follow my directives. It was a pertinent thought that played a discordant tune within the harmony of my own determination to control the future of my son. I would need an ally to speak with parliament, who would sit in the Royal Council. My own role would inevitably be curtailed by my being female; I needed a man on whom I could rely to be a bulwark for Richard against the storms of government, a man whom I could trust to set aside his own ambitions for those of a God-Anointed child.

Therein lay the problem.

Who knew better than I that men did not always consider the consequences of their actions? Thomas: marry and depart, sure in the knowledge that a wife would be waiting after months of silent absence. William: incarcerate a hostile wife in the belief that she would become compliant. Ned: wield a heavy sword in Aquitaine and expect the powerful lords to fall to their knees in loyalty. Whereas, I, since that distant occasion when I had exchanged vows with Thomas Holland which cast us all into the mire, considered the consequences of all my actions. Since then, with maturity and experience, I had taken no thoughtless step. It was the same driving force that I was forced to admire in Alice Perrers, for all her sins and power-grabbing.

But the incisive power of women to think and plan – woefully overlooked – would not change within my lifetime, so I must work to keep the reins in my own hands as securely as I might. When Edward was dead, when Alice Perrers was removed from the scene, when Richard, my son, wore the crown: then I would be in a position to bring the proud creature that was England under my dominion in my son's name.

I will make Richard a King of whom you would be proud.

It was a promise I made to Ned every night. A role that was mine to grasp, I would not retreat from it when my love was dead and gone from me.

I held my hands up to the light, turning them. They were small and fine-boned, heavy with jewels. They were capable, clever, skilled. Was not Joan of Kent still known for her beauty and grace? But these hands could not carry the burden that lay on my heart with increasing heaviness. Without doubt I needed an ally, a confidante.

I allowed the men of my acquaintance to replace the march of claimants to the throne, considering them, discarding them with unnerving rapidity, particularly when they were one and the same, both possible ally and enemy. Was there no one suitable to stride beside me to ensure the unquestioned succession of my son and my own position in his household?

Not Will Montagu, as steady and reliable a man as one of Edward's new gateposts beyond my window, but before God he had no flair for plotting.

My sons, Thomas and John. They were too young, too lacking experience, neither of them near his thirtieth year. Their loyalty to their half-brother was unquestionable, but I needed a man with years and a honed ability under his belt.

Then there were Richard's royal uncles who would regard it as their right to wield power in the name of their young nephew. Edmund of York was too weak; Thomas of Gloucester not to be trusted. As for Edmund Mortimer, Earl of March, Richard's uncle by marriage, he might prove to be no friend to Richard and his royal claim. None of them appealed.

Why was I procrastinating? I knew who I needed; some would say not a wise choice. An uncertain choice. Nor was I even certain that I could shackle such a wayward talent to my own desires. He was a man who would go his own way, who would place his own ambition before that of others. I would have him as my compatriot in arms but I did not yet know how to ensure his compliance.

Opening a different coffer as Richard continued to turn the pages of the book, exclaiming at the beauty of the gilded images, I considered, then pushed a fine ring, a ruby, onto my finger, admiring its glow in the sunlight. One day fate would thrust this man into my hands. And if it did not, then I would take fate and twist it, mould it into my own creation, so that he had no choice but to become my ally. One day…

Sometimes the burden of my past was becoming too great to bear alone.

★★★

The King sat beside his son, his hand resting on Ned's, lax on the bedcovers as if he could tie this departing soul to the earth, oblivious to the coming and going of servants and physicians, until he became aware of the crush in the doorway as a small crowd gathered.

'Close the door,' he ordered. 'My son needs peace.'

But I read an unspoken demand in Ned's face, the sudden feverish fire in his eye.

'No.' I raised my voice so that all should hear. 'That must not be.'

The King stood, his face as ravaged as Ned's. 'You would dictate to me, your King?'

'Yes, my lord. Leave the door open. Admit all who wish to come close.'

'Would you drain the life from him so fast? My son has not the will to receive visitors.' Edward raised his hand towards the servant who awaited the outcome between us. 'Close the doors, I say.'

'No, my lord.' I addressed the servants. 'Leave the doors open.'

This was a battle I must not lose.

'Why would you do this?' Edward said, turning once again to countermand my order, frustration lining his brow, grief bowing his shoulders. 'Have I no power in my own land?'

And all my determination to impose my own will drained away into utmost compassion, so that I walked to him, to place a hand on his shoulder and lead him back to the chair beside Ned. This was the brightest gem in his crown, the son who was the best of knights, who should have made the best of kings.

'You will see,' I said, kneeling before him as the most unimportant of subjects. 'Are you not still King? Do I not kneel before you? But Ned has a need that we must not hinder. It would be cruel to do so.'

Edward looked down at me. 'Then do it.' He clutched my hands. We were at one perhaps for the first time, to bring what comfort we could to his son.

I nodded at the servants.

I knew what Ned hoped for, what would happen. Had we not talked of it in the early hours before dawn? I had sent out the word that the hours of the Prince of Wales, once Prince of Aquitaine but no longer, were drawing to a close. Thus they came, all the household who had known him through their life and his. Servants to kiss his hand. His former knights who had fought long and hard at his command to kneel at his side, in honour of their once-great captain. The citizens of London to make their final farewells. His brothers of York and Gloucester paid their final respects in low tones. My sons Thomas and John paid due respect to the man who had taken their careers under his guiding hand as would any father for his son. Perhaps it had, after all, been good to return to Westminster. The affection in which Ned was held proved to be shatteringly emotional for all.

When I thought I could withstand no more, here was a face I recognised, and the familiar heraldic achievements, a mass of red;

and white and silver lozenges on the breast of his entourage that stood in the doorway. He knelt beside the prince, head bent, and kissed his hand. They had fought and won together. As he had fought alongside Thomas. But he had lost to Thomas, and not just on the battle field.

I watched him, my attention momentarily taken from my suffering lord, my heart softening with an old affection in spite of everything. Will had grown into the man he would always become. Still gentle, still easily brought to the brink of emotion, but a fine soldier and a fine man who had made his name without the royal blood of a bride. He had been as good a servant to Edward as his father had ever been. I smiled a little sadly. I had brought him nothing but heartbreak and trouble.

Our paths had crossed little since my return from Aquitaine, only in a superficial way. Now I walked across to him, unsurprised that his eyes were full of tears, which he hastily wiped away before taking my hand, saluting my fingers as an old friend.

'Forgive me, Joan. This is no time for being unmanned, but we will lose a great knight. A fine king.'

I squeezed his hand, quelling the tremor of my own emotion as well as his. I had discovered that I had need of friends who would mourn with me.

'He will have been pleased to see you.'

'I'm not sure if he realised.'

'I am certain that he did. You were one of his most trusted comrades in arms.' I steered the talk into kinder waters so that he might recover his control. 'Is your wife well?' Although I cared little, except as it affected Will. He deserved some happiness at the hands of a better wife than I had been to him. A surge of compassion and regret for my own behaviour washed over me. This was indeed a morning for regrets.

'Elizabeth thrives,' Will said. 'And so does my son. I'll make a soldier out of him. I don't expect the peace with France will outlive me.'

'No, I don't expect that it will. The Treaty of Brétigny has finally disintegrated into dust.'

He cleared his throat. 'I am sorry that you lost your son in Bordeaux.'

'Yes.' I retreated from the bitterness that still had the power to waylay me when I least expected it. 'But Richard will be a worthy heir.'

Our eyes jointly centred on Richard who stood with his tutor at the foot of Ned's bed, my son encouraging a reluctant monkey to sit on his shoulder, oblivious to the scene being played out before him, until the monkey escaped and fled, chattering in anger, the gold links of its chain clinking on the tiles. Will shuffled from one foot to the other so that I could almost read his thoughts. Was this indeed the makings of a potent ruler?

'Of course he will be,' he said. 'And we will serve him well. My son and I.'

Service. Duty. How fortunate I had been. Perhaps I had more friends who would mourn with me and stand with my son than I had realised. Will must have seen my melancholy for he touched my hand to restore me to the present.

'You will not be Queen of England, if that was your ambition.' His glance sharpened, became speculative. 'I imagine that rankles.'

'Yes. It does.' I would be honest with him, for there was no reason not to be so. 'But I will be a superlative King's Mother.' Will cleared his throat. I lifted my chin. 'Say it,' I commanded. I was in no mood for secrets and innuendo.

But there was none, merely a promise from a friend on whom, I knew in my heart, I could rely.

'If you ever need a man who will raise his sword in your defence, if you ever need a man who will remain loyal through all the vicissitude to come, I will be that man. As I will be for your son. I will always be your servant.'

So simple, so heartfelt born out of long affection and not a little strife. I felt tears begin to well as memories rushed back. 'I remember,' I said. 'I recall the day when your late lamented mother informed us all that you would never be half the man your father was. I was angry that she said it then, because it hurt you. There, you see. I was not always selfish.' My smile was wry. 'Now I know she was wrong. You will be everything your father was, and more. And thank you. I will value your friendship as will my son.' I turned my head to look over my shoulder to where Ned received another of his military comrades, to where Richard stood, wishing to be anywhere but in this room of pain and utter misery. I was no seer and yet I said: 'I think that somewhere in the future our paths will cross again, Will, hedged about by severe difficulties. It will be good to have a friend.'

His face was flushed with emotion.

'There will be no question of it. For all that has been in our past and in our present.'

He kissed my hand, bowed, and moved quietly to speak final words to his admired commander in battle. I watched him go, my emotions tumbling. There was no happiness in me on that day, no contentment, but one day when emotions were less raw, perhaps there would be.

There was one final step I wished Ned to take. Before his energies quite waned, I knelt and whispered in his ear, seeing the intelligence return, the quick understanding. Nothing could keep death from Ned's door, but between us we could make the path of our son straight and true.

'You know what you must do,' I urged.

'Yes...'

'He is too weak, madam,' the hovering priest intoned. 'He is sinking fast.'

I waved him aside. 'Then all the more necessary that this is done now.'

Ned's mind sought mine. I could sense it, feel it as his wasted hand closed over mine, as I had never sensed it in life. Never had I felt so close to him as at that moment in this urgent need. There was the bright intelligence once more, behind the suffering, as our thoughts held fast.

'Bring him here,' Ned gasped.

Richard was brought forward, trembling in awe at the assemblage, and in fear, his eyes flickering to the King, to his father, to me. He hesitated when the Prince stretched out his hand then approached when I placed my hand between his shoulder blades.

'My lord.' Ned's eyes were on the King, his speech halting as he struggled. 'I ask that you swear that you will acknowledge my son as your heir. To be King of England after you. I ask that you swear it now, before all witnesses. So that there will never be doubt or question of it.'

Standing now, finding the strength from some deep well of resolution, Edward placed his hand on Richard's shoulder. 'Be it known to all here-present. This boy is my heir. Richard will be King when I am gone. I give you my promise.'

'And your brother too must swear,' I murmured, my hand gentle on Ned's as it lay, fingers splayed and dug deep into the linens.

Ned's eyes sought the ranks of his family. All his brothers. I knew what he would do.

'John,' he said.

My heart beat loud in my ears as the terrible drama was played out. As Lancaster came and knelt. There was moisture on his cheeks.

'You too will swear, John. To put all your weight and power behind
my son. That you will see him crowned and you will be his dearest
counsellor. If you love me, you will promise me.'

I willed John of Lancaster to swear.

John knelt, head bent. 'I swear that I will be all things to your son.'

'And you will swear to be executor of my will.'

'I do so swear.'

I remained at Ned's side and bore witness to the vows. This
was what I had needed. This oath had superbly eliminated the
Lancastrians from the direct line of succession. Lancaster could not
inherit while Richard lived, nor could his son Henry. Here was an
oath even more binding on Ned's deathbed than the one John had
made to me.

The relief was like a wash of cool water over heated limbs. I would
be the one to guide Richard, I would direct Richard's steps and stitch
the tapestry of his future life. But Lancaster's allegiance was essential to
the final stitching. Together we would make of Richard a fit monarch
to follow in the royal line of Edward of Woodstock.

Then I let my hand drop away from where it had rested, taking
a step back so that Ned was free to make the final ordering of his
affairs with his father and brother. I had begun to learn the value of
a woman adopting invisibility in a world where men held sway and
paid little heed to female tongues. I would continue to be discreet,
even though I would be the power behind the throne, for a little
time at least.

Ned was speaking still.

'My dear wife and consort will advise my son. She will be his
counsellor too.'

I could have asked for nothing more than this recognition of my
own role in England's future.

'I will. On my honour, I will do that,' I said, making my own oath.

Ned sank into death on that day, sprinkled with holy water and holier prayers, surrounded by those who loved him most, asking forgiveness from all who had suffered at his hands. It was a peaceful end on Trinity Sunday, the best that I could have hoped for him after those days of unrelenting agony from which his physicians could find no respite. If I had wished for some solitude together, I was unable to voice it, forced to accept this very public leave-taking. It could not be otherwise, even as I wished to shriek my denial and cast them all out so that we could be alone for the final infinitesimal stretch of time.

I stood beside him throughout; not touching him for this was so formal a leave-taking that it denied intimacy between Prince and Princess. When others wept, I did not. I had been well schooled in what was acceptable and appropriate and what was not. No, I did not touch him flesh against flesh, but our eyes held as he said all that needed to be said.

'Will God forgive all the deaths at my hands?' he asked me, in an interlude between one petitioner and the next, his eyes dark with pain. A question that I would never have expected.

'He will. I am certain of it.'

'So much destruction. So much loss.'

I tried to reassure. 'It is the cost of war. Every soldier risks his life, as you did. God will receive you as the greatest warrior England has ever seen. He will see in your heart that you would bring glory to England. God will undoubtedly bless you for your service to the duty you have known was yours since the day of your birth.'

At my side, one of the priests murmured his assent.

'Hold my hand, Joan. I would not be alone at my passing.' And Ned managed to hold out his hand with all the old power.

'Nor will you be.'

Here at last was the permitted intimacy. There was nothing more to say, and Ned did not have the strength to say it, whereas I no longer cared that we were surrounded by a crowd. I knelt beside him and held his hand, afraid to watch the shadow that was drawing across his face. It was as if the light in his soul was dimming minute by minute until there was barely a spark. As I tightened my clasp, he no longer responded but in his eyes I saw that his love for me still lived, fathomless, infinite. Silently, I returned it.

The ending was clear to all, where men bowed to honour the Prince, but I continued to kneel, unmoving, in a scene that had played out in my mind so many times since our return from Aquitaine. A cup was brought, the fair and fatal juice of the poppy which Ned drank as if he sought oblivion. My lord would never have sought oblivion, but the pain was too great and he accepted the draught as a precious gift. I had lived through this one moment again and again, accepting that it would not be long in coming. Now here it was, in grim reality, no longer a dream from which I would awaken to some sense of renewed hope.

I kissed his brow, his mouth then bent my forehead to our clasped hands. Those who watched meant nothing to me. I had no dignity.

Without a sigh, without a word, Edward, Prince of Wales, once Prince of Aquitaine, my heart and my soul, departed this life. Thus died the hope of England. And mine too.

When I walked from the room, the great lords of England bowed so that I walked along a corridor of deep obeisance. Once it would have mattered. Now it did not.

My world had become a desert, a wasteland. How would I survive in it? I was inconsolable, if anyone had cared to ask.

Chapter Seventeen

My first thoughts in those early days, when grief was a merciless conqueror and I a grovelling supplicant at its feet that my whole world had lost its boundaries, its direction. There was no centre to my existence, no beating heart. In those early days I floundered in uncertainty with no confidante. No Philippa, no Isabella to hear my complaints and give me succour. On my knees before the Blessed Virgin I poured out my sorrow, to no avail. My emotions were numb with an irreparable loss. Was this to be my experience for the rest of my sorry existence, frozen into a lonely incompleteness? Did I accompany my sister by marriage into her nunnery, walling myself away in my everlasting mourning?

Until one morning I rose from my bed aware of an unexpected calm, for no reason that I could fathom unless it was the blessing of early sunlight sliding across the red velvet of the hangings, enhancing the embroidered ostrich feathers of silver, bringing the leopard heads of gold into life. It was as if I was renewed, recognising that I had a purpose that I could not neglect, even though the grief hammered unceasingly at my mind and my heart. Ned would never forgive me if I refused to tread this path. And as the leopards seemed to breathe fire rather than leaves from their mouths, I accepted the path along which I saw my future unfold. Life would not end for me with Ned's death. I patted the leopards, and took the first steps. I had never been lacking assurance; now it directed all my days, for I knew what must be done.

My immediate purpose: to ensure that Ned's final wishes were carried out with exactitude, regarding his burial near the chapel of St. Thomas the Martyr at Canterbury. How detailed they were, which was no surprise to me since Ned rarely left anything to chance, and I was grateful, for the intricate arranging filled my thoughts with who and how and to what effect. What other minutiae of my day to day life would occupy my mind from waking to sleeping if I did not have Ned's final great project to fulfil? I went to my bed exhausted, I rose from it to pick up the threads from where I had left them. There was no solace for me, but there was at least a dedication that deadened my emotions. I drove myself to accomplish what must be accomplished.

'Why will he not be laid to rest in Westminster?' Edward fretted in one of his now increasingly rare moments of lucidity, anger beginning to grip him as if it were my doing. 'Westminster is the place for his tomb. If it was good enough for Philippa. I too will be buried there...'

Tears stained his cheeks.

'Your son, the Prince, wished it to be Canterbury,' I replied. No other explanation was necessary, yet I touched the King's arm in compassion, for it had been a grave blow to him. Edward's tears almost brought me to my knees.

'Then you must do as you wish.'

And so I moved in a carefully constructed pool of calm and supreme efficiency, directing craftsmen and clerics with a mask of gentle demeanour until all was done. I had learnt much in the years since Aquitaine. I requested and persuaded until I had achieved what it was that Ned had desired. The muscles of my face were strained with preserving a smile of gratitude for completed tasks. Only then did I take Richard to Canterbury to see the finished result, to pay his respects and learn a lesson in kingship.

'Look!' I commanded him.

And I looked too, for this was my first visit.

There in awe-inspiring effigy lay Ned, fully armoured in plate of war, his great leopard helm set beneath his head. As splendid in death as he was in life, the engraved bronze was gilded and burnished until it shone in the shadows of the great cathedral, drawing all eyes. His face was exposed in stern repose. The sheer dominance of his tomb, on seeing it complete for the first time, shocked me, into a new realisation of his death, but I would not submit to the deep beat of pain. This was not Ned. This was Edward, Prince of Wales, heir to the Crown of England. This was a man born to rule, robbed of his destiny by rank disease, buried beside his beloved Saint Thomas in the Trinity Chapel. There was no smile on these carved features, only an austerity, a grandeur that demanded that the onlooker stand and admire.

I pushed aside a new wave of desolation. I must concentrate on the purpose that had brought me here, and so I commanded, with a short gesture, that a servant should lift Richard so that he might see his father's engraved face.

'Your father was a famous soldier, Richard. So will you be one day.'

Richard's small hands spread, fingers wide, over the hilt of the sword.

'I don't like swords,' he said.

Which I knew to be true. I swallowed any words of censure, of disappointment that he should be so unlike his father. There was time. There was plenty of time. I would see to it that he was trained by the best swordsmen in the country.

'When you are older you will like them better,' I said.

'I like to ride.' He was running his hands over the intricacy of the great helm.

'You will ride as well as your father,' I said. As emotions crowded in, however much I might fight against them, I was finding it difficult to control my breathing.

'Set me down!' Richard commanded. And when he was lowered to the floor, he fell to his knees as he investigated the three ostrich feathers, Ned's emblem, carved with the words *Ich Dien*. 'What does it mean?'

'I serve.' My reply was little more than a whisper.

'But he was a Prince. Whom would he serve?'

'Your father served his country and his people. And his God. As you will.'

Richard looked up, over his shoulder to me, suddenly imperious. 'I will not serve any man. I will be King.'

His words were older than his years, and unwise. I lifted him, a hand beneath his arm, prepared to take him to task but he pulled free, darting away to the items laid beside the tomb.

'I like the gold gauntlets. I wish to have a pair like them.'

There they were, laid out on a fair cloth in which they had been enclosed for their journey from Kennington, so personal a statement of Ned's life. And with them his tabard and shield and golden helm. They would, later in this day, be lifted high above his tomb, to remind every pilgrim who it was who lay here in everlasting peace. The colours, Ned's heraldic achievements as a royal prince, glowed as brightly as the bronze effigy. It was what Ned would have wanted. Battle had been his metier. He would lie here with the symbols of his greatness above him. This was my doing, not Ned's; but I would have it so. I knew that he would approve.

But there was Richard thrusting his small hand inside one of the gauntlets.

'Leave them,' I said, my voice cracking in the stillness, unbearably moved.

I looked at him dispassionately, the child created by Ned out of my womb, doubly royal. Would this child ever grow for his hands to fill Ned's gauntlets? Small, slight and angelically fair, he had everything to learn about duty and service.

In a brief moment of unutterable despair I turned away, and then my eye was caught. Caught and held, as Ned would have planned it, as if he stood beside me to marvel at what I had wrought in his name. If I turned my head, would I not see him with that straight regard, that smile that I had discovered had the power to sap my will?

Ned had chosen an epitaph. I had had no hand in this, merely instructing the craftsman to have it carved as Ned had requested so that all who passed by might read it. The words had not interested me, I had taken no account of them, thinking that I knew him well enough to know his choice. It would be some vaunting praise, enabling him to be remembered in death as he was in life, a man of courage and valour and supreme authority. Now I read the truth.

I little thought on the hour of death
So long as I enjoyed breath.

My eye travelled down the flow of lines. I had been wrong, completely wrong. Was my knowledge of him so superfluous, after all those years? Here was no princely grandeur. Here was Ned anticipating death with deep regret.

But now a caitiff poor am I.
Deep in the ground, lo here I lie.
My beauty great is all quite gone,
My flesh is wasted to the bone.

Those two final lines. How Ned had humbled himself in death. Where was all the hauteur, the pride, arrogance, the extravagance for which he had come under attack, the vanity too in his physical glory?

All gone. All brought before the eye of the passerby to be censured. All now lost in death.

For the length of a breath I resented it. This was wrong. Ned was no caitiff. And what a remarkable choice of word for a royal Prince. Ned was never a contemptible wretch, he never could be. I imagined him kneeling at the Heavenly throne in his golden armour with all the glory and presence that he had had in life. Would he kneel in abject misery? He had made his peace with God and would kneel before Him in reflected majesty.

But there was more. For a blink of an eye I was reluctant to read on, fearing what I might learn more:

For God's sake pray to the heavenly King
That He my soul to heaven would bring.

I could no longer deny Ned's meaning. Wretched caitiff indeed. Here was the humility in death, deep below his majesty, here in engraved script was his ultimate acceptance of his soul's need. I doubted that I had ever seen such humility during his lifetime. His enemies never saw it, nor I thought did his friends. Even when our marriage had lacked recognition there had been no regret in him. Ned had demanded compliance from the Church, we both had, with no sense of our wrongdoing. And yet, perhaps I, his wife, had seen it at the end when there had been a true need for prayers and God's forgiveness for deeds in warfare. A need for redemption.

How death brings us low. Ned's penitence was heartbreaking.

Pray God Ned was granted God's forgiveness, for he was beyond my sphere of influence now. I would never again bring him solace. My throat was full of tears, my heart aching as I absorbed Ned's plea for absolution, as I saw his helm and gauntlets laid out as if he had only to don them so that the splendour would once again be his. But he never would. This was a campaign from which Ned would never return, the gilded bronze nothing but an empty shell, as were his garments, and I was alone. Tears fought for mastery, but the pain was so great in my heart that I could not accept the release of it in so paltry a fashion as tears.

Was this love? This wrenching apart, with no one to hold me together?

Love is wretched misery. To live with, it's despair.

But to live without it when my lover was dead was an even greater desolation.

So intense was the hurt that I spread my hands against my breast, as if I might contain it, control it, but I could not. All I had was the agony of parting after the terrible years of Ned's suffering, and the knowledge that we would never be together in the same room, in the same space.

At last I bowed my head in acceptance. It fell over me in a deluge of wretched loss, so that all hope was obliterated. My love was dead and gone from me and I was more alone than I had ever been or could imagine. There were tears on my cheeks, sliding, landing silently, marking the dark hue of the damask.

'What is it, *maman*?'

Richard stood before me.

'It is nothing.'

'Will I have armour like this?'

'Yes, you will.' I did not want to be here longer. All was empty and valueless to me. 'Now we will go. We have much to do.'

I stopped a little way distant, waiting until Richard had gone on ahead, before looking back. Then returned, reaching up to touch Ned's arm as I had so often in life.

'Farewell, my dear lord. I did indeed grow to love you with my whole heart. I thought you should know. If you were ever in any doubt.'

I had loved a knight whose prowess knew no peer. And he had loved me.

A single thought came into my mind, startling me, carrying me back over the years. Was it Ned or Thomas, my gifted, peerless knight whom had I loved?

Both of them, of course. And both had loved me.

I had been blessed indeed. Doubly blessed.

And then a second thought assailed me, as the grandeur of the Trinity Chapel pressed in on me with its incense and carved saints. Where, in all this holiness, would I command for my own resting place when the day came to end my earthly existence? Here, rendered insignificant by the proximity of Prince and Holy Martyr? I would be cast in the shade, interred to one side perhaps, or at Ned's feet if room could be found. A wife. A minor player in his life.

'This is not the place for me, Ned,' I said as if he would hear and understand. 'I think that keeping Thomas company in Stamford would be a more fitting place. Where I can demand some recognition of my own that is not cast into the shadows by your regal presence.'

I could imagine his acceptance. The nod of his head, conferring princely permission.

'When my time comes. But not yet.' There was really no more to say. 'Farewell, my lord. My thoughts remain with you, always.'

I followed Richard from the cathedral, turning my face to London, all trace of tears wiped away. There was a task to be done to ensure Richard's safe inheritance. Nothing must stand in the way of my son's wearing of the crown; nothing must threaten it.

January 1377: Kennington Palace

I must win the high regard of the citizens of London, those who were wealthy, with an increasing influence on affairs of the realm. If Richard was to slide seamlessly onto the throne of England when Edward died, I needed the unequivocal support of the City of London for the God-given rights of a child. When I had received Ned's gold plate, with fair words and gracious gesture, I had won their approval. Now I must also appeal to the common element with its crude pleasures and wayward alliances. It was not beyond my powers to bring the rabble to heel when I dropped my demands into appropriate and willing ears. Who did not enjoy a celebration? In my son's name the people of London rose to a magnificent occasion.

Parading through the streets of London as night fell, feted by the crowds drunk on free ale and good humour, a vast group of masked mummers, well over a hundred of them, all tricked out as squires and knights, cardinals and papal legates, leapt and cavorted, blazing torches creating tortuous shadows. Revelry that would not be forgotten for many a day. From there, at my specific invitation, the mummers arrived at Kennington with huge din, to where we were met, a festive family of Richard's royal uncles and powerful magnates.

What a prescient evening it was to be, full of laughter and good will, when, presented with a pair of loaded dice by a crafty emperor in purple and tawdry gilt, Richard cast them again and again onto a square of black silk to win objects of true gold from the obsequious emperor, Richard crowing with childish delight, unaware of the trickery. At my behest but in Richard's name, gold rings were dispensed to the mummers, ale to the crowd that had followed them. Music played to which all danced, lords and commons alike, even the royal uncles, urged on by the charged and wine-fuelled atmosphere

of the moment. My satisfaction was beyond expression, not to any
degree overshadowed by the amount of coin and subterfuge it had
taken to achieve such a lavish display. It was worth the stench of
unwashed bodies and the thick reek of the torches, their flames
blackening Ned's beautiful Kennington stonework.

'Clever.' Lancaster at my shoulder, still hot and short of breath,
his hair curling, knew at whose door the planning lay. 'Richard the
Fortunate: Richard the Munificent. You are to be commended.'

'Am I not?' I continued to watch, aware of every nuance in the
crowd.

'Were the dice yours?'

'They were Ned's. And before you ask, the gold rewards were
provided by me. It cost the mummers nothing but their compliance.'

'I thought I recognised the jewelled knife that Richard won. I gave
it to Ned, many years ago.' He laughed softly, perhaps recognising
an ambition as strong as his own. 'Nothing is too much for your
son, is it?'

'Nothing.'

I followed the line of his sight to where Richard still danced in
procession with a cardinal and a handful of scruffy knights in make-
shift armour. This was what I wanted for my son. Leaving Lancaster,
I ensured the cups were kept full and, rescuing Richard for now he
was weary, I kept him circulating at my side, his fair hair gleaming,
his eyes bright with the adoration on the unmasked faces. The perfect
Prince, who would be well-beloved, a King on whom fortune smiled,
even if fortune needed a smart kick on the ankle.

Across the chamber, Lancaster was accepting another cup of wine.
I considered the possibilities of speaking with him. But no, not yet.
This was neither the time nor the place, but soon. The King's life
was assuredly drawing to a close. I must be patient for this was a time
of waiting.

I had drunk nothing. My perception of events on that night was incomparable.

The time came to pursue my plans further in February when I least expected it, and in a manner that was as compelling as it was unnerving, showing me once again how vulnerable we all could be. Late at night, as Compline had pronounced its blessing on us, my household at Kennington was disturbed by a hasty arrival. After a brief conversation and my consent, my chamberlain admitted Lancaster, damp, ruffled, angry, who, marching into my private chamber, dismissed my women with a brusque gesture that asked no permission from me.

I allowed him to do it. Matters in the city, news of which had been reaching us daily, had clearly come to a head. Exerting patience, I allowed him to pace the room, tossing off his cloak, his artistically folded chaperon, scattering raindrops as he went, while I assessed his mood which was dark with fury.

'Don't speak until you have drunk this,' I said at last.

Rising from my chair I poured him wine which he drank in one gulp, while I sat again and waited as another cup of wine was dispatched.

Then, into the silence, he told the tale in short phrases, all but spitting out the details. He had been dining with friends, a private occasion at the house of one of the powerful Percy family retainers. News had arrived of an approaching mob, intent on taking revenge on Percy and Lancaster for their attack on the liberties of parliament, clergy and city.

'And are you surprised?' I asked with deliberate calm.

For I had made it my business to keep abreast of happenings in London. Why was it impossible to trust any man to act with good sense? Lancaster had thrown a blazing torch onto the bonfire of parliamentary and clerical sensibilities. And what a conflagration that had caused. I was furious with him, even as I admitted that I should not have been surprised. He could rarely govern his words when his temper was compromised. I could accept that he was a choleric man, a man whose haughty mien was second only to that of Ned, but this was beyond forgiveness.

Calling on his supporters, Lancaster had set about either reversing or ignoring the earlier legislation of the Good Parliament, even, for some inexplicably altruistic motive that was beyond my understanding, reinstating Alice Perrers to her position at court as the King's constant companion. The Speaker who had led the vocal opposition was arrested, replaced by one of Lancaster's creatures, ensuring that the new parliament forthwith granted a generous sum in taxes to the Crown. Many frowned at Lancaster's control, too heavy-handed, too indiscriminate. It made him few friends when he enhanced his own regal power and thoroughly damned parliament, denying that they had any power at all.

Not the wisest of policies since parliament controlled the taxation for a crown that was increasingly in debt.

As if that were not enough, the antagonism had grown worse. Why did Lancaster feel moved to support that radical clerk John Wycliffe so openly and so violently? I too might have had sympathy with the man but sometimes principle must be subsumed by expediency. Yet when the august Church Assembly of Convocation met and moved against John Wycliffe to stop his subversive views attacking the power and wealth of the clergy, summoning him to appear before them and answer to the charges of heresy, what did Lancaster do? Nothing but push his way into St. Paul's to rescue his protégé from the mob, threatening to drag the Bishop of London from his see by the hair. The clergy were as instantly up in arms as was parliament.

'I had no choice but to take to my heels,' Lancaster now said, choosing to ignore my cynicism. 'They were fired up with anger at their so-called dishonour, they were past conciliation. Someone spread the rumour that I intended to behead the damned bishop. I might think about it, but only a fool would do it.'

'Whereas you are no fool. And you were quite ready to negotiate.'

'Jesu! No, I was not. They'll get no conciliation from me. A mob has already threatened The Savoy. Did you know that? I found a stinking boat and an equally stinking boatman to row me across the Thames. I've a gouge in my shin bigger than my fist, and had to forgo a better dish of oysters than any I've eaten for a month. I tell you, Joan, it cuts at my pride to have to run for my life from the gutter-rabble. A Prince of the realm... !'

So! Lancaster was under threat. And he had come to me. The possible consequences leapt fully formed into my mind like Athena from the head of Zeus.

He was pacing again, and as he did so, venting his spleen against the Londoners who had dared to proclaim him traitor to his knighthood, pinning his coat of arms, disparagingly inverted, on the doors of St. Paul's and Westminster Hall, it seemed that events had fallen beautifully into my lap. This was the man I needed as my ally. If I had asked advice from any man of my acquaintance, he would have warned me away from Lancaster with his ambitions and wayward moods. But I knew better. I would harness my future to that of Lancaster, and here he had presented me with the perfect opportunity to tie him to my sleeves – and those of Richard. Here was a juicy morsel of bait for me to throw to capture this enormously important fish.

But would he allow it? Pride was a Plantagenet besetting sin. Would Lancaster not consider his oath to Ned, with all the drama of a deathbed, to be sufficient? It was not sufficient for me. I would land him, thrashing and desperate for help. I would make him mine.

'So you have come here to me,' I observed lightly as he finished the tale, pouring yet another cup of wine, growling over his ruined hose.

'Where else would I go? They'll not attack you. You are honoured as if you are the Blessed Virgin herself. Such a change in your fortunes.' He hissed on an inhalation. 'I need your help, Joan.'

I remained unmoved, even as I saw the wound to his pride in having to ask for aid.

'You need a miracle. It is your own fault.'

'Should I bow the knee to such rabble? Do they think that they are Kings and Princes? Have they forgotten who I am, how powerful I am?'

'They will not have forgotten. You could try compromise.'

'While they spread rumours that I am a changeling.'

Which I knew came closer to the grain than any other accusation, scurrilous talk in the stews of London that he was the son of a Ghent butcher, substituted for a dead royal child. It hurt his pride like nothing other. But I would allow no sympathy.

'Did you have to threaten the Bishop of London?'

'Yes. But now I am painted as England's enemy. They are out for the blood of any who support Lancaster.' At last he sank down on a stool at my side. 'I fear for The Savoy. I fear for the safety of my people. Yet I know not how to safeguard them other than dispersing the peasant mob with a troop of retainers to give them safe passage.' He scowled at me. 'I expect you will say that is bad policy too, to put my armed men on the streets. You could be right.'

At last. Some contrition.

'What do you want from me?'

For a moment he sat, hands planted on his knees, energy shimmering round him.

'Mediation?'

'I think I might refuse.'

'Refuse? Why would you?'

'You allowed Alice Perrers to return to court. I am not pleased with you.'

'I dislike parliament's power to remove her more than I dislike the woman herself. It pleased me to untie parliament's knots. They have no power other than that allowed by the Crown. By me.'

I did not think that I could ever forgive him, all my hard work undone, all my plotting gone awry, in the interest of Lancaster's ongoing conflict with parliament. Curbing my irritation, dismissing Mistress Perrers, for I would deal with her at a later date, I gave a little shrug as I announced. 'You need to fight your own battles, Lancaster. I have my own concerns.'

'Do you then turn me over to the mob?'

He looked astounded that I should not immediately spring to his aid. But my compassion was roused. This was the man who had undertaken the burial of my tiny son in Bordeaux. This was Ned's dear brother, who had fought beside him when his health was draining his strength. This, in the King's decline, was the most powerful man in England. It would be ill-advised to throw this fair chance to the winds.

'I will help you,' I said, standing so that for once he must look up at me. 'But you must be conciliatory towards those who attack you.'

'By the Rood!'

'There is no other way. You must agree to do as I say.'

'I have no choice do I? They will tear me limb from limb if I step beyond your door.'

I smiled, resting my hand on his shoulder.

'Wait here.'

I gave orders to send out three of my knights into the hotbed of London streets.

When I returned, he was where I had left him, the lines on his face sharp-etched. It had been a novel experience for him to be hounded through the streets. Yes, it would work to my advantage.

'Go to bed,' I advised. 'You can do no more. Or only damage.'

He went to bed, but I did not. I waited for the return of my knights.

Both risen early next morning, I refused to relay any information until we had celebrated early Mass. Lancaster looked as if he had slept ill, but was otherwise his usual peremptory self.

'Well? What news?'

Groomed, impressive, clothing replaced by me from some of Ned's garments that fit him well, we had barely stepped out of the chapel. Anger still throbbed below the surface.

'Not in public.' I drew him into a silent antechamber.

'This is what I have done, in your absence. The citizens of London, who were self-righteously considering burning The Savoy to the ground, have dispersed to their homes through love of me. I have arranged that a deputation of Londoners appear before your father, the King, at Sheen, to answer for their riotous behaviour that has threatened the peace of this land. When their sins were laid before them in my name, they were sufficiently contrite. You will be there at Sheen at your father's side. You will speak softly. You will make them your friends again. Furthermore I will come with you, to remind you of what is inappropriate when you start to snap and snarl like an untrained hound.'

He was not convinced. 'Before God, Joan! You ask the impossible.'

'It is the only way. Yes, you are a Prince, but it is not good to have London as your enemy.'

He considered this. Then he considered me with a more than sceptical gaze. He nodded. 'I'll do it. But I'm not sure why you have put yourself out to such a degree. You are not given to altruistic gestures, Joan.'

I smiled with great sweetness. 'Times change, John. How could I abandon you? A Prince should not be seen fleeing through the streets with holes in his hose. The thigh-length tunic suits you, by the way.'

He reminded me so strongly of Ned. The stance, the lift of his head, the dark wave of his hair against the rich sable edge of the borrowed collar.

He touched my hand as if he had read the direction of my thoughts. 'I miss him too. Sometimes more than I can bear. I know that you grew to love him too.'

My heart softened, ached, full of unshed tears.

'More than you will ever know. He became the love I never expected,' was all I would say.

It was an uneasy meeting at Sheen. Very few of the summoned citizens presented themselves in spite of my encouragement, doubt-less fearing Lancaster's retribution. If I had thought Lancaster would curb his temper I was wrong. While he continued to rage at their attack on his person and his status, I smiled and offered the citizens safety when they returned to their homes. While Lancaster waxed eloquent and furious about the insults shown to the King and his sons, for which London must be punished, I offered them ale to wet their parched throats. When Mayor and aldermen fell to their knees and begged for mercy, I suggested conditions on which they might be pardoned. The erection of a pillar in Cheapside and the offering of a candle at St. Paul's must be acceptable although all quailed at death for those responsible for the reversing of the ducal arms. Throughout it all King Edward sat in an isolated silence, not understanding.

Oh, I worked hard in that hour, until it ended as an apology of sorts from the Mayor, a grudging acceptance from Lancaster, the dispute patched over even though my stitching was lamentably weak.

'I am grateful.' Lancaster admitted this gratitude to me through a jaw-clenched demeanour that had not softened to any degree.

'You owe me a debt, my lord of Lancaster,' I replied in all serious-ness. 'One day I will demand its repayment.'

'I pray it will not be too high a price for me to pay, madam.'

'I assure you that it will not. Besides, how could you refuse?' My smile was of the most dulcet. 'It may be be that I have saved your life as well as your dignity.'

'I will not forget.'

In the end, I sent for him. John of Lancaster. A man who could be a threat to me and to Richard, for despite those who decried him, Ned's death had left Lancaster the most powerful man in the land and Edward's chief councillor, in effect governor of the realm. A dangerous precedent, which roused fears that he had sinister designs on the crown for himself and his own son. If the line of inheritance through Lionel's daughter was rejected as a female line and so of no merit, then Lancaster was heir presumptive after Richard. And what if he saw it in his mind to remove Richard, or govern through him as a puppet?

My putative power in England would be destroyed overnight.

Deep respect and trust between Ned and his brother had always been apparent, most keenly in those final days in Aquitaine, but Ned could be blind in his affection for his family. For me there was the everlasting kernel of uncertainty. Did I fully trust John of Lancaster, in spite of the oath he had made when Ned lay dying? He was a man of ambitions, after my own heart. It would indeed be good policy to ensure his loyalty. I must harness it quickly, for I could wait no longer.

He came promptly.

'I need your help,' I said as soon as the door was closed at his back.

'What can I do?'

There was no hesitation in me. Nor were there any social graces. This was a matter of pure business and although I had learned the value of discreet persuasion, on this occasion I wanted no possibility of misunderstanding.

'It is this.' I flung back the lid of the little coffer with its crowned white hart, conveniently sitting at my feet, exposing all that it contained. 'Look if you will.'

So he did, dropping on one knee beside it to begin lifting the documents, sifting with fine fingers, reading occasionally, then returning them to their home, closing the lid on them again as if it might be a danger to expose them to the air. He turned the key and handed it back to me.

Here were the documents I had kept so carefully in my possession. The dissolution of my marriage to Will. The formal and undeniably legal proof of my marriage to Thomas Holland. The complex decisions over my marriage to Ned: the revoking of the first, the proof of my second. All so essential. More weighty than gold. More precious than the gems on my fingers.

'Do you understand?' I asked, keeping my hands resting lightly in my lap when they would have preferred to curl into fists of uncertainty at the fickleness of fate. Here was the whole debate over Richard's legitimacy as heir to King Edward, contained in this one small box, and here was the man whom I did not fully trust on whom I must cast my son's fate.

'I think that I do.'

'I am full of fear.'

His brow creased. 'Surely you have all the legality here that you need?'

'But do I? You know all about my past.' My eyes were wide, commanding on his, forcing him to see the hazards that could still threaten me. Willing him to be won over by what might become a real threat to the stability of the kingdom. 'You know about the legal difficulties of my first marriage.'

'But it was upheld in the face of Salisbury's opposition, wasn't it? You were returned to your rightful husband. I was too young to take much note, but is that not so?'

'And I wed Thomas again before King and Court and a clutch of Bishops, but Popes have come and gone since Clement granted my legal status. Will Pope Gregory pipe to the same tune? Not if he decided it would be in his interest to support France rather than England. He might reverse this papal decision, simply to be mischievous.' For here was an unexpected entanglement. Popes were not immune from reversing the decisions of their predecessors when put under pressure by temporal powers.

Lancaster frowned over the possibility then demurred.

'I don't think His Holiness is smiling on either, since neither France nor England agreed to his suggestion of a diplomatic meeting to break the deadlock over who should have ascendancy in Aquitaine. My father would not reject his sovereignty, while the King of France has refused to remove his troops, so all is held in a vice of rank vituperation. I think you have no need to fear Gregory leaping into bed with either.'

'Gold can sway the argument most effectively.' I was not convinced by Lancaster's reading of the politics of Pope and temporal powers. 'What if His Holiness is persuaded to rescind his predecessor's decision and pronounce my true marriage to be the one fully witnessed with William Montagu? If that is so, then my marriage to Ned would be called bigamous. That would make Richard illegitimate. What's more, I would still be married to Will, since he is clearly not dead.'

'A tale of terrible complications, I agree.' He continued to frown at the coffer as if its contents were to blame, rather than merely the commentary on past choices. 'But will it ever happen? Are you looking for rats in corners that don't exist?'

'I don't know what will happen. And they may well become very visible rats.' I took a long, slow breath, studying my whitened knuckles as if this were all new to me, whereas it had been a longstanding nightmare. This would be the challenge to Lancaster's own loyalties, despite his oath-swearing. How would he respond?

'It might well come about, if there are those who would prefer Richard *not* to inherit the crown,' I stated carefully, weighing each word. 'It might well, if there are those who would prefer the crown to pass elsewhere, to a King who is a man rather than a boy. There might well be a reason to drop a hint or two into the papal ear and a purse of gold into his open hand, that a change of policy would be desirable to some in England. His Holiness might be open to persuasion to rescind past decisions and bastardise Richard.'

I lifted my eyes to regard him with all the power of my insecurity, and he looked at me, a sharp light in his eye. He rose from his knee to stand over me, forcing me to look up.

'Do I understand you, Joan?'

'I think that you do.'

'Do you believe that I would work against your son, to take the crown for myself?'

'There are rumours.'

'There are always rumours. Which have no foundation.' There was the rumble of anger that I had expected, the hardening of his mouth into denial.

'Your power, Lancaster, is vast.'

'My power is vast, as you say, because my father is incapable.'

'But what will happen in the future?'

'I will support Richard, if that is what you are asking. Have I not already sworn to do so?'

'There are those who might not be so ready to bow the knee to my son.'

He nodded with brusque acknowledgement. 'Lionel's descendants. The Mortimers.' He shrugged, dismissing the possibility. 'What can they do?'

We both knew what they could do. How easy it would be to question Richard's legitimacy, bringing into the light of day my matrimonial adventures as evidence.

We were long past subterfuge now.

'Look, John. You know the story of it. My marriage to Ned was also *verba de praesenti*. Illicit and invalid this time, through both consanguinity and compaternity. Yes, I know that we received a papal dispensation and were legally married, and the Pope instructed Canterbury to ensure there was no problem in the annulment of my previous marriage with Will. Here is the evidence of it all.' I placed my hand over the dome, inlaid with a frivolous riot of flowers and tendrils and the collared hart that had taken Richard's interest. 'There should be no question of the legality of Richard's claim to the throne. But I fear. I fear that it could all be resurrected to threaten Richard. If someone saw it in their interest to do so.'

And then there was another layer to my fear. Now I stood to confront him. It was not an accusation to make while seated.

'Richard is so young,' I said. 'Until he is old enough to take a wife who will carry his heir, he is in grave danger. If he were to die tomorrow, who would become King of England after Edward? It is my duty to preserve his life from malign conspiracy.'

'Conspiracy such as those God-forsaken chroniclers say is in my mind, I suppose. That I will work to remove Richard to claim the crown for myself and my own son.'

'The court will always gossip about the predictions of Merlin,' I observed, intrigued to see Lancaster's reaction in the face of such an accusation. It was explosive, of course.

'God damn Merlin for a pernicious meddler. I would wager such treason never came from his lips, more from a Mortimer source, endowed with magical significance by this attachment to King Arthur's court. And yet you summon me here because you think there might be an element of truth in it. What would you have me do? Swear on God's name that I will not kill my nephew? Shame on you, Joan! Are we to be guided by empty prophesies and dreams?'

With his voice and face hardened into defiance, when he bent to pick up his hat and gloves and began to stride towards the door, I called him back. A woman could not get her own way by berating a man of Lancaster's calibre.

'If you want an apology from me, Lancaster, you have it. It was not my intention to question your loyalties.'

He stopped, but kept his back to me. 'Was it not? But you did exactly that. My loyalty to my brother is beyond reproach. What right do you have to question it? Deathbed oaths are sacrosanct.'

I stretched out my hands, an action that contained no element of dissembling, even as I knew he could not see me. My desperation had taken control so that my voice shivered over the words. Here at the end was the depth of my need, making a plea to the only man who could help me.

'You are my only hope, John. Richard needs a man at his side, a powerful uncle at his shoulder who will guide and advise and support. If you will not act as counsellor, what can I do, a woman alone?'

'You can use your own influence. I have seen you do it. You got what you wanted in becoming Princess of Wales.'

An accusation I could not deny. 'Yes, I married Ned for ambition.' I would not talk about the love that grew between us. 'Now, in Ned's name, I need you to be Richard's man when he is crowned King.'

'Why me?'

Oh, I would be more than honest with him. 'Because you are as ruthless as I in getting what you want.'

His mouth tightened. 'How can I resist such a reading of my character.' I saw his shoulders flex, straighten. 'I will be Richard's man, for you and for myself. Are we not both surrounded by enemies?'

'Yes. I can imagine them, in the pay of some self-interested party, screaming bastard at Richard as the crown is lowered onto his brow. I do not wish to live to hear that. The sins are mine, but Richard should not have to carry them.'

Slowly Lancaster turned and, face softened, walked back to me, reading all the fear in me that I no longer had a need to hide. His own anger had quite gone as he once more cast aside gloves and hat and took my hands, held fast in his.

'I swore to Ned that I will be counsellor to Richard. So will my son Henry. Nothing will destroy the loyalty of Lancaster to Ned's heir. I will swear it to you, if you wish it.'

'Yes, I do wish it. For my own peace of mind I would command it.'

'And this is the debt that you are now calling in?' His lips twisted into not quite a smile.

'Yes, it is. You owe me for past services. I am calling in that debt of honour.'

I would anchor him with an oath he would not break. As for Lancaster, he was always a man who could make an impact, simply by walking through a doorway, for good or ill. Now he sank to his knees before me, lifted my hands and kissed one palm and then the other.

'I will dedicate my loyalty to Richard, in God's Name and that of the Blessed Virgin. I will do all in my power to smooth his road to the throne. It will be my father's wish too. He will never disinherit Ned's son. I dedicate myself to your service too, to preserve your reputation and your ultimate position as King's Mother.' Then, once more on his feet but my hands still clasped, he nodded in the direction of the little coffer. 'Do you wish me to keep those documents safe for you?'

'No. I'll keep them under my own eye. When Richard comes of age they go into his keeping. He will understand the need to win his subjects to him, and rule them wisely.'

'And meanwhile we support each other.'

'A perfect alliance.' My smile was genuine but transient. 'There is something else I need from you, John.'

I could not mistake the malice in his eye. 'So I am John again rather than Lancaster. Why did I ever think that swearing an oath on the sanctity of my soul would be enough for you, Joan?'

'I have no idea. But you will approve of this. You must prevent any further discussion in parliament of the deposition of Edward. Can you do this? It can only harm future kings if it is allowed to fester. It can only harm Richard.'

'I promise to hunt down those who would speak against us.' His smile widened. 'What do you want me to do about Mistress Perrers?'

'Nothing. I will deal with her myself.'

There. It was done, all done, as much as I was able. I summoned all my strength for the days ahead. I knew that I would need it. As for Mistress Perrers, women who made a bid for power above their status were to be admired. Mistress Perrers had many talents, but there was no room for both of us at court. I would have no rival.

Chapter Eighteen

July 1377: Westminster Abbey

I was tense notwithstanding our meticulous planning, my nails dug hard into my palms. Despite the heat pressing down on the crowds in the streets, all was ice beneath the heavy luxury of my furs, all cut in a seemly manner for this auspicious occasion. The light silks of Aquitaine had long since been packed away or refashioned to suit this new life where my dignity and honour must be paramount, my hair never again worn loose under a light veil but braided with all seemliness within a jewelled caul and coronet. I forced myself to breath evenly. Nothing could stop it now. Surely nothing could. On this day Richard would be crowned King of England and Ned's hopes would be fulfilled.

And yet my heart fluttered, my mouth was dry. Nothing was certain. Prophecies and rumours could not be overlooked as mere gossip to pass an hour over a cup of ale. They held significant power, to be harnessed and used by those who might still wish me ill. Those who would see a ten year old boy as too dangerous to be King of England.

Ah, but this was what I had been waiting for. There it was being held aloft in all its mystical glory, in a blaze of sunlight striking hard through the Abbey windows. The royal crown of the Kings of England was in the act of being held above Richard's head, the Archbishop on one side, on the other Richard's Mortimer cousin by marriage, the Earl of March. Between them my child, so small; the crown so heavy. Lord and cleric took the weight of the gold and jewels that one day Richard must carry for himself.

Too young. Too vulnerable.

The echoes in the abbey, silk against damask, fur against gold chains, all rustled and formed into warnings. Was I the only one to hear them?

The crown was lowered until, lightly, it touched Richard's brow. My breathing eased.

What need of warnings now? There were those who would shield Richard until he grew, to protect his power, to encourage him in good governance. All had been set in place: he had a Royal Council; he had John of Lancaster; he had my two Holland sons, Tom and John. Will Montagu, of course. And I would be there. I would fight for him as viciously as any vixen to safeguard her cubs from the wiles of the hunter. All my concentration was on Richard's face, willing him to remain strong through this interminable service, to which I had been party despite my misgivings.

'It is too long,' I had said to John of Lancaster when the plans were being made, each step carefully written down by the clerk at his side who noted every demand. 'He is only ten years old.'

'It is necessary,' John had replied, preoccupied with detail, reading over the scribe's shoulder.

'Why? As long as it is done, and seen to be done. What need for all this, to sap his young strength.'

John looked up at the sharp protectiveness in my voice.

'Every detail is necessary. It will turn this child into a monarch answerable only to God. It will show my enemies that I have no designs on the crown for myself. It will show those who despise your unfortunate past that this child is the legitimately-born heir and fit to be ruler.'

'Do I not know that?'

He watched me, struggling with his habitual impatience, as I failed to mask my displeasure.

'Don't rail at me, Joan. You asked me to protect your son. That is what I will do. At the same time you and I will emerge as the seraphim, clothed in white and crowed with heavenly diadems, above any suspicion. Richard will need us in the years to come. And so this lengthy ceremony, with every holy auspice I can think of, is more than essential.' His smile was suddenly feral. 'It might even prove to you that I have no designs on the throne which belongs to your son. I will protect him until the day of my death. Did I not swear it?'

Each point was driven home by his finger into the wood of the clerk's desk. I saw his plan. I should have seen it for myself, for it was worthy of my own planning. I was forced to admit that I had still much to learn, but here I had the man with the skill of political manoeuvring at his fingertips. I would learn fast and I would learn well.

'And you will instruct Richard that he must sit still, follow orders and concentrate,' John continued. 'This is no day for wilful childishness and disobedience. We need nothing for the carrion-crows of ill-omen to pick up and chew over.'

It was in my mind to object, to make excuses of so blighting an indictment of Richard's occasional truculence.

'You know he has an uncommonly purposeful mind of his own beneath all that fair innocence,' John added, before I could.

'Very well! We will do it!' I was still tight-lipped, but convinced. 'And if we are talking of chewing over ill-omens, you had better make sure that all the jewels in the crown are secure. I don't want any to fall at Richard's feet.'

'Already done! There will be no portents of disaster!'

He was as irritated as I, but proving a worthy ally. And so we had closed hands as if a treaty had been agreed. We would make of Richard a worthy successor to his famous grandfather. The King that Ned should have been.

Now it was almost at an end. The processions, the prayers, the acclamation of the lords and clerics in the congregation, had passed as smoothly as the silk and heavy velvet of Richard's outer garments, those garments that had been ceremonially removed behind a golden tapestry to allow the sacred anointing with holy oil of his frail body on hands, chest, shoulders and head. Now the sceptre and the ring were his too. And the crown.

I sighed softly. It was done. No one, *no one,* could question his God-Anointed right to be King of England. For the first time I felt my body relax since the minute that my cousin Edward had passed from this life and been buried, now eleven days ago. Robbed of the power to move, and eventually the power to speak, he had become a sad remnant, shut away in the palace at Sheen, to die alone except for a priest and the redoubtable Alice who it was said stripped the rings from his fingers. What an inglorious end to the man who had made England's name superlative for military power at Crécy and on the field of Poitiers, building and furnishing castles and palaces with impressive luxury during a time of peace. Who had made the commendable companionship of Garter Knights. A tragic end, his mind wandering, enclosed in bitter grief, unable to survive the death of Philippa and Ned. Now he lay at peace beside his beloved wife in Westminster Abbey.

I had not seen him in those final days, except for the occasion of his celebration of St. George's Day at Windsor, in the same spirit as he had done so many years ago when he had made Thomas and Ned and Will knights of the Garter. How he had found the strength to stand there in his robes I knew not, but it had been an occasion to tear at my heart. Richard, together with Henry, the young Lancaster heir, had been knighted, the sword touching lightly on his shoulders. Joy warred with pain that Ned was not there to see it.

But after that, in truth I had not tried to see the King again, when Alice, restored to his household, held sway in the royal chambers, dictating who should and should not approach as the King neared his end. It was beneath my self-esteem to request permission from a royal concubine. I would never forgive her for flaunting Philippa's jewels, the famous rubies gleaming like blood, when she rode through the streets of London as Edward's ceremonial Lady of the Sun. Nor of secretly marrying a man as immoral as she, William de Windsor, a man of much charm and even more political ambition, which might just have finally broken Edward's heart. I knew all about the damage caused by secret marriages.

But here at last was the culmination of my victory. Mistress Perrers was not here today. Nor had I allowed her to be present at Edward's solemn interment. I had taken pleasure in barring her path at the cathedral door. No royal doors would open to her again.

'This is no place for you,' I said as Edward's funerary procession drew close. Her sorrowful demeanour appeared genuine, but I would not be swayed. 'I rule here now.' Any compassion had fled with the scandal that one of the youths knighted by Edward at his last Garter ceremony, kneeling with Richard and Henry Bolingbroke, had been John Southeray, the King's bastard son with Alice. I would have no more scandals to mar this new reign. Alice and her offspring, whoever fathered them, must retire from public gaze.

'I have a right.' Her chin lifted, her dark eyes direct, as they had always been.

'No longer. The King is dead.'

Her eyes were bright, some might have said with unshed tears. I did not trust her.

'You know what it is to lose a man whose love means all to you,' she said.

'I do. I would deny that my loss bore any comparison with yours.'

'How would you know? Yet you would deny my right to kneel at the King's tomb, when I have loved him for more than a decade.'

'You have no right. It was an immoral love.'

Alice stepped back, as a body of mourners pushed forward between us. 'I had hoped for understanding from you at least, my lady. I was wrong.'

I watched as she retreated, her figure disappearing into the crowds, surprised that it gave me no satisfaction. I felt that I had lost that clash of will, even though she had obeyed me. Should I have seen her pain, allowing her to make this last gesture of respect if not love? Uneasily I accepted that I should have shown her mercy. Almost I called her back as guilt laid an unexpectedly heavy hand on me.

But I did not, shrugging off any finer feelings. There would be no place for Alice Perrers. And yet I did know of the power of love, when love overcame sense and clear thought. Who in England would know better than I? Was I any better than Alice? In birth of course, but not always in choices, and I knew that I would not rest until Alice was stripped of all she had gained in her infamous career.

I cast thoughts of Alice aside. Far more important to me was that Edward had made his will, in which he had been sufficiently in his right mind to make the succession clear. It was to be Richard, of course. Edward had bequeathed to him his best bed with all the armorial hangings as well as four lesser beds and tapestries for his rooms. Richard would never be short of furnishings. His bequest to me of a thousand marks and restitution of the jewels I had once pledged to him was an irrelevance beside his final wielding of royal power, for by Edward's decree, only males were to inherit the throne. First Richard, then Lancaster and his sons. Which neatly removed the Mortimer descendants of his dead son Lionel. Thus Edward at the end made it plain that he would not countenance any claim to his crown through his granddaughter Philippa.

Security for Richard. Security for Richard's descendents.

Did I have any hand in Edward's decision? Who was to say? I might have talked of the problem of the Mortimer claim to the throne on occasion, when my cousin was lucid.

The choristers were beginning to sing, the perfect clarity of their high voices drawing me back to this ceremony, but Richard was weary, his head seemingly too heavy for his slender neck. Now he must withstand the High Mass and the performance of homage by the great magnates of this realm. His uncles of York and Gloucester knelt before him, took their oath of loyalty. So did Lancaster and his young son Henry Bolingbroke.

My triumph was supreme.

With the placing of the crown over Richard's head I had been deemed King's Mother. This was my metier. This was why I was born, it seemed. Not to be Princess in distant Aquitaine. Not even to be Queen of England. This was my fate, to mould and guide a new king to further England's greatness. This is how I would be remembered, for under my hand Richard would administer fair justice, issuing pardons and grants to those who deserved royal favour. He would claim his rights against the aggressive states across the sea. He would become a leader of men, as his father had been. I would ensure that it was so. And first of all, a new barge would be ordered, I decided in a moment of deplorable whimsy as the vision opened before me. Richard would travel in a new barge, gilded overall, drawing every eye as he travelled the

Thames. And so would I, seated beside him, catch the attention of those who came to see us pass by.

But I would tread carefully. My experiences with the nobility of Aquitaine had taught me well. A woman had need to be self-effacing, to be guided by honour and discretion, even humility. I would be that woman. No one would ever question my garments or my demeanour again. The days of my scandals were over. Here was a new reign with new challenges, a new dance with new steps to learn.

The singing coming to an end, the echoes dying away, a breath of warm air shivered over us as the great west door of the Abbey was opened to a dramatic entry, a clash of armour, a clatter of horse's hooves. It was as if a hand of ice had closed over my heart, all over again. I had been too precipitate. All was not well. Again I swept the noble congregation, to note whom might be absent, who might pose a threat. But here were all Richard's uncles. Here was the Mortimer family out in force, all willing to take the oath of allegiance. Had not the Earl of March himself held the crown?

My hands were clenched hard in the ermine lining of my cloak, as I glanced across at Lancaster. Why did he show no sign of anxiety? Surely this military intervention was not within his encompass? There he stood, calm and implacable beside Richard.

So if he showed no concern…

I looked towards the west door, all my fear draining away at what I saw there. I had forgotten. I had forgotten this element of heraldic tradition that would accompany the coronation of a King. This was expected by all, not a sign of danger, merely a moment of dramatic charade, and I sighed soundlessly at my foolish insecurity. Here was Sir John Dymock, King's Champion, come to issue the customary challenge to any man who would question the newly-crowned King's power. A mighty finale to the whole proceedings, enjoyed by all for its flamboyant performance of an ancient custom, even though no one was likely to accept the challenge.

But no, this would not be!

Richard was wilting, no longer interested in the proceedings, his eyes huge in his face which was as pale as the candle-wax on the altar. I would intervene.

Taking a step forward, I caught John of Lancaster's eye, before looking towards my son. Whereupon Lancaster nodded, then a whisper in the ear of a squire to carry a message. Sir John Dymoke, expression masked by his great helm, saluted, and the challenge was postponed until the evening. It would all have been too much, far too much for the boy.

Richard was carried out of the Abbey on the shoulder of Simon Burley, whose importance as a member of the Royal Council I tried hard not to resent - I must remember to smile on him - so that the crowds might see their King and acclaim him as had the lords. The cheering was a stunning acceptance of this child-king. Richard's bright visage was turned to his people as he raised his hand in acknowledgement as he had been taught. He would indeed melt hearts this day in England.

But I frowned at what I saw. Richard, in the crush, had lost one of his shoes.

Had it been noticed as he was held up in Burley's arms? I held my breath, waiting for a murmuring of concern, of superstitious comment. The gems in the crown had been closely inspected by a master goldsmith. I had had no thought of so trivial a matter as the loss of a shoe, yet some might say this was an ill-omen. I thought it a piece of rank carelessness, determining to talk to those who had dressed him. It must not happen again, nor anything of like nature. I would see to it that there was no sly rumour to undermine the God-Anointed authority of the new King of England.

I was not the only one to notice.

Bowing my thanks to Lancaster who rescued and replaced the gilded leather slipper, suitably reassured I moved to stand beside my son. The cheering redoubled in fervour. I had truly been forgiven. I bowed before the recognition of me as King's Mother, taking Richard's hand as he was placed on the steps beside me, smiling down at his over-excited face.

My dear and beloved Ned. I will make of him such a King as England has never seen.

And so it began. I rose to a new dawn. This day, with circumspection, with well-planned discretion and prudence, and perhaps with the hand of fate, I would make my presence felt. The crown, so recently marking Richard's elevation to his legitimate inheritance as King of England, was barely packed away into its travelling coffer before the doors were flung back by my chamberlain and I was announced into the Council Chamber. The new members of Richard's Council, not all of them pleased to see me, rose precipitately to their soft-soled feet.

They were an impressive grouping. The Earls of March and Arundel, the Bishops of London and Salisbury, the rest of them familiar faces at court or in the company of Ned in his lifetime. They were a worthy group to give advice to my son and I was not displeased although I had had no influence in their creation. The great magnates of the realm had seen fit to choose themselves on the morning of the coronation.

I would make it clear, in seemly fashion, that they must not ignore the wishes of the King's Mother. I would not be banished to the realms of the solar.

It interested me that John of Lancaster had not been named, but with power to supervise all aspects of government he could attend the Council if he so wished. At my direct request, he too was present.

We would see what we would see. I would, as far as it was possible, mould this Council into my own creature. And yet I did not have the assurance that my demeanour might seem to invoke. All lay in the balance as I well knew. Even now I might fail.

'My lords. Gentlemen.' I approached even as they were still bowing, adopting a fair expression, bowing my head to honour Lancaster and the two earls, then the bishops. My manner was most decorous; they would see no female guile.

A stool was quickly brought forward for me, then, as I gazed for more than a moment at the lack of comfort, a cushion, the whole being set for me at the head of the table, replacing the Earl of Arundel. I sat, indicated that they should do likewise, and placed the document before me, my hands closed flat over its weighty folds, my costly rings an expression of power as I sent out a clear message. This matter was for me and me alone.

'We did not expect you, madam.' The Bishop of London did not consider my presence either seemly or necessary.

'No, my lord. Nor will I attend all your meetings, even though my interest is paramount, for I am aware that I was not appointed to do so, but I am certain that I will be made welcome on this occasion, sir. You must know that I value your advice for the care of my son, the King.' A long pause as I allowed my eye to rest on every man. 'Your knowledge in these matters will be invaluable as neither I nor my son the King have any direct experience in the government of England.' I paused again. 'Although I, of course, have been Princess of Aquitaine.'

Did they think that I had absorbed no experience of government in Aquitaine? I smiled winningly at those gathered to dictate the direction of the kingdom under its new monarch. Flattery would carry me over many a mile. Any latent hostility at my treading on their toes evaporated in the morning sunshine, but would they bow to my dictates? I pressed my hands hard against the document so that no shiver of light from my rings would display my uncertainty.

'You are welcome, madam.' Lancaster's expression remained as uncomfortably bland as a herb custard.

'There is a matter I wish to discuss with you.' I tapped the document.

'Is this a matter of great urgency, madam? We have much business to attend to.' The Earl of Arundel, a man of some pride and much impatience. Would he be the one to stoke the fires of tradition against me? Queens rarely sat in Royal Councils, the King's Mother even less frequently. 'Finance is as ever critical,' he was saying. 'We were considering a royal progress for our young King to make the acquaintance of his subjects...'

I allowed my smile to fade as I turned my regard on him.

His words dried. 'If that is your wish, of course, madam,' he added.

'I am certain that would be good policy,' I agreed at the same time as I slowly, painstakingly, unfolded the document so that all might appreciate the weighty seal, and the fact that it was in my hands and not theirs. 'We will discuss the provision of new royal barge for the King's enjoyment. But royal progresses can wait. Here is the prime issue for our discussion.'

They craned their necks.

I took a breath and smiled with great serenity, aware of the shades of the past around me. Edward, burning with authority, gracious Philippa and Ned, forever glorious, all standing at my shoulder. But their role was at an end now; the burden and the achievement for the future now fell to me.

'My son the King needs a wife. Here is our first approach,' I announced, 'as we might have expected. From the puissant Charles the Fourth, Holy Roman Emperor. He offers the hand of his eleven year old daughter Anne. The Emperor, it would appear, is not one to allow grass to grow under his feet, nor under ours...'

I waited, as the discussion, much as I expected, began.

'Would such an alliance be in our best interests?'

'Perhaps not. Yet it would be a magnificent alliance for a young king.'

'Surely the Emperor is a friend of France in his policies? Would that suit us?'

Much as I thought, as I sat and listened. Division and indecision. Lancaster did not participate, which again intrigued me. I saw his policy. While I played the woman in need of advice, he kept his counsel so that no man here present could accuse him of using overbearing power. There were many who would be happy to so slander him.

'Do we consider it, or do we reject it, my lords?' I spoke, cutting through the comments.

'We should not reject it. Not out of hand, madam.'

The Earl of March, whose interest in the throne thorough his marriage to Richard's royal cousin Philippa still found occasion to trouble me whatever Edward's pronouncement. Edward was dead and this Mortimer Earl very much alive.

'I would never be so hasty, my lord. We all know the value of diplomacy. But...' I turned to Lancaster, my trusty ally. 'Is there any value to us in considering this alliance?' I pushed a little. 'Would an alliance with the Emperor further our own English policies?'

His reply was prompt. 'No madam. I think it would not. There is no prospect of diplomatic gain for us here. The Emperor is in too close collusion with the French for my liking. We can do better.'

'So I think. Are we then agreed? We will thank the Emperor but look elsewhere.'

They bowed their heads in acknowledgement, while I folded the document and passed it to a waiting clerk. A rejection would be suitably and regretfully penned.

'My thanks, my lords.' I stood, so that they must do so too. 'I am sure that you will understand if I suggest that there will be no agreement on the subject of a wife for my son without my consent.'

No voice was raised against me as I swept out.

Lancaster, paying me a visit later in the day, had acerbic judgement writ large in the lines of his face when he lounged at his ease in my chamber, much as Ned would have done, while I prowled in restless thought.

'Well done, Joan.'

'It was, wasn't it?'

I had done it. I had achieved all I had set out to achieve in these initial days of Richard's reign, marking my place in the Royal Council, showing these proud magnates that I would be a force in Richard's life. *I* would dictate the direction we would take with Richard's marriage, not my lords of Arundel or March, nor the Bishop of London. Nor even Lancaster. I would continue to invite myself to Royal Council meetings when I felt the need. The Councillors, with soft handling, must become used to my presence. I knew how to wear velvet gloves when necessary.

It was always necessary.

Interference many would call it. I had seen the austere criticism in the face of the Earl of March. As for a wife for Richard, did I not know the value of a wife for a powerful man? I would ensure that the future queen was of my choosing, fair and well-born and fertile, a formidable bride for my son, as I had been for Ned. Richard would be the most sought after prince in Europe.

I assessed what my ambassadors were telling me from the courts of Europe. There was a Valois princess to be considered, but one to be rejected since England would not warm to being tied with the enemy. An offer from Scotland? What value to us in a Scottish alliance, another nation for which Englishmen had no love.

'I hear on the diplomatic grapevine that the Visconti Dukes of Milan were sniffing out the possibility of providing a wife for Richard,' John offered with deceptive insouciance when I told him of my thoughts. 'Lionel's second wife was a Visconti so I think they look to renew the connection.'

I regarded him, neither accepting or rejecting, merely walking round him to place a hand on his shoulder, in recognition of his kindness. 'It may be possible. Equally I may have been too quick in my rejection of the young girl Anne. If the Holy Roman Emperor will step back from his French sympathies, forging his own interests in Europe now that his French wife is dead, it might provide an interesting alliance. It is an idea that appeals to me.'

So I would change my mind. It was my prerogative to do so in the interests of England. I had much experience of changing my mind when unfolding events suggested it would be to my advantage.

I pressed a little harder with my hand so that John would know my purpose.

'There are more immediate concerns. Mistress Perrers may have been stripped of her influence, but she is still in possession of her ill-gotten wealth,' I advised. 'It would be far better filling the coffers of my son than feathering her own multiplicity of nests.'

'And you look to me for a fellow conspirator against her?'

'Who else?'

There would be no conspiracy. Legality was now engraved on my soul. It could be accomplished with a recourse to law, to accuse her of embezzlement before parliament. Perhaps even banishment might be considered, once her possessions had been seized. I had not won every battle with Alice, but, with John's help, I would be victorious in the war.

'You might find an appointment for her husband, William de Windsor, somewhere in Europe,' I suggested. 'Does not Cherbourg require a new Governor? Windsor might be unscrupulous but he is able.' My smile was thin. 'Mistress Alice can take herself out of England to accompany him.'

Standing, stretching, John of Lancaster bowed and saluted my fingers, departing to set all in motion while I, pleased with the result, returned to my devising of the perfect, most advantageous, matrimonial alliance for Richard.

Ned would approve.

Acknowledgements

My grateful thanks, as ever, to my agent Jane Judd, who enjoys the complexities of the lives of medieval women as much as I do. She provides me with a constant presence in my writing, full of insight, calm good sense and advice, in a sometimes frenetic world.

My appreciation of the work of my editor Sally Williamson at HarperCollins cannot be overstated when she is willing to indulge me in chatting about historical characters, existing six hundred years ago, as if they still live and breathe today. Her oversight and advice are invaluable when I am swamped with detail.

And of course my gratitude to the whole editorial team at HarperCollins. They turn my ideas and writing into a book. Without them Joan of Kent would not exist as *The Shadow Queen*.

My debt to Emma Draude and Sophie Goodfellow at EDPR must not be neglected. I am most appreciative of their expertise and enthusiasms when bringing my historical characters to the notice of the reading world.

Finally my thanks to Helen Bowden and all at Orphans Press, who answer all my internet questions and without whom my splendid new website would not exist.

What inspired me to write about Joan of Kent?

Who was she?

Joan of Kent, during her eventful life, was Countess of Kent in her own right, Princess of Wales, Princess of Aquitaine and ultimately King's Mother. She was a woman of royal birth and unsavoury reputation. What was it about this woman who made an impact on the court circles of the late fourteenth century that appealed to my imagination?

A Plantagenet princess, she was first cousin to King Edward III, a woman of royal status although her father's name was tainted with treason. Joan was by tradition beautiful, raised in the royal household, but was salaciously notable for her three marriages, two of them clandestine and one certainly bigamous. Thus she has intrigued readers of history as much as she has invited condemnation. Was she '... the most beautiful lady in the whole realm of England, and by far the most amorous.' Was she 'beauteous, charming and discreet'? Or was she 'given to slippery ways'?

But scandal was not the only element of fascination in Joan's life. So was her ambition. As wife of Edward of Woodstock, later to be known as the Black Prince, she blossomed as Princess of Aquitaine where she made as many enemies as friends. As King's Mother to the boy King Richard II she succeeded in the early years in keeping a firm grip on the power behind the throne. But her past scandals could undo all that she had achieved, threatening to destroy her secure hold on power. Would it, because of Joan's marital history, be possible to accuse Richard of illegitimacy and so dethrone him?

How was the proud woman to be able to protect herself and her son? Always subtle and carefully manipulative, Joan exhibited a range of talents drawing into her political net the Royal Council and the powerful prince, John of Gaunt, Duke of Lancaster.

There is so much here to entice the lover of medieval historical fiction. Was Joan simply a pawn in the pattern of royal alliance-making, forced into marriage with a powerful family against her personal wishes, or did she take her future into her own hands? Was she a woman of perfect compliance, or did she have a will of iron? Was her marriage to Prince Edward one based on a childhood love affair, or were Joan's motives far deeper in her bid for personal power?

A character of much notoriety, some charm and considerable ambition. This is Joan of Kent, *The Shadow Queen*.

In the steps of Joan of Kent

How unfortunate for us that so many of the castles and palaces that Joan would have known and enjoyed in her lifetime no longer exist or are in a critically ruined state. Others have been much developed so that Joan would recognise very little of what exists today and we would find it difficult to catch a trace of her. But here they are, for your enjoyment:

Palace of Berkhamsted, Hertfordshire, a royal place much enjoyed by Edward III and given to the Prince of Wales for his own use, was originally a motte and bailey castle but was greatly added to as an important centre throughout the medieval period. It became the Prince's favourite home and it was where Joan first lived after her marriage to him. Becoming unfashionable, it gradually fell into ruin and was only saved from extinction by English Heritage.

Palace of Kennington, north of the Thames, although a favourite residence of Prince Edward, and where he and Joan spent some of the early months of their marriage, sadly no longer exists.

Havering-atte-Bower, one of the favourite residences of Queen Philippa, no longer exists. No walls were visible by 1816.

Bisham Manor, Berkshire, or what is left of it, is now a health club.

Wallingford Castle, Oxfordshire, where Joan probably died in

1385, is ruined but at least there is some element of the home she would have known. She lived here in her final years when she retired from Richard's court.

Castle Donington, Leicestershire, the most important of Joan's own family properties, has been demolished. The church of St Edward, King and Martyr at Castle Donington, would have been known to Joan.

Palace of Woodstock, Oxfordshire, built as a hunting lodge, was where Edward was born and where Joan spent some of her childhood with the royal children. Badly damaged during the Civil War in the seventeenth century, it was further demolished and what was left of the stone used in the building of Blenheim Palace nearby.

The Church of the Grey Friars in Stamford, where both Thomas Holland and Joan were buried, suffered in the Dissolution of the Monasteries. All that is left today is the gatehouse. We have no record of the chapels and monument that Joan planned for her first husband and herself.

Arundel Castle, Sussex, where Joan was probably born and spent the early months of her life, is one of our most notable castles but has been much rebuilt in the centuries after Joan's time. The original stone keep still exists.

Palace of Westminster, mostly destroyed by fire in 1512 so that what we see today would not be familiar to Joan except for its position on the River Thames.

St Andrew's Church, Wickhambreaux, Kent. Wickhambreaux

was the only manor in Kent owned by Joan. It is probable that she visited and stayed at the manor on her annual pilgrimage to Prince Edward's tomb every June after he died. The church of St Andrews dates from the fourteenth century so Joan would have known it well.

But here are other major English historical sites, used by the royal family over the centuries, for living accommodation, celebration and religious ceremony and burial, where we might catch more than a glimpse of Joan:

Windsor Castle and St George's Chapel, Berkshire, where Joan lived as part of the royal household. She was married to Edward of Woodstock in St George's Chapel.

Canterbury Cathedral, Kent, where Edward, Prince of Wales is buried. The Black Prince's Chantry was founded by Edward Prince of Wales in 1363 in a act of piety in response to a Papal Dispensation to allow him to marry Joan of Kent who was related to him within the degrees of forbidden consanguinity. There is a roof boss of Joan of Kent in the chapel.

Westminster Abbey for the tombs of Richard II and Anne of Bohemia as well as King Edward III and Queen Philippa.

And Afterwards:

Joan of Kent continued to remain a constant support for Richard until her death in 1385, possibly at Wallingford Castle, it is said suffering from a broken heart caused by the vicious conflict between her two sons, Richard II and John Holland. She was about fifty-eight years old when she died, and not in the best of health in these final years. In her will, it was the beds, symbols of wealth and power, that were important:

> *To my dear son the King, my new bed of red velvet, embroidered with ostrich feathers of silver, and heads of leopards of gold with boughs and leaves issuing out of their mouths. To my dear son Thomas Earl of Kent, my bed of red camak [sic.] paled with red and rays of gold. To my dear son John Holland, a bed of red camak.*

King Richard II ruled, not always wisely, until 1399 when he was overthrown by his cousin Henry Bolingbroke, thus beginning the House of Lancaster as King Henry IV. There was some truth in the old predictions. Richard died, probably in February 1400, a prisoner at Pontefract Castle, it seems from starvation, for which Henry must accept the guilt. Richard's first wife was Anne of Bohemia, as Joan had planned.

Joan's two Holland sons, Thomas and John, switched their allegiance from Richard to Henry Bolingbroke, but then participated in the Epiphany Rising of 1400 to kill Henry and his four sons and restore Richard. When the rising was crushed they both fell foul of Henry's vengeance. Both died as a result but both had descendents to carry on Joan and Thomas Holland's line. Joan's two daughters also married well to carry on the Holland and Plantagenet line.

John, Duke of Lancaster, never did fulfil his ambition to become King of Castile in more than name. He remained in England as counsellor to Richard, married his long-time mistress Katherine Swynford and died in 1399.

William Montagu, Earl of Salisbury, remained Joan's close friend until the end of her life. A soldier by repute, he was also a valuable counsellor of King Richard, advising him to treat the peasants in the Revolt of 1381 with mercy, and serving the King on various commissions until the end of his life in 1397. He was buried at Bisham. Tragically he killed his only son in a tournament in 1382, the earldom ultimately passing to William's nephew John after much bitter dispute.

Epitaph of Edward of Woodstock, Prince of Wales

Edward's title, the Black Prince, frequently used in history, was not found in evidence until the Tudor period, and so it would be wrong to use it to assess either his character or his reputation. The reasoning behind such a title is obscure, and will remain so. Was it attributed to his black armour? No, since his armour would not be black when burnished for battle. Was it a later comment on his autocratic temper, or even an example of presumed French propaganda, painting him black as their most notable enemy? There is no evidence of either of these.

The epitaph on the Prince's tomb in Canterbury Cathedral is strikingly lacking in either arrogance or autocratic pride, but portrays him as a 'caitiff', a man worthy of contempt. It is not an original composition but was based on an anonymous 13th century French translation of the *Clericalis Disciplina* written in Latin by Petrus Alphonsi who was physician to Henry I. On the tomb it is written in French, but is here translated by the antiquary J Weever in *Ancient Funerall Monuments, 1631.*

> *Who so thou be that passeth by,*
> *Where these corps entombed lie:*
> *Understand what I shall say*
> *As at this time speak I may.*

Such as thou art, some time was I,
Such as I am, such shalt thou be.
I little thought on the hour of death
So long as I enjoyed breath.

Great riches here I did possess
Whereof I made great nobleness.
I had gold, silver, wardrobes and
Great treasure, horses, houses, land.

But now a caitiff poor am I
Deep in the ground, lo here I lie
My beauty great is all quite gone,
My flesh is wasted to the bone.

My house is narrow now and throng,
Nothing but Truth comes from my tongue:
And if ye should see me this day
I do not think but ye would say
That I had never been a man;
So much altered now I am

For God's sake pray to the heavenly King
That he my soul to heaven would bring,
All they that pray and make accord
For me until my God and Lord:
God place him in his Paradise,
Wherein no wretched caitiff lies.

Here Edward, Prince of Wales, wretched caitiff, lies for all time, as a supplicant for human prayers and divine mercy. Death levels us all, even a Plantagenet prince.

HQ Young Adult
One Place. Many Stories

YOUNG
ADULT

The home of fun, contemporary
and meaningful Young Adult fiction.

Follow us online

 @HQYoungAdult

 @HQYoungAdult

 HQYoungAdult

 HQMusic